BYWAYS TO EVIL

BYWAYS TO EVIL

A VICTORIAN MYSTERY NOVEL

LLOYD BIGGLE, JR.

Edited by

KENNETH LLOYD BIGGLE
&
DONNA BIGGLE EMERSON

WILDSIDE PRESS

WITH SPECIAL THANKS TO DAVID DATTA
AND STEPHEN LUCCHETTI
FOR THEIR VALUABLE ASSISTANCE

Published by Wildside Press LLC.
www.wildsidebooks.com

CHAPTER 1

The year was 1900, the place was London, and the night, an unusually warm one for September, began and ended with horrors. I was caught up in them almost without warning as I turned into a narrow, poorly lit, cobbled lane and instinctively slowed my pace. Ahead of me, where the passage took a sudden bend to the right, a small gas lamp glowed feebly, and its uncertain, wavering light produced oddly distorted shadows.

A man loomed up suddenly on my left—instantly recognizable despite the eerie dimness. It was John Thurtell, the notorious murderer. At one time his likeness—with clean-shaven, pock-marked face, closely cropped hair, and affectedly informal dress—had stared out of thousands of newspapers, posters and broadsheets. He had a fine, athletic figure, and had it not been for the diabolical sneer on his face, he might have been taken for a gentleman down on his luck. The sneer revealed his true character. Probably it was the last thing his victim saw when Thurtell, after firing two pistols into William Weare's face, made the gun shots more emphatic by cutting his throat.

On the other side of the lane, standing with the dark silhouette of a barn behind him, was William Corder. In better light I might have been able to pick out, through the open door, the exact spot where he had just buried the mangled body of Maria Marten.

A few paces ahead of me were two sinister, shadowy forms, one short and stout, the other tall and thin—Burke and Hare, the "resurrectionists," heavily burdened with a large tea chest in which they were conveying the corpse of their latest victim to Doctor Knox's School of Anatomy.

A ghastly phantasm was at work in the shadows behind them: Jack the Ripper, bent over a victim to perform his perverted mutilations.

Under the dim lamp, the most fearsome figure of all stood quietly conversing with a neatly-dressed young woman. This was James Canham Read, the Royal Albert Dock cashier. Father of eight children, holder of a responsible business position, trusted and respected by all who knew him, he was horrifying because he was so eminently respectable both in reputation and appearance. He had made a sordid pastime of seducing young women until, only a few years earlier, he murdered one of them and was hanged for it. His career tainted every decent man's reputation. It made respectability suspect.

Probably worse horrors lurked around the corner, but a quite ordinary door opened abruptly at the end of the lane, and light flooded the waxworks's Dungeon of Horrors. The figures shrank to mere sculpted images, grotesque but harmless. Lady Sara Varnley called, "Is that you, Colin? We've been waiting for you."

I entered a bright workroom where I found Lady Sara; Stephen Lynes, a young sculptor and protégé of Lady Sara's whom I already knew well; and a second man—tall, middle-aged, wearing a frock coat—whom I had never met. He looked like a tired tradesman dressed for a night on the town. Lady Sara introduced us. He was Evan Vaughan, an artist from Leeds. She introduced me as Colin Quick, her secretary.

I was at most twenty years of age—my exact birth date had been lost in the mists of an East End childhood—but despite my youth, she never hesitated to confer on me whatever title or function a situation required. I was sometimes her assistant, sometimes her chief investigator, sometimes her secretary, sometimes a visiting official or technical consultant. Needless to say, I had to devote considerable effort and ingenuity to appearing and acting older than I was. Lady Sara's own mentor, a retired actor, had coached me in applying quick touches of make-up and making minute changes in dress and manner in order to alter my appearance completely.

Lynes affected a beard, a cape, and a beret in the manner of young artists. Like beginning artists everywhere, he had to take any work he could get until he made a name for himself. "Any work he could get" had been extremely difficult to find, so he was attempting to earn money with a waxworks and at the same time set new standards in the realism and artistic representation of wax effigies.

Lady Sara was, as always, Lady Sara. The daughter of the deceased Burke Varnley, Earl of Ranisford, she was about forty years old at this time. Men her own age often told me how beautiful she had been as a girl. I thought she was still beautiful. She was unusually tall, for a woman, and she wore a simple gown of some rich, dark blue material. There were no flounces or frills of any kind. She wore no jewellery. Her straight black hair was arranged with the same simple directness—parted in the centre and gathered into a soft cluster behind her. She not only eschewed elaborate coiffures and curls, but she also disdained the Royal, or Alexandra, fringe across the forehead made so popular by the Princess of Wales.

Her oval face was capable of an astonishing range of expression. Many of her friends thought she might have been a great actress if she had come from a different social background, but it simply was not done for the daughter of an earl to choose a theatrical career. I thought her face the most expressive when she was simply being herself. No one walking into that room could have had the slightest doubt that she was the person with authority. That was true of any room and of any company. Lord Salisbury once took her to a cabinet meeting to discuss police problems in Britain. I had no doubt that she instantly took charge of that group, also.

An artist meeting her for the first time was certain to want to paint her. Any stranger knew at once that she was a woman of high distinction, but only her intimates had an inkling of her true métier. She was the foremost private investigator in England.

She took me aside for a moment, scrutinized my face briefly, and then remarked, "The steam-launch wasn't the answer, I see. Never mind. Sooner or later we'll find an opening."

This was the most disconcerting thing about her. She didn't have to ask what I had been doing or how my day had gone. One glance, and she knew.

Rampant thievery from London's riverside warehouses had been going on for several years. Although the thefts actually took place along the shore, newspapers and even the police were calling the perpetrators "river thieves." Goods under lock and key and close watch were disappearing by the boatload or waggon-load, and Lady Sara was asked to look into the situation. She arranged with the Thames police for me to observe their procedures, and I had spent the day on one of their steam-launches.

I hadn't told her I intended to do that. I hadn't known it myself until I arrived at Wapping Police Station, the river police headquarters. How could she possibly have known it? Not until I chanced to see myself in a mirror did I understand. There were smears of soot on my face. She knew I was going on the river, and, on a bright September day, where would I have exposed myself to soot if not on a steam-launch? Probably my frustrated air told her I hadn't learned anything. In this fumbling fashion, I sometimes succeeded in making my own reconstruction of a deduction she arrived at instantaneously—but only one slow step at a time and with considerable effort.

"A launch is too conspicuous," I told her. She was impatient of anything that wasted time, and years before she had ordered me to stop addressing her as "my lady" in private conversations. "Tomorrow morning, I'll leave early and spend a few hours in one of the oared police galleys. They should have an advantage, especially at night. Unfortunately, they follow set schedules."

She nodded. "The thieves will know those schedules at least as well as the constables do. Have a look, and then we will plan our next move."

She turned to Lynes. "We are ready, Stephen."

There were numerous waxworks in and about London, an indication of the steady growth in popularity of this form of entertainment. Most were temporary exhibits, hastily prepared to dramatize the most recent newspaper sensations. When their novelty faded and their custom fell off, they moved to new locations. The crudeness of such knocked-off displays was readily apparent, and their owners attempted to compensate by offering additional entertainments in the form of palmists, clairvoyants, or conjurors. Of the half-dozen or so permanent waxworks, the most prominent were Madame Tussaud's, on Marylebone Road, and its principal rival on Edgware Road. These not only were artistically superior, but they offered far greater variety in their attractions, and their patronage reflected this.

Lady Sara considered the best waxwork figures to be pathetically inept, and she was encouraging Lynes in the hope he could achieve more life-like representations. The result was this new establishment on Tottenham Court Road—close enough to its rivals to compete with them but far enough away to attract a following of its own. With Lynes's undoubted talent and Lady Sara's critical assistance and financial support, it seemed bound to succeed.

Its opening was only a few days away, and we had been invited to preview what Lady Sara called the *pièce de résistance*, an effigy of Hob Hagan, the giant axe murderer, who had been hanged only two weeks previously. Hagan was a man of genuinely gigantic proportions, and I had expected a monstrous effigy, but the contours of the sheet-draped figure that stood in the centre of the workroom seemed preposterous. The top was at least ten feet above the floor. "Surely he wasn't that tall!" I protested.

Lynes chuckled. "Just wait!" he said.

From the care with which he unwrapped the statue, one would have thought it fashioned of egg shells. Finally Hagan's effigy stood revealed to us, and it was a fearsome thing, a *pièce de résistance* indeed. John Thurtell had displayed a sneer in his effigy; Hagan turned the furious snarl of a demented wild beast on the world. His huge, swarthy face had a nightmarish ugliness, and his massive arms looked equal to any kind of brutal iniquity. He held the axe poised above his head for another blow, and its blood-stained blade was dripping crimson gore onto his clothing and the turf at his feet. The wax effigies of the hacked victims—Hagan had murdered three people with his axe—were not yet completed.

"Excellent!" I exclaimed.

"Very well done," Lady Sara agreed. "You've caught the climactic moment. The public should be delighted. Did he really pose for you?"

"He did, my lady," Lynes assured her. "The authorities wouldn't let him have an axe, but I rolled up a piece of newspaper to serve as an axe handle, and he posed and produced a number of appropriate facial expressions for my sketch pad. He seemed delighted that he was going to be in a waxworks."

"Astonishing!" Lady Sara murmured. "Was he at all repentant?"

"Not in any way. In his view, the victims brought it on themselves. They shouldn't have angered him."

Lady Sara turned to Vaughan. "What do you think, Evan?"

"It is very capably done, my lady," Vaughan said condescendingly, "but I can't imagine Hob Hagan producing a facial expression like that, even by request. I knew him, you see." Then he moved closer. "There's one other thing. What have you done with his birthmark?"

"Birthmark?" Lynes echoed. "He had no birthmark."

"But he did," Vaughan said confidently. "A port wine mark on his left cheek. Just about here." He pointed at his own face. "From a distance, it looked like a bug." He walked around the statue. "And that mole on his right neck. Surely you're wrong about that. Hagan had no mole."

"But he did!" Lynes protested excitedly. "I'll show you!"

He dashed to his desk and returned with the sketches he had made of Hagan in prison. He brandished them like a barrister producing telling evidence in a court of law.

Vaughan went to a chair in the corner for a large folder he had left there. He opened it and took out his own sketches, which he brandished in the same fashion.

Lady Sara watched the developing argument with a wisp of a smile on her face. Not only had she known this would happen, but she had invited Vaughan in order to make it happen—I hadn't the slightest doubt about that. One of Lady Sara's friends claimed her true talent was that of an impresario. She arranged confrontations in real life the way a theatrical manager arranged them on the stage. There was some truth in this, but the friend failed to grasp its significance. She thought Lady Sara improvised these scenes for her own amusement, whereas they were planned with great care and always with a purpose. In this instance, she already had formed her own conclusion about Hob Hagan, and she brought Vaughan with her in order to confirm it.

"Just a moment," she said when things seemed about to get out of hand. "You should know, Stephen, that Evan sketched Hagan when he was in prison in York for assaulting some men there. Let's sit down and compare the sketches."

We gathered around a table, and Vaughan laid out his drawings. "These were done almost eight years ago, my lady," he said. "Hagan interested me because of his size. I was living in York at the time, and I visited him several times while he was in prison and got to know him well. He always seemed like a very gentle person, slow to anger. I've been astonished at the reports of his subsequent career. He is supposed to have committed one hideous crime after another while all the police of England searched for him. Finally he was caught with the bloody axe in his hands. I still find that difficult to believe. All I know is that I sketched him exactly as I saw him in York, and the Hob Hagan I knew wasn't a man who would savage anyone."

"Tell us what did happen in York," Lady Sara suggested.

"Hagan was a farm labourer. The farmer who employed him said he had a way with animals. Because of his enormous strength and willing attitude, he was an excellent worker. One day he happened upon three men who were mistreating a worn-out old horse. When he remonstrated with them, they turned their scorn on him. What happened next is a bit vague because there weren't any witnesses. All three of the men ended in hospital, and one was injured critically. The magistrate was disposed to be lenient, because the original offence lay with the three men, but he had the severity of the injuries to consider. He gave Hagan two months and ordered him to pay the men's medical expenses. It amounted to a severe fine."

"Was Hagan repentant?" Lady Sara asked.

"Extremely so. He hadn't meant to harm anyone. He just wanted to stop them from tormenting the horse. When they began to ridicule his size, he lost his temper. He swore it would never happen again."

Lady Sara turned to Lynes. "How do you reconcile that gentle giant—with a birthmark on his face—with your axe murderer and his mole?"

Lynes shrugged. "Obviously he lost his temper again despite his good intentions. As for the mole, I drew him exactly as I saw him in his prison cell. Who can say a man wouldn't grow a mole in almost eight years?"

"True enough," Lady Sara said, "but what about the missing birthmark?"

Lynes shrugged again. "If it had been there, my lady, I would have drawn it. Maybe it faded away."

"I doubt that!" Vaughan protested. "It was a deep red, and he said he'd had it all his life. It could have faded gradually as he got older, but it wouldn't have vanished completely—not even in eight years."

"I've been following Hagan's career ever since he first came to police notice in York," Lady Sara said. "Giants aren't common in England. When I was a child, the Egyptian Hall exhibited a Chinese giant at the same time that a French giant was on display at St. James's Hall. It was rare to have two such exhibits in London simultaneously. I made my father take me to see both. I found them fascinating, and I've been interested in giants ever since. Midgets never appealed to me. They were too close to my own size. A genuine giant seems breathtakingly gigantic to a child."

"Are giants really that rare?" Lynes asked. "From time to time I see them advertised in squalid sideshows."

"Along with fat women, tattooed men, fraudulent savages, and any other freaks the showmen have been able to find or fake," Lady Sara agreed, "but giants in sideshows are rarely very gigantic. The French and Chinese giants I saw were genuinely huge. So is or was Hob Hagan—however he was sketched. There is more of a problem here than a disappearing birthmark or a newly grown mole. The reports indicate a remarkable personality change. I noticed it long before he killed three people and was caught with the bloody axe in his hands. What transformed the gentle, repentant giant of York, whose only offence was coming to the aid of a helpless animal, into the vicious murderer who emerged later?"

Neither of the artists said anything.

Lady Sarah smiled at me. "Chief Inspector Mewer will be along shortly. I wonder what he'll have to say about this."

"Something profane," I suggested.

She laughed appreciatively. "No doubt, but he'll keep that to himself. I wonder what he'll have to say to me. I am amazed that such a capable police officer can function with so little imagination. When I invited him to meet us here, he said, 'Waxworks? Waxworks? What's that got to do with the police?' Sometimes the questions I ask him, or the objections I raise, or the way I interpret evidence, almost makes him forget I am a lady. His own deductions make me want to forget it myself. We'll find out shortly."

But the Chief Inspector never arrived. After waiting for an hour, we went back through the Dungeon of Horrors and climbed the stairs to the office on the ground floor, where Lady Sara telephoned Chief Inspector Mewer's home and had a brief conversation with his wife.

"He was called away by an emergency," she told the artists. "He won't be available tonight. Mrs. Mewer conveys his apologies. Because the waxworks isn't open yet, it didn't occur to him to let us know by telephone. If I have a chance to talk with him, I'll try to arrange for him to see your sketches tomorrow.

We left the artists to continue their discussion of moles and birthmarks.

"I intend to look into this," Lady Sara told me on the way out. "I consider it a certainty that there were two giants. Their careers have been confused not only by press and public but also by the police. Our legal system has called one of them Hob Hagan and hanged him for murder. The other may be just as vicious, and we must find out what happened to him before there are more victims." She added, "This may be a case for the board."

"A case for the board" was a crime or a mystery that merited an exceptionally thorough investigation. It was her standard of measurement. Cases for the board came along but rarely. If she considered the problem of the two giants worthy of a place there, it meant that the issues involved were either extremely serious, or they offered a fascinating perplexity—or both.

One of the workmen unlocked the door for us, and Old John Quick, Lady Sara's congenial coachman and my foster-father, urged his horses forward when he saw us emerge from the building.

She paused on the step as I was handing her into the carriage. "Sorry, John. We have a long ride and perhaps work to do. Shadwell Market."

He turned quickly and stared at her, and so did I. The crime had to be an extremely serious one to cause her to drive half-way across London at that time of night. I leaped aboard and closed the door, Old John flipped his whip, and the horses started off. We clattered our way down Tottenham Court Road to Oxford street and turned east, from which point the route to Shadwell was considerably more direct than those between most distant points in London.

Lady Sara kept her eyes on the countless dramas being enacted in the patches of illumination we passed. She loved to travel about at night, but she much preferred to do the driving herself. She would disguise herself in men's clothing, take her place on the box beside Old John, and terrify him with the pace she set. Because such conduct while dressed as a woman would have scandalized London, on this night she had to confine herself to the carriage.

The streets had a restless, anticipatory air about them—a "between happenings" atmosphere. The early night crowd was tucked away in theatres or restaurants; the late night crowd, which would include much of the early crowd when it finally emerged, had not yet arrived. Because it was mid-week, traffic was light. Little knots of people stood gathered about food vendors, and sometimes they sent guarded, apprehensive looks at us as we passed. Such indications of guilt were seldom without justification, and I suspected these casual bystanders of all sorts of stratagems and treasons.

Here and there the dim presence of a solitary vendor could be glimpsed—a baked-potato man; a peanut seller; a shawl-muffled woman with a pipe in her mouth and a basket of unsold vegetables at her feet. They were desperate for custom and determinedly sticking to their posts long after all hope had vanished and their competitors gone home. They were the failures of their profession, a few of the many for whom costering provided not a living but only another way of starving. Lady Sara gave employment and survival to many such. She made them her agents, and if they sold little, they observed much, repaying her with information that was well worth the weekly shilling or two she gave them.

While we rattled our way toward Shadwell, Lady Sara told me what she had been able to learn from Mrs. Mewer about the emergency that forced the Chief Inspector to break his appointment. "She was reluctant to discuss it, but the little I was able to coax out of her suggested another Jack-the-Ripper is on the loose—this time with a male victim."

"Do you mean the victim was deliberately mutilated?" I asked.

"That is the impression I got. Mrs. Mewer wouldn't or couldn't supply any details. London has never got over Jack-the-Ripper. It would stand this city on its head if he started operating again. The official view is that he drowned himself shortly after his last murder back in 1888, but the evidence wasn't as clear as the police would have liked. The authorities may have been guilty of wishful thinking."

Huddled into a corner of the carriage, I thought about the horror I was about to see and the horrors I had seen earlier—among them, the waxworks monster with an axe. Was his brutal twin at that moment stalking another victim?

By the year 1900, the East End, at least in its main thoroughfares, had become so regularized and sanitized that visitors to London sometimes made daring forays along Whitechapel or Commercial Road on Saturday night just to see the sights, which included enormous crowds of people, flaring naphtha lights on stalls and barrows, confused surges of passers-by, and the noisy bellowings of vendors. The crowds were much smaller on week nights, and the show was more restrained, but it was still worth seeing. Even St. George Street, which once was the notorious Ratcliff Highway, offered nothing that visitors to London would find offensive. The side streets were another matter entirely. A stranger venturing into them could quickly encounter more curiosities than he cared for.

Compared with the brightness of central London, St. George Street was dark and rather quiet. It was named for St. George's in the East, one of the great churches of London. Establishments like the Seamen's Mission Hall and the Seamen's Chapel indicated how close we were to the docks. There also was Jamrack's, where you could place an order for any living creature that interested you, from a humming-bird to an elephant, and eventually get it. At that hour of the night, long stretches of the street were deserted except for scattered groups of people talking or sitting in front of open doors. Perhaps they were already discussing the horror that had occurred at Shadwell Market.

In neighbourhoods near the docks, an apparently deserted street conveyed no impression of emptiness. Every second or third house was a pub, and all of their patrons were seamen with wives or sweethearts. From the open doors came strains of robust sailors' songs, sung with an excess of enthusiasm and a marked absence of musical talent.

When we reached the turning to the market, we found the street blocked. Three constables were directing traffic away—not that there was much to direct. Shadwell Market had been established as a fish market to compete with Billingsgate. It did not seem to be thriving, but it tenuously survived. It did its business in the morning, however, opening at five o'clock. During the early hours of the night, the area should have been all but deserted, but police milled about with flares and bull's-eye lanterns. Points of light flitted here and there as though someone had mobilized an army of fireflies.

Old John brought the carriage to a halt, and Lady Sara leaned out. "What's going on here?" she demanded of the constable.

He turned his light on her for a second and then directed it away apologetically. All of the police in the metropolitan area knew Lady Sara well and admired her. They considered her their friend and supporter, which she was, but the constable seemed reluctant to discuss this particular crime even with her.

"There's been a n'awful murder, my lady," he said. "I have to ask you to move on."

"Where is Chief Inspector Mewer?"

"The Chief Inspector is busy. I'm sorry, but you'll have to move."

"So am I busy," Lady Sara said. "Tell the Chief Inspector I want to see him."

The constable hesitated helplessly. At that moment a sergeant arrived, and the constable said in hushed tones, "Lady Sara wants to see Chief Inspector Mewer."

The sergeant knew how to deal with a problem like that. He went looking for his inspector. Old John was allowed to make his turn and wait for instructions.

Eventually Chief Inspector Mewer appeared. He had his regular duties, but within the confines of Scotland Yard he was known as Commander of the Lady Sara Branch, the commissioner having decided years before that making one senior officer responsible for handling Lady

Sara's complaints, requests, suggestions, and revelations would be time saving. The Chief Inspector bore the burden of that responsibility with gloomy resignation.

He murmured, "Evening, my lady." Then he demanded, "What are you doing here?"

He was not exceptionally tall, but he was unusually sturdy-looking, a Gibraltar of a man, and his mere presence at the scene of a crime brought comfort to victims and fright to anyone with a guilty conscience. When he chose to display it, he had a gentle refinement that seemed entirely out of character, but usually he hid this behind his bristling moustache. He might have been the prototype of the music hall joke that asked, "Who's that gentleman?" And answered, "That's no gentleman. That's a police officer."

"What am I usually doing?" Lady Sara asked.

"Something horrible has happened," he said. His voice was sharply accusatory as though she were somehow responsible.

"I heard. Your wife made it sound like another Jack-the-Ripper murder."

"That's what the constables who found the body thought, but they were far off the mark. As near as we can make out, there's some kind of wild animal loose along the waterfront. It's killed a man—mutilated him horribly. As you know, animals like lions and tigers are imported from time to time for zoos and other exhibitions. We're checking to see if one could have escaped from a ship. We're also trying to get hold of someone from Jamracks to see whether they are missing an animal."

"How did the animal kill him?" Lady Sara asked.

"He was clawed—as I said, horribly. Practically had his face torn away."

"That killed him?" Lady Sara asked sceptically.

"He also suffered a blow to the head and claw marks on his arms from trying to defend himself."

"I want to see this corpse myself," Lady Sara said.

The Chief Inspector looked at her angrily. Lady Sara was always challenging his sensitivities by demanding to see and discuss things that he felt compelled to protect her from.

"Come along," he said finally. He had learned that arguing with her was a waste of time.

The police were still awaiting the arrival of the divisional surgeon, and the body lay on its back where it had fallen—not in the market area, but in an adjoining street. It was a ghastly horror. The animal had swiped the unfortunate man's face twice, or done it simultaneously with both front paws. Flesh had been ripped from the face. The left eye had been torn out. The Chief Inspector showed us how the victim had raised his hands to defend himself. Claws had ripped his coat sleeves away and cut vicious stripes along almost the whole length of the back of his forearms. The blow to his head had crushed the skull on the left rear side.

For more than a minute, Lady Sara stood scrutinizing the corpse. It was always a moment of high drama when she stepped onto the stage where a crime had occurred, but she behaved so quietly, not to mention decorously, that the police, and especially Chief Inspector Mewer, never seemed to comprehend what was taking place. I had seen it happen so often—her level, emotionless gaze, her complete indifference to what was happening around her, her intense examination of the entire scene, and then the sudden question or revelation—that I always held my breath while I waited. I performed my own scrutiny at the same time, but only rarely did my deductions keep pace with hers.

It was a moment of high drama, but it was not a performance. She never displayed her deductive abilities merely for effect or to impress bystanders. She said only what the occasion called for, and she was careful not to burden anyone, especially the police, with flights of deduction they would not be able to follow.

She took a step backward and asked a constable to direct his lantern at the cobbles surrounding the corpse. They looked bare, but she studied them with care anyway. Then she returned her attention to the dead man.

"There doesn't seem to be much blood," she observed suddenly.

"There isn't much to be seen," the Chief Inspector conceded. "There may be a pool of it under the body."

"Or there may not be," she said. Leaning over, she placed her fingers next to the dead man's face, using them to measure the spacing of the claw marks. Then she raised his head. Again she called for light, and when she had examined the cobbles under the head, she lowered it gently.

"Do you know who he is?" she asked.

"Not yet. A decent labouring type from the looks of him."

"Why are your men wandering about like that?"

"They're looking for tracks. We've got to find out where the creature went before it attacks someone else. We also would like to know what sort of animal we have to deal with. An expert can tell us that with a glance if we can find an impression of its foot or pug-mark. My guess makes it a tiger, but I suppose it could have been a leopard, and Sergeant Grower, who has travelled in America, thinks a grizzly bear could have done it. If we can find just one pug-mark, we'll soon know."

Lady Sara returned her attention to the corpse. She regarded it for a few moments with calm reflection, and then she walked in a slow circle around it. "If I were you, I wouldn't waste time looking for an animal," she announced finally. "I would search the victim's background. Either he was a considerable threat to someone or someone was threatening him. This man was murdered. He was hit on the head and killed. The clawing was done afterward for effect." She paused, continuing to study the mutilated corpse. "And it is effective, isn't it?"

The Chief Inspector shook his head. "It'd be a rare 'someone' who'd leave claw marks like that!"

"But 'someone' did," Lady Sara said. "Not only did someone want him dead, but he wanted to leave his body in the most gruesome condition possible. I congratulate you, Chief Inspector. You have a remarkably interesting case on your hands. Come and see me tomorrow afternoon, and I may be able to tell you something about it. Shall we say—two o'clock? Come, Colin. You've had a long day."

We turned away, leaving the Chief Inspector staring after us.

In the carriage, I asked, "Is this another case for the board?" After a doldrums that had lasted through much of the summer, a night that turned up two worthwhile cases would be one to remember.

A dearth of important cases did not mean Lady Sara hadn't been busy. She was always furiously busy, but the trivial problems she handled daily were mere grist to keep her mind sharp until something significant came her way.

She reflected for a moment. "It's too early to say. I'll point the Chief Inspector in the right direction and see how he manages. Stripped of its bizarre embellishments, this may be a simple case. If he muddles it completely, which wouldn't surprise either of us, then of course we'll have to help him out."

She paused, and then she added thoughtfully, "A deliberately disfigured corpse is rare in Britain. This wasn't done in a frenzy of lust or blood lust like the Jack-the-Ripper murders. This murderer had a purpose, however deranged and perverted, and the mutilation was done for coldly calculated effect. The murderer has left his own distinctive signature on the corpse. I wonder whether his purpose was fully achieved with one murder, or whether he will require more."

We made our turn onto St. George Street, and the unusually warm September night had suddenly began to feel chill and threatening.

CHAPTER 2

It rained during the night—a rain such as London rarely experiences, with savage thrusts of lightning tearing apart the darkness while thunder rolled like the artillery of a besieging army. Water fell in cascading floods. Sleep was impossible, so I lay awake thinking about the search for a ferocious animal among London's wharves and docks and wondering how Lady Sara could be so certain there was none.

I had no doubt she was right. She always knew; she always saw what no one else saw, or she had information everyone else had overlooked or hadn't bothered to acquire. Chief Inspector Mewer never seemed able to grasp that fact. With every case she interested herself in, he had to grapple with it anew as though there were something unnatural about a woman from a titled family becoming a criminal investigator.

I tried to think what she could have seen in her scrutiny of the mutilated corpse. Of course I had seen it, also, but it meant nothing to me. Too frequently I lacked the essential bits of knowledge that made deduction possible. Such detective talent as I possessed could be exercised only with intense effort. Lady Sara seemed to use hers with ease though she claimed to have worked as hard as I did in the beginning.

She was often asked how she happened to acquire an interest in crime, and she answered that she came by it honestly—she inherited it. Her mother, Lady Ranisford, the Dowager Countess, was, like so many titled ladies, a great enthusiast of murders and murder trials. It was a lifelong interest. One of Lady Sara's earliest memories was of her mother sending a maid or a footman to buy copies of broadsheets—penny plain or tuppence coloured, the Countess of course bought the tuppence version—or the latest newspaper from street hawkers who shouted an account of a murder. The Countess also was an avid frequenter of murder trials at Old Bailey, one of a number of stylishly dressed, bejewelled ladies of family, position, and wealth who never missed a session of a sensational trial.

Lady Sara vividly recalled her mother's jubilant return home at a late hour in 1877 with news of a conviction in the sordid Penge murder trial. A man named Louis Staunton had married a feeble-minded girl for her money. Once he gained this, he, his brother, and two females of irregular status had maltreated and starved the poor girl to death.

Lady Ranisford's delight over the verdict changed to absolute fury at Charles Reade, the author, when he wrote a series of letters for the Daily Telegraph claiming that Staunton was innocent because the wife already had a fatal disease, tubercular meningitis. "As if it were perfectly all right to starve an ill person to death!" the Countess exclaimed indignantly. She banished all of Reade's books from the house forthwith, a severe hardship on her because she was fond of them, especially The Cloister and the Hearth.

When the Earl of Ranisford was looking for a London town house, it was understandable that his wife would direct his attention to Connaught Place. For one thing, the architect ingeniously placed the entrances in the rear, leaving the splendid terraces with unobstructed views of Hyde Park and allowing access to them from a lightly travelled side street rather than busy Bayswater Road. For another, the address was eminently respectable. Caroline, Princess of Wales, had lived there in the early years of the nineteenth century. Finally, the location—at the convergence of Oxford Street and Park Lane, which earlier had been called Tyburn Street or Tyburn Lane—was the site where the notorious Tyburn Tree once stood. The "tree" had been replaced at an early date by a gallows, and the gallows was repeatedly enlarged until as many as twenty-four criminals could be hanged there simultaneously. The place had been the nemesis of London's convicted malefactors from the twelfth century until 1783 when the gallows was moved to Newgate Prison. It was estimated that as many as sixty thousand people were executed at Tyburn over the centuries.

If this weren't titillation enough for a murder enthusiast, during the excavation for the Connaught Place terraces, quantities of human bones were uncovered, relics of those same malefactors. At least a cartload was hauled away to be buried in a pit in Connaught Mews. When Lady Ranisford discovered this, the Connaught Place address became irresistible to her.

But Lady Ranisford's interest in sensational crimes could not begin to account for Lady Sara's amazing talent for serious criminal investigation. Lord Anstee, a long-time friend of the Earl of Ranisford and Lady Sara's confidant after her father died, once told me this about her: "The first thing you must understand is that she is brilliant. She has blazing intelligence—one of the best minds in England. I would go book with her against the best. And because she was born a woman, she grew up with nothing for that wonderful mind to do. Women doctors are a rarity; they were almost unheard of when she was young. Nursing was becoming a recognized profession, thanks to Florence Nightingale, but it was still battling for respectability, and it was no career for a noblewoman. Other than that, there was nothing. It wasn't even possible for women to obtain a good education without extraordinary effort. Oxford and Cambridge grudgingly allowed them to attend lectures and take university examinations, but even today, at the beginning of the twentieth century, women aren't eligible for degrees at either place, no matter how much higher their scores are than those of the men competing with them. What was she to do?

"People who know very little about her work say she has made a hobby of crime. They could not be more mistaken. She has made a profession of it, and the profession is one she invented herself. She applies research, along with analysis and synthesis, to criminal investigations—not the ordinary kind of research done in libraries nor the analysis and synthesis practised in laboratories, but an intense mental application that brings the full spectrum of human knowledge to bear on criminological problems, even including such a newfangled thing as psychological medicine. She had one enormous advantage—her social position and wealth opened doors that otherwise would have remained tightly shut, and it also enabled her to call upon the many professional men and scholars of her acquaintance for assistance. Scotland Yard can't begin to match her resources. She is the only investigator in the world who works like this, but she will never receive credit for it because she is a woman."

Most of her titled friends thought she had an eccentric quirk for solving mysteries—certainly an odd pastime for a person in her position but a harmless one. They condescendingly came to her for assistance with their own petty domestic and business puzzles. Few of them had any conception of the enormous scope of Lady Sara's activity, or they would have considered it far more disreputable than acting.

Her greatest difficulty was and always had been gaining professional respect from the men she had to work with. It was a challenge she faced anew each time she encountered another pompous ass in a position of authority. Lord Anstee described a confrontation he had witnessed between Lady Sara and two of Scotland Yard's assistant commissioners: "She encouraged them to talk until they had made resounding fools of themselves. Then she began to ask questions neither of them could answer. When she had them sufficiently embarrassed, she answered the questions herself, and from that point they had to listen to her."

That may have been her method with politicians and bureaucrats; where artists, or scientists, or professional men were concerned, she encouraged them to talk because she wanted to know what they knew. Her memory was astonishing, and that, coupled with her wonderful intelligence, enabled her to analyze and compare things no one else noticed. She delighted in assembling a panel of experts, hearing everything they had to say on a subject, and then watching with amusement while they argued themselves into a conclusion she had already arrived at.

Lady Sara's headquarters were in nearby Connaught Mews, where a block of stables had been remodelled to meet her requirements. The end rooms on the first floor, formerly the quarters of grooms and coachmen, were now a comfortable apartment where her sometimes highly irregular comings and goings, at all hours and in odd dress or actual disguise, would not perplex her mother's staid servants or titled guests.

The ground floor below, which had been occupied by stables, had become her workrooms, and it contained a study as well as a laboratory where all kinds of odd experiments and investigations were conducted.

Adjoining Lady Sara's headquarters were apartments for her employees, including my own residence. Beyond these were carriage houses, stables, and more living quarters for employees. Lady Sara owned a carriage as well as her own private cabs, both hansom and four wheeler, which meant she was always prepared for whatever kind of foray a crisis called for. In addition, there was a cart that could be adapted to various highly useful functions, from impersonating a greengrocer to costermongering.

She also owned a splendid Spider Phaeton that she favoured for her own daytime excursions because it was a socially acceptable vehicle for a woman to drive. She could take the reins herself and occasion no more severe criticism from her mother's friends than "There goes Lady Sara being eccentric again." Once out of their sight, her driving became decidedly unladylike. I often occupied the phaeton's rear seat garbed as her groom.

She kept six horses and a donkey, which made it possible for her employees to use several vehicles simultaneously if an investigation, or several investigations, required it.

Lady Sara had remarked that the case of the two giants might be one for the board. The "board" she referred to was the world's largest cribbage board. It had been designed by Burke Varnley, her father, a cribbage fanatic from the moment he learned the game as a child until his death.

The Earl had two passions in life—besides women, his Countess would have quickly added—cribbage and eating. He acquired the latter obsession in Spain at Madrid's famous Restaurante Botin. That venerable establishment introduced the Earl to many delicacies he was fond of describing in lyrical terms, but its great specialty, and the Earl's favorite, was cochinillo asado, roast suckling pig.

When, much later, he learned that the invention of cribbage was ascribed to Sir John Suckling, a seventeenth century poet and cavalier with the army of Charles I, the notion that the inventor of his favourite pastime had the same name as his favorite food came to him as a revelation. He considered it a divine command to merge his two passions.

He founded the Suckling Club, which offered its members an elaborate roast suckling dinner weekly and access to Sir John Suckling's game at all hours. Unfortunately, true gourmets rarely proved to be cribbage players. They were more prone to nap after a meal than gather around a board for a challenging session of cribbage, and the club was not a success.

The Earl invented a six-handed game of cribbage especially for the Suckling Club. It required the enormous cribbage board and three packs of cards. The board had rarely been used because of the difficulty the Earl experienced in assembling six players of the quality he insisted on. Now Lady Sara kept the board in the centre of a large oval conference table in her study, and she used it to peg her progress in her more important investigations. She could keep six cases going at once on it, but she rarely had more than one or two that were sufficiently interesting to merit a place there. The board was more than six feet long and used pegs almost as large as a man's fingers, and the six tracks, of 121 holes each, looped and entwined to form fantastic patterns. I often wondered how the Earl's inebriated friends—which, according to his Countess, they frequently were—had accurately pegged their points on that complicated board.

Because the tracks were so convoluted, Lady Sara referred to them as byways—her Byways to Evil.

If criminal investigation was an unusual pastime for a noblewoman, so was my presence in Lady Sara's household. As her principal assistant, I considered myself the most fortunate of mortals. In inventing a profession for herself, she also devised one for me. But first she had to invent me!

I remember very little of my early childhood. I have read that a baby is born in London every five minutes, and it is only to be expected that most of them arrive in undistinguished homes. It was not quite correct to say I was a street arab—a homeless, unwanted child—from birth. Someone wanted and loved me, and cared for me, and kept me in health until the age of three or so. Then both my parents died. Whether they met death separately or together, from sickness or from an accident, I have no recollection. I find it difficult to believe they simply abandoned the child they had loved and cared for until then. Since I have neither records nor recollections of them, I can only assume they had no relatives or close friends, and their suddenly orphaned child somehow got overlooked.

The East End was a crowded place—much more crowded then than now—and there were far too many homeless, parentless children about anyway. One more or less made no difference.

I must have wandered for a time, desperately seeking food and shelter, and I had the astonishing luck not only to survive but to escape the kind clutches of the various charitable organizations intended to succour children in my situation. Dr. Barnardo's National Waifs Association would have cared for me and taught me a manual trade—and stultified my imagination. A number of similar organizations that look after homeless children, such as the Orphan Working School, Princess Mary's Village Homes, the Church of England Association for Befriending Waifs and Strays, or the Metropolitan and City Police Orphanage, would have taken me in, but I managed to avoid them. An even worse fate would have been to fall into the hands of charities like the Marine Society, which prepared homeless boys for careers as sailors, or Miss Annie Macpherson's Home of Industry, which would have trained me and then sent me to Canada for a new start in life.

Fate guided my steps. I escaped all of the well-intentioned societies and sought refuge in the cattle-shed of an Irish dairyman. He and his wife were childless, kindly people of middle age—poor, of course, but I had never known anyone who wasn't. They adopted me, jokingly calling me Colin Kine—Colin meaning child or young animal, and kine being their word for cattle. Colin Kine I remained until, long afterward, Lady Sara's coachman adopted me. The dairyman and his wife had a surname of their own, but it never occurred to me that I had any claim to it.

I already had my start in life. I was learning the shabby parts of London as few people ever know them.

When I was eight or nine, my adoptive parents died of a fever, perhaps typhoid. Sickness and death were and are an ever-present reality to the London poor. I was sick myself but survived. Perhaps my foster parents fed and cared for me better than for themselves. The relative who took over their dairy business didn't like my looks, and I didn't care for his, so I left. My luck at avoiding well-intentioned charities continued. Simply by surviving in the London streets, I continued to educate myself as though I were deliberately preparing for the career I eventually followed.

I must have been almost twelve when I met Lady Sara. I had happened onto a crowd of boys tormenting a dog that had been run over by a carriage. When they wouldn't stop, I attacked the whole group in a fury, even though several were larger than I. In the end, with both eyes blackened and a bloody mouth, I routed all of them.

Then I heard a woman's voice say, "Bring that boy here." Her coachman grabbed me and took me to her carriage. She had watched the entire fracas, not intervening until it was over because she wanted to know what the outcome would be. She asked my name.

"Colin Kine, Ma'am."

"Where did you get a name like that?"

"I useter to look after cows, Ma'am."

"It's the wrong name for you. You deserve something heroic. It takes character to fight a mob over an injured mongrel."

She continued to question me. When she found I had no parents and no home, she opened the carriage door. "That won't do. Come along— I'll find a place for you." She was given to such kind impulses, and she always made up her mind quickly.

She seemed as beautiful as a fairy princess, and the carriage and coachman marked her as fabulously wealthy, but none of that meant anything to me. My mind was still on the dog. I said, "Please, Ma'am, I wants to look after the dog."

She regarded me with interest. "Of course. That was the cause of it all, wasn't it? We mustn't forget the dog. I'm afraid it has a broken leg, but something might be done for it. Bring it along."

We drove directly to the Harley Street surgery of Thomas Tallmage, who was one of London's most prominent young physicians. Once Lady Sara made up her mind to succour a mongrel dog, it wouldn't have occurred to her to offer it anything but the best medical care available. As Dr. Tallmage himself said, laughing, when he learned what our errand was, "Lady Sara never does anything by halves!" He expertly reduced the dog's fracture, and Lady Sara took it and me home with her. At that time she was still living in Connaught Place, so the street urchin and the mongrel joined the household of Earl of Ranisford, to the consternation of the Countess, her mother.

But it was quickly evident that I could not be comfortable in such a fashionable residence. I was removed to Connaught Mews to the home of Lady Sara's coachman, John Quick, who even then was known as Old John. He and his wife were wonderful people, and their own children were grown-up. Old John was almost as vain about his surname as he was about being Lady Sara's coachman. He claimed to be descended from Robert le Quic, of Cornwall, a thirteenth century notable and the first of a long line of nimble ancestors. At Lady Sara's suggestion, he formally adopted me, and I proudly became Colin Quick.

Old John and his wife looked after me like a father and mother, but Lady Sara took the responsibility for my education and employment. She began by giving me menial chores to perform in her workrooms.

When I demonstrated some potential, she began to trust me with more complicated tasks. The dog and I became known all over London. Much of my education developed out of the errands she gave me. She also took me with her when she travelled about the city, pointing out things and questioning my reactions.

The errands were odder than I realized, and as I grew older, I gradually began to grasp the strangeness of this profession she had invented for herself. At the same time, there were large quantities of book learning for me to catch up with, and in this, as with everything else, she was a stern taskmaster. For one thing, I had to master different accents and dialects. My native cockney was invaluable but only when I was supposed to be one. Anywhere in the West End, or in fashionable society, or even in a middle-class suburb, it marked me disastrously. My struggles with English grammar, which I learned from a book by a Mr. Meiklejohn, will haunt me all my life. Pitman's Shorthand Dictionary became my support in matters of pronunciation, a useful connection because as soon as I had the rudiments of reading and writing, Lady Sara set me to learning Pitman's shorthand. As my skills improved, she began calling me her secretary when she needed one, and she kept drilling me intensely at shorthand until I had attained a speed somewhat better than a hundred and fifty words a minute. She was not about to lose valuable testimony because her secretary couldn't keep pace with a witness.

I was indebted to the Countess, Lady Sara's mother, for another important aspect of my education. The Countess frequently asked me to accompany her on shopping expeditions, ostensibly to run errands but actually to receive instruction in matters she suspected Lady Sara was neglecting.

She knew the city as few people knew it, but the attractions of London that interested her most were not listed in an ordinary visitors' guide. They were places known and cherished only by connoisseurs such as herself: the dwelling celebrated for its strange assortment of ghosts; the public house outside which, ten years previously, the dead body of a man had been found in the gutter, his throat cut and a half-guinea piece clenched between his teeth; the place where the poisoner Neill Cream met one of his victims; the theatre where, concealed at the back of a closet, a skeleton had been found with a knife between its ribs; the square in Highgate haunted by the ghost of the chicken Sir Francis Bacon had beheaded and used for his famous experiment to prove that stuffing a carcass with snow would preserve it. The Countess had an amazing repertoire of such tales, and she knew where each had occurred.

Lady Sara drove me to master an entire curriculum of skills and disciplines until I became a capable investigator myself though certainly not on her level. She had invented the profession; she invented me because she needed an assistant. She solved crime after crime—some highly public and some in the highest degree confidential; some of utmost importance and many trivial—and for most of these triumphs she received no credit or acknowledgement of any kind. Only a few of her closest friends and associates were aware of her achievements. Whether a mystery concerned missing jewellery or a fortune in stolen goods, it posed a question mark and a challenge. Lady Sara made a career of removing such question marks, and her success was the only reward she required.

Now she had three unusually sinister problems to consider: the missing giant, who might be rusticating in a peaceful rural surrounding where his unusual size was accepted or who might be hiding somewhere in the depths of the London Underworld and waiting to strike again; the beast in human form who deliberately mutilated his victim; and the river thefts in which large quantities of valuable merchandise was stolen without leaving a trace.

It was too early to say what Lady Sara intended to do about the missing giant or whether she would leave the Shadwell murder to Chief Inspector Mewer. As for the river thefts, we had hardly begun our investigation. We were still attempting to understand the problem. The one thing we knew for certain was that solving them would not be easy.

"If it were, the shippers and importers would handle it themselves," Lady Sara said.

A hundred years earlier, thievery in the old Port of London had become a national scandal. Ships' crews were bribed routinely; waterside workers regularly joined the thieves in pilfering cargos. More than half a million pounds worth of goods was stolen annually, most notably from West Indian ships loaded with rum, sugar, and tobacco. Part of the problem was London's ancient restrictions on imports, which required that all ships be unloaded between London Bridge and the Tower.

The modern dock system, with docks built like fortresses, was the result. Ships could be unloaded quickly, and large-scale theft was practically eliminated. Obviously someone had found chinks in the system, though as far as we knew, the major docks had not yet been victimized.

None of those chinks had been visible from a police steam-launch. On the morrow, I would find out whether there was more to be seen from a slow-moving, oared galley.

The storm faded, finally, and I dozed off still futilely puzzling over the mysteriously vanished merchandise from the river warehouses.

CHAPTER 3

I rose at the dawn, accompanied by a twittering of sparrows. There was no point in my waking another of Lady Sara's employees just to drive me to the river, so I walked to Bayswater Road, marvelling that the city was still intact after such a furious storm, and whistled up a four wheeler, the famous London cab sometimes called a growler because of its creaking noises, or its driver's grumbling, or both. The route we followed was similar to the one Old John had taken the night before. Wapping Police Station was a short distance upstream from Shadwell Market.

The Wet Bobs, the water constables, were sterling fellows with a nautical air—they were recruited wholly from the ranks of expert seamen and boatmen. They were bronzed and hardened by their constant exposure to the weather and by long hours of labour at the heavy police oars. On their caps and coat-collars they wore nickel anchors, the badge of their office. In severe weather they donned watermen's shining straw hats, and on the river they always had their "toe bags" at hand—waterproof sacks with a warm inner lining, which they wore over their legs when they were rowing.

They did a six-hour tour of duty. Then they were off for twelve hours before their next tour. They regarded night-work as their worst ordeal, and snowstorms, fog, and piercing head winds as well as rain-swollen tides could make the Thames a place of torment for them. To row for six hours under such conditions was trying even for these hardy individuals.

They patrolled the Thames continuously, day and night, year in and year out, from Fulham to Crayford Creek. Two duty boats left Wapping police stairs every two hours. One proceeded "up along," where it was met by a boat from the Waterloo Police Station; the other made its way "down along" to meet the boat from the lowermost station at Blackwall. There were in addition supervision boats commanded by senior inspectors, the steam-launches, and the disguised boats of their detective staff. The river thieves somehow managed to elude all of this diligent attention.

That morning I joined a regular duty boat headed downstream. There was an inspector in command; he sat in the stern to steer. There were two constables at the oars, and I took the bow seat as surplus ballast. Shadwell Market, as we passed it, seemed bustling with its usual morning business, apparently untouched by the previous night's tragedy. My companions had already heard about the murder, and all four of us scrutinized the wharves and warehouses from time to time for some sign of a large, ferocious animal, but there was too much traffic to attend to on the thronged river for us to devote much attention to the shore.

We pulled in and out among the crowded shipping, now skirting the wharves, now rounding the stem of a deserted schooner to make certain thieves weren't at work in it, racing to overhaul a suspiciously evasive wherry, checking flotsam, capturing a derelict skiff, searching a barge for contraband goods. We passed row after row of moored black hulls with their riding lights still burning brightly. Steamers slipped past us, their sirens and hooters hoarsely warning river craft to make way. There were dapper passenger ships; grimy colliers; fish trawlers whose reeking cargo advertised their presence even when we passed them upwind; blunt-nosed coasters; Dutch eel scoops; sailing ships carrying timber from Norwegian pine forests; barges from the Medway, hay-laden halfway up their stubby masts.

A brig had caught fire and run aground, but fire floats had that problem in hand before we reached it. Several times we narrowly missed being run down by faster vessels.

My mates kept reminding me to watch for floating bodies, for—the night's storm excepted—the weather had been lovely for a number of days, and lovely weather is drowning weather along the Thames. Not all of these deaths are accidental. Suicides happen far more frequently in nice weather.

"But not very often in winter," one of my mates said. "The cold water puts 'em off, seemingly."

At mid-morning, I had them land me at a convenient wharf, and I took a cab back to Connaught Mews. I now had seen the Thames from a steam-launch and from an oared duty boat, studying the crowded river traffic and pondering ways in which thieves might make off with goods by the boatload. I had no answer to the problem, but Lady Sara wouldn't expect one at this early stage.

I reached Connaught Mews in time to change my clothes and make myself presentable for Lady Sara's coffee hour. She held this at eleven o'clock in her drawing room whenever anyone from her own social class asked to discuss a personal problem with her. Her friends would have been offended if she had received them in her study and positively insulted if she refused to waste her valuable time on their trivialities. The coffee hour answered both objections.

Lady Sara liked to have me present to take notes—and also, I suspected, so I could practise conducting myself with propriety under her severely critical gaze, for despite my many years as a member of her household, I was still attempting to acquire social ease in the presence of lords and ladies.

On this day, the annual social Season being over and most of Lady Sara's friends having left town, there were only three guests. The first to arrive was the elderly Lady Cowlan, Viscountess of Durgess. She was a remote cousin of Lady Sara's on both sides of her family. Her face was a mass of wrinkles, and she wore a heavy, fur-trimmed gown on that pleasant autumn day.

She was escorted in by Charles Tupper, one of Lady Sara's two footmen. Except for his small stature, he looked the part perfectly. His uniform, demeanor, deferential expression, and humble politeness in the presence of such a dazzling noblewoman were impeccable. He also was poised to perform any necessary service, which he demonstrated by deftly recovering the scarf the Viscountess dropped and returning it to her with a bow. There was nothing unusual about this except that his performance in other capacities, including that of an investigator, was equally polished. Both of Lady Sara's footmen were trained to act any part required of them—as were her other employees. In those days even a small domestic establishment like Lady Sara's required a large staff of servants, and her housekeeper, cook, maids, footmen, coachmen, grooms, stable-boys, and such supernumeraries as she retained from time to time, all had to become adept at following a suspect, watching a suspicious address, or making enquiries in situations where their special talents could be useful.

The Viscountess ceremoniously settled herself in a comfortable chair and looked about disapprovingly. It was her first visit to Lady Sara's drawing room, and she probably thought the place threadbare. Lady Sara's simple tastes were completely unlike those of the Dowager Countess. At Connaught Place, the rooms occupied by her mother were filled with expensive clutter: gold tea and coffee services, heavily engraved; fruit stands and side dishes, also of gold, supported by arching palm trees with sculpted animals and cherubs about their bases; cruets blazoned with sea or land battles; silver urns crowded with sculpted flowers; trays with an entire ballet represented on them; statuettes of every kind; stoneware that displayed the history of England; clocks ornamented with Egyptian obelisks; mechanical figures that moved to music. In Lady Sara's quarters, everything was plain and functional, like her gowns, and in exquisite taste.

Before the Viscountess could state her problem, Lord Woolston ambled in. He was an elderly baron with white hair and a spectacular white, drooping moustache. His black frock coat was set off by a gold-coloured embroidered waistcoat and a gold-coloured silk cravat. He had come directly from home; his trousers were not even wrinkled. He ceremoniously removed his gloves, gold-coloured to match his waistcoat, before he accepted Lady Sara's hand and gave me a condescending nod.

The third arrival was the Honourable Blanche Dillion, a shy young woman about twenty, who was a younger daughter of the Viscount Dillion. She might have been almost pretty had she not been so obviously distressed. She was dressed much too severely for her age in a brown coat and skirt with just a passing nod to fashion in the lace trimming on her blouse. Her face was pale, and she behaved in an extremely subdued fashion.

Lady Sara got everyone seated. Her maid poured coffee and served an assortment of biscuits. The previous night's storm dominated the conversation for a few minutes. Then Lady Sara diplomatically suggested that she see them one at a time in her library if they had anything to discuss with her.

Immediately all three turned shy and wanted to be last. Lady Sara was never willing to waste time on social trivialities. "Very well," she said. "Usually it is ladies first. Since the ladies are reluctant, Lord Woolston, why don't we start with you?"

He nodded and smiled. "Jolly good idea. Let's get on with it."

Lady Sara led him into the library and I followed, leaving the maid to keep the two ladies supplied with coffee and biscuits.

We seated ourselves comfortably, and Lord Woolston harumphed twice, bit his lip, and then announced, "London after the Season is a stupid place. Nothing to do, don't you know. My granddaughter is about to have a baby, and Lady Woolston insisted on staying in town to be near her. That's women's business, nothing to do with me, but Lady Woolston insisted I stay, too. London is a thundering dull place with everyone gone."

"It must seem so," Lady Sara said sympathetically. Since Lord Woolston seemed reluctant to come to the point, she added, "You haven't been quarrelling with both Lady Woolston and your valet, I hope."

"Why do you say that?" Lord Woolston demanded.

"If you had been on speaking terms with either of them, you wouldn't have been allowed to leave the house wearing that cravat with that waistcoat."

Lord Woolston gave his cravat a bewildered glance. "Really? Never gave it a thought. Edward went to Cornwall for a few days to visit his parents, and to tell the truth, both Lady Woolston and I were upset. I went to one of my clubs last night, White's, and the place was practically empty. I met a friend there, though. At a loose end himself, but he said he knew where we could have a friendly game of cards. So we went together."

"How much did you lose?" Lady Sara asked.

Lord Woolston winced and chewed on his moustache. "Matter of a bit more than five thousand pounds," he said finally.

Lady Sara nodded gravely. "Not what I would call a friendly game. What were you playing?"

"Baccarat."

"How did you manage to lose so much?"

"Never saw such a run of luck—good and bad. Mine was all bad. This other fellow won, and won, and won. Remarkable."

"Did your friend lose, too?"

"He did. He also lost the night before. That's why he went back. Thought his luck had to turn."

"But it didn't," Lady Sara said thoughtfully. "Were you planning to have another go at it tonight to see if your luck would turn?"

"At first, I was. But I told Lady Woolston what happened, and she threw a fit. Insisted I tell you about it."

"There are several possibilities," Lady Sara said. "One is that you really had a run of bad luck, but such runs rarely last an entire evening—or, in the case of your friend, two entire evenings. Another is that your own inept play was responsible, but I have played cards with you, and I doubt that."

"Never considered myself an expert," Lord Woolston said, "but I usually hold my own."

"So the third possibility is the more likely one. You were cheated. The methods of cheating at cards are legion. The cards could have been marked, or the sharper could have marked them himself in the course of play. In addition, several varieties of sleight-of-hand or manipulation are possible in baccarat. A reflector—there are numerous kinds—could have enabled the sharper to identify every card as it was dealt. A holdout could have been used. There are many types, and all are devices to conceal one or more cards until it or they can be played advantageously. In connection with this, extra cards are sometimes smuggled into the game. How many players were there?"

"There were five of us."

"Then the sharper could have had one or two collaborators, which introduces other possibilities for cheating. However it was managed, you were cheated outrageously. The question is—what can be done about it?"

Lord Woolston harrumphed. "Don't want any fuss, you know. No publicity."

Lady Sara smiled. "Believe me—neither does the man who cheated you. On the other hand, if nothing is done to stop him, he'll go right on cheating. This is what I suggest. Go back there tonight and play again. Take two 'friends' with you. One of them will be my footman, Charles Tupper. He can spot a sharper across the room and give him back more than he bargains for. The other will be a police officer who is just as good. You'll get your five thousand pounds back. You'll also give the sharper a good scare. An official record will be made so the police can keep an eye on him from now on."

"All right," Lord Woolston said. "I'll do it."

"You can call here after dinner for Charles and the police officer—would nine o'clock do? Along the way, you can give them the information they will need, and they can give you your instructions. Done?"

"Done," Lord Woolston agreed.

I ushered him out, and Blanche Dillion took his place in the library. She looked at me timidly. Then she turned to Lady Sara. "Does he have to be here?"

"He is my assistant," Lady Sara said kindly. "We will probably need his help, so it is important that he know what your problem is. He will do his best for you just as I will."

The young woman sat in silence for a moment. Then she burst into tears. "He said he loved me," she said.

"Let me guess," Lady Sara said. "You gave him your jewellery."

"How did you know?"

"Because you aren't wearing any of it."

"He said he needed money to pay some debts so we could get married."

"And your father didn't like him?"

She shook her head tearfully.

"Have you seen him or heard from him since you gave him your jewellery?"

She shook her head again.

"Describe him as best you can."

She did so and also gave us the Bloomsbury address where he had claimed to be living. One of her father's grooms—his daughter had been her nurse, and she felt able to trust him—had made enquiries there after the man stopped seeing her. The landlady claimed the man wasn't known at that address.

She had met him at Lord's at the Oxford-Cambridge cricket match. She had thought he was with some friends of hers. Later, when her father enquired, the friends denied any knowledge of him. Her father considered him an interloper looking for a girl to pick up, which was one reason he had taken such a violent dislike to him.

The man told her his name was Kingsley Lyman. He seemed very pleasant. He did nothing at all improper, then or later. When she introduced him to her parents, they said he was no gentleman, but he had been to Oxford—

"Or so he said," Lady Sara observed. "I know the rest of the story. You kept meeting him, and you fell in love. Finally he asked you to marry him as soon as he was able to pay his debts, so you gave him your jewellery."

She nodded. Sobs shook her body.

"All right. I know all about this man. He has been involved in shady business before—a lot of shady business. Sit down at the desk and make a complete list of every item of jewellery you gave him. Describe it as carefully as you can and don't leave anything out. It may be possible to recover some or even most of it."

Once Blanche Dillion had accepted my presence, she paid no further attention to me. During her sad tale of deception, she did not send a glance in my direction. Her attitude was not uncommon among Lady Sara's titled friends. A girl like Blanche could fall madly in love with a crook pretending to be a gentlemen, but she was unlikely to make this kind of mistake about Lady Sara's secretary and assistant, however upright and presentable he might be. Only too obviously, he was no gentleman—he worked for a living.

At one time Lady Sara had been concerned that I might fall in love with one of these young women from titled families. That could have been devastating for me; like Blanche Dillion, all of them accepted my presence without really being aware of my existence.

But Lady Sara need not have worried. After my association with her, they and their fluttery lives that revolved so exclusively around their social concerns seemed shallow and frivolous, not to mention downright silly.

While Blanche was making her list, we returned to the drawing room for a talk with Lady Cowlan.

"So sorry to bother you, Sara, dear," Lady Cowlan said gushingly when the maid had poured more coffee for her. "My brooch is missing—the gold one with diamonds. It was my mother's, you know, and her mother's, and her mother's, and I don't know how far back it goes, it's a family heirloom. I'm afraid it's been stolen, and I had so counted on giving it to Melantha."

"When did you first miss it?"

"Oh, days and days ago. I don't often wear it, and at first I thought I had mislaid it. I often do. But now I've searched and searched, and the servants have searched and searched, and it isn't anywhere. I just realized yesterday that it must have been stolen."

"Do you suspect anyone?"

"Goodness, no! If I suspected anyone, I would have got rid of them. I wouldn't have a servant in the house who stole things."

"Would you describe it for Colin?"

"Well it's an oval, about—" She waveringly held up two fingers. "—this big." She could have been indicating three inches or six. "It's gold, of course, with little diamonds around the edge and a big one in the centre."

"Very well, dear," Lady Sara said. "You finish your coffee, and then I'll send Colin home with you. The first thing is to make a really thorough search. When he has done that, he can talk with your servants."

She turned to me. "Oh! Would you?"

"I should be honoured, my lady," I told her.

While she gulped her coffee and finished the biscuit she was eating, Lady Sara took me aside. "What a parcel of dreary problems," she said wearily. "It's a gold antique brooch that Lady Cowlan is missing, oval, two and a half inches long by an inch high. It has ten small diamonds around the perimeter and a large one in the centre about a half carat in weight. Because it is so old, its value as an antique would certainly be far greater than the value of the stones and the gold separately, but a thief might not know that. If it really was stolen, it probably has been broken up and disposed of by now. Her servants are highly reliable, and they dote on her. I'm sure none of them took it nor would any of them cooperate with a thief. I think it much more likely that she lost or mislaid it. Find out when she last wore it and what gown she wore it on."

We had a short ride down Park Lane in the Viscountess's carriage. Dorothy, her maid, a sensible, middle-aged woman who had been with her for years, told me she had searched every drawer and container that could possibly have contained the brooch.

"What gown was the Viscountess wearing when she last wore it?" I asked.

This occasioned an argument between Dorothy and another maid. Neither of them remembered, and of course the Viscountess had no recollection of it. Finally Dorothy went to a wardrobe crammed with dresses, one of several such wardrobes, and took out a gown, a showy arrangement of silk that must have looked odd on the elderly Viscountess.

On the breast of the gown was pinned the brooch.

It was a typical triumph for Lady Sara—a brilliant solution to a problem that proved to be trivial only because of her brilliant solution. As was usually the case, someone else got the credit. I was warmly embraced by the Viscountess, congratulated by Dorothy, and viewed as a miracle-worker by all of the servants, who had been extremely distressed over the Viscountess's loss. Her butler presented me with a bottle of a fine old port that I knew I didn't have the palate to properly appreciate.

I took it home with me and gave it to Lady Sara. This was one of the few times her prowess brought her a tangible reward.

After I returned to Connaught Mews, Lady Sara and I discussed the river thefts. She first wanted to know about the Thames Police's detective staff.

"The detectives use disguised boats and follow no schedules at all, but there are too few of them," I said. "Occasionally they happen onto booty that's been sunk in waterproof bags and buoyed with an innocent-looking float of some kind, but almost always this turns out to be smuggled goods. The smugglers cache them here and there in small quantities, and the occasional discovery of a hiding place is no great loss to them. As far as the police are concerned, these are worthwhile 'finds,' but they have nothing to do with the river thefts."

"What are your impressions?" she asked.

"I never realized what a welter of confusion exists on both sides of the river," I said. "It is packed with wharves, warehouses, and docks all the way to Greenwich and beyond. There are ships of every kind docked, or anchored, or arriving, or departing, or moving from one place to another. It is difficult to make any sense of it."

There was laughter in her voice. "Spoken like a true landlubber. Successful thieves have the ability to turn such confusion to their advantage. That is why they are successful. What are their chances of being overlooked if they boldly move goods through that clutter of shipping by daylight?"

"None," I said confidently. "They might manage it once or twice, but they would be caught sooner or later and probably sooner. The police and customs authorities keep a closer watch on things than seems possible."

"In any case, the actual stealing would have to be done at night when there are few people about," Lady Sara mused. "The first question is whether the stolen goods are being removed by waggon or by boat."

I had no answer to that, but I felt certain of one thing: If by boat, they weren't being transported far. "When boats move on the river at night, someone knows all about them or quickly becomes suspicious," I said. "They couldn't navigate through London's harbour night after night in unlighted boats of whatever description without both police and customs authorities investigating. Even if the boats are properly lighted, someone will soon get curious as to who they are and where they are going. They aren't transporting stolen goods from Tilbury to somewhere beyond the upper pool, for example."

"All the thefts to date have occurred between London Bridge and Greenwich," Lady Sara said. "The thieves probably have a haven somewhere along those reaches. Or several havens. Even so, it seems strange that the authorities have never caught sight of them. Chief Inspector Mewer considers this a simple case. 'One not worthy of Lady Sara's attention,' was the way he put it to a subordinate. He regards the thieves' success as a question of luck, but he has to concede they have been uncommonly lucky."

"There has to be more than luck involved," I said.

"A great deal more. The thefts have been managed so cleverly that the firms robbed haven't been able to decide when or what time of day it happened or what employees were on duty. That suggests an organization of highly skilled thieves. But to return to the waggon or boat question—however the thefts are managed, almost certainly the goods are being taken somewhere quickly by boat."

"Why not by land?" I asked, remembering those sharp-eyed police on the river.

"Think how many waggons it would require, or how many trips by one waggon, to transport the quantity of goods stolen. That would attract far more attention around the looted warehouses than a single unlighted boat. I am certain the thefts occur at night with the goods being removed by boat to a warehouse or warehouses along the river."

I thought for a moment about what I had seen from the river. "If the thieves were to use a boat small enough to nose into narrow openings, they could move closely inshore and keep out of sight by threading their way among anchored or docked ships. That might enable them to escape detection indefinitely."

Lady Sara shook her head. "The boat would have to be large enough to carry worthwhile loads. Also, a boat behaving in the manner you describe would arouse suspicion the moment anyone glimpsed it. The thieves may find boldness more effective than stealth because it isn't so likely to be suspected. They may keep to the centre of the river and follow in the wake of a large boat. Or they may work up one side and then drift back downstream on the other side. They may change their tactics repeatedly."

The idea of a small boat hiding in shadows along the shore appealed to me, and I was reluctant to give it up. "Sentries posted on the bank could detect them easily if they really are moving close inshore," I said.

"But we don't want them 'detected,'" Lady Sara said. "Capturing one boat wouldn't solve anything. They would simply change their tactics. We must find out where they are taking the stolen goods. Their warehouse, or warehouses, will have to be our first objective. These may belong to a firm handling a large volume of legitimate business. Only in that way could quantities of stolen goods be disposed of without eventually arousing suspicion. We also need to know something about the way goods are handled along the river. When you can spare the time, give some thought to that."

CHAPTER 4

The meeting with Chief Inspector Mewer was scheduled for two o'clock, and Thomas Tallmage, the doctor who, years before, had reduced a mongrel dog's fracture for me, arrived shortly before two. He was now Sir Thomas Tallmage, one of London's most distinguished physicians. He was tall and handsome, greying despite the fact that he wasn't much older than fifty, the calm and poised master of any crisis because he had seen so many. He had been Lady Sara's suitor for more than twenty years.

He once told me how, as a young doctor, he had attempted to persuade her father, the Earl, that his prospects, both for wealth and distinction, were excellent, and he would make a worthy husband for a nobleman's daughter. The Earl cut him off with a laugh. "You don't have to convince me, my boy. Convince her!"

Sir Thomas had never been able to, but he was still trying.

Lady Sara was her father's favourite child. He would have left the peerage to her if the law had permitted it. He often announced, pridefully, that she did everything he could do, and did it better, except chase women. When she came of age, the Married Woman's Property Act had not yet been passed, and a husband had absolute control over a wife's money and property. Lady Sara told her father she wanted no man meddling with her patrimony. He decided he didn't, either, and he settled a generous life income on her in such a way that her husband, if she acquired one, would be unable to touch the principal or even the income.

"The day before that happened, I had about four hundred suitors," Lady Sara remembered with a laugh. "The day afterward, the number had dropped to four."

She had nothing against marriage. She thought it a splendid institution for a man but not for a woman. Lord Byron had written, "Man's love is of man's life a thing apart,/'Tis woman's whole existence." To Lady Sara's extreme irritation, men were fond of quoting this to her, and she liked to point out acidly that they always quoted it out of context. Lord Byron's lines were not for her.

There was so much she wanted to do with her life, so much to learn, so many things to accomplish, and when she looked critically at the lives of her women friends, she saw that marriage had all but consumed every one of them. Marriage left a woman little time for anything else. Even women of her own class, with no financial worries and houses full of servants, had to supervise constantly; dismiss inept maids and fight daily battles with housekeepers and butlers; conduct their own employment bureau so as to always have a full staff available; plan elaborate social occasions; struggle heroically with catastrophe when, with a dinner party in the offing, a cook or butler or housekeeper left without notice; look after their children's welfare and education; work unremittingly to make certain their homes were efficiently and peacefully and economically run. To what purpose? So their husbands could be freed from all domestic concerns in order to occupy themselves with more important matters. Lady Sara chose to remain single and invest her large income in the work that was her vocation, her profession, and—yes—her religion, the detection of crime.

When I joined Lady Sara and Sir Thomas, they were already seated at the oaken conference table in her study. In the centre was the enormous cribbage board Lady Sara inherited from her father. At the moment there were only two sets of pegs on the board. One represented our investigation into the river thefts. Those pegs were still in their starting holes because we had not yet turned up a single clue. The other set represented the mystery of the two giants. The artists' sketches provided enough information for a beginning, and Lady Sara had moved the pegs two holes forward.

The Shadwell murder had been left in Chief Inspector Mewer's hands. I once suggested giving the Chief Inspector a cribbage board of his own to record his cases on, but Lady Sara said no, he wouldn't know how to use it. This was probably true. I had never been able to understand how Lady Sara used hers. She had her own subjective system for rating her progress on cases.

Sir Thomas greeted me with friendly scrutiny. He liked to make jokes about the state of my health. He remarked, "Colin has been unusually reticent of late. Is he in love?"

"He has been reading Mrs. Humphry's Manners for Men," Lady Sara said. "In the last chapter, she lays down rules for speaking with royal persons, and Colin is grappling with the notion that during such conversations he must leave it to the royal person to originate subjects of discussion and never, under any circumstances, introduce a topic of his own. If you want him to talk, you have to suggest a subject and invite his comments."

"But I'm not a royal person," Sir Thomas protested.

"You are a knight," Lady Sara said. "That, with your other qualifications and achievements, would fully entitle you to royal treatment if 'royalty' really meant anything." She added thoughtfully, "It's an asinine rule. Most royal persons have nothing in their heads but lumber. They're completely incapable of suggesting subjects worth discussing. Quite apart from that, it was silly of Mrs. Humphry to include such a topic in her book. How many of her readers will ever have occasion to converse with royalty?"

"Not all royal persons are empty-headed," Sir Thomas said loyally. "You'll have to concede we are blessed with a great queen."

Lady Sara shook her head. "Her Majesty's only accomplishment is to be herself. She has never done anything else. She was popular in her youth, extremely unpopular in middle age, and now she is popular again. All of that has been the result of her being herself. In any situation that requires nothing more of her than that, she performs magnificently. A truly great queen should be able to reach beyond herself when a great occasion demands it."

"What does the royal family think of you?" Sir Thomas asked.

"Princess Louise is a good friend," Lady Sara said. "As you know, she is a talented artist, and we have interests in common as well as mutual friends in London's Bohemia. When I first came out, the Prince of Wales thought I was fascinating until I made it clear that I thought he wasn't. The others don't think of me at all except when something I do is forced on their attention. Then they dismiss me with tones of deep regret."

Like Lady Sara's rooms upstairs, her study was furnished severely. There were no bric-a-brac. Everything had a place and a use. The books that lined the walls were on every imaginable subject. Although crime was Lady Sara's principal concern, she was interested in everything about it, and since crime touched every sphere of human activity, she was interested in everything.

The two artists, Stephen Lynes and Evan Vaughan, had just arrived, and Lady Sara was still greeting them, when the Dowager Countess, Lady Ranisford, swept into the room. She was small, plump, and as unlike Lady Sara as could be imagined. She had come over from Connaught Place because Lady Sara had told her Sir Thomas would be there.

She brought with her Reginald Dempster, a cousin of hers and Lady Sara's several times removed. He was a man about forty, slight of build except for an ample stomach, with a small, almost frivolous moustache. He was always impeccably dressed, and he had the air of waiting for some higher calling, although no one who knew him, least of all himself, had the slightest notion of what that might be. When he was younger, he had been, for a time, heir presumptive to a baronetcy. Then the present baronet remarried, taking a second wife much younger than himself, and in short order produced a large family that included several sons. This naturally was a considerable disappointment to Dempster and his wife— especially to his wife, since she had married him on the presumption of his inheritance. He lived on a limited fixed income, a legacy from an aunt. He was always short of money and apparently incapable of earning any even though he had received a Third in law from Oxford and had been called to the bar.

Lady Sara considered him both a bore and an ass, and years before she had, with effort, cured him of his attempts to borrow money from her. He both thought and spoke in clichés, which she found irritating. When he delivered himself of some such profundity as, "I can't make head nor tail of it," she would reply lightly, "That possibly is because it has neither a head nor a tail." We had seen little of him in recent years except when we encountered him at the Countess's home. The Countess tolerated him because she found him amusing. He was a wonderful source of gossip about persons of note, and if she needed someone to complete a foursome for whist, or she merely wanted someone to chat with, Dempster was always available. He had nothing else to do.

The Countess greeted Sir Thomas with formal affection, gave me a friendly nod, and graciously permitted Lady Sara to present the artists. Then she turned to Sir Thomas and asked, "Did you really see that unfortunate man?"

"A murder victim is beyond feeling," Sir Thomas said with a rueful grin. "I'm the unfortunate one. Lady Sara routed me out at sunrise and hauled me off to a makeshift mortuary down by the docks. Yes, my lady, I saw him."

"Was he really clawed by an animal?" the countess asked breathlessly.

"He undoubtedly was clawed. I should have said 'by an animal,' but I've suspended judgment because Lady Sara has promised to show me otherwise. We can't start until Chief Inspector Mewer gets here."

"Police officers," the Countess said scornfully, "are never on time and never where they are needed." She turned to me. "Did you see him, Colin?"

"The murder victim? I saw him last night, my lady."

"What did he look like?"

"Like someone had fed part of him into a sausage machine," I said.

She uttered a peal of laughter. "Dear Colin. He always has the right word."

"He wasn't pretty," I said defensively.

"You can't expect a corpse to be pretty. It is totally incapable of presenting its best profile, or rearranging its clothing to advantage, or striking a pose, or doing any of the silly things people are always doing to improve their appearances. This one sounds deliciously gruesome. Will you join me for tea, Sir Thomas?"

"No, thank you, Lady Ranisford. I must get back to my neglected work as soon as we deal with the Chief Inspector. Lady Sara would never admit it, but her patient, being dead, could have waited. My patients, being alive, have to be kept that way."

"Lord Anstee is coming," Lady Sara said. "You may be able to persuade him to stay for tea."

The Countess stared at her. "Why would he be coming to town at this time of year? He hates London after the Season is over."

"I asked him to come," Lady Sara said.

Reggie Dempster was taking everything in with open mouth. Casual descriptions of hideously-mutilated corpses were obviously not his cup of tea, but he was coping as best he could. His mouth opened wider when the next guests arrived. The first was Chief Inspector Mewer, but his entrance went almost unnoticed because Lord Anstee, mutton chop whiskers fluttering, dashed in right behind him.

"Sorry I'm late, Sara, dear," Lord Anstee announced. "The trains I take never run on time. Ah, Hildegarde!" He gave the Countess a sweeping embrace. "You are more charming each time I see you. Sir Thomas, you look too unhealthy to be a doctor. Better let me mix a tonic for you. Hello, Colin. Glad Sara hasn't worked you to death. But it'll come, it'll come."

Lady Sara greeted him with a kiss. "Did you bring it?" she demanded.

"Of course I brought it. Did you think I would come without it? But it still isn't clear to me what you wanted with it. On the telephone, you sounded as though the Houses of Parliament would collapse, the Thames would reverse its flow, and war would break out with France if this museum piece weren't placed in your hands at precisely two o'clock. I wouldn't have dared not bring it. Sorry the train was late."

Chief Inspector Mewer, always fearful that London would be ravished by crime while he was absent from his office, was becoming increasingly impatient. He harrumphed twice, but Lady Sara was too occupied with Lord Anstee to notice.

Lord Anstee handed her a package. "I removed the handle," he said. "Awkward to carry on a train with the handle attached. Hope you can manage without it. I'd hate to think war broke out with France because I left the handle at home."

"I can manage splendidly without the handle," Lady Sara assured him. "As for the train being late—bosh. I know when your train gets in. You would have arrived early if you hadn't made a detour to the Caledonian Club."

"How did you know?" Lord Anstee demanded.

"By the whisky Mac on your breath. The odor—or perhaps you would rather I said 'fragrance'—of Scotch whisky and ginger wine is unmistakable, and nowhere else are the whisky Macs as potent, and as fragrant, as at the Caledonian Club."

Lord Anstee laughed sheepishly. "The Caledonian wasn't so very much out of my way, and train rides are a dull, dry business. A man has needs, you know."

"I do know," Lady Sara said with a laugh. "To tell the truth, you weren't even late. Would you like me to mix you another?"

"Thank you, no. For all your talent, you don't have quite the right touch for mixing drinks. A moderate drinker never does." He nodded at the package. "Now that you've got it, do you need me?"

"I may," Lady Sara said. "The Chief Inspector is a hard man to convince."

The Chief Inspector was on the verge of exploding with impatience, but there was further delay while the Countess settled the question of tea with Lord Anstee. She departed, finally, taking the still-awed Reggie Dempster with her, and Lady Sara got everyone seated around the oaken table.

Because of his sturdy build, the Chief Inspector should have dominated the scene. He dominated most scenes he was a part of, but on that occasion, sitting next to Lady Sarah, an earl's daughter, and across the table from Lord Anstee, a marquis, he shrank noticeably. Not only was he ill-at-ease, but he seemed to be following Mrs. Humphry's credo concerning conversation with royal persons. He was waiting for someone to address him before he dared open his mouth.

Sir Thomas had a look of anticipation on his face.

Lady Sara turned to the Chief Inspector. "Have you found any animal tracks?"

He shifted his feet uneasily. "Well—no. Last night's storm pretty much settled that, but we're still looking. One might have been left in a sheltered place. If it was, we'll find it. We only need one. Doctor MacIver—he's the divisional police surgeon—agrees with me. Only an animal could have clawed the man's face like that."

"Have you identified the man?"

"Yes. His name is William Havill, usually called Bill, and he was employed at the London Docks as a night-watchman. He had always been steady and reliable, and he never missed work—until last night."

"Then he was killed on his way to work," Lady Sarah mused.

"The market wasn't on his way to work. He came down Broad Street from his home—he lived over in Limehouse—and he should have continued straight ahead to the Shadwell New Basin warehouses. There was no reason for him to wander down toward the market. We're wondering if he encountered the animal somewhere along Broad Street and was trying to escape from it."

"Probably he encountered his murderer—murderers, more likely—and they forced him into a place where there would be no witnesses when they disposed of him. The area around the market is pretty much deserted early at night, isn't it?"

"Well, yes."

"Lord Anstee has brought something that will help you identify the animal. He has a remarkable collection of medieval torture instruments. This one is called a 'Spanish Tickler.'"

She unwrapped the package Lord Anstee had given to her and took out a bar of iron about four and a half inches long and an inch thick. Curving out from it were four claw-like iron projections, each terminating in a razor point. There was a hole in the end of the bar where a round shaft could be inserted to serve as a handle.

Sir Thomas leaned forward and studied it intently. Then he smiled and shook his head in amazement. "You've convinced me," he told Lady Sarah.

The Chief Inspector stared open-mouthed at the iron claws. He said nothing.

"It's also known as a 'Cat's Paw,'" Lord Anstee said. "There are illustrations in early books showing how it was used. They would string a nude victim up, hoisting him high into the air by his thumbs or wrists, and then, with a long handle on this thing, they could rake his entire body with it—make a bloody mess of him in very short order. These points are sharp."

Chief Inspector Mewer was still staring. "I'll be—" He cleared his throat apologetically and then reached out a finger and tested the point of one of the iron claws. "You think something like this tore Havill's face?"

"I'm sure of it," Lady Sara said. "No animal would have raked both sides of his face simultaneously, and if he had raised his arms to protect himself, he wouldn't have had the backs of both forearms raked—it would take an extremely awkward position to make that possible, try it. The claw marks would have gone across his arms, not down the length of them. Someone killed him with a vicious blow to his head. Then, with him lying on the ground dead, claw marks were produced on his face and the backs of his arms with an instrument like this. Because it was done after he was dead, there was very little blood."

The Chief Inspector harumphed indignantly. "Then someone applied a fancy touch in an effort to confuse the police."

"Possibly, but I doubt it," Lady Sara said. "I take it you've found no reason why anyone would want to murder a steady, reliable worker like Havill. He couldn't have been carrying much in the way of money or valuables. Since there were no witnesses, the police would have been confused enough without the claw marks. Someone had a reason for mutilating his face and arms. It may have been a ghoulish reason, but it was a reason. It does seem strange that there were no animal tracks, though."

"But you just said there was no animal!" the Chief Inspector protested.

"There wasn't. But if the murderers could mutilate the corpse with claw marks, they easily could have left a few fake animal tracks. It would have been the right artistic touch. I wonder why they didn't."

"I'm going to have a hard time convincing my superiors about this," the Chief Inspector said ruefully. "Could I borrow this thing for a few hours?"

Lord Anstee nodded his assent.

"But don't lose it," Lady Sarah cautioned. "It is rare and immensely valuable to a collector."

"It is that," Lord Anstee agreed. "It is continental in origin, and I don't think there is another in England—not even in the Tower of London." He turned to Lady Sara. "Do you need me for anything else? Then I'll have a chat with your mother." He nodded at the artists and at the Chief Inspector, told Sir Thomas he was always happy to see him as long as he didn't have to see him professionally, and added a cautionary remark for me.

"I'm afraid you'll come to a bad end, Colin, brought up in crime the way you were. Keep an eye on him, Chief Inspector. With the training Lady Sara has given him, he can make a master criminal of himself any time he feels so inclined."

The Marquis headed for Connaught Place to find Lady Ranisford, and Lady Sara took up the business that had started all of this, the giant axe murderer. She began by describing the circumstances under which each of the artists had come in contact with a giant. Then she asked them to show Sir Thomas and Chief Inspector Mewer their sketches. It took the Chief Inspector a full minute to grasp their import.

He demanded indignantly, "Are you suggesting there were two seven and a half foot giants?"

"I'm not suggesting it," Lady Sara said. "I'm stating it. One giant had—probably has—a birthmark; the other, the executed murderer, had no birthmark but a mole. Because they looked remarkably alike, it wouldn't surprise me if Hob Hagan had a brother, even a twin brother. And it was the brother you hanged, not Hob Hagan."

"If you're thinking we hanged the wrong man, that's nonsense. He was caught bending over his victims with the axe in his hands."

"There can be no question about that," Lady Sarah agreed. "You caught the axe murderer, and you hanged the axe murderer. But you didn't catch or hang Hob Hagan."

"Several people identified him!" the Chief Inspector protested. "He admitted himself that he was Hob Hagan!"

"Let's consider what we know about him," Lady Sarah said. "Hob Hagan first came to the attention of the police in York. He injured some men who were mistreating a horse. He was a gentle, repentant sort of person, but he did resent jokes about his size. Everyone who knew him had the impression that he desperately wanted to live a normal life. The manager of a travelling sideshow approached him when he was in prison and offered to make him rich. Hagan would have nothing to do with him.

"He drifted on, and there were several police reports concerning violent behaviour committed in very similar circumstances. Someone was mistreating an animal, or someone tried to poke fun at his size. Finally he reached London, and in this violent city there were more acts of violence. There were reports of men being beaten by a giant but not severely and only with his fists. Probably they taunted him, but he had learned to react with restraint.

"Suddenly he acquired a knife and a drastically different personality. He badly injured a number of people before the report of his first murder entered the police files. There were two more such reports before he was caught standing over three victims with the bloody axe in his hands."

"He confessed to all of the murders," the Chief Inspector protested.

"Why wouldn't he? He was caught in flagrante delicto. There was no way he could escape hanging, and he knew he could only be hanged once. But was he really responsible for all of those crimes, or was he taking the blame for his brother because he knew he was doomed anyway? Was Hob Hagan the gentle giant he appeared to be, or did he become as violent as the axe murderer and commit some of those murders himself?"

"You have a unique talent for thinking up police problems where there shouldn't be any," the Chief Inspector grumbled. "If there really is a brother, and he really is a gentle giant, why bother with him? We have enough criminals to worry about without that."

"It is important to find out whether one giant or two has been committing violent crimes. Officially, Hob Hagan has been hanged. That's a wonderful situation for a criminal to be in. It gives him licence to commit all the crimes he pleases. No suspicion can fall on him because he is already dead."

"So what are we to do about it?" the Chief Inspector asked.

"Ask police everywhere to be on the lookout for a giant. He should be easily recognized if anyone sees him. If he has turned violent, we must try to find him before he kills someone else."

"I guess we could do that without too much trouble," Chief Inspector Mewer conceded. "It's just that I'm not clear in my own mind what I would do with him if I got hold of him."

"If you find him, let me know at once. I'd like to talk with him."

"Well—I can do that."

"I can tell you where a giant is," Sir Thomas said.

We all turned to him expectantly.

"He is an Irish giant," he said. "Officially, he measures seven feet nine inches tall, which is three inches taller than Hob Hagan. He lived during a period in the eighteenth century when there was a competition between anatomists to acquire interesting specimens. This giant, whose name was Charles Byrne, had a horror of suffering such a fate. He made elaborate arrangements to avoid that, but the eminent surgeon John Hunter coveted his skeleton and shamelessly bribed officials to obtain it. It is now in the Hunterian Museum. I can testify of my own knowledge that Byrne is a sedate, well-behaved skeleton, totally without such frills as birthmarks or moles, and the police have no cause to concern themselves with him."

"Fifty or sixty years ago, there was a Norfolk giant named Hales," Lady Sara said. "The most interesting thing about him was that he had a sister who was said to be only seven inches shorter than he was—and seven inches taller than any man in the county when her brother was out of it—proving that giantism can run in families."

Chief Inspector Mewer cleared his throat twice and changed the subject. "Just this morning I convinced my superiors that there's a wild animal prowling the docks. Now I have to explain why there isn't any. They may decide to give me thirty days' leave for my health."

He left. Under his arm, and carried with exaggerated care, was the Spanish Tickler, which he couldn't have broken by throwing from an upper storey window.

CHAPTER 5

Sir Thomas, on being assured he was no longer needed, returned to his round of patients. The rest of us continued to discuss the missing giant.

"The original Hob Hagan may have dropped from sight because he found a quiet rural corner where he can live a normal life without being harassed about his size," Lady Sara said. "If so, routine enquiries will bring us word of him sooner or later. If he really has been committing crimes in London, that's another story entirely, and he will be much more difficult to find. For one thing, he'll have learned how to keep out of sight. For another, someone may be sheltering him."

"Someone may have been intimidated into sheltering him, my lady," I said. "And supporting him."

Lady Sarah looked at me quickly. "One peg for you. But even if he doesn't have to support himself, he can't remain in hiding forever. He'll need an occasional breath of air. Chief Inspector Mewer's problem is that he has no curiosity and very little imagination. Also, he is well-versed only in police matters. He knows all about the regulations for this or that, but he hasn't begun to comprehend how fantastic the Shadwell Market crime is. Or, for that matter, how fantastic it is to have a missing giant."

"Are we still leaving the Shadwell murder to him?" I asked.

"For the present. We have two investigations of our own to launch. One of them concerns the giant—to find out what has become of Hob Hagan and to learn who the giant axe murderer really was. The other concerns the river thefts."

Lynes looked crushed. "Does that mean I can't exhibit Hagan, my lady?"

"Of course you can," Lady Sarah said reassuringly. "The axe murderer pretended to be Hob Hagan. We want the real Hob Hagan to think we believe that. Go ahead and exhibit him complete with mole and minus his birthmark. In the meantime, we will launch the most thorough search possible for him."

"One would think a man that size wouldn't be difficult to find," Lynes said.

"Obviously he has mastered the art of keeping out of sight," Lady Sarah said. "The one advantage we have is that anyone who does see him will remember him. Sideshow owners, for example. Apparently Hagan wasn't interested in joining one, but a sideshow owner would certainly try to recruit any giant he saw, and if one has caught a glimpse of Hagan recently, he'll be able to tell us where he saw him. London's Bohemia would be another place to look. Artists would find a giant-sized model fascinating. What a find Hob Hagan would be for an artist painting a David and Goliath scene!"

"He could hardly make a career of that," I objected.

"No, but if an artist has made use of him, or tried to, he'll remember him. Other artists will remember that so-an-so had a giant model. There are a number of occupations where his height or his strength would be of enormous advantage to him. We'll have to begin our search at once and spread our net as widely as possible to find out whether anyone re-members seeing him and to alert all of our people to watch for him. We may be lucky. If we aren't, we will still be looking for him at this time next year."

"We'll start tomorrow," I promised. "I'll tell Rick and Charles."

Rick Allward and Charles Tupper, Lady Sara's two footmen, were not often called upon to function as footmen, but they were invaluable to her in other capacities. Tall footmen were considered a mark of distinction for a household. The taller they were, the higher their wages. Lady Sara's footmen were somewhat below average height—this was considered by her friends to be another of her eccentricities—and they were paid fifty pounds yearly and also provided with living quarters for their families in Connaught Mews, which amounted to extremely generous wages. They were masters of disguise, could lose themselves in a crowd in a twinkling, could follow a suspect from the docks to the Houses of Parlia-ment or Hampstead Heath without being detected, and were invaluable support in any kind of a fracas. They were, in fact, expert investigators. They loved their work and loved working for Lady Sara.

"We will take a day and a night," Lady Sara said. "I want all of our agents and informers alerted to look for the missing giant. Those near the river should also be asked to watch for suspicious activity around the warehouses. We can begin the two searches at once."

"Charles has Lord Woolston's sharper to deal with tonight," I remind-ed her. "That will make tomorrow a long day for him."

"He will have a full night's sleep," she said confidently. "It won't take him long to settle the sharper."

The artists left, and the moment the formalities of their departure had been attended to, Lady Sara turned her attention to the work that still lay ahead of her. The next item on her agenda was Blanche Dillion's errant lover.

"His real name is Roy Koby," she said. "Sometimes he calls himself Kingsley Lyman or Lyman Kingsley, but he also uses other names. He has been living on his good looks for years by using ingenious variations on this dodge. Sooner or later someone will be outraged enough to make a formal complaint to the police, publicity or no, and his career will be temporarily interrupted. Our task is to make him think this is the time. Shall we go?"

We first enquired for Kingsley Lyman at the Bloomsbury address he had given to Blanche Dillion. The landlady, a severe-looking, elderly woman, disclaimed any knowledge of him.

"Obviously she is in his pay, but it doesn't really matter," Lady Sara said. "I'm sure Koby only used this as an accommodation address. Now that he has written Blanche off, he already has a new one."

We next visited the Bishopgate Police Station to borrow a constable named Perkins who sometimes worked with Lady Sara. She told his inspector she wanted to frighten someone, and he understood at once that she was dealing with a law violator the police couldn't touch.

Constable Perkins was elderly, for a constable, with a solemn face and an air of such profound gravity that anyone not familiar with his slow, fumbling thought processes immediately received the impression of a trusted official regularly consulted by the commissioner and privy to all the secrets of police officialdom.

Our next objective was "The Malt Worm," a flourishing pub near Aldgate High Street. "Malt worm" was a term applied to habitues of taverns in Elizabethan times. It had no special significance in Aldgate High Street except perhaps to suggest that this particular public house once had a landlord with a historical bent.

We didn't enter the public house. Instead, we went round to a side entrance and rang the bell of the most exclusive club in London. No directory of clubs listed it—which was not surprising since it had no name. The members jocularly called it "The Crib," a term commonly used for addresses far more disreputable than this one. Its membership qualifications had never been written down nor did they need to be. The basic requirement was a simple one. All of the members were, one way or another, crooks.

It was an excellent club. It never closed. It had no licence, but the best quality ales, liquors, and wines were always available. It was full of nooks and corners where confidences could be exchanged and jobs planned without any danger of being overheard.

And it was, as I said, exclusive. Merely being a crook didn't qualify one for membership. One had to be a respected craftsman, admired for the deftness with which that crookedness was exercised.

I jerked the bell-pull, and a panel opened in the door. A youngish male face with sharp eyes studied us. "I want the Gaffer—quickly!" Lady Sara said.

The panel closed. After a brief delay, it opened again. This time the face was infinitely old and bearded. The eyes were pale and watery. A thin, cracked voice said, with as much politeness as a voice with that timbre could manage, "Afternoon, Lady Sara."

"Gaffer, I've got to see Roy Koby immediately. He is going to be nicked if nothing is done to queer it."

The pale eyes studied the three of us and settled on Constable Perkins. The cracked voice said perplexedly, "You've brought a peeler with you to keep Roy from being nicked?"

"The constable is in with us," Lady Sara said impatiently. "Where do you think I get my information?"

The door opened. "I'll send for Roy," the Gaffer said. "Make yourselves comfortable."

He was surprisingly erect and quick on his feet for one so old. Probably that quickness had saved him from many an arrest.

We found ourselves in a long, narrow room. An alcove at either end was furnished with chairs and sofas. Here members conducted business with outsiders they didn't want to take into the club, and outsiders waited to be vetted before they were admitted.

We seated ourselves in one of the alcoves and waited.

Lady Sara's relationship with the London underworld was peculiar. The criminals knew she worked hand and glove with the police and had a chief inspector at her beck and call. Perhaps for that very reason they were tempted to consider her a friend with high connections, able to put in a good word that would get a sentence reduced or a charge dropped.

And occasionally she did get a sentence reduced or a charge dropped—sometimes in the interests of justice but more frequently because there was bigger game in the offing and the favours she did were likely to be returned. Criminals who received help from Lady Sara, or whose families were helped while they were quodded, considered her a colleague with whom one could jaw without restraint. The gossip she picked up was always interesting and sometimes invaluable.

As a result, Lady Sara was made welcome in the club any time she chose to visit it, and so was I when I accompanied her—but not when we had a constable with us. This was why we were kept waiting outside.

Finally Roy Koby joined us. He was fairly good-looking but rather old to inspire a girl Blanche Dillion's age to fall so precipitously in love. Though his face bore no obvious signs of dissipation, I marked him at once as a heavy drinker, and this would do him in eventually if some angry father or brother didn't settle him first.

Perhaps he had been to Oxford. He had that confident self-assurance about him, and he was impeccably dressed even though he had been summoned unexpectedly. He greeted Lady Sara with exaggerated courtesy—he had a pleasant, beautifully modulated voice, which probably served him well—and nodded politely to me and to Constable Perkins when Lady Sara introduced us.

She invited him to sit down. Then she said, "You really soaped Blanche Dillion. Didn't you know how young she is?"

He said with a frown, "Surely she is in her twenties—"

Lady Sara was shaking her head. "You should have checked. She isn't twenty yet."

Koby raised his eyebrows.

"Did you know she stole some of that jewellery from her mother and also gave you some her aunt had lent to her?" Lady Sara asked.

"No," he said slowly. "I didn't know that."

"Her father doesn't like you," Lady Sara observed.

Koby shrugged. "Fathers never do. As long as the daughters like me—"

"This father is a Viscount and an MP. Her uncle is a judge. The Home Secretary, who is the highest police authority in the London area, is her godfather. You certainly made a muck of it this time. Her family is furious and determined to make a muck of you in return."

"They wouldn't do that to the girl," Koby said confidently.

"Think again," Lady Sara said. "They've got you dead to rights. She'll turn crown's evidence and claim you goaded her to steal the jewels. She'll be let off with a reprimand—would a judge send a Viscount's daughter to prison for taking her mother's jewellery when there's a character like you to blame the entire mess on? It'll be the lag for you. The sentence will give you something you haven't had for years, a permanent address."

Koby looked at me. I nodded slowly. He looked at Constable Perkins, whose nod had the solemn authority of an Act of Parliament.

"Understand—none of this is Blanche's idea," Lady Sara said. "Her family won't leave her any choice."

He didn't want to believe her. He had been so successful for so long, had made fools of so many women, that he had difficulty grasping the possibility that for once something had gone wrong. On the other hand, here was Lady Sara—with a constable who certainly looked as though he ought to know—and Lady Sara had never been known to give anyone a bad shot. His pause was a long one while all three of us sat looking at him sternly. It was his move.

"What's to be done?" Koby asked finally.

"The jewellery," Lady Sara said. "If you have it in my hands within an hour, I'll see that Blanche puts it back where she got it. That will stopper things. Nothing missing, nothing to fuss about however angry her father may be."

"I haven't got all of it," Koby said.

"Your problem. Get it."

"I'll do what I can," he said. "Will you wait here?"

Lady Sara nodded.

He hurried away, and Lady Sara announced to us confidently, "This shouldn't take long."

It took him only thirty minutes. Lady Sara told me afterward she knew he'd had several successes recently, and he wouldn't have been in any hurry to fence Blanche's jewellery. He might have given a few choice pieces to the woman he was living with, though, and that could have delayed him while he persuaded her to give them up.

She checked the jewellery against the list Blanche had made for her. "Right," she announced finally. "That's the lot. We'll have everything back in place no later than tonight."

As we started to leave, she turned to Koby. "I feel certain this will quiet things, but if for any reason it doesn't, I'll let you know at once so you can clear off. I hesitate to give advice to an old hand like you, so just consider this a friendly suggestion. In the future, try to concentrate on older women, preferably those whose relatives aren't peers or politicians."

When we returned to Connaught Mews, we found an impressive-looking brougham outside Lady Sara's residence. It was drawn by two splendidly matched horses, and there were two splendidly matched and uniformed coachmen on the box. Inside Lady Sara's apartment, two visitors were waiting. One was the Earl of Spalton, a wizened little man whom I had never met, though Lady Sara seemed to know him well. I had heard much about him. He was rare among England's peers for his extensive business interests. He had disposed of most of his land holdings and invested the money in a diversity of commercial enterprises. Instead of a landed peer, he now was a merchant prince.

The Earl introduced his companion, Sir Cecil Elliman, whose name was one to reckon with. It was frequently mentioned by the newspapers in connection with his business affairs. He was what reporters liked to call a magnate. In the City, where he was active in a number of major enterprises, he was of towering importance. It required only a glance to see that he was active in them to his own considerable profit.

The Earl, one of the wealthiest men in England, looked shoddy beside Sir Cecil, who was a substantial-looking man in every respect. His suit certainly had been built by the best bespoke tailor on Saville Row, his custom-made boots came from Lobb, and his hat, from James Lock, was distinctive enough to have been a special design the maker reserved for him. He had the air of always knowing what the best was and insisting on getting his money's worth. His gloves put the Earl's to shame and could have been used for a window display in the most expensive shop on Regent Street. His shirt, also custom-made, had a front that bristled with diamonds. He was middle-aged, with an ample moustache and long side-whiskers. His hair was deep black with no sign of thinning.

He seemed pleasant enough, but he had a narrow, calculating way of looking at a person that was disconcerting—as though everyone he met had to be weighed in terms of profit or loss. For all I knew, perhaps this was characteristic of all magnates. My experience of them had been severely limited. When we were introduced, his searching glance left me grateful I wasn't an employee of his summoned to walk the carpet. Having studied me and found me wanting, he turned his attention to Lady Sara.

"I must confess, my lady, that I persuaded my good friend the Earl to come along and introduce me so I would be certain of a hearing," he said. "I know much about you and your achievements, and I have come to ask for your advice if you would be so kind."

Lady Sara was consulted frequently by business proprietors, from the elderly woman who kept a tiny sweet shop to directors of large companies, but none of them, not even those of Sir Cecil's class, had ever brought along an earl to introduce them. She modestly replied that she could offer no guarantee, but she would be pleased to give his problem her full attention.

We seated ourselves in the drawing room. Lady Sara suggested tea or coffee, which both men politely declined.

"I hold a substantial interest in the Tradesmen Life and Accident Assurance Company," Sir Cecil announced, coming to the point immediately. He impressed me as the sort of man who would always come to the point immediately. Probably he had never in his life opened a conversation with a remark about the weather. "In fact, I am its chairman. I will illustrate the problem by describing three cases I have had to deal with recently."

Lady Sara nodded. "Please do."

Sir Cecil reflected for a moment. "Eric Hodson was a wool merchant in Bradford. His firm, which seemed prosperous, had been founded by his grandfather. He was in good health, was highly respected by friends and business associates, and had an affectionate family life. The Tradesmen Life and Accident Assurance Company had insured his life for a thousand pounds. Two weeks before the incident I am about to describe, he applied to increase that amount to five thousand pounds, and his application was accepted.

"Shortly afterward, returning home from a neighbouring town, his carriage was struck by a train, and he was instantly killed. It appeared to be a tragic accident until we looked at it closely. Hodson had the reputation of drinking infrequently and then very little. On this night he reeked of alcohol, and there was an opened gin bottle in his smashed trap—presumably he had been holding it in his hand when the train struck him. He had somehow managed to turn onto the tracks and drive along them for a considerable distance, but his horse, which he had owned for many years and was extremely fond of, had miraculously turned aside and then stopped, leaving only the trap in the path of the train. When we looked into Hodson's business affairs, we found he had been speculating and had lost almost everything he owned. The assurance was, in fact, the only resource that stood between his family and destitution. It was obvious to us that he had craftily committed suicide. The gin was to give credence to his actions. He had driven down the track, turned his horse aside so it would survive, and waited for the train. He deliberately selected a location where the track emerged from a wooded area on a curve and it was impossible for the engine driver to see him until the train was upon him. Do you concur?"

"Of course—on the basis of what you have told me," Lady Sara said. "Was the assurance payable in the event of suicide?"

"It was not."

"Did you refuse to pay it?"

"We did not. We paid it promptly, conveying our deepest sympathy to his family."

"Why?" Lady Sara asked.

"Our solicitor advised us that suicide would be devilishly difficult to prove in a court of law, my lady, however obvious it might seem to us. Further, the attempt would put the company in the position of denying an assured's family the security for which he had worked so hard and paid premiums for so long. It would give us an unfavourable reputation that would cost far more than the five thousand pounds, so we paid.

"Second example. Edward Pannier was a trusted employee of the North Wales Steel Company. His life was insured for two thousand pounds. He was middle-aged. He had married late and had a young family. His health was excellent, and he was a sailing enthusiast. He took his family to Tenby for the holidays and hired a small sailing boat, which he sailed himself. He failed to return; the boat was recovered later. It had capsized, and obviously he had fallen overboard. The verdict: an accidental drowning. It was a choppy day on the water, and a freakishly large wave could have taken him by surprise. Everything seemed in order until the company audited his accounts and found them twenty thousand pounds in arrears. He had been gambling with the company's money. He knew an audit was scheduled, and obviously there was no possible way he could have made good the shortage. We were convinced his death was suicide."

"How long had he been insured?" Lady Sara asked.

"More than seven years."

"And you paid the claim?"

"Yes, my lady, for the same reason that we paid the first claim. Third example: a widow, a Mrs. Geffen, was providing a home for her grown son and his family. She was in arrears on her mortgage payments, and the lender had threatened to have the bailiffs in. The stove in her bedroom inexplicably malfunctioned, and she was found asphyxiated. The stove was not defective; the damper had been turned. The coroner's verdict called it an unfortunate accident—the damper lever must have been bumped inadvertently. By coincidence, the amount of her assurance was slightly more than the amount needed to pay off the mortgage. We felt certain that the malfunction had been deliberately arranged. She killed herself. These are only three cases. Obviously we have no idea how many of our death claims represent suicide masquerading as some other kind of death. The cost to the company must be enormous. My question: To what extent would a careful investigation of each applicant for assurance avoid this kind of claim?"

"How long had the widow been insured?"

"For nine years, my lady."

"In your first example, a careful investigation should have resulted in your declining the application to increase the assurance but not the original application. In the second and third examples, since the causes of suicide occurred long after the subjects were insured, an investigation would have been of no help at all. A really careful investigation, by a skilled investigator with ample time and resources, would be far more costly than you realize. Obviously it would not be economically feasible except where unusually large amounts of money are at risk."

"Thank you for your time, my lady. That is what I needed to know." Sir Cecil got to his feet, nodded to the Earl, who emulated him, and the two of them very politely took their leave of us. In parting, Sir Cecil once again scrutinized me and found me wanting.

After they left, Lady Sara did something completely out of character for her. She went to the window and watched them out of sight.

"Sir Cecil has the reputation of being highly intelligent and imaginative in all of his business dealings," she said. "Too often when a man of business is flattered in this way, people are attributing his success to the wrong qualities. What he really has is a grasping acquisitiveness.

"On the basis of today's performance, Sir Cecil is neither intelligent nor imaginative. The head of a large company is like a captain steering his ship through dangerous waters, and he controls a number of such ships. His days are filled with engagements and conferences, with an endless procession of callers wanting something or wanting to sell him something, with cheques to be signed, with important decisions to make, with solicitors to consult, with meetings to preside over, with personal responsibilities to deal with. He took time away from all that to ask for advice an intelligent and imaginative man wouldn't have needed. His assurance company surely has extensive data on suicides in its own files, and he has an army of clerks available to shape it into reports."

She paused. "Unless, of course, he was after something else," she added thoughtfully.

"He doesn't look like the sort of man who would be reluctant to state what his true purpose is," I suggested.

"I'm not so sure. We can only wait and see."

CHAPTER 6

One evening each week Lady Sara put her social status aside, dressed in a flowing, brilliantly patterned gown and shawl, did things to her face with theatrical make-up to give an impression of infinite age and wildly staring eyes, called herself Madam Zarno, and went beyond the pale. I had a costume of my own for these occasions—a long robe ornamented with glittering, completely meaningless symbols and a turban of gold-coloured silk.

The occult and the mystic have always fascinated humanity, and in the London of 1900 there were thousands of men and women of all social classes and every degree of educational background who daily resorted to fortune-tellers of every nuance, whether occultists, or prophets and prophetesses, or seers and wizards, and believed in their ministrations as firmly as a businessman of that year believed in the Bank of England.

The type of oracle a person consulted depended very much upon his—or, more often, her—social class. The preferred occultism of wealthy or aristocratic women was likely to be palmistry, and they consulted their favourite diviners in stylish apartments in fashionable West End thoroughfares, contributing heavily to the upkeep of those expensive establishments each time they called. Servant girls, factory girls, and wives of workingmen would seek out "wise women" who lived in small back rooms in their own neighbourhoods and for a few pence would have the cards told for them. Some wise women also dabbled in charms and potions. For an extra fee, a girl could obtain a mysterious powder to slip into her young man's beer and induce an immediate offer of marriage.

Clairvoyants, crystal gazers, and spiritualists also thrived but were less popular.

Lady Sara kept four fortune-tellers on her list of informers. All of them told the cards for their clients and performed a few rudimentary tricks with crystals. She paid them no wages, but she set them up in untenanted shops that she'd had remodelled to her own specifications. All four establishments had a small waiting-room, a parlour for consultations, a second, special consultation parlour that was kept locked except when Lady Sara was using it herself, and, in the rear, comfortable living quarters. In addition, Lady Sara made certain the police did not bother them.

In return, the fortune-tellers informed her immediately concerning any confidences they received that had a bearing on crime—past, present, or future—and they assisted Lady Sara when she appeared in the special consultation parlour as Madam Zarno. It was a highly advantageous arrangement for them. They had the free use of an excellent place to live and work, and they had no worries about police interference.

Lady Sara visited all four establishments each Wednesday evening. The first she called at occupied what had once been a shop off Mile End Road. On one side was a chemist who also functioned as a leech merchant. He was a jovial Irishman, and he kept a place in the country with a large pond where he bred his leeches. He stored them in aquaria in the shop's basement. Because English leeches weren't suitable for medical purposes, he'd had to import a breeding stock from France and raise his own. He was cheerfully willing for curious customers to plunge a hand into a tub of leeches and find out for themselves how painless leech bites were. The demand for leeches had fallen off in recent years, but he still did a brisk business with doctors, hospitals, and a few brave persons interested in curing themselves.

On the other side was the chemist's competitor, a herbalist who sold all kinds of dried herbs by weight. Sir Thomas Tallmage thought very little of his concoctions, but once, when I had a violent headache, he gave me powdered root of Lady's Slipper to take in sweetened water, and it cured me promptly.

The setting was perfect for a fortune-teller's establishment. She gained clients from the customers of both shops because people consulted her on all kinds of health problems.

When we called that Wednesday evening, the fortune-teller, a cockney whose real name was Mabel Fuller but who now called herself Madam Furneaux, greeted us at her rear door as was her custom and invited us into her kitchen. We left stabling the horse to Rick Allward, the footman, and two grooms who had accompanied us, Ed Geffer and Tom Ness.

The fortune-teller was a plump, dark, friendly woman who could have been a capable actress herself—probably all who dabbled in the occult needed that talent. Her living quarters consisted of a large kitchen, which also served as her private parlour, and a bedroom. A young niece lived with her.

She made us comfortable in her kitchen and served tea and a cake she had baked before she handed Lady Sara the names of clients who were waiting to see Madam Zarno. She discussed them while we sipped our tea.

"Two of your regulars are here," she said, "and two of my regulars want to consult you—they wouldn't tell me why. They've heard about you, and it's you they want to talk with. I told them it was up to you whether you would see them or not. Then there's one stranger."

Lady Sara glanced at the names. "Anything of interest?" she asked.

"I would swear Jane Gape is afraid of something. And Mary Tibbs has been coming to me for several years but suddenly she refused to talk with me. She insisted on seeing you. The stranger is Jared Rance. At least, he says he's called that. I've never seen him before. He wouldn't tell me why he wanted to see you. I suppose all three are hoping your magic is more powerful than mine. Otherwise, it has been a dull week. I haven't turned up a thing that would interest you."

"Let's go over the list," Lady Sara said.

Rick and the grooms had joined us by then carrying a heavy box. All three of them were in ordinary street dress. While Lady Sara and Madam Furneaux talked, I followed them into the special parlour and helped them make the necessary preparations for Madam Zarno's interviews. From the box we took an elaborately carved wood stand with a large crystal mounted on it. Crystal and stand had been made to Lady Sara's own design. The carving featured mysterious symbols she had devised, and the crystal contained a liquid with streaks of colour in it. A concealed spirit-lamp illuminated the crystal and heated the liquid. The heat made the colours swirl impressively. I had seen it virtually hypnotize some of Madam Zarno's clients.

We placed crystal and stand on a draped table and lighted the spirit-lamp. A shaded gas lamp diffused a soft glow around the client and kept Madam Zarno's face shadowed, which accentuated the effectiveness of her make-up. Madam Zarno's chair was slightly higher than the chair opposite, and this permitted her to look down into the crystal and watch the client at the same time. It also made the client look up at her. She thought this gave her a subtle advantage.

At one end of the table was a piece of brightly-patterned rug where I squatted while the interview was in progress. I had practised for hours coming out of that squat to a standing position. As the interview progressed, the client quickly forgot about me. When it was over, or if the client became unruly, I was able to materialize like magic. One moment I was concealed by the table and virtually invisible; an instant later I was standing over the client, impressively garbed in my robe and turban and ready to take whatever action the situation called for.

Rick took his place behind a screen in case I needed assistance. The two grooms waited in the kitchen, watching through a concealed opening for a signal that meant Lady Sara wanted a client followed.

As she took her position at the crystal, she handed me the list of waiting clients with numbers showing the order in which she wanted me to summon them. I straightened my turban, gave Rick a wink, waited for Lady Sara's nod, and then went for the customer she had marked number one.

She took the "regulars" first because these clients were actually informers. They brought her information whenever they had any. Some were paid for it, and some were repaying Lady Sara for substantial favours they had received in the past. Their spouses, or relatives, or landladies saw nothing unusual in their regularly consulting a fortune-teller.

I ushered in Sally Smeed, a timid-looking, middle-aged woman. Her husband had served several short prison terms for minor offences. Lady Sara had helped her during the most recent of these. Now he was out and supposedly on the straight. She perched on the edge of the interview chair, looked around her cautiously—I had dropped onto my rug out of sight—and spoke in a whisper. "Mannie's dealin' smash again."

"Mannie" was a cousin of her husband's who had got him into trouble several times in the past. Obviously she was afraid it would happen again. "Smash" referred to counterfeit coins.

"'e's been at it more'n a week," she added, continuing to whisper.

"I'll try to have something done about it before your husband is tempted to join him. Anything else?"

"Ifan Jones is plannin' somethin'."

Ifan Jones was a dragger, a robber of freight waggons. He had been convicted several times. "Is he trying to rope your husband in?"

She nodded.

"Did he drop any hints about the job?"

She shook her head.

"Keep your husband clean, and I'll have Ifan watched. Anything else?"

She shook her head again.

Lady Sara leaned forward. "I'm looking for a giant," she said quietly. "An enormously tall man. Seven and a half feet, and he is big all over. Ask your friends and let me know if anyone has seen one."

I was on my feet before Sally left her chair. In response to a nod from Lady Sara, I slipped her a shilling as I showed her out. It was little enough, but it probably paid half the week's rent on the slum room she occupied with her family.

The other regular was Sadie Walker, who kept a low rooming-house in Stepney and allowed her tenants and their friends to shake an elbow—play at dice—in her kitchen on Friday and Saturday nights as long as they bought their drinks from her. Lady Sara protected her in this doubly illegal operation; in return, Sadie overheard much and passed anything interesting along to Lady Sara.

She was an older woman, in her fifties, and much better dressed than Sally Smeed. There was nothing shy about her. She said, "Lattie is onto somethin' big."

"Has he been flush?"

"No. Tried to buy drinks on tick. I told him I'd be glad to mark him up if he'd talk my landlord into lettin' me pay my rent on tick. He's been spongin' on his friends."

"He might have been putting them on about his prospects," Lady Sara suggested.

Sadie shook her head. "He didn't tell nobody but Rob Slade, and that was when he thought no one else was listenin'. Asked Rob if he wanted in on it. Rob said, 'Sure!'"

"Excellent! Anything else?"

There wasn't, so Lady Sara told her about the giant and also, because men came some distance to visit her kitchen, she asked her to listen for clues to the river thefts. There was no shilling for Sadie nor did she expect one. She was well off, and Lady Sara's help with the police more than repaid her.

Jane Gape, the woman Madam Furneaux thought was afraid of something, was young, pale of face, and extremely nervous. She sat down, placed sixpence in the small dish placed on the table for that purpose— sixpence being Madam Zarno's fee for a consultation—and stared into the crystal; Lady Sara pretended to do the same, but she was watching the client.

"Do you want to ask me something, or would you rather I told you what your problem is," Lady Sara asked in kindly voice.

Jane Gape started. "You tell," she said.

Whenever this occurred, I put myself in Lady Sara's place and tried to guess what she would say to the client. Usually I failed.

"You're worried about your husband," Lady Sara said confidently.

Jane Gape nodded.

"Do you want to know if there's another woman?"

"I seen him with her," Jane Gape said bitterly.

Lady Sara scrutinized her. "He isn't missing work, and he still gives you plenty of money," she observed.

Jane Gape nodded again. "But he don't come home. And he's spendin' money on her. I seen him."

"And you're worried about where he is getting the extra money." Another nod.

"When you asked him about it, he beat you," Lady Sara said.

"'e slapped my face."

I had noticed the bruise on her cheek.

Lady Sara said slowly, "The next time you see him, tell him the police have been enquiring for him. Ask him what he's been up to. Tell him you have a right to know. If he keeps it up, your children will be missing their father, and you'll have to support them on your own. If he values his family, he will mend his ways."

"I'll tell him," Jane Gape promised fervently.

Such problems posed a moral dilemma for Lady Sara. Without a doubt there was a clue here to a crime or a series of crimes; but if the husband went to prison, the family would be ruined. In the crush of the pitiless poverty that enveloped London's poor, few women could hold a family together and support it. Many slipped into prostitution while trying. As long as the crimes were petty in nature, Lady Sara attempted to frighten the husband into reforming. If that failed, and often it did, something more drastic had to be done.

"Has your husband ever mentioned a giant, an extremely tall man?" Lady Sara asked.

Jane Gape shook her head dumbly.

"If he does, or if you see one yourself, or hear of one, tell Madam Furneaux at once, and she'll tell me. Otherwise, severe misfortune will follow. Beware the giant!"

I escorted her out and brought in the waiting man, Jared Rance. He was about twenty years old, intelligent-looking, and well-dressed. He seemed almost respectable, but I didn't care for his shifty look. Neither, as it turned out, did Lady Sara. He placed his sixpence in the dish, seated himself, and announced, "I got a scheme for a put-on. Never mind what it is. It looks foolproof. What I want to know is, will I get caught if I use it?"

Lady Sara passed a hand over the crystal and then looked into it. She sprinkled a powder into the spirit-lamp, which resulted in a puff of scented smoke. She had acquired the effect from a good friend of hers, Sir William Samper, Professor of Chemistry at the University of London. It was highly effective. Rance drew back in alarm.

"Yes," Lady Sara announced after a dramatic pause. "You'll be caught. The police know all about your put-on. They are watching you now."

Rance started. He stared at her for a moment, muttered, "Thanks," and left. Lady Sara nodded to the grooms, which was the signal for one of them to find out everything he could about Rance. She wanted to be ready for further action in case she hadn't frightened him sufficiently.

I waited until the smoke cleared before I brought in the next client, Mary Tibbs. She was about thirty, neatly dressed, and almost pretty. The contrast with Jane Gape was startling. She contributed her sixpence, hesitated, and then spoke while still standing. "I want to know whether I should get married."

Lady Sara regarded her with interest and then studied the crystal. "Do you want to get married?"

"I don't know."

"You do and you don't," Lady Sara suggested.

Mary Tibbs nodded her agreement.

"There's much that you like about the man, but there is something mysterious about him that is holding you back," Lady Sara said, continuing to study the crystal.

"It's my employer. I work in a dress shop. He seems to be well off. He wants to marry me and keep it secret."

"Did he tell you why?"

"He asked me to trust him."

"You haven't known him long," Lady Sara said confidently.

"Only as long as I've worked for him—three months."

Lady Sara continued to study the crystal and added another puff of scented smoke for effect. "If it were an honourable offer, he wouldn't care who knew about it," Lady Sara said. "The reason he wants to keep your marriage secret is because he is already married." Mary Tibbs winced as though she had been struck. "Tell him you'll think it over," Lady Sara went on. "Use the time to find another position."

She left dazedly. Lady Sara signalled to the remaining groom, and he left right behind her. The groom would find out who her employer was, and we would make discreet enquiries to learn whether he made a practice of seducing his shop assistants by pretending to marry them.

And so it went. The popular view that criminal investigators handle one fascinating case after another, all with world-shaking implications, could not be more wrong. "Work" is the most apt synonym for the word "investigate." Our Wednesday evenings often turned up nothing at all. Sometimes there were a few hints; occasionally there was something Lady Sara thought worth looking into or sufficiently interesting to pass along to Chief Inspector Mewer. Cases for the board in Lady Sara's study were almost never to be found amidst the sordid problems Madam Zarno dealt with.

From Mile End Road, with our party reduced to three because the grooms were following two of Madam Furneaux's clients, we went to a similar establishment in Limehouse. There, because it was much closer to the docks, Lady Sara not only asked her informants about a giant, but she told all of them to be alert for clues to the river thefts.

Our next stop was an address in Southwark near what had once been the land of Shakespeare. The area was now sadly impoverished. Pathetic, dilapidated dwellings filled the old courts that abutted on the river bank near where the Globe Theatre had stood—Moss Alley, Ladd's Court, Bear Gardens, White Hind Alley. These were abodes of waterside labourers who earned a precarious income and were unemployed half the year. Wives and children took what work they could get to help the family survive. When the tide was out, crowds of boys could be seen wading in the mud of the Thames. These were mudlarks who tried to find anything of value that might have fallen into the river from passing boats. A handful of copper nails was a treasure for them, redeemable for a few farthings or even a penny or two. Despite the poverty, when these people had a little money, they often spent it recklessly, and the fortune-teller who had their confidence thrived.

Finally we visited Seven Dials, which not too many years before had been so crime-ridden that even police officers feared to go there alone. It still had pockets of severe poverty. Madam Zarno's fee in Seven Dials was only a penny, and she waived that if a client pleaded penury. It was unfortunately true that many of the residents didn't have a penny, and crime was still rampant. Because the two grooms had quickly learned what they needed to know about the subjects they were following and were able to catch up with us in Southwark, Lady Sara arrived in Seven Dials with ample support.

As with the other locations, we collected a few hints that might or might not lead to something and asked all of the clients to be on the lookout for clues concerning giants and the river thefts.

Up to that point, the night had gone as most Wednesday nights went, but even humdrum cases such as these could take surprising turns, and this happened just often enough to make the investment in time seem worthwhile. Then there was the rare genuine surprise that struck with disconcerting suddenness like a bolt of lightning.

A woman named Betsy Cameron visited Madam Zarno in Seven Dials that Wednesday to ask for a pregnancy charm. She was a much abused prostitute, probably still in her twenties though she looked fifty. Her body had been wracked by disease since puberty. Pregnancy, even if Madam Zarno had possessed the magic to confer it, would have been a health hazard for her and a disaster for her child.

Madam Zarno caressed her crystal and added a puff of scented smoke. "There are shadows across your future that make parts of it unclear to me," she announced gently. "I am not able to see whether there is a child in it." Then she asked, "When did you go to church last?"

Betsy Cameron was too startled to answer. Probably she couldn't recall.

"Babies are God's bounty," Madam Zarno said. "Go to church, pray, talk with your priest or pastor. Perhaps God will answer."

This thought certainly had not occurred to Betsy Cameron. She gave Madam Zarno her dazed thanks. She was about to leave when Madam Zarno asked a parting question about giants.

Betsy turned. "I see'd one once."

"Where?" Madam Zarno asked quickly.

"'e come walking along Monmouth Street."

"What time of day?"

Betsy consider that. "Three in the morning."

"But you saw him clearly?"

"There's a lamp there."

"And you're sure he was a giant?"

Betsy described how he had towered over her. There could be no doubt that she had seen an extremely large man.

"How long ago was this?"

She couldn't remember, but Madam Zarno's questions quickly established that it had happened several years before. The height of the man had been so unusual that she still remembered him vividly. When it became obvious that she had nothing more to offer, Madam Zarno let her go.

Dim as it was, this was the first giant footprint we had found. It seemed like a good omen for the search that would begin the next morning.

CHAPTER 7

Lady Sara had built her organization of agents and informers on two levels. One was made up of impoverished people all over London. They were reliable, honest citizens who deserved far better of life than a constant struggle to find food and rent money. An extra shilling or two each week to a crossing sweeper, a costermonger in poor health, a buyer of discards or second-hand articles, any of London's immense army of scavengers, not to mention poorly paid porters, messenger boys, or street performers, meant the difference between survival and abject poverty.

All of these regularly paid agents were immensely grateful and willing to do anything, or go anywhere, for Lady Sara. They learned to use their eyes and ears and quickly became expert witnesses and informers. They feared no one because they knew Lady Sara would protect them. Each carried three emergency tuppences that were never to be spent except to telephone Lady Sara when there was urgent information for her. Since few of them had ever talked on the telephone before, one of my tasks was to instruct new agents in the use of one and make certain they knew where call offices open to the public were located—in post offices, public libraries, underground stations, and occasionaly in shops—where tuppence would buy three minutes of conversation. They also had to be cautioned to speak in guarded terms on the telephone. We always assumed that an operator was listening in.

Lady Sara had the firm conviction that no investigator worthy of the name, private or public, could function in the London of 1900 without ready access to a telephone. An efficient investigation simply was not possible if one foolishly relied on the fumbling delays of the telegraph system, and she could cite cases by the hour to prove that. She had a telephone in her living quarters and also one in her study, and she considered it a national scandal that London's police stations were still without telephones even though the nation's telephone system had been functioning efficiently for almost two decades. All of her agents and employees used the telephone as a matter of course. The telephones in Chief Inspector Mewer's home and his Scotland Yard office had been installed at Lady Sara's insistence.

To the list of paid agents was added an enormous number of volunteers who were somewhat better off—cab or omnibus drivers, reporters, hotel or market or railway porters, lamplighters, coffee stall operators, watermen, an occasional clerk or shop assistant, artisans, labourers. All were indebted to Lady Sara for one reason or another—financial assistance when sick, employment found for them, a helping hand extended when in trouble. Lady Sara's own social contacts, as well as her coffee hours, covered the upper levels of society. The result was an enormous net whose meshes enveloped all of London and its suburbs and caught all kinds of law violators.

Most of those it snagged were the authors of routinely sordid and often petty crimes. Information about them was promptly turned over to the police. The really interesting or complicated mysteries Lady Sara kept for herself. Even among them, a crime or puzzle worthy of a place on the board was a genuine rarity. When one occurred, the entire organization had to be alerted.

I always carried a notebook with a complete directory in it—written in shorthand for compactness. Rick Alward and Charles Tupper, Lady Sara's footmen, did the same. The three of us shared the chores of making payments and receiving information, which kept us in touch with everyone on a regular basis. If we needed assistance in any part of London, we always had someone to turn to.

Our immediate task was to query all of the agents about giants and alert them to look for a duplicate of the recently hanged Hob Hagan, whose size and features were still fresh in everyone's memory. At the same time, those who lived and worked near the river had to be asked to be on the lookout for suspicious activity around warehouses at night.

Rick, Charles, and I met for breakfast in Lady Sara's apartment and divided London among the three of us. The two footmen were about the same age, in their forties. Both had grown up in towns remote from London and had handled and cared for horses almost from their infancy. Both had moved to London with their families in an attempt to better themselves. They had little success until they met Lady Sara, but the variety of jobs they knocked about in stood them in good stead later.

Rick had dark, curly hair; Charles was a blond. Their facial features were totally unlike, but so similar were their builds that Lady Sara's visitors could not have told them apart had it not been for their dramatically different heads of hair.

While we ate, Charles described the trapping of Lord Woolston's card sharper, who had been caught in the act of cheating with a panoply of illegal gambling aids on his person. The police officer had frightened him thoroughly. Lord Woolston and his friend had got their money back, the sharper had been put on police notice to behave, and all concerned except the sharper and his collaborator had considered it a successful evening.

When we finished breakfast, Rick and Charles each took one of Lady Sara's cabs, and, after dressing myself appropriately, I took the cart, heaped some bundles of wood on it that I could pretend to be delivering, hitched up the donkey, and set out.

My beat was the East End, and I followed a tortuous route, stopping at intervals to converse with Lady Sara's agents: A coster girl with a plaid shawl and a cotton-velvet bonnet who sold apples from a stall; a bearded crossing-sweeper with a crippled hand who wore a comical miscellany of discarded clothing (most of the male sweepers were disabled, elderly, or of infirm health, and the pittance gained from their sweeping was a thin margin between them and the workhouse); a costerman with a barrow selling vegetables (I heard his high-pitched cry, "Penny a bunch turnips!" long before I saw him); a father and son piano-organ team whose musical careers had been launched by Lady Sara through the simple expedient of giving the father the required deposit, ten shillings, so he could rent an instrument (the father, a wizzened little man with no teeth, had a wonderfully powerful singing voice, and the son, a husky, feeble-minded youth, good-naturedly pulled the piano organ about on its two wheels and turned the handle when his father stopped for a performance); a man who propelled himself about in a small cart selling bootlaces and pipe-cleaners (he had lost his legs in one of the colonial wars, and his subsequent career tragically illustrated how harshly the government—any government—treated its "thin red line of heroes" when a war was over); a poorly-dressed woman offering clockwork toys for sale (she was one of a row of ragged kerbstone merchants who eyed her enviously when I stopped to have a word with her); an elderly man selling newspapers; an Arab wearing a long, shabby coat and a soiled turban who sold rhubarb and spices (he was villainous looking but gentle and friendly, and he would have walked through fire for Lady Sara).

So it went, and I checked off names in my notebook one by one: Houndsditch to Aldgate High Street; a stop to converse with several vendors caught up in the turmoil of the Petticoat Lane Market—while there, I refused a miserly offer for my entire load of wood; through Whitechapel High Street, Whitechapel Road, and Mile End Road to the Regent's Canal; south to Commercial Road; back west again with loops through Stepney, Limehouse, and Whitechapel.

There was a tendency on the part of the rest of London to pity people who lived in the East End—entirely without cause. Those East Enders who had regular employment thought it a fine place to live. Mile End

Road was a splendid, wide, bustling street. People knew each other and were always friendly. In summer, the fruit stalls were almost continuous. I had been told that more fruit was eaten here than anywhere else in England. The young people were as frank and unconcerned in their courtships as West Enders were in their shopping. They would stop and embrace anywhere.

But even the more prosperous East Enders had their problems. For one thing, there seemed to be more funerals there than in other parts of London. One always encountered several on any trip along Mile End Road, sometimes in an ostentatious procession: the glass hearse ornamented with ostrich-feather finery and bearing a splendid coffin almost buried in flowers, followed by numerous mourning coaches—four wheelers, hansoms, crowded wagonettes—filled with men and women in black. More often it was a baby funeral, a single, threadbare carriage with the poor little coffin under the box seat and the driver and bearer in white hat bands.

I made stops at dolly and swag shops, at pawnbrokers, at cabmen's shelters. No one I talked with had seen a genuine giant or noticed suspicious night-time activity along the river, but at least I left a large number of sharp-eyed observers looking for both.

Dusk found us ready for another assault on the city—made necessary by the fact that London changes both its aspect and its dramatis personae by night. An entirely different cast of characters is to be found abroad in darkness. Because night poses its own special problems, we used a different approach. We worked together from the four wheeler, with Lady Sara driving and the three of us accompanying her as passengers or ranging ahead of her on foot. We changed costumes according to the neighborhood. All of us were equipped with revolvers, police whistles, and dark lanterns—essential items for a pedestrian's safety in some parts of London.

We continued to check off names on our lists and to ask the agents about giants or suspicious night-time activity along the river. They were to telephone at once if they caught so much as a rumour of either. In addition, we now were on the look-out ourselves for anyone casting a longer-than-normal shadow. If the giant emerged from his lair at all, it was likely to be at night when he could veil his abnormal size in darkness. Lady Sara considered it no coincidence that the one giant sighting we had heard of—that of Betsy Cameron—occurred at three in the morning.

The route we followed was an odd one, and the great monuments so eagerly sought out by visitors to London were passed by without a glance. We did not expect to find our giant at Buckingham Palace, or the Tower, or on the steps of the National Gallery.

There were other strangenesses about our meandering search. For one thing, except when an agent we were looking for was likely to be found there, we avoided bright lights and crowds. London's night life was concentrated on Piccadilly Circus and its tributary surroundings: Leicester Square on the east, lit by thousands of electric lamps and ornamented with a statue of Shakespeare that grotesquely reflected the red, blue, orange, or green tributes paid to it by lights flashed from the nearby Empire and Alhambra Theatres; busy Shaftesbury Avenue on the north where the bright illumination merged into that of another important centre of night life, Soho; and the tongues of light radiating outward along Regent and Bond Streets and the Pall Mall. The Haymarket was once an important centre of night-time activity. It had faded, but it was still too bright for our purpose.

Our giant, if he were anywhere in London, would not come near those areas where a multitude of lights would make him look more enormous than he was. He would avoid crowds as much as illumination. There was no point in searching for him among theatre patrons or in the gay throngs patronizing fashionable restaurants. Even the dimmest corners of Piccadilly were far too bright for him. Neither could we envisage him as a prostitute's bully, lurking around corners to rob the men she attracted. If he engaged in crime, it would be solitary—a snatch from the shadows with the villain never seen by the victim; then a swift retreat into darkness.

We performed a meticulous search of low neighborhoods, looking into one decrepit pub after another. We continued checking off names of Lady Sara's agents, some of whom emerged only at night to sell sandwiches at theatre doors, or fried fish from pub to pub, or baked potatoes wherever crowds gathered. The East End pubs, especially those near the river where sailors thronged, were already rocking with song.

But even in the East End we did not expect to find our giant in well-patronized public houses or in brightly lit main thoroughfares where enormous crowds of people thronged in the flaring naphtha lights of barrows and street stalls. Neither would he be lingering in the neighbourhood of a Penny Gaff, an East End theatre—often a large, untenanted shop with a crudely-constructed stage where singing, dancing, and even melodrama could be enjoyed for a penny admission.

Instead, we searched dim, narrow lanes where cabs were rarely seen even in daylight. While one of us remained with Lady Sara, the other two proceeded on foot, poking into unsavoury courts and shining our lanterns along seldom-used footpaths. Moving purposefully with a steady tread, we routed a number of thieves of the sordid class sometimes called "mutchers," who were loitering near drinking establishments to rob drunken patrons as they emerged. Thanks to our forays, on that one night more than a few inebriated sailors kept their money—and perhaps their clothing and even their lives—longer than they otherwise would have.

By the time the midnight clangour of Big Ben could be heard echoing along the Thames from Chelsea to Greenwich, probably all but half a million or so of Greater London's six million inhabitants were safely abed. The more respectable pubs had already closed. "Time, please, gentlemen," sounded across the city in others as twelve-thirty approached. Here and there a coffee stall was opening for business. Giant presses were pounding out their papers' country editions on Fleet Street. In the center of the city, crowds were waiting for the last omnibuses or hurrying to catch the last trains of the central London underground and the "inner circle" railway. The streams of cabs were thinning, but this had little effect on London's traffic. All night its streets were traversed by heavy waggons bound for docks, depots, or markets. Along the main streets, wherever crowds lingered, so did the barrows of the sellers of baked potatoes and other viands, and their chants cut shrilly through the darkness. The cry, "Fresh mussels, eyesters, and periwinkles! All 'ot!" was repeated over much of central London. A newsmonger touting his unsold papers added his piercing call to the clamour.

The crowds thinned gradually; then, with what seemed like abrupt suddenness, they separated themselves into two kinds of people: Men and women walking quickly and purposefully—they are going home. Others who lounged about, dawdled, moved uncertainly—they had no homes. They were the elderly, the unemployed, the perpetually destitute. They drifted toward the benches and flagstones of the Thames Embankment, Trafalgar Square, or some similar place. This was a dry night, not too cold, so the ordeal wouldn't be as punishing for them as it would be later when winter approached. Some would lie down in doorways until a passing constable chased them on. As we continued our search, we began to scrutinize those recumbent forms, dim in distant electric or gas light, in squares and parks and along the streets we passed, but none of them seemed to be of an unusual size.

We looked into railway stations that were open all night to accommodate incoming trains. Derelicts sometimes tried to sleep there under the guise of waiting for relatives or friends to arrive, but sharp-eyed porters kept them on the move.

We, too, kept ourselves on the move, making few stops except for a whispered word with one of Lady Sara's agents. At a coffee stall where the owner was known to us, we paused to talk with him while we refreshed ourselves with penny cups of coffee and wedges of cake. Two young "Juliets of a night," also drinking coffee, sent hopeful glances in our direction and turned away resignedly when we paid them no attention. Four young men—who should have been home in bed long ago and probably were up to no good—eyed us warily. When they finished their cake and coffee, they slunk away into the darkness. We finished our own coffee and paused long enough to break up a fight between a middle-aged man and his wife, both of whom were drunk. The man wanted to go home; the wife insisted the night was young. It was she who started the fight.

By two o'clock, London was as hushed as it ever gets. The immediate vicinities of the markets and the General Post Office seethed with activity, but they were exceptions. We returned to Connaught Mews for a fresh horse and then looped through the East End again. Silence was settling over it like a ragged blanket except for the grinding noise of traffic in the main streets and, coming from several directions, muffled sounds of workmen who were making street repairs. In one street men were laying an electric cable. They laboured in deep trenches while great sheets of flame danced in the breeze above them and lit their work.

We were moving through a narrow lane in Limehouse, Charles Tupper and I walking some distance ahead of the cab, when we heard a scream.

"The giant!"

Instantly we were off and running; behind us, Lady Sara whipped up the horse and blew her police whistle, and Rick, who had remained with the cab, sprang out to follow us. The scream sounded twice more. Charles and I quickly reached the victim, who was lying senseless on the pavement. The assailant had paused to search his pockets, a fatal error. We left the victim to Rick and followed a tall, fleeing figure into a narrow alley.

It was a cul-de-sac, and in a moment we had him cornered, caught in the light of our lanterns. A knife flashed in his hand. Then he saw our revolvers and thought better of it. He dropped the knife and stood pinioned to a stone wall by the lantern beams. We eyed him disgustedly, savouring our disappointment.

He was no giant. At six feet or so he wasn't even remarkably tall, but probably he had looked gigantic to his victim when he leaped on him suddenly. With Charles following alertly, revolver in hand in case our captive experienced a change of heart, I frogmarched him back to the scene of his crime. He contented himself with cursing us. Two constables had arrived with commendable promptness, and they cheerfully took charge of our non-giant, who had the victim's pocket-book and watch in his pockets. The constables thanked us sincerely and applied manacles.

The victim had regained consciousness, but when we questioned him, he could only say, defensively, "Well—he *looked* like a giant." We were about to leave him to the police when Lady Sara asked suddenly, "What happened to your hand?"

His hand was heavily bandaged, but I hadn't noticed anything suspicious about that. Certainly it had nothing to do with the robbery. I couldn't think what had directed Lady Sara's attention to it, and I preferred not to expose my ignorance by asking. She reacted to everything with the instincts of a great investigator.

She told the constables, "Maybe he's hurt worse than he thinks. Let's have a look at it."

They agreed; the victim didn't. He resisted strongly, which increased everyone's curiosity, including that of the constables. While they kept the prisoner subdued, Rick held the victim, and Charles stripped off the bandage.

The back of his hand had been raked with four deep, parallel slashes, all heavily clotted with blood. If we hadn't known better, we might have thought he had been clawed by an animal.

"You do need a doctor," Lady Sara told the victim. "Who are you?"

He gave his name, address, and place of employment as reluctantly as he had shown us his hand: Alf Rixon, a night worker at the West India Docks. He'd had an accident—a crate had fallen on him and cut him. Because he was in pain and not able to do his work, his foreman had sent him home. Along the way, he stopped to give a helping hand—his good hand, of course—to a friend, which was why he was so late.

"The only help your friend needed was in emptying a few bottles," Lady Sara suggested.

Rixon admitted that the two of them had drunk a bit.

"Maybe your injury set your nerves on edge," Lady Sara went on. "That was fortunate for you. If you hadn't been startled into screaming 'the giant!' at a robber who wasn't very gigantic, you would have lost your money and watch. The constables will find a doctor for you, and a detective will visit you tomorrow and get the whole story."

She took one of the constables aside. "Write your report carefully," she told him. "This is far more important than you realize. See that Chief Inspector Mewer gets a copy. I'll tell him to expect it."

The constable hadn't recognized her in her cab driver disguise, and he stared at her dumbfoundedly.

The constables took assailant and victim away, and we resumed our giant hunt.

London begins to awaken at four o'clock. The earliest of the markets open then, and we looked in on some of them, but there were no giants among the costermongers waiting to load Yarmouth bloaters or "Finney haddick" at Billingsgate or cabbages and carrots at Covent Garden. We didn't expect to find any, but there is work around a market where a giant's physique would prove invaluable—on Billingsgate's oyster-boats, for example, unloading the immensely heavy, dripping black oyster bags, so we thought it worth a look.

I changed my clothing before I entered Billingsgate. One attending a fish market should never wear anything except the oldest togs he owns. Sometimes the air there seems filled with fish scales, and spray and slime fly everywhere as the fish are flipped and handled.

Billingsgate was the noisiest of the markets, with traders and salesmen trying to shout each other down, porters bellowing insults, and an entire community of hucksters crying their special wares through the barn-like square where fish were sold—waterproof capes, hardware, newspapers, baskets, food and drink for both customers and market workers.

Because regular fishmongers had first pick of the day's catch, the army of costermongers was just beginning to form at that early hour. I moved through the market quickly, talked with a few porters I knew, looked the scene over without seeing a giant, and returned to our private cab, where I stuffed my fish-tainted clothing into a bag and made myself presentable for Covent Garden.

Saturday was the Garden's busiest day, but even on a weekday it bustled with activity. Carts and barrows filled the surrounding streets; porters hurried this way and that with tiers of baskets on their heads; and its piles and heaps of fruit and vegetables in vivid colours, along with pots of flowers, made it far more attractive to the eye and immensely more pleasing to the nose than Billingsgate. Again I looked the scene over quickly, talked with a few porters, and came away.

After calling at several more markets, we returned to the London docks, where heavy labour abounds and a willing giant would find work when others were being turned away. Dock labourers gathered an hour or two before "call on," nosing about and trying to find out where the work would be that day. When hiring began, they had to scramble for tickets or tallies handed out by foremen, and they never knew whether this magic token represented half a day's work or employment for a week. Sometimes, when there were few ships to unload, the fight for the available jobs became violent.

There were hulking specimens waiting for tickets, but I saw no giants among them, and the officials I talked with did not remember seeing any. We were off again, this time to call on the casual wards of workhouses. These offered paupers a cold bath, a bed, and meals of bread and watery oatmeal with an occasional bit of cheese. In return for this, they were expected to perform a long day's work making oakum—fibers produced by picking old rope to pieces—or breaking stones. It was the harshest conceivable kind of charity, but starving men waited in line for hours for admission, and many were turned away each day.

The workhouses we visited had harboured no giants within anyone's memory. Neither had any of the other shelters for the homeless we called on.

By this time the vast city was fully awake. Workers from the suburbs were converging on it in trains, omnibuses, trams, on foot, on bicycles. The hordes of women and girls of the East End's sweated dress factories, who rode the "marrowbone stage" to work—meaning that they walked— were already filling the streets there. Street sweepers were beginning to deal with the night's accumulation of horse droppings. Coffee stalls were closing. Our giant, even if darkness drew him from his hiding place, had long since returned to it. Like the trolls of old, he would fear the daylight.

But we now had a small army looking for him, and he couldn't elude us indefinitely. We also had turned up two extremely odd clues: the robbery victim's wounded hand and his strange cry when the robber set upon him: "The giant!"

We returned to Connaught Mews, and Lady Sara told us to get some sleep. When I awakened, four hours later, she had left on an errand, so I resumed the search by myself.

I once heard a visitor describe London as a perpetual Vanity Fair. Much of that vast show was free, but many attractions could be seen or experienced only for money. Some were priced at a penny; others, depending on the location of the seat, cost one to ten shillings or more. Sometimes the fee was only a ha'pence dropped into a slot. An entertainment hall's automatic picture machines, where the pay slots were located, had become so popular that often the traditional penny sideshow acts had been banished upstairs.

It was the upstairs acts that interested me. They featured bearded ladies; Africans licking red hot pokers that sizzled on their tongues; Oriental jugglers; tatooed men or women; an "electric lady" who conveyed shocks to those who touched her; a "noble savage" whose features belonged more to the Middle East than to America; fat women of stupendous dimensions; a human skeleton or two; a two-headed pig preserved in spirits; strong men who lifted enormous weights and had stones smashed on their chests with sledge hammers; and assorted riff-raff. But I found no genuine giants nor did the shows' proprietors know of any.

It wasn't the best season for investigating sideshows. In summer and autumn, many of the freak acts toured in caravans and exhibited at country fairs and markets until cold weather drove them back to London. At that time they hired untenanted shops for their exhibitions or took engagements with regular shows. Rather than extend our investigation to all of rural Britain, it seemed far simpler to wait for cold weather and visit the freak shows again.

I next went to Chelsea and called at the studio of an artist I knew. He was at work on a large painting, and I had to wait until he decided he had done enough for the day and dismissed his model. Then he went with me to call on a number of his friends. I quickly established that no artist working in or near London had ever used a giant as a model. Several thought the idea had excellent potential—they especially liked the notion of painting David and Goliath from live models—if I would furnish the giant.

Once more I returned to Connaught Mews.

Lady Sara arrived shortly after I did, and she was in an unusually cheerful mood. Without any ceremony, she placed a third set of pegs in starting holes on the oversized cribbage board. "I'm adding the Shadwell murder to our cases," she said. "Chief Inspector Mewer has muddled it already. There has to be a direct connection between the mutilated robbery victim, Alf Rixon, and the mutilated murder victim, Bill Havill, even though the Chief Inspector refuses to see it that way. Both are dock workers, the Spanish Tickler was used on both, and they have almost identical character references. According to Rixon's foreman, he is an excellent worker. Completely honest and very steady and dependable— just like Havill." When I looked puzzled, she asked impatiently, "Don't you see the implications?"

"Are you including the robbery, too?" I asked.

"The robbery of Rixon was a fortunate accident for us, coming at that particular moment. Otherwise, it had nothing to do with the Shadwell murder, but Rixon's injured hand certainly does. Now do you see the implications?"

"The connection—the Spanish Tickler—is obvious," I said. "But I don't understand what it is connecting."

"It is connecting our cases," she said impatiently. "The giant—some kind of giant—also has a role in this. I refuse to believe Alf Rixon screamed 'The giant!' merely because he was imagining things. Don't be surprised if all of our Byways eventually merge."

CHAPTER 8

I spent the next morning searching for agents we had failed to find during our first forays—often an agent became sick, or died, or moved, or simply dropped out of sight for a time, and we were constantly adding new names to the list. I also looked up some of my own contacts all across London. Rick Allward and Charles Tupper did the same. In the afternoon, Lady Sara held a conference to discuss both the giant and the river theft investigations and consider what should be done next.

Our gathering was breaking up when Reginald Dempster, Lady Sara's nonentity of a cousin, arrived in a rush to ask if Lady Sara could spare him a few moments. "Happened onto something queer this afternoon," he said to her. "That's your department, so I thought you would want to know about it."

Interruptions of this kind, with new problems to investigate, were commonplace for Lady Sara. Her morning coffee hour always brought her a triviality or two to deal with, and her Wednesday night excursions as Madam Zarno brought more. Tips from her agents were received frequently, and many of them had to be acted on at once.

But she rarely received information from the likes of a Reginald Dempster, who impressed me as a person who wouldn't recognize a queerness if someone hit him with it. Despite this, Lady Sara was sufficiently tempted to give him a hearing. She asked me to remain, dismissed the footmen with a final instruction or two, and returned to the oaken conference table with Dempster and me.

"How is Cicely?" she asked politely as we got ourselves settled there. Cicely was Dempster's wife.

"Bored," Dempster said. "We usually spend August and September in Harrogate with Cicely's mother. But the old woman decided to go to Bath this year, and prices there are a bit steep for us. Just to complicate things further, this year the relatives we usually visit for the shooting-season for some reason failed to extend their hospitality. A careful scrutiny of my pass-book convinced us we might as well stay in London, since we have to pay rates and taxes here anyway, rather then run up fresh bills in some dreary watering-place. A penny saved is a penny earned, don't you know."

"A penny doesn't amount to much however it is used," Lady Sara said, "but there are compensations for staying in London. I enjoy spending autumn here."

Dempster shrugged. "We've been doing the City churches with Mr. Hare's Walks in London for our guide, and we've looked up long-forgotten friends in the suburbs and even attended a few Promenade Concerts—though not with unabated joy, I must confess. I find that kind of music tiresome. It is wearying enough to listen to sitting down, and the promenade part seems wholly unnecessary. Of course none of these things take up much time, but Cicely has a new passion to sustain her flagging spirits. She has gone in for bridge. She doesn't just play it, she studies the oracles and in odd moments comes out with strange remarks about 'calling' and 'passing' and 'doubling to the score,' and the advisability of 'strengthing a heart lead on a passed diamond call.' It is all Scandinavian to me, but it keeps her occupied."

"You mentioned something queer," Lady Sara reminded him.

"To be sure. With everyone away, both my clubs are closed for cleaning, and we are quartered on our neighbours, which introduces a rather unwelcome element of novelty into one's social experiences. So I now hobnob with a bishop or two and a few sedentary M.P.s at the Athenaeum and an assortment of colonels and captains and even an occasional general at the the Rag—the Army and Navy, don't you know. I've always wondered how I would look in a scarlet tunic, and at one point I considered the army as a profession, but my aunt—the one I had expectations from—was against it. She reminded me, very properly, that there was always the risk of war."

"Something queer," Lady Sara murmured again.

"To be sure. Even with depleted membership this merging of members of several clubs can be unsettling. Has the effect of dumping a group of strangers into an atmosphere where things usually don't change much. Very confusing to the porters and waiters, too, having to extend all the courtesies of membership to a parcel of interlopers. It's the Oxford and Cambridge that is temporarily quartered on the Rag. The queer bit happened there an hour or so ago when I heard a chap indentify himself as David Clarke, a member of the Oxford and Cambridge."

"Isn't David Clarke a member of the Oxford and Cambridge?" Lady Sara asked.

"Indeed he is. I know him well."

"So what was queer about that?" she persisted.

"This chap wasn't David Clarke. As I said, I know him well. The real David Clarke is spending the month in Devon."

"Is the man using his name still at the Rag?"

"He may be."

"Is he respectable looking?"

"Not entirely so, no, but they wouldn't keep him out for that reason. The Oxford and Cambridge is known for its unrespectable elements. Unfortunately."

Lady Sara turned to me. "He may be taking advantage of the holiday confusion to find a temporary haven. On the other hand, the fact that he took the trouble to learn the name of a member who was away is suggestive. See what you can find out."

Because we were feeling our way into three important new cases, the interruption came at an especially awkward time. I had hoped to finish contacting Lady Sara's agents that afternoon, but obviously she thought Dempster's story merited looking into. I went to my quarters and quickly changed my clothing. I didn't want to be as unrespectable looking as Clarke. A few minutes later, Dempster and I were in a hansom rattling our way toward Pall Mall and the Army and Navy Club.

I wanted a good look at the imposter, close up, and we took a moment to discuss how this could be managed. Otherwise, Dempster had little to say during the ride except that once he muttered, "Called himself David Clarke. Deuced odd to meet a stranger using the name of someone you know well."

Hyde Park, already replanted for the autumn, looked splendid, and I envied those with the leisure to enjoy it. They included swarms of tourists who recently had persuaded themselves that Buckingham Palace was the Tower of London and now were looking doubtfully at the Serpentine and wondering if they had discovered the Lake District. The more energetic had hired boats. It was an altogether lovely day.

We swung into Picadilly and then took St. James Street to Pall Mall, where we pulled up in front of a gloomy building I once heard Lady Sara refer to as a misplaced Venetian palazzo, the Army and Navy Club. It always bewildered me that so many of the exclusive private clubs looked like public buildings.

I was not surprised when Dempster jumped out and engaged the porter in conversation, leaving me to pay for the cab.

He introduced me as his guest, and we mounted palatial stairs, passed through a palatial hall, and entered one of the palatial rooms. Dempster nudged me and indicated with a nod two men engaged in quiet conversation. "The one on the left," he whispered.

As we had planned, Dempster led me to a nearby chair and said, loudly enough to be overheard, "Why don't you wait here? I'll be back directly."

Then he left me. I picked up a newspaper and pretended to read while I studied the man calling himself David Clarke. He was about forty years old, with sandy hair and a neatly-trimmed moustache, and he seemed presentable enough even though his suit was out-of-date and on the shabby side. In one respect he definitely was not a typical London clubman. His paunch needed nourishing. This would not have been noteworthy for a member of the Rag—many army and navy men managed to preserve slender, ramrod figures—but David Clarke was impersonating a member of the Oxford and Cambridge Club.

He was talking with an older man, a barrister by his conversation, who had enough paunch for the two of them. The barrister's face was alert and good-humoured, and he seemed amused by the younger man's conversation. He also was being quartered on the Rag while one of his clubs was cleaned—in his case, the Junior Carlton, the Rag's next-door neighbor.

After some desultory chatter concerning the bleakness of London at that time of year, the false Clarke began to complain about his wife. It seemed she had her heart set on a diamond necklace. Less than a year previously, it had been pearls. He had given her the pearls, and a deuced expensive gift it was. Looked beautiful on her, though. Still looked beautiful on her. So why would she want another necklace, he grumbled, especially when she already had a diamond brooch, and diamonds didn't look nearly as nice on her as pearls?

I looked over the top of my paper to see how the solicitor was taking this. He was grinning broadly.

The imposter caught my momentary glance and broadened his appeal to include me. "What gets into a woman?" he demanded.

Both men turned my way, prepared to be amused by a younger man's reaction to feminine contrariness. I said, in a matter-of-fact way, "The real question is why men react to these things the way they do. Some of them buy expensive harnesses to ornament their horses. Some buy expensive wines to ornament their wine cellars. Some buy expensive jewellery to ornament their wives. It depends on which of their possessions they want to display to the best advantage."

The barrister's face crinkled with laughter. The imposter looked at me with interest. "That's a deuced good line," he said. "Display to the best advantage, eh? But diamonds aren't to my wife's best advantage. What then?"

"Give her something that is—if you want to display her," I said. "If you don't, then display your horses or your wine cellar."

"You have a wisdom far beyond your years," the barrister said. "Where did you come by it?"

"I had a wise father," I said. But of course I knew nothing about my father. The wisdom came from Lady Sara.

The two men began to discuss friends who had ornamented their wives—or cellars, or horses—in various flamboyant ways. I had learned as much as I needed to know about Clarke. When I saw Dempster glance into the room, I excused myself, wished Clarke well in his attempt to satisfy his wife with something short of diamonds, and took my leave of them.

"Anything in it?" Dempster asked curiously as we walked away.

"I think so," I said. "Whether there's anything to be done about it is for Lady Sara to decide. Right now I want a telephone."

From the cubicle to which the Rag confined its telephone, I called Lady Sara. Her maid told me she had gone to have tea with her mother, the Countess, so I telephoned the Connaught Place address. The Countess tolerated a telephone only for Lady Sara's convenience. Her servants seemed terrified of it, as though they were afraid of being electrocuted or mesmerized, and every one of them tried to speak into it while holding it at an extreme distance. They would have had good reason to be shocked and horrified if they'd had to take some of the messages Lady Sara's housekeeper or maids handled when there was no one else around to answer, but any communications directed at the Countess by telephone were certain to be thoroughly innocuous.

By exercising patience and raising my voice to a shout, I managed to have Lady Sara called to the telephone.

I told her what I had observed and heard.

"What do you make of it?" she asked.

This was part of my continuing education. If my deductions were correct, we would proceed from there. If they were not, she would show me where I had gone astray.

But I had no doubt about the false Clarke. "He is a 'putter up,'" I said. This was an informer who supplied information to thieves. A servant, for example, who knew there were things of value in a house and where they were to be found, might—for a price—put up a thief to steal them. Clarke was connected with a ring of burglars. He obviously was interested in learning which club members had ornamented their wives with expensive jewellery. At the same time, he would try to find out whether they had gone to the country—women were unlikely to take their best jewellery with them unless their destination was a fancy watering-place or a stately home where they wanted to make an impression. If the servants who remained behind were careless, or if Clarke's associates could get around them in some way, the members' London homes could be burgled during their absence.

"Ingenious," Lady Sara murmured. "I wonder how long it has been going on. Perhaps for years. It won't have occurred to the police to include a victim's clubs in their investigation of a burglary. We will have to make our own list, which will take time."

"What about Clarke?" I asked.

"I'll send you some help. As soon as possible we need to identify him and learn who his associates are. There is one thing that should be done immediately. Is Reggie anywhere nearby?"

He was waiting outside the door. I called him to the telephone, and Lady Sara congratulated him on his astute observation. Dempster said modestly, "It wasn't the sort of thing a man could very well overlook. I knew he wasn't Clarke."

She asked him to call the Rag's secretary to the telephone, and she informed that worthy individual that I, Colin Quick, was her personal representative engaged on an important investigation. She wanted the secretary to extend his fullest cooperation to me. If he had any reservations about that, he was to tell her at once, and she would see that he received instructions from the Rag's committee—naturally she knew most of its members personally—and also the police.

The secretary already knew about her, and he had no reservations. He hung up, and we retired to his office. He was a severe-looking man, somewhat aloof with an exaggerated military bearing, which seemed appropriate for a secretary of the Rag, but he received me courteously enough and was dignified and attentive when I began talking with him. Before I finished, his face had become flushed, he was on his feet waving his arms wildly, and I almost had to use restraint to prevent him from dashing out and personally pitching the false David Clarke into the street.

"We don't want to alarm him in any way," I said. "There may be serious crimes involved, and we must find out as much as we can about his associates and collect evidence to convict them."

"Then what's to be done?" the secretary demanded.

I gave him Lady Sara's instructions. He agreed reluctantly. Pitching Clarke into the street would have given him far greater personal satisfaction. He got on the telephone himself, and a short time later we had waiters from several nearby clubs—the Athenaeum, the Travellers, the Guards, Boodles, the United Service, Brooks, the Carlton, White's, and the Reform—assembled in his office. We sent them, one at a time, to have a surreptitious look at Clarke.

Six of them recognized him, indication enough that Clarke's scheme had an astonishing scope to it. That autumn or during those of previous years he had visited their establishments under various names when they were temporarily hosting members of other clubs. As far as they knew, he had conducted himself with propriety and done nothing irregular except that he never signed a chit for anything and he talked at great length with anyone willing to converse with him. Signing a chit would have given his game away the moment the clubman he was impersonating started receiving the bills, so he ate or drank only when another member was treating him. As for the conversations, he must have had a rare gift of friendliness and a knack for getting to know people because most London clubmen resented overtures from strangers.

I imposed secrecy on everyone concerned, sent the waiters back to their clubs, thanked the secretary and Dempster, and went outside to wait for the help Lady Sara had promised to send. It was already there—a hansom cab driven by a smartly-dressed cabman who looked thoroughly at home in Pall Mall. He was Lady Sara's footman, Charles Tupper.

Charles had a passenger in his cab—a young man of a collegiate type wearing a cap and blazer. The passenger winked at me. It was Lady Sara. Once again she had been unwilling to sit at home and leave the fun of the chase to her employees. Her own original method for following a suspect with a cab was to have passenger and driver change places whenever there was an opportunity to do so unobserved. The position of a horse-drawn cab's driver, either of a hansom or a four wheeler, was much too conspicuous for a lengthy pursuit without the subject becoming aware of it. With the frequent switches Lady Sara trained us to make, the cab always had a new driver unfamiliar to the suspect; the former driver, now a passenger, had ample opportunity to alter his appearance for his next turn on the box. Changes of jackets, coats, and hats were kept in the cab. The horse, of course, had to be nondescript, and alternate ornaments for its harness were also kept in the cab. The scheme worked superbly.

The other footman, Rick Allward, already had the cart parked around the corner in St. James Square. It was loaded with odds and ends of furniture. Allward was dressed like a poor carter and could simulate the tragic aftermath of an eviction in case Clarke led us into a shabby neighbourhood.

I described the situation to Lady Sara. "The waiters will keep a list of the names of everyone Clarke talks with," I said.

She nodded her approval and then looked at me critically. "You're too well-dressed to work with Rick. You'll have to change into something dingier—or would you rather join me?"

"I'll join you," I said. "Some whiskers and a few facial lines are all the disguise I need. Rick may not be necessary. Clarke is the shabby genteel type. I would place him in a neighbourhood that only recently was almost respectable."

"Or a middle-class suburb?" she suggested.

"That would be a come-down for him. He's been to Oxford or Cambridge, and he seemed perfectly at ease in the club. A tradesman turned to crime couldn't do that. He may be a well-off family's younger son."

It was an awkward problem for Rick—his shabby cart looked ludicrously out of place in London's Clubland—but he was equal to the situation. He had got himself positioned to follow quickly once the chase began. Then he removed a hub and a wheel and pretended to have a breakdown on his hands. Fortunately traffic was light, and no one paid any attention to him.

We were equipped for any eventuality, but all of that careful planning went for naught. Clarke finally emerged—about nine o'clock—and shook his head when the porter offered to call a cab for him. He walked off along Pall Mall. I followed him on foot with the hansom hanging back inconspicuously and the cart bouncing along far to the rear.

Clarke walked with the easy, swinging, purposeful pace of a man with a distant destination. He showed no signs of suspicion about being followed. There was no reason why he should have if he had been practising this dodge for years without detection. He turned into the Haymarket and strolled past the theatres there without a glance at the play-bills. Probably he'd had ample opportunity to study them on previous walks.

From the Haymarket he turned into Shaftesbury Avenue; from Shaftesbury Avenue he turned into Wardour Street; and Wardour Street took him to Old Compton Street. I walked along quietly a dozen strides behind him; the hansom lagged far behind, then closed its distance, then dropped back again. It is awkward following a man on foot with a cab. Somewhere in the rear, the cart was keeping in sight of the hansom.

The procession ended at the Hotel Suisse, an almost excessively unpretentious establishment that offered rooms as cheaply as two shillings and six pence with meals comparably priced. Breakfast was one shilling. Clarke entered the hotel; I waited for a measured minute to allow him to get clear of the lobby, and then I dashed after him as though trying to overtake him.

"Was that Mr. Jones who just came in," I asked the porter.

He denied it.

"I saw him in the street," I said. "I'm certain it was Mr. Jones."

"It was Mr. Ivatt—Mr. Edward Ivatt—from Birmingham," the porter said. "He stays with us every autumn."

I apologized, gave him sixpence for his trouble, and withdrew to confer with Lady Sara.

"We were both wrong," she said. "He lives somewhere outside of London. He comes here each autumn to take advantage of the state of confusion the clubs are in at that time. Perhaps he picks up enough information to keep his friends occupied the remainder of the year. They aren't paying him lavishly, though, or perhaps he is addicted to frugality. Not only did he choose a hotel so cheap that it is just barely respectable, but he chose one within walking distance of the clubs so he can save cab fares. You drive the cart back, and I'll take the cab. We will leave Charles and Rick here tonight. Tomorrow you can find out all about Clarke-Ivatt and organize a proper watch on him."

Lady Sara and I returned to Connaught Mews. A groom took charge of the horses, and we went to her study, where she placed two more pegs in a starting position on the cribbage board, thought for a moment, and then pegged the first five holes. We already had the beginning of a case.

"How quickly we resolve it depends on how much difficulty we encounter in connecting Clarke-Ivatt with his confederates," she said. "If he communicates by mail, this could take time. We might be reduced to feeding him false information about a house and then keeping it under surveillance."

"But we do have a case," I said.

She nodded happily. "Four Byways in use. It has been some time since we had four cases on the board at once."

The next morning, Saturday, I quickly picked up as much as was known around the Hotel Suisse about Edward Ivatt from Birmingham. Of course his real name was neither Edward Ivatt nor David Clarke, and he certainly did not come from Birmingham, but the problem of further identification could be left until later.

As the porter had told me, he stayed at the hotel every autumn. Apparently this had been going on for years, and his visits always lasted for a month or two. The hotel employees thought he liked London when it wasn't crowded.

It was almost noon when he finally made an appearance. As he headed in the direction of London's Clubland, I made him known to a street vendor trained by Lady Sara who was to follow him for the day and report which clubs he visited. The vendor was adept at changing his appearance and also his trade—he carried stocks of several items in his voluminous pockets, and at one moment he could be selling penny short-hand cards; at another, race-cards; at a third, perfume; at a fourth, boot-laces.

Having got him fairly launched on Clarke-Ivatt's heels, I went back to Connaught Mews to plan my own day. First, I wanted a list kept of the men he talked with. Second, I wanted to make certain he was not interfered with in any way. Third, I wanted to find out whether waiters from any of the other clubs could identify him. All of this would require careful disguise on my part because he'd had ample opportunity to scrutinize me the day before.

I reported my plans to Lady Sara. "Very well," she said. "But after to-day, we'll have street people keep an eye on him and inform the secretary if he changes his operations to another club. This investigation is going to be protracted, not to mention tedious, and I don't want you wasting your time on it. It is simply a matter of watching him carefully until he leads us to his confederates. If he leaves London without doing that, then we will need a different approach."

I agreed. "I would very much like to know how long he has been practising this dodge," I said.

"The thing that amazes me is that Reggie Dempster noticed it. I never would have believed a feather-headed ass like him could recognize any crime more subtle than a gross assault. Perhaps he could be useful to us in other ways."

I spent the remainder of the day in Clubland, completing Lady Sara's arrangements to make Clarke-Ivatt the most carefully watched man in London. When I returned to Connaught Mews to report, I found Lady Sara in deep meditation over the cribbage board.

"It is strange," she said, "how quickly we have accumulated information about this new case, and how slowly information has turned up about our older cases. I've hardly touched the other pegs since I put them in the starting holes. Our efforts haven't produced a scrap of new information about the missing giant, or the river thefts, or the Shadwell murder." She thought for a moment. "Perhaps that is the most important clue we have. I wish I knew what it means."

CHAPTER 9

On Sunday I finished alerting Lady Sara's agents to our searches for a giant and for clues concerning the river thieves. At the same time, Lady Sara was sending enquiries of her own throughout Britain and even abroad. As far as the giant was concerned, there was little more to be done. We could only wait until someone saw him.

On Monday morning, I made certain that the watch on Clarke-Ivatt was continuing, even though nothing of interest had happened. He spent his afternoons and evenings at clubs that were temporarily harbouring members of other clubs. The names of the clubmen he talked with were being noted by employees so they could be interviewed privately later. Clarke-Ivatt continued to walk between the clubs and the Hotel Suisse. Away from the clubs, he met no one.

I turned my own attention to the river thefts and began looking for likely places to conceal stolen goods. For several days I visited the Thames at random points from the Isle of Dogs all the way through the city, trying to understand the dimensions of the problem before I planned a systematic search.

It was on the fourth day of these excursions that I reached the slope of the hill between St. Paul's and the river where a series of old, narrow lanes wound down to the water from Upper Thames Street. Strange little businesses thrived in these oddly named passageways: Trig Lane, Distaff Lane, Little Divinity Lane, Garlick Hill, Stew Lane, Broken Wharf; and, despite the cramped, out-of-the-way, inconvenient location, they were bustling and noisy throughout the day. Nowhere else in London did horses' hoofs make such a clattering, echoing racket as they did hauling waggons and drays up these narrow, sloping, cobbled lanes from the wharves and piers below.

The old brick buildings had the weathered aspect of having stood there forever. So had the shops and warehouses that occupied them. They relied on a long-standing clientele that knew where they were located, and they wasted little effort in attracting the attention of passers-by. The dust of ages had dimmed windows and formed a thick coating on any merchandise displayed. Each shop seemed to be concealing its own mysterious history.

Stibbit Lane was typical of these narrow streets. Many of its shops had a nautical flavor. There was a ship's chandler with a display of running lights arranged in a circle around a quadrant, a compass whose card trembled with the vibrations of passing waggons, and a bright brass sextant. Next door, a shop offered uniforms and gear for ships' officers. Across the lane, a faded little establishment displayed old maps and much-used charts that looked crinkly with salt spray. The proprietor of the latter shop sat near the window in a robe, smoking a long-stemmed pipe. A cat dozed on his lap, and he held an old book in his hand. Both he and his shop looked as though customers were rare and always unwelcome.

A short distance down the slope was a slop shop, an establishment selling cheap sailor's togs, and the front of the shop was all but covered with bright red and blue flannel shirts, well-oiled nor'-westers, canvas trousers, and rough pilot-coats. A pile of sailor's hammocks almost blocked its doorway.

There also were odd little import houses tucked into out-of-the-way corners: a button shop offering buttons made from all sorts of materials imported from all over the world; a shop displaying grotesque metal ornaments from the orient; another that sold exotic, alien birds. I once called at the latter shop out of curiosity; inside, I found the squalking of parrots, macaws, cockatoos, and mynahs deafening; outside, it was scarcely noticeable above the din of the street.

My favourite establishment was a bow-fronted shop in whose windows stood ancient tobacco jars and snuff canisters. This was the venerable firm of Wightman & Co., Tobacconists, a concern that had thrived through five generations of Wightman ownership. The present generation would be the last; the current proprietor, Jasper Wightman, had neither son nor son-in-law to succeed him.

I had become acquainted with Wightman several years earlier when my investigations first brought me to Stibbit Lane, and I often stopped there to buy tobacco or a tin of snuff and chat with him when I was in the neighbourhood. I used neither of these products myself, but I always carried them. The timely offer of one or the other to addicts who had long been deprived was wonderfully effective in encouraging them to talk.

Despite the humble location, Wightman did a flourishing business with customers scattered not only throughout Britain but around the world, and he once showed me, in an old ledger, lists of the favorite snuffs of George IV and other notables. Snuff-taking was once socially fashionable, but it had gradually dwindled to use by night-watchmen, labourers, policemen, and others, including clergymen, who were not allowed to smoke tobacco when on duty. The company's own snuff tins carried announcements in ornate, difficult-to-read type of the personages to whom it had once been purveyor of tobacco and foreign snuff. Among them were various dukes and duchesses—including the Duchess of Kent, the mother of Her Majesty, Queen Victoria.

The use of snuff had fallen off sadly since the days when kings and peers routinely indulged in it. According to Wightman, one of the things that helped to kill the snuff habit among the socially prominent was the fashion for white handkerchiefs. This had little effect on the sailors and dock workers who constituted the majority of the shop's present snuff customers.

On my previous visit I had been enquiring about giants, and Wightman, a tiny, elderly man who seemed not much larger than a dwarf himself, remarked that while he sometimes saw unusually large men among the passers-by, none of them impressed him as being gigantic. On this day I was curious about the volume of traffic passing his door. The stolen merchandise always consisted of goods in common use with a high value per volume. No cargo of grain had disappeared, but large quantities of tea, tobacco, wine, and liquor had been taken. If such merchandise was being handled by one of the wharves below, it should have resulted in a noticeable increase in the clatter of waggons struggling up the hill.

"The traffic certainly is worse than it used to be," Wightman agreed, "but it has been getting worse each year for as long as I can remember. This means the wharves are handling more merchandise each year, and that is good for business. I would worry if it were otherwise."

Our conversation was interrupted by an altercation outside the door. A cart had taken on a heavier load than its single, elderly horse could haul up the steep, meandering lane to Upper Thames Street. The warehouse manager had told off a group of workers to assist, and five or six of them were pushing, with whoops of encouragement, while the horse laboured in front. They certainly were big men, in every dimension, but I wouldn't have called any of them gigantic. The cart moved slowly up the slope past the shop's door.

A short time later, just as I was taking my leave of Wightman, the workers trooped past in the opposite direction. One of them, a hulking, perspiring fellow with sleeves rolled up and a good-natured grin on his face, entered the shop and asked for a large tin of a Spanish snuff I had never heard of.

When he had paid for it, he broke the seal, dried his forearm on his trousers, and laid down a thick line of brick-red tobacco powder the entire length of it. Then he lowered his head and absorbed it in one rapid, swooping sniff as he moved his nose along his arm. Nothing was left of the powder after his nose passed but a few scattered grains. It was like watching a sailor consume several glasses of rum, neat, in rapid succession.

He straightened up and grinned at me.

"Isn't that hard on your health?" I asked.

"Never had a cold in m'life," he said, still grinning. "Never even sneeze. Best medicine going. Makes a good tooth powder, too. Hardens the gums and preserves the teeth." He gave Wightman a nod and hurried off to join his mates, and I trailed after him.

The shops were fascinating, but on this day my interest was centred on the river bank below. The Thames had long been infested by river pirates, petty thieves who boarded a ship or landed at a wharf under some pretext and grabbed whatever they could carry off in their pockets. The thefts Lady Sara was investigating were an entirely different kind of crime. They were carefully planned and carried out by an organization large enough to handle an enormous quantity of goods. She had cautioned me again that a respectable-appearing firm with a substantial volume of entirely legitimate business probably was involved. Either it controlled the thieves, or it was controlled by them. Its position would enable it to dispose of the stolen merchandise without raising suspicion.

Her theories usually were correct, so I directed my search at finding the warehouse or perhaps several warehouses belonging to such a firm.

I followed one lane after another down to the river. The Thames was alive with ships—not the huge iron vessels to be seen below London Bridge, but smaller craft of all kinds. The barges, their brightly-coloured sails taut in the morning breeze, added flower-like touches to the scene as they tacked among the drab shipping. The shore buzzed with activity— lighters coming and going, barges being loaded and unloaded, waterside labourers swarming over them, cranes swinging overhead. I studied the warehouses with care, but none of them on this reach of the river aroused even a suggestion of suspicion. For one thing, they were too small to be handling huge volumes of stolen goods and their legitimate businesses as well. For another, they all had a decrepitly honest air about them.

Eventually I came on a wharf where bundles of heavy iron bars were being unloaded from a barge, and I paused for a moment to watch the workers. The younger men were fine physical specimens with hugely developed muscles. Their strength must have been Herculean. I had heard it said that they carried as much a two and a half hundredweight on their backs with ease as they ran along the narrow planks connecting ships with the wharves. Older men, racked by years of this punishing labour, groaned and gasped under the heavy loads, but they staggered bravely on. They knew too well that a single failure would cost them their employment.

One of the failures stood nearby, looking on sourly. He was not elderly, but years of heavy labour on the docks had maimed and destroyed him. His right hand had lost two fingers; the others were so swollen he had difficulty gripping the stub of the empty old pipe he sucked on. He looked much smaller than he was because he was permanently stooped from the burdens his back had borne for so long. His unshaven face, above his ragged beard, was deeply wrinkled with premature old age and the permanent sense of gloom that enveloped him. I thought he meant to beg, but he was merely whining complaints because the foreman had passed him by at the morning "call on," and he had no work for the day. The foreman would have known this worn and crippled docker could not carry those bundles of iron, but so desperate were the impoverished for work that he would have tried even if it killed him—and such work frequently did as men toppled overboard under their loads or fell into holds.

A younger, healthier man would have hurried off to try his luck elsewhere. This man found work so rarely that a single refusal had defeated him. He remained there, snivelling, afraid to go home and face his family with empty pockets.

I offered him my tobacco pouch. He gave me a look of stark astonishment and then filled his pipe with his fumbling, swollen fingers. I held a vesta for him and watched while he sucked in the smoke.

"Takes a strong man for that kind of work," I suggested, nodding at the barge.

The tobacco revived him. "Used to do it," he said. "Could do it now if they'd let me."

"Big men have an advantage," I observed. Then, because I was looking for clues to the river thefts, I added, "Ever try for a warehouse job?"

His mind was still gloomily meditating my last remark. "Big men get called first. I 'spects foremen have orders. There ain't many big'uns 'round here, but I knew one once could 'a carried two of those loads. Or three."

"He must have been really big," I said.

"Really big," he agreed. "A bloomin' giant."

I immediately lost interest in the river thefts. "Let's have tea, and you can tell me about him," I said.

We had coffee instead at a ramshackle stall near the river. I added two hard-boiled eggs to his repast, and he ate them as though he hadn't had a solid meal for days. When he finished, I bought him a piece of cake and more coffee. He brightened with that small amount of food in him and thanked me sincerely for the "corfe, stones, and kike." We talked while he was eating, and by the time he licked up the last crumb of kike and swallowed the last of his corfe, I knew that his name was Ungles, that he had a wife and four children, and that the big man he mentioned had lived for a time in the building where the Ungles family occupied a room.

"Don't know nothin' 'bout him," he confessed. "Maybe he only kipped with someone as lived there. But I seen him now an' again."

His wife might be able to tell me more if she had time to talk, but she worked all of her daylight hours making matchboxes. When I mentioned a shilling, he brightened at once and offered to take me home with him.

Few people who weren't impoverished themselves had any notion of how the poor lived in this wealthiest of the world's cities in the year 1900. Residents called their cramped Spitalfields alley Pig Lane. Perhaps there were or had been pigs kept somewhere in the vicinity. The passageway was littered with children and filth. The house had once been a substantial dwelling, but now it was the most dismal of slums with each room sheltering a separate family—or families. Landings and halls were heaped with refuse. The stairs were of stone, but railings and bannisters were missing. So were the panels of nearly all the doors and sometimes even the doorposts, not to mention cupboards and shelves. All had been wrenched free or chopped down for firewood. As we passed open doors and door holes on our way to the top of the house, I saw in every room ragged women and sometimes several ragged children bending over tables or old sugar cases and silently and swiftly making matchboxes, making umbrella tassels, making artificial flowers, making hatboxes, making paper bags, making scrubbing or laundry or shoe-brushes, making fly-paper, repairing clothing or even boots. Thus did the London poor labour all their waking hours for their pitiful scraps of food.

I knew the scene well. I had lived in a similar slum before I met Lady Sara.

Mrs. Ungles was a care-worn slattern with an ugly, pock-marked face and untidy hair. The room contained a few sugar boxes that held domestic clutter, a mattress, and a rickety table. There was a crumbling fireplace with a small pile of coals on the floor near it, but despite the chilly morning, there was no fire on the grate. No doubt the coals were being saved for genuinely cold weather.

The woman was working at the table, which was placed under the room's one window. She did not even look up as we entered. Her face was expressionless; her fingers moved swiftly with a wonderful deftness. The air was filled with the cloying scent of paste. The only sounds were the slight cracking of thin wood and the soft slopping of the paste brush.

Ungles had told me his two younger children were among the crowd of infants we had seen in the street. The two older children, whose ages were seven and nine, worked beside their mother until they had to leave for school, and they resumed their places as soon as they returned. There was little food in evidence; probably one or another of various charity organizations fed the older children at school, and the younger ones ate whatever scraps their parents could provide.

Ungles explained my errand, mentioning the promised shilling. Mrs. Ungles continued to work as though she hadn't heard him. He spoke to her again; she shook her head and muttered something. Finally I understood. She was refusing to answer my questions unless I first paid her two and three-quarters pence, which was the amount she earned for making a gross, or twelve dozen, matchboxes. She insisted on being compensated in advance for the time she would be wasting. The shilling promised her husband was none of her concern. She knew she would never see it.

Once I had counted out pennies and farthings, and she had put her work aside, she proved to be wonderfully loquacious. Her outbursts flowed like the incoming tide, liberally laced with obscenities and street cant, and it was difficult to point her conversation where I wanted it to go, at the giant.

She was full of complaints about the Charity Organization people, "them enquiry blokes." She was eager for her children to get their schooling done—not to acquire valuable knowledge, but so their days could be spent helping her with the pasting, which would give her a little ease. She worried about her girls; she had a sister who had once earned a living, of sorts, making artificial flowers but who had "fallen."

As for the big man her husband had mentioned, she knew nothing about him, didn't even know his name. He had been living with, or visiting, the neighbour who lived in the next room, a man known to her only as Nick, who had long since moved away. She saw the giant come and go regularly for a few days, and then she never saw him again. He had been shy and polite, but he lost his temper in a flash one night when he found her struggling with a drunken man who was trying to force his way into her room when her man was in hospital.

She laughed hoarsely and gestured with her hands to show what had happened. The giant picked the intruder up by his collar with one hand and slapped his face—hard, like to broke his neck—with the other. Then the giant pointed him toward the stairs and gave him a kick, and the intruder rolled all the way down to the landing and lay there. She didn't know how badly hurt he was. In any case, he was gone in the morning, and she never learned whether he was a resident, or a visitor, or a stranger who had sneaked into the house to kip. People came and went all the time, and few of them actually belonged there.

The giant shyly asked whether she was all right and then went to the neighbour's room. That was all she knew about him. Her husband, who had only seen him a few times coming or going, knew even less.

"How big was he?" I asked.

She pointed to the door, which was about six and a half feet high. The giant had to stoop "way over" to get through it. And everything about him was big, arms, hands—he had huge hands, and when he slapped a face hard, the neck really snapped back. It was a wonder he didn't break the intruder's neck.

I asked whether she had noticed a birthmark on his face or a mole on his neck. She shook her head bewilderedly. The only time she had seen him close up was when he came to her rescue, and that was at night with only one candle lit. Anyway—with so much of him to notice, she wouldn't be likely to see a little thing like that.

How long ago did this happen? She and her husband speculated for a moment or two about the age of one of their children, the second youngest, and then decided it was four or five years ago. The trail would have faded completely by now. Even so, it was a genuine giant footprint and, with Betsy Cameron's Monmouth Street giant, the second we had found.

I thanked the couple, gave the husband his shilling, gave the wife a few more pennies, and told them I might come on the morrow and bring someone with me who was interested in giants.

I brought Lady Sara, who had a costume for such occasions—a ragged dress and a shawl. She mimicked the accents of a street sweeper we both knew. The giant was her nephew, she said, and she had lost touch with him and was eager to find him again. She took the couple over the same ground I had covered without learning anything new. Then she talked with the landlady who presided over the ruined building, but that dissipated individual—there was gin on her breath at nine in the morning—was unaware she'd had a giant for a tenant. She seemed content with collecting her rents and allowing the building to decay without any interference from her. She remembered very little about Nick, who had taken a room, paid his rent after a fashion, and vanished without notice.

"Even if the giant only came there at night, he wouldn't be easily overlooked in that building," Lady Sara remarked when we regained the street. "One of the other tenants must have noticed him."

"All of these people come and go like Nick," I said. "It may be hard to find another tenant who has lived there for five years, but I'll try."

The following day I made a thorough search, but the giant had left no more footprints—in that building or in any of those nearby. As the woman's husband suggested, probably he had kipped with the man called Nick for a few nights and then found another refuge.

Like the first giant footprint, this second one led nowhere.

When I returned to Connaught Mews, I learned that I'd had a visitor. A friend of mine, an elderly cobbler named Nat Daniels, had called not once but three times hoping to see me. He called again, bursting in on us while Lady Sara and I were still savouring our disappointment over the blind alley our giant hunt had become entrapped in.

Despite his age, Daniels was still a superb cobbler. He stoutly refused to fuss with the latest styles of footwear, but the ordinary, everyday shoes he made were excellent. He had been my cobbler from the day I first became able to buy shoes for myself, rather than scrounge them, and when I told Lady Sara about him, she also patronized him.

Normally he was a congenial, easy-going type, but on this day he was almost too angry to speak. He had to pause to catch his breath. Then he gasped, "Burglary!"

"Who, or what, was burgled?" I asked.

The story came out in bursts of sentence fragments. He lived above his shop. He had heard something in the night—or maybe he hadn't, he wasn't sure of that himself. In any case, he had paid it no notice. His was a busy, crowded street with traffic throughout the day and night. In the morning, two shoes were missing from a rush order for two pair that he had finished the previous night. The thief had taken one shoe from each pair.

"And," he added with breathless anger, "this is the second time it has happened!"

"Two shoes each time?" I asked.

He nodded dazedly. Then he added, "Two left shoes. Both times he took the left shoes." He shook his head bewilderedly.

Lady Sara spoke for the first time. "Are there any one-legged men living in your neighbourhood?"

"That's what Constable Hardy asked, my lady," Daniels said. "He looked into it. There aren't any, and there've never been any, and no one saw a one-legged man loitering there."

"It is an obvious question to ask in a case of stolen left shoes," Lady Sara said with a smile. "Another possibility would be a shop that caters to one-legged men—but in that case, why not steal the right shoes as well? A clientele consisting only of left-legged men would be unthinkable. Further, if there really is, somewhere, an unimaginable market for left shoes, why didn't the thief steal as many as he could carry while he had the freedom of the shop? He must have had some very special object in taking only two both times. How was the break-in managed?"

"It wasn't, my lady," Daniels said. "All the doors and windows were locked. Constable Hardy checked."

Lady Sara arched her eyebrows. "Come, Colin. We must look into this ourselves."

Charles Tupper drove the three of us in the four wheeler. The cobbler's small shop was located on the ground floor of a building on Marylebone Road, and Constable Hardy, who had heard that Daniels had gone to consult Lady Sara, was there waiting for us. He and Daniels demonstrated to us how both front and rear doors had been double-locked. All of the windows were kept locked. There was no other way to enter.

"What about that window?" Lady Sara asked, pointing to a small, unwashed pane of glass located near the ceiling just above some shelves on which shoes were displayed.

Constable Hardy chuckled. "It'd take a mighty small thief to get through that, my lady."

Lady Sara nodded to me. I called for a ladder and checked both the top shelf and the window. The window opened easily. There were confused smudges in the dust on the top shelf—unmistakable marks of someone coming and going.

I described what I had found.

The constable was abashed.

We then went round to the back of the shop and traced the route of the thief—from a barrow onto a dustbin, and from there onto the roof of a storage shed, which gave him access to the window.

"You were quite right on one point," Lady Sara told Constable Hardy. "Our culprit is a mighty small thief. Equally obvious is the fact that he has both of his legs and feet. Otherwise, he couldn't have negotiated that entrance and exit. How large were the stolen shoes?"

Daniels pointed to my feet, which are larger than average.

"Then he wasn't stealing the shoes to wear," Lady Sara said. "He could have been stealing them for someone else, but—how long ago did the other theft happen?"

"A month," Daniels said.

"Few one-legged man would need four new shoes in such a short time. This brings us back to our earlier deduction that the shoes were stolen for some special purpose. What would their salvage value be? Could the shoes be ripped apart for the leather?"

"Why would anyone go to all that trouble?" Daniels demanded. "There is plenty of leather in the shop if he wanted leather."

"Then our problem is to discover the special purpose that required two left shoes on two separate occasions."

The rest of us looked at her blankly.

"Or perhaps," she went on meditatively, "a special purpose that required two shoes. Any two shoes. We don't know for certain, yet, that the left-shoe shape was essential. Let's have a look at the neighbourhood."

She strode briskly along the pavement with Constable Hardy, Daniels and I trailing after her.

It was a perfectly ordinary neighbourhood. Like most London locales, there was a blend of social levels ranging from wealth through extreme poverty. Lady Sara dismissed the row of shops—a clothier, a tobacconist, a chemist, and a green grocer—after one glance, but the crowd of kerbstone merchants that hovered about the corner of Marylebone Road and York Place interested her. Several were offering elaborate clockwork toys—a small hansom cab that moved in circles, a black poodle dog that hopped like a frog and barked; a pair of pugilists engaged in a lively boxing match. The more complicated ones cost as much as eighteen pence. Other toys, including bagpipes and Jews' harps, went for a penny.

Lady Sara looked them over thoughtfully and then turned to the other merchants. At first I was able to follow her line of thought easily. She gave momentary attention to a man offering cheap purses, but it was immediately obvious that larger pieces of leather were required to make them than could be salvaged from shoes, and the leather had to be thinner and more flexible. A man with toy microscopes also interested her briefly, but the tubes, through which children could see all the wonders of nature for a penny, were of metal.

The merchants watched her hopefully as she moved among them. For many, the day's receipts decided whether they slept on a doorstep or in a comfortable bed in a lodging house; whether they ate or went to bed hungry.

Lady Sara paused for a moment to consider a couple of tiny puppies that one of the merchants produced from his pocket as she approached—perhaps she was wondering whether shoe leather might be used for dog collars. She gave a searching glance to a stack of umbrellas that had leather trim on the handles but paid no attention at all to the men offering iced drinks or sherbet. An offer of leather boot-laces made her pause and frown with concentration.

Then she lost me completely by settling her full attention on a girl of about ten who was offering pots of flowers for sale. I thought perhaps the small, subdued beauty of their blossoms—in contrast to the showy blooms flower girls usually sold—were what caught Lady Sara's attention. They were ordinary woodland and meadowland wild flowers, which many persons, particularly those with rural backgrounds, were extremely fond of.

Lady Sara paused to question the girl, who obviously felt flattered by her interest. "Where do you get such unusual flowers?" Lady Sara asked.

"My aunt grows them," the girl said.

"Your aunt grows them—where?"

"In her rooms," the girl said.

"I would like to see how your aunt manages this. Where does she live?"

The girl recited the address, which was on Crawford Street. We turned in that direction with cobbler and constable still following us—the constable curious; the cobbler hoping for a miracle.

When we reached the Crawford Street address, the child's story seemed totally unlikely. It was a tall, run-down building with narrow windows. It had been divided into numerous flats, and it seemed impossible that enough light could be collected in any of them to grow a single blade of grass. Lady Sara chatted briefly with a resident who was just leaving the building and confirmed the aunt's address. Then she resignedly turned to the stairway.

The aunt lived on the top, or fourth, floor, and it was a long climb. Once arrived, Lady Sara tapped on the door, introduced herself, and expressed her curiosity as to how the aunt managed to grow such lovely flowers at that address. The aunt, a plump, cheerful woman, beamed at her and invited us in.

It was a former artist's studio, with a row of large skylights in every room. Living arrangements for the woman and her family were crowded into a minimal space; the plants were everywhere else. Her own three children, along with the niece we had spoken to, sold the flowers.

"Remarkable," Lady Sara mused. She headed directly for the far side of the room where, on a long plank, was a row of seedlings that had been started in very unusual trays. They were growing in old shoes.

There were men's shoes of every kind, but almost all of them were in a sadly decrepit condition. They had been worn to a point of total uselessness. The woman had cut the tops away to produce a very satisfactory receptacle for new seedlings and also an economical one, since it saved buying expensive pots.

Scattered among them were a few shoes that looked almost new. Nat Daniels uttered a cry and sprang forward. "My shoes!"

Lady Sara explained to the woman that those four shoes had belonged to pairs of new, unworn shoes that had been stolen from the cobbler's shop. The woman was mortified. Neighbourhood boys brought her worn-out discards, she said. They were of no use to anyone—except her—and she gave the boys a pittance for them. As for those particular shoes, the boy had said he found them. They were badly scuffed when he brought them to her, and, anyway, who had a use for two left shoes? So she had bought them.

"'E scuffed 'em 'isself to make 'em look old," Constable Hardy announced. He was wise to the ways of young thieves.

"What did you pay for them?" Lady Sara asked the aunt.

"I give him a farthing."

"For two of them?"

She nodded. "Shoes make fine pots. Before I put potting soil in, I stuff sand into the toes. It holds the moisture. But I had no idea—left shoes, who would have thought—" She turned to Daniels. "Do you want them back?"

Daniels shook his head sadly. "All that work wasted," he muttered. "Four pair of shoes ruined."

"Who was the boy who sold them to you?" Lady Sara asked.

"His name is Tim Noakes. I don't know where he lives."

"I do," Constable Hardy said grimly.

From that point, the law took charge. Constable Hardy led us to the apalling slum where Tim Noakes lived. His father, a costermonger, was away at work trying to earn his daily pittance. His mother was giving a pathetic supper of bread and jam to a large family of young children. Tim, the eldest, was about ten. He went pale and made a break for it when he saw the law at the door, but Constable Hardy was expert at capturing escaping thieves.

He also was expert at extracting confessions. Under his stern interrogation, the blubbering Tim poured forth his pathetic story. He had, several times before, sold the flower lady shoes he had found in the street. He had noticed the cobbler's high window when prowling the mews behind his shop for salvageable trash, so when he needed a farthing for sweets and couldn't find any shoes, he slipped out one night, squeezed through the window, and took two shoes.

"How did you happen to pick two left shoes?" Lady Sara asked.

Tim didn't know. He just reached down from the top shelf and grabbed the first two shoes he encountered. The next time he wanted a farthing for sweets and couldn't find any shoes, he repeated the feat.

The thief's tearful mother apologized. Agony throbbed in her every word as she told Daniels, "I will pay for the shoes. It may take a long time, but I will pay. This family pays its debts."

She slumped onto a chair and buried her face in her hands. Her body shook with sobs. The boy sat snivelling in the corner, crushed by the sudden awareness that his thoughtless acts had bankrupted his parents.

Lady Sara turned to the cobbler. "You sometimes hire a boy for deliveries and odd jobs. Why don't you let Tim work off his own debt?"

Daniel stared at her. "Me? Hire a thief?"

"Why not? He'll be especially anxious to make amends. He just might be the best helper you've ever had. He is resourceful, and agile, and he seems to be smarter than most boys."

Daniel continued to stare at her. Finally he turned to Tim. "Do you want to work for me?"

The astonished Tim looked at him dumbly for a moment and then nodded.

Cobbler and thief left together. Lady Sara and I returned with them to Marylebone Road, where Charles Tupper was waiting with the four wheeler.

"It was an obvious deduction," Lady Sara said when I asked her what inspired her to link the stolen shoes with flower pots. "If the shoes weren't being taken to wear, and if they weren't being used for salvage, someone had to be putting something into them. Our happening onto the woman's niece selling flowers was a stroke of luck, of course, but never forget this—luck comes in strange guises. It only brings good fortune to people who are able to recognize it."

After a pause, she delivered her own summation of the case. "Crime is a tragedy for everyone concerned. There are small and large tragedies, and sometimes the small ones cut far more deeply than the large ones. But perhaps this will be one of the rare cases with a happy ending."

CHAPTER 10

Lady Sara was becoming restless and increasingly worried. She continued to solve trivialities and occasionally a serious problem for her friends during her coffee hour. Rarely she failed, as in the case of a titled lady whose jewellery had been taken by her titled but impoverished husband, who vanished along with it. As always, she picked up numerous tips as Madam Zarno and as many more from her agents around London, made use of a few of them herself, and passed most of them to the police. While this activity kept us fully occupied, unfortunately it did not advance the cases on the cribbage board by a single peg hole.

There had been no more giant tracks. Not one of Lady Sara's sharp-eyed informers had caught a glimpse of a clue concerning either the missing giant or the river thefts.

Clarke-Ivatt was still routinely visiting clubs. Otherwise, he went nowhere and saw no one. On the Shadwell murder, we had made virtually no progress. Chief Inspector Mewer was still galloping off in all directions and had made even less.

Lady Sara worried constantly because she felt certain that the Shadwell murderer, and perhaps the giant as well, would strike again. Daily she searched reports of the debris churned up from the depths of the city—victims of murder or of vicious assault—and examined descriptions of victims for traces of the Spanish Tickler or a giant's flash of temper.

"It will come," she said gloomily. "I am convinced it will come."

After a long evening spent in brooding over the pegs stalled in four cribbage board byways, she announced her verdict. "We'll have to do something drastic."

In my wanderings along the river, I had become acquainted with Ben Lyle, a former fisherman from somewhere in Kent. He was a lazy, humorous scoundrel who probably remained in port whenever he had the price of a pint in his pocket. His wife had died years before, and he had moved to London to be near his married daughter. Now he was about sixty years old and as lean and muscular as he had been when he was hoisting sails on a fishing smack.

The daughter's husband held a responsible position with a Southwark chemical factory, and he had arranged employment for Lyle—as a doorkeeper, the most undemanding job the establishment had to offer—but the stench and rush and noise and confinement of a factory were not for him. He found his own jobs, working on river boats whenever he felt like it or needed money. When he did not, he passed his time leaning over the wall along the Thames with his hands in his pockets, spitting into the eddies and commenting on the ineptitudes of men on the sailing barges.

"Twenty yards inshore there's a current would take 'em down three miles an hour faster, but ne'er a one of 'em seems to know that," he would grumble.

This is what he was doing when I met him. He told me that in the old days he never touched an oar, sails being his business and oars being against nature; but it was obvious that he loved boats and loved being on the water. He viewed a day of rowing on the Thames as recreation, and he offered to scull me down to Greenwich and back for a pipe of tobacco. What he couldn't abide was having someone who knew far less about it than he did telling him what to do.

He had lived in London for little more than a decade, but he knew the river like the back of his hand. When I remarked on this, he responded with a shake of his head. "I know it better. Never paid much mind to my hand."

He lived with his brother Bob, also a former fisherman, and the two of them must have been a sore trial to their landlady.

I told Lady Sara about him, and she asked to meet him. The two of them got on famously together. As a result, the Lyle brothers hired a large skiff, equipped it according to Lady Sara's instructions, and they met us at dusk at Battle Bridge Stairs, just below London Bridge on the Surrey side of the Thames, for a night of adventuring on the river.

This was the "something drastic" that had to be done. Despite the huge quantity of goods stolen from warehouses along the river, no one had noticed any suspicious activity around these sites. Lady Sara wanted to know why. There was far less river traffic at night, but there always was some, and she especially wanted to know why no one on a passing ship had observed anything. Was it because those travelling the river in darkness had problems enough without trying to scrutinize the shore, or was it because night and its shadows enshrouded the thieves in invisibility? There was a third possibility. The thefts could have been observed regularly by witnesses who thought it wise to look the other way and say nothing.

Hence our nocturnal expedition. We had no expectation of discovering anything. We merely wanted to see how difficult it would be to detect a theft in progress when one occurred. We were trying this because nothing else had worked.

Lady Sara, wearing sailor's togs, took the skiff's tiller; I sat in the bow with a paddle, ready to assist in an emergency. Our watermen turned us into the current, and we turned downstream. Since the tide was going out, the current would take us at a leisurely pace with very little rowing unless sudden speed were required. It was the return trip upstream that would require work, but our watermen were accustomed to it.

Lady Sara had told Ben that our passage was to be as silent, and as close inshore, and as invisible as possible. We would keep our boat dark unless something threatened to run us down. Ben took her at her word and even muffled the long oars—to her considerable amusement.

Lights were coming on along the shore; tug boats were already showing their red and green running lights. Ahead of us, a large iron passenger steamer, illuminated from stem to stern, her hooter sounding a hoarse warning, was headed down with the tide, and Tower Bridge raised its bascules to let her through.

Moving slowly, we passed alongside docked or anchored freighters and dredgers, turned toward shore whenever an opening permitted, and then veered out again. After brightly lit Tower Bridge Wharf, where a freighter was unloading the last of a shipment of skins and hides, we drifted under the bridge and passed close by the Anchor Brewhouse. We turned toward midstream to avoid the ships at Butler's Wharf and edged shoreward again at Horselydown New Stairs. And so it went, with all four of us watching the riverside wharves and buildings as we moved slowly but steadily past—watching to learn what an observer on the river was able to see of the shore at that time of night. We drifted past mills, past graineries, past wharves handling all manner of specialized trade.

Occasionally strains of song reached us from a riverside pub. In Rotherhithe, the Jolly Waterman had an unusually roisterous clientele. Darkness was settling in rapidly by then, and the church tower of St. Mary, Rotherhithe, a riverside landmark, was only dimly visible against the night sky. Ben Lyle quickly developed respect for Lady Sara's skill as a helmsman. He spoke to her only once. We were skirting the Lower Pool, and as we passed Trinity and Durand's Wharves, where large timber rafts frequently were anchored, he suggested she give them plenty of room because the wood rode low in the water and was difficult to see.

When Greenwich finally hove into view, we set running lights. Lady Sara and I were able to scrutinize the Surrey bank a second time while our watermen rowed us back upstream. We went ashore at Kings Stairs and had refreshments at the Dover Castle, where Lady Sara had no difficulty passing as a seaman. Then we continued upstream, and after we passed the long barrier of light thrown over the river at Tower Bridge, we crossed over, doused our lights, and drifted down the north side of the river.

It was a repetition of our earlier trip except for the hour, which now was well after midnight. The already diminished night traffic on the Thames had thinned further. Lights of the city hazed the sky to the north-west, but darkness prevailed along the shore, where the most momentary illumination was visible for long distances over the water.

As far as our experiment was concerned, we now understood why nothing suspicious had been seen from the river at the time of the thefts. Except where an occasional wharf was brightly lighted for legitimate night work, virtually nothing could be seen from the river.

Again we set our lights and started another return trip with our watermen rowing energetically. Ben, who knew the currents perfectly, muttered an occasional instruction to Lady Sara. We gradually put the concentrations of heavy riverside industry behind us and, having negotiated the Limehouse Reach and the Lower Pool, passing both Shadwell Market and the Wapping Police Station, we were almost on our home stretch. The lights of Tower Bridge were beckoning ahead of us; along the shore were dim shapes of a series of low buildings typical of small general merchandise wharves.

A splash sounded, followed by a confused murmur of voices. A light flashed on the shore and went out just as suddenly. At a sharp whisper from Lady Sara, we doused our own lights. She pointed the skiff toward a gap between anchored barges; Bob rested his oars, and Ben worked his as silently as possible.

The sudden, brief illumination had given us a momentary glimpse of activity on a wharf. Someone was loading, or unloading, cargo. The picture lingered in the mind's eye long after the light had gone out: A ship of some sort, perhaps thirty-five or forty feet long; a few dock workers, two of whom were kneeling on the edge of the dock as though fishing for something in the water; two others carrying a large box or chest.

What intrigued all four of us, instantly, was the fact that this scene was being enacted in dumb show. Any sound made there would have carried to us easily, but there was none. Except for the splash, obviously caused by something dropped accidently, and the flutter of excitement that followed, the men worked in an unnatural, uncanny silence. Their movements were so measured and cautious as to produce no sound at all. They must have worn special shoes, for even their foot treads were silent.

And the scene was being enacted in darkness.

If the loading or unloading had been legitimate, the work area would have been brightly lighted, and no attempt would have been made to muffle the routine noises produced when merchandise was moved. Why bother? Who would have cared?

Our first concern was that someone on the dock might have noticed our approach and become suspicious when we doused our lights. Ben, working his oars carefully, kept us approximately in the same place—we moved upstream a short distance with each stroke and then drifted backward. We waited, offering silent thanks for Ben's foresight in muffling the oars. I scarcely dared to breathe.

Those on the dock seemed unaware of us, but if they continued to work, they did so as quietly as before. Time passed with all of us straining to see through the thick veil of darkness. Suddenly Lady Sara whispered a sharp command, Ben rested his oars, and we drifted backward downstream just as a large, dark shape moved toward us. It slipped through the opening between anchored barges where we had been hovering and headed toward midstream.

Then it veered, and at the same moment it showed running lights.

"It's a small steam-launch!" Lady Sara whispered. Ben and Bob leaned to their oars, and I tended our own lights.

What followed was the most unequal race since the hare and the tortoise. The lights of the launch easily pulled away from us, running swiftly downstream along the north, or London shore. We were rapidly falling further and further behind when, abruptly, the launch's lights went out.

Ben and Bob continued to row, churning the water with their utmost strength. They had the advantage of the current, now, but so did the invisible steam-launch. We knew approximately where we were, but we had no idea where the launch had got to except that it must have passed the Limehouse Basin of the Regent's Canal. An accidental alignment of lights, both on the river bank and far inshore, helped us. A dark shadow moved across them.

All four of us took sightings on the black stretch of river bank that the launch seemed headed for. Then it was swallowed by the darkness. When we reached that area, we hovered in the current as we had before, staring at the shore and listening, but this time no accident resulted in sound or light.

"Know where we are?" Lady Sara asked Ben Lyle finally.

"Just off St. Anne's, Limehouse, my lady," he said.

"Are you sure?"

"I can just barely make out the clock tower. There's a little reflection on it."

"Right. It's been a good night's work. Let's go home."

In the morning, with Lady Sara again wearing sailor's togs because we had another river excursion ahead of us, we made the acquaintance of St. Anne's, Limehouse, one of the churches built under a grant made by Queen Anne. Its architect was the celebrated Nicholas Hawksmoor. The splendid old church had a fascinating history. It had burned in a spectacular fire on Good Friday, 1850, and only the walls and the clock tower were left standing. The roof and fittings had been quickly restored, and additional renovations had been made during the past decade.

It merited far more attention than we gave it, but our interest centred on the riverside, and the church was located some distance away, in Commercial Road. Its hundred and thirty foot clock tower was a river landmark, and it was this that Ben Lyle had glimpsed, dimly, from the skiff.

We made ourselves acquainted with the stretch of river nearest the church. It was one of the few places in the entire dock area where the road ran close to the river. Lady Sara pointed out the advantage this offered in moving stolen goods. A wagon could be quick-loaded at night almost while it was driving past.

The road was called Narrow Street. Fronting on both it and the river were several eighteenth-century buildings. One of them was a famous pub, the Grapes. Otherwise, the buildings functioned as offices for small wharves given to barge repairing or lighterman businesses. On the downstream side was a much more modern brick building known as Prout's Mill. Its landing-stage was Prout's Mill Wharf. Its name suggested that it once had been a mill. Now it was occupied by a general importing firm called Eynon Brothers Company.

Beyond Prout's Mill was Duke Shore and Stairs, a decrepit wharf with a chequered history that was currently being used for barge repairs. Next came Taylor Walker's new brewery, a fine, large, modern building little more than a decade old.

Despite the presence of Prout's Mill and the brewery, this was a ramshackle-looking stretch of river-bank.

After a casual survey and an innocent question or two, we came away. We didn't want our enquiries to arouse anyone's suspicions. We next joined Ben and Bob Lyle in their skiff so we could drop downstream through the colourful clutter of daytime shipping on the Thames and view the stretch of bank along Narrow Street by daylight. We were looking for a steam-launch. There was none to be seen, which was disappointing but not unexpected. The stolen goods would have been unloaded quickly and concealed; the launch could have been underway again long before daylight.

There were two barges at Duke Shore and a miscellany of small craft at the wharves upstream. At Prout's Mill, there was only a single-masted sailing ship.

"That's her!" Ben exclaimed suddenly as we drifted past.

Lady Sara looked at him inquiringly.

Ben chuckled. "Now wouldn't that spiflicate you! They took off the funnel and rigged a mast. Made her a clumsy sloop."

"Are you sure?"

"Saw her clearly against the light last night, my lady. She's got funny lines—her deck-house is unusually high, 'n there was somethin' else about her I couldn't place. Now I understand—she's got a small crane amidships. Don't often see a crane on a ship that size. Never see one on a sailing ship, which don't need one 'cause its boom can load or unload cargo, but she's got one. That's her, all right. Funnel gone, mast rigged. Wonder how she sails. Not somethin' I'd like to put to sea in, but I 'spect she gets by on the river."

Her name was painted in small, almost suspiciously inconspicuous letters. We had to drift close to her in order to make it out. She was called the Molly Mae.

Ben chuckled again. "On a board! Not painted on the ship but on a board! I'll wager there's another name under it. She'll be called somethin' else when she's a steam-launch."

"Or whenever the owners need a ship of another name," Lady Sara suggested.

Ben nodded happily. "I never see'd the likes of it."

We headed back upstream to look for the place where we had seen the goods being stolen. We had noted the location as carefully as we could in the dark—along the stretch of river above the Wapping Entrance to the London Docks—but there was little to be seen there. The river bank was lined by low warehouses and wharves that were too small to accommodate coasting ships. Most were used for storage of goods transported by lighter or barge directly from ships or from other wharves.

Lady Sara gave the Lyle brothers their instructions before they put us ashore. They were to keep an eye on the Molly Mae as well as they could from the skiff. We returned to Connaught Mews, where Lady Sara retired to her own quarters to discard her sailor's togs. She emerged triumphantly as herself. Back we went to the river, this time with Charles Tupper driving us in Lady Sara's private hansom. One at a time we called on every business in the entire row of buildings located along the stretch of river where we had witnessed the theft. At each establishment, Lady Sara's card gained us instant access to the manager.

Lady Sara explained her errand carefully. We had received a report of a theft the previous night at some wharf in that vicinity.

We were met with blank faces everywhere we called. None of the firms had had anything stolen.

Neither had any of them been loading cargo in the early hours of the morning. It was a complete dead end for us. Through an enormous stroke of luck we had seen a theft in progress and knew where the stolen goods had been taken, but there had been no theft!

Lady Sara wasn't finished. She called on a friend who operated a shipping company and enquired about a sloop called the Molly Mae. It was properly registered to the Eynon Brothers Company, a well-known importing firm.

After Lady Sara asked a few routine questions about ships' funnels, we left.

"What was it about the funnel?" I asked her when we were headed for Connaught Mews again.

"It suddenly occurred to me that a funnel doesn't have to be a cylindrical pipe. If it were tapered slightly, it could be made in sections, and with a very simple mechanism, each section could be telescoped down into the one below. The entire funnel could be collapsed out of sight in seconds and the hole in the deck-house roof covered. Perhaps a mast could be constructed in sections as well. Its base could be made a solid part of the ship, and the sections of mast added when they wanted to convert to sails. As Ben remarked, one wouldn't want to go to sea with it, but it might do passing well on the river. If the mast isn't in sections, it could be kept lying on the deck. With that arrangement, one could convert a steam-launch into a sloop in very short order. Any necessary piping or drainage could be concealed just as quickly. It is further proof that these river thefts are planned by someone with intelligence, imagination, and considerable organizing ability."

"Are you going to tell Chief Inspector Mewer?" I asked.

"No. We still haven't made a beginning. The Chief Inspector would be all for getting a warrant and raiding Prout's Mill. Our few glimpses of an unidentified place in the dark, and our guesses about the boat, don't begin to provide the necessary evidence, but the Chief Inspector certainly would try. If he succeeded, even if he found substantial quantities of stolen goods, he would be reduced to arresting a few warehousemen who would protest, perhaps truthfully, that they knew nothing about them. We don't want the warehousemen. We want the person who plans the thefts and gives the orders. Otherwise, the organization will be left intact to transfer its operations somewhere else."

Later that day we heard from Ben Lyle. It was probably his first experience of talking on the telephone, and he sounded deeply suspicious about the process.

He also sounded tired out—tired, but happy after a day of hard work on his beloved river. The *Mollie Mae*, under full sail, had dropped down the river to a wharf below Greenwich, where she loaded chests of tea and then headed back upstream. The Lyle Brothers hadn't been able to keep pace with her on the return trip, but when they reached Prout's Mill Wharf she was docked there, and she was still being called the *Mollie Mae*. I told Ben to get some rest and take another look the next day.

It was evening when Chief Inspector Mewer called. He brought with him Mr. Horatio Narramore, a small, tidily dressed man whose appearance and mannerisms loudly proclaimed that he did something in the City. Obviously he did it to his considerable profit though not so exorbitantly so as did Sir Cecil Elliman. He was impeccably attired, and his tie-pin flashed a large diamond. Beside him, the large, carelessly-dressed Chief Inspector looked slovenly.

"This morning, my lady, you and Colin called at Harkin's Wharf and asked whether a theft had occurred there recently," Chief Inspector Mewer said. "You were told none had. Why did you ask?"

"Because we saw it taking place," Lady Sara said calmly.

"You actually saw—"

"We were in a boat on the river, and we caught a glimpse of something happening on the shore that looked highly improper. Someone was loading or unloading a ship, and not only was it being done in darkness, but the activity was virtually noiseless. It was carried out in an incredible, unbelievable silence. Since it was night-time, and since we saw it only momentarily in an accidental flash of light, we weren't sure what wharf was involved. This morning, Colin and I called not only at Harkin's Wharf but at all of the wharves in the area trying to identify the one we had seen. None of them had a theft to report."

"One has now," Chief Inspector Mewer said. "Mr. Narramore will tell you about it."

"It was our tea, my lady," Mr. Narramore said. "I am chairman of the Narramore Importing Company, a fine old firm that was founded by my grandfather. We operate Harkin's Wharf and two others. We aren't the East India Company, but nevertheless we import large quantities of tea. We produce our own blends—the Narra Blends. I thought of that name myself. Perhaps you have tried them?" He looked at Lady Sara hopefully.

"Of course," she said soothingly. "My mother, the Dowager Countess of Ranisford, serves them regularly." She firmly believed no capable detective should ever hesitate to lie in a worthy cause.

Mr. Narramore beamed at her. "Late this afternoon, my lady, the Harkin's Wharf manager informed me that a large quantity of tea was missing. He also told me that you had been inquiring about a theft. Naturally I informed the police immediately, and Chief Inspector Mewer suggested we call on you. You actually saw it happening?"

"We saw a ship being loaded—or unloaded, the glimpse we had was too brief to say which—in that area, some time after three o'clock this morning. Why was the theft so long in being detected?"

"We have an annex for tea storage," Mr. Narramore said. "As it happened, it was filled with tea chests—was supposed to be filled with tea chests. Those stacked in front of the door were left as they had been before, and no one could see that the room was empty behind them until they had been removed. The theft might not have been detected for days or even a fortnight if we hadn't received an unusually large order today. There had been no reason to visit that annex for some time, and my employees are completely bewildered as to when the theft could have happened."

"Was it a large loss?" Lady Sara asked.

"A considerable loss, my lady," Mr. Narramore said. "Three o'clock this morning, you said?"

"Yes, but we couldn't testify in court that the activity we saw was occurring on your wharf. Just that it was somewhere in that vicinity."

"You've given us what we needed," Chief Inspector Mewer said. "Obviously the night-watchmen were bribed." He regarded Lady Sara querulously. He always seemed to have mixed emotions about any information he received from her. It wasn't that he was ungrateful but that he couldn't help thinking she shouldn't have done it. "What were you doing on the river?" he demanded.

"Trying to find out whether it would be possible to see a theft taking place on shore."

"Since you saw one, I presume it was possible."

"But we only saw it by accident," Lady Sara said. "It was an incredible stroke of luck. The question is how to make the best possible use of it."

"We'll use it to make those watchmen talk, my lady," the Chief Inspector said grimly. "This is the break we've been waiting for. Thank you." He got to his feet. "Coming?" he asked Mr. Narramore.

Mr. Narramore scrambled after him, and the two of them rushed away to confront the night-watchmen.

"Will they find out anything?" I asked Lady Sara.

"They might extract a confession, but the watchmen won't know who they were dealing with or where the tea was taken."

"Now that we know what was stolen, if the Chief Inspector were to raid Prout's Mill—"

"He would find tea," Lady Sara said. "He also would find documents to prove the tea is there legally, and all of the tea chests would be marked accordingly. They have had plenty of time. Have you forgotten what the *Mollie Mae* picked up below Greenwich?"

"Some chests of tea," I said.

"Exactly. There would be ample proof that the sloop picked up all of the tea the Chief Inspector found at Prout's Mill—from there and elsewhere. Someone plans these operations with great care and provides for every contingency. It is going to take more than one accidental sighting of a theft in process to put an end to this business."

"So what do we do?" I asked.

"First, we find out as much as we can about the Eynon Brothers Company. Second, we keep a close watch on Prout's Mill—and hope for another accident. At least we now know how they operate: surreptitiously, without lights, when leaving shore or returning to it so no one can be certain where they have been or what their destination is; boldly and properly lighted in midstream when they have far to go; and in a steam-launch that probably can outdistance anything else on the river in an emergency. They will know exactly where the police patrols are and plan their movements accordingly. It would not surprise me if they have an informer at Thames Police Headquarters who lets them know in advance where the unmarked detective boats will be. Even if the police had the incredible luck to intercept them, they would find our thieves equipped with valid documents to support whatever they claim to be doing. This gang leaves nothing to chance."

I began my investigation of Prout's Mill the next morning, passing it several times in a hansom driven by Rick Allward, studying the surrounding buildings, looking for posts from which the Prout's Mill building and wharf could be watched. I spent the remainder of the day wandering about the area on foot.

When I returned home, I found Lady Sara bemused by a letter that had arrived in the late afternoon mail. It was typewritten on the crisply engraved, expensive-looking stationery of the Tradesmen Life and Accident Assurance Company, and it invited Lady Sara to become a director of the company, pointing out that she would be the first woman in England to be accorded such an honour and responsibility—which she was, of course, eminently qualified for.

The letter was signed with a flourish by Sir Cecil Elliman.

"Now you know why he took the trouble to call here with such a trivial problem," I said. "He was vetting you!"

"Not likely," she said. "First woman in England, indeed. Why has it taken so long?"

She dictated a reply—to be written by hand, not typewritten—informing Sir Cecil that her present committments did not permit her to take on additional obligations. "I am still wondering what his object is," she said as she signed it.

Lord Anstee came up to London on business the following day and stopped by, as he always did, to see what Lady Sara was up to. When he heard about her latest honour, he laughed loudly.

"Lady Sara wants to know what Sir Cecil's object is, my lord," I said.

"I can answer that," Lord Anstee said. "Sir Cecil is a businessman—a highly astute businessman. He has a reputation for being far-sighted, and this is excellent evidence of that. There has been much agitation about women's suffrage and women's rights. The Married Woman's Property Act has been a help, but women still lag far behind men in their legal status. As every businessman should know, however, their legal status is no indication of their economic importance. Women from wealthy families are beginning to buy substantial assurance policies for themselves. Further, women can have an enormous influence on purchases of assurance or anything else made by the men in their lives. It would be a brilliant business move for the Tradesmen Life and Accident Assurance Company to appoint a woman to its board of directors—especially a woman from a titled family. The potential benefit to the company's business would be immense. Sir Cecil's motives are always the same. Whatever he does, he expects to make money by it, but of course that is no concern of yours. You should have accepted if only because it would help the women's movement take one small step forward."

Lady Sara shook her head. "That explanation is far too simple."

"The truth often is," Lord Anstee said with a smile.

She shook her head again but said nothing.

Lord Anstee grinned at me. "Lady Sara is resentful of anyone who attempts to give her equality with men because she already has superiority."

CHAPTER 11

The owner of Eynon Brothers Company proved to be the Reverend Theobald Eynon. He also was listed as Vicar of Pangstead, Kent. If, in addition, he was presiding over a vast theft operation, he was keeping himself almost excessively busy. His combination of activities sounded unlikely enough without the thefts.

I had naïvely thought that England's network of railways gave a traveller easy access to every part of the country, but Pangstead proved surprisingly difficult to reach. It had the disadvantage—or supreme virtue—of not being near anywhere. After a train ride and a tiresome, hilly drive in a rented trap, behind a horse that clearly found the trip far more tiresome than I did, I arrived in an exquisitely remote rural town less than forty miles from London. It was far larger than I expected. Perhaps not being close to anywhere added to its importance for the surrounding farmers. I drove through its several streets and pondered the variety of shops and businesses—the most prosperous of which seemed to be that of Z. Farncombe, the local blacksmith, whose sign ungrammatically proclaimed, General Smith and Shoeing.

Adopting a favourite role of mine, I became a visiting estate agent. I was looking for parcels of land which would form an estate for a gentleman who preferred to remain anonymous. Locals immediately assumed that some great nobleman wanted to build a stately home remote from the city for rural living, fishing, and shooting, which would have provided an important new source of money for the locality, and they reacted enthusiastically. They not only answered my questions eagerly, but they virtually pressed information upon me.

In less than an hour I knew all about Pangstead and its Vicar, and I felt far more confused than I had been when I arrived. The Reverend Theobald Eynon was not merely a rural clergyman; he was a saint. He helped the poor. He sent deserving young men to the university. He gave support to the sick and the elderly. The fine old medieval church that had been falling into disrepair when he arrived had been renovated and restored by him. A complete inventory of his virtues would have occupied me for a week. No one had an unkind word to say about him.

I next drove to the church and passed some time there before proceeding to the vicarage. I gave it a thorough inspection, first outside and then, under the watchful gaze of the sexton, inside. The sexton greeted me warmly, gave me the freedom of the place with a wave of his hand when I said I merely wanted to see the church, but kept an eye on me anyway.

The church dated from the thirteenth or fourteenth century. It was surprisingly large, like many of the old churches. It couldn't have been in better condition if it had been built the previous year. From the outside, a new roof was evident along with numerous touches of restoration. The Vicar had had the entire fabric gone over with no thought to the expense. Townsfolk were especially proud of the stained glass windows he'd had added during the renovations. Observed from the inside, they proved to be of surprising beauty. The interior featured a magnificently carved rood-screen; bright, colourful wall paintings; a finely carved pulpit; a richly embroidered altarpiece; an ornate chest whose secure lock proclaimed that it contained the church's plate—the inventory became staggering. An obviously new organ; box pews and benches with carving; a carved lectern; new choir stalls, also carved; the Reverend Theobald Eynon had invested a fortune in refurbishing and renovating a church that had been old but in no way remarkable.

Finally I allowed the sexton to relax and went to call on the author of these staggering improvements. At the vicarage, which also showed signs of recent renovation, a maid greeted me with the unwelcome news that the Vicar was down for the day. That startled me but only for a moment. The modest account of his personal history in Crockford's Clerical Directory had mentioned that he was an alumnus of Lincoln College, Oxford; obviously he still employed the college expression for being in London, and the maid was mimicking him.

"When will he return?" I asked.

"He is always down on Tuesdays and Wednesdays. He has a business to see to. He leaves Monday night and usually returns Thursday morning." She paused. "But not always. Would you care to consult with one of the curates?"

I concealed my surprise. The townsfolk hadn't mentioned curates. The Vicar was given credit for everything. "How many are there?" I asked.

"There are three."

A parish with an absentee vicar was, unfortunately, not a rarity, but this humble rural parish not only had a restored and refurbished church upon which huge sums of money had been lavished, but it had three curates to assist a vicar who should have been able to manage its affairs by himself.

Not wanting to stir up curiosity, I thanked the maid and told her I would prefer to call again on a day when the Vicar wasn't down. I had ample time to spare before my return train, so I wandered about the village and picked up what additional information I could. Then I set out on the tedious journey back to London.

"I know where the profits from the river thefts are going," I told Lady Sara when I arrived at Connaught Mews.

She frowned. She disapproved of what she called impetuous deductions. "Tell me," she said.

I described Pangstead and detailed the repairs and improvements lavished on the church and vicarage. "Not only that, but the Reverend Theobald is benefactor to all of the poor families in the parish," I added. "The local people revere him. He is the most popular spiritual leader the parish has ever had. This raises a fine point of religious dogma. If a vicar steals and uses the money for noble and generous purposes, is that as great a sin as if he were to steal and greedily spend the profits on himself?"

"You said he was down today and tomorrow. Call on him tomorrow before he goes back to Pangstead."

She briefed me on what she had learned about Eynon Brothers Company. It had been founded with a family inheritance when Theobald was still a child, and he had been a one-third owner from the beginning. His two elder brothers ran the firm with immense success for many years, but from the time he left Oxford, he had spent one day a week in London keeping tabs on the family business. When, several years before, both of his brothers were lost at sea on one of their own ships, he became sole owner by inheritance of a thriving importing business. He decided to take charge of it himself until he found a suitable buyer, and, to his immense surprise, he found that he enjoyed the work and was able to make a considerable success of it.

"Can one learn to run an importing business successfully by spending one day a week at it?" I asked sceptically. "I had no idea it was so easy."

"It was one day a week for almost thirty-five years," Lady Sara pointed out. "What he accomplished would depend on how he spent that one day."

Since then, he had been devoting two or three days a week to the business. Running Eynon Brothers Company on two or three days a week struck me as even more improbable than learning to run it on a one day a week.

The next morning I called at the Eynon Brothers Company headquarters, which was located a short distance below St. Katharine Dock at Brothers Wharf. The date over the door of the stately neo-gothic warehouse building informed me that it had been erected two decades earlier.

I sent in a card identifying me as Colin Quick, secretary to Lady Sara Varnley, and the Reverend Theobald sent for me at once, greeted me effusively, and asked what service he could offer me.

I expected to find a gaunt, ascetic type of person who had dedicated his life to good works. Instead, I found a plump, jovial, balding man who obviously enjoyed life, enjoyed people, and was enjoying the sense of power he experienced both in running a prosperous company and in disposing of an unneeded large income on worthy projects.

"I called to ask a small favour," I said. "Lady Sara was traveling in Kent last summer, and she had the pleasure of visiting your church. She was impressed with all that you have done for it. Now she is considering a similar project with the church on her family's estate in Somerset. She wonders if you would be so kind as to furnish her with the names of your artists and architects."

He beamed his pleasure and wrote out names and addresses for me himself. We exchanged pleasantries, I remarked on the splendid view of the Thames he had from his office, and he took me to one of the windows and enthusiastically directed my attention to this and that. I mentioned in passing that he must have found the transition from cleric to trading magnate an odd one to master even though he obviously was thriving on it. He said candidly that it was far easier than he had expected, and he was enjoying it. I thanked him for his time and took my leave of him.

I told Lady Sara later, "Either he is innocent, or he is the most hypocritical villain I have ever encountered."

"You have fallen into the deplorable habit of confusing your opinions with your facts," she remarked irritably. "A fact remains a fact in any association. An opinion without facts to support it is no better than speculation." She paused. "It is a fact that the river thefts started about the time the Reverend Theobald took over sole ownership of Eynon Brothers Company. It is also a fact that his church connection provides him with excellent cover for illicit activities. One puzzle remains, as you have already pointed out. Would he be able, during the two or three days a week he spends in London, to successfully run his trading company and a large and enormously complex theft ring as well?"

She had been curious about the attitude of the Reverend Theobald's bishop toward such highly irregular activity, and she had telephoned him. Not only did the bishop know all about it, but the situation had his full approval. Eynon certainly wasn't neglecting his parish duties. The bishop viewed Pangstead as the best-run parish in England. He was not aware of a single complaint, either on the part of parishioners or outsiders. The parish—in fact, the entire country—was benefiting enormously from Eynon's two or three days in London. The wealth he acquired was supporting not only charities and church improvements in Pangstead but church projects all over England.

The next step was to maintain a continuous watch on Prout's Mill and on the Eynon Brothers headquarters. This proved difficult, but Lady Sara equipped several costermongers with hidden cameras—one of the new models from the Eastman Company that took numerous photographs on a roll of film—and kept one or two of them in both neighbourhoods all day long. They were to photograph a certain type of caller. Our assumption was that the Reverend Theobald had to have help in his illicit enterprises. Two or three days a week simply was not enough to create the overwhelming crime wave we were contending with, and his background argued against his running such an enterprise by himself. We were looking for his partner or partners. They would be men of considerable affluence who were accustomed to controlling large enterprises and who had the ability to create an ingenious scheme for large-scale theft as well as the organization essential for carrying it out. In short, we were looking for Magnates of Crime.

Well-dressed businessmen were not often seen around the docks, and the results were meagre. The first week produced only four likely photographs. With the help of friends in the business community, Lady Sara was able to identify them, and she passed the names to me for further investigation and moved one set of pegs two holes forward on the cribbage board. Our river theft case finally had some suspects.

Malcolm Gavin owned and ran Malcolm Gavin Ltd., which impressed me as a piddling excuse for a trading company. Gavin, on the other hand, was surprisingly wealthy, and his insignificant company seemed to be his only source of income. He was the swashbuckling type with a tall, powerful body, and drooping moustaches. I told Lady Sara, "He should have been a pirate or a highwayman." She answered, "Perhaps he is."

Alban Ryman never would have attained magnate status if his father hadn't founded and developed a successful business, Manley Ryman Ltd. The firm specialized in the Baltic trade. Ryman himself was a colourless individual who lived a quiet life with his family. Since his father's death, he had extended the company's operations—overextended them, some said—and he had been in financial difficulties a few years earlier. Now he was said to be recovering.

Innes Cameron was the head of Cameron & Company Ltd., a Scottish importing firm. He was a dour middle-aged man with a florid face. He was said to be generous to friends and totally unforgiving to enemies and competitors.

Grant Stoffer was another son who inherited a business and promptly overextended himself. George Stoffer & Company had been highly successful under his father's guidence. Grant Stoffer merged it with two other firms and almost ruined it in the process. The firm had barely survived, but now its health was said to be improving.

With the Reverend Theobald Eynon, this gave us five candidates for the Magnate of Crime role or roles. I made my own choice at once— Malcolm Gavin, who not only had unexplained wealth, but who was the only one of the five who actually looked the part. Of course his adroitly making use of ships and warehouses belonging to Eynon Brothers Company pointed to the involvement of the Reverend Theobald as well.

We were debating this matter on a dreary, rainy Sunday afternoon when the routine watch on Clarke-Ivatt ended suddenly. There was a telephone call. Clarke-Ivatt had jumped his rails and taken a trip to Fulham. Parsimonious as ever, he had walked—in the rain—from the Hotel Suisse to Charing Cross Station, where he took the Metropolitan Railway to Gloucester Road. From the Gloucester Road Station he took a cab to Fulham. His destination was a house in a neighbourhood near Munster Road.

Lady Sara had prepared for this eventuality by stationing three street vendors near the hotel. They were men who worked for her often and could be relied upon. All three had followed Clarke-Ivatt by cab from Gloucester Road. Two were watching the house while the third telephoned his report.

"Clarke-Ivatt is finally passing along the information he has gathered," Lady Sara told me. "Perhaps he is also collecting his wages. That means he may be leaving London soon. The vendors will watch the Fulham address until we can make other arrangements. Needless to say, we must find out who lives there as quickly as possible. You can go to Fulham now and decide what should be done. I'll send Rick and Charles to watch the Hotel Suisse. They will be ready to follow Clarke-Ivatt when he leaves."

One of the grooms drove me to Fulham in Lady Sara's four wheeler. On a rainy Sunday, Munster Road was a thoroughly unattractive thoroughfare, though it probably bustled with excitement and commerce on Saturday nights. The neighbourhood Clarke-Ivatt was visiting also looked dreary despite the fact that someone had tried, unsuccessfully, to add a touch of elegance to the long, bleak rows of brick terraces by giving every house in the street a balcony over its front door.

There were no shops nearer than Munster Road, and, on a Sunday night, there was no traffic. Probably there was little traffic at any time. It would be a difficult address to watch by day. On a rainy night there were no problems, however, and I noticed a "Vacancy" sign in a window across the street that could be investigated the next morning.

I left the three vendors to their chore of watching the house and went in the four wheeler to search for a public telephone—a frustrating task on a rainy night in a London Suburb where no post office was open. I finally found one in the Kensington High Street Metropolitan Railway station.

I telephoned Lady Sara. I knew without enquiring that none of the vendors would have been acceptable as a tenant in that neighbourhood. I thought the situation called for a quiet, respectable-looking, elderly couple. Lady Sara agreed.

Clarke-Ivatt left shortly before midnight, having had a conference lasting more than six hours. His host saw him to the door. Unfortunately, it wasn't possible to see what the host looked like in the dim light that leaked out when the door was opened. Two of the vendors followed Clarke-Ivatt back to the Hotel Suisse, where they turned the watch on him over to Rick and Charles and went back to Fulham.

About the time the next morning that Clarke-Ivatt was boarding a Great Western train at Paddington with Rick and Charles on his heels, a polite, elderly couple, a Mr. and Mrs. Barugh, were calling at the Fulham home of a widow, a Mrs. Adnett, to discuss her "Vacancy" sign. By noon, they were settled in their new quarters. The three exhausted street vendors were permitted to go home.

Later that day, I called to see the Barughs and their new residence and was introduced to Mrs. Adnett as Mrs. Barugh's nephew, a solicitor's clerk. The moment the door closed, I went to the window and made use of a telescope the Barughs had brought with them in their luggage. The view was excellent.

The Barughs were soon on familiar terms with their landlady and several of the neighbors, and they learned as much as was known locally about the occupants of the house Clarke-Ivatt had visited. The head of the household was known as Douglas Forbes, a railway employee who frequently had to work nights. Every caller was studied carefully with the telescope and photographed when possible. The three street vendors kept a remote watch on the house during the day, a close watch at night, and followed those who called there.

Within three days, we had identified Mr. Douglas Forbes and several of the callers. Forbes was Fast Freddy Lipford, a veteran burglar with a long record of malefactions. He was called "Fast Freddy" because of his fleetness afoot, which sometimes enabled him to avoid the consequences of the occasional miscalculation or bad luck all burglars suffer from time to time. The visitors we identified also were burglars well known to the police.

In the meantime, Rick and Charles had learned that Clarke-Ivatt was one Travis McGill, black sheep of a respectable Scottish family that had educated him well, repeatedly paid off his debts, bought his way out of frequent scrapes, and finally given up and threw him out. Now he was a staid and well-to-do citizen of Bristol with a wife who had been his housekeeper, several small children, and a stationery shop his wife ran for him while he was away for several weeks each autumn on unexplained business. Although the shop was a small one, it seemed to be flourishing, and McGill the stationer always paid his bills promptly, caused no one any trouble, and was highly respected by his customers for his politeness, his willingness to be of service, and the variety of his stock. His only character defect seemed to be a ridiculous frugality, which his friends and neighbours found amusing—the more so because it was so obviously unnecessary in such a thriving shopkeeper.

Lady Sara frowned when she read the report about the wife and small children. The consequence of crime—and the apprehension of a criminal—weighed on her the heaviest when the criminal had a family. However, the burglary ring was making McGill and several others prosperous and had financed the move to Fulham of Fast Freddie and his family, and it had to be stopped.

Lady Sara jubilantly moved the Clarke-Ivatt pegs on the giant cribbage board two thirds of the way to the game holes and sent for Chief Inspector Mewer. The only question remaining was how best to bag the lot.

The Chief Inspector left the conference with a pleased look on his face. Fast Freddie's elevation of himself and his family to social respectability in Fulham had escaped police notice. Scotland Yard was wondering what had happened to him. The breakup of his entire ring was now only a matter of time, and the Chief Inspector relished the prospect.

Lady Sara did not share his elation. This single success in no way compensated for the three byways where pegs were still stalled near the starting holes.

CHAPTER 12

Lady Sara thought Reggie Dempster should be told what his casual sleuthing had accomplished. She invited him to stop by after her coffee hour. He arrived promptly, impeccably dressed as always, all smiles and expectations as though he expected her to announce a legacy for him.

Lady Sara looked at him critically. "You've changed your barber," she observed.

Dempster blinked at her. "The old one died. Left me feeling totally deprived, don't you know. Like losing an old servant. How did you find out?"

"Your new barber trims your moustache differently."

"Does he really? I suppose it's plain as the nose on my face, but I hadn't noticed."

"Not quite so plain as that," Lady Sara said. "The difference is more like a hair's breadth."

She made him comfortable in her drawing room, had the maid serve coffee, and then explained what Clarke-Ivatt had been up to. "Thanks to your astute observation, the police will soon have the entire gang in prison. As a result, numerous houses it had targeted will not be burgled, and their owners have good reason to be grateful to you—though of course they will never know that."

"You don't say!" Dempster seemed overwhelmed. "Being a hero on the side of law and order is a new experience for me. Is there anything else I could do?"

Lady Sara smiled. "I'm afraid Clarke-Ivatt was a fluke. Your contacts with criminals must be extremely infrequent, which is, of course, a good thing. For example, we have a gruesome murder on our hands that took place down by Shadwell Market."

Dempster shook his head. "I see what you mean. That's a bit out of my orbit. Can't remember the last time I was down there. The whole neighbourhood stinks of fish and other unmentionables, and I prefer to avoid that sort of thing. I only expose myself to the river, or vice versa, at the Henley Regatta. If there's ever anything you need investigated at Henley—"

Lady Sara smiled again. "We are also looking for a giant," she said. "Unfortunately, very few members of the Oxford and Cambridge Club or the Rag could meet the necessary specifications."

Dempster threw his head back and laughed. "I'm afraid not. I don't recall meeting anyone at either club who impressed me that way if by 'giant' you mean 'tall.' Some of the members have well-developed horizontal dimensions, but they lack the vertical qualification. But hold a moment. I believe I did see a giant recently."

"Really?" Lady Sara was humouring him. "Where did you see him?"

Dempster meditated for a moment. "It was in Regent Street."

"You saw a bona fide giant in Regent Street?"

"If being tall makes a giant, I certainly did. Towered over everyone and everything. He was big all over—not fat, just big." He looked from one of us to the other. "What's so unusual about that? Is there some regulation against being a giant in Regent Street?"

"The giant we are looking for is more likely to hang out in an East End slum," Lady Sara said. "Tell us how you happened to see a giant in Regent Street."

"'Happened' is the word. I was in a cab. It was about noon, and workmen had the street up. Somewhere between Conduit Street and the New Gallery, I think it was. They always choose the time and place that will create the most ghastly chaos. We waited, and waited, and waited. Having nothing else to do, I watched pedestrians going about their shopping, and this giant walked past. Had a little old woman on his arm. She didn't look half his height. They went into a shop. At that moment traffic cleared, and we left."

"How old was the giant?" Lady Sara asked.

Dempster reflected. "Not a stooped old man with a beard or anything like that. Youngish, meaning twenty-five to forty. Spiffed out, too. Acres of checkered suit topped by a boater. Straw hats are always in poor taste, and a straw hat on a giant looks preposterous. I remember thinking what a valuable account he would make for a tailor or a hatter."

"What about the little old woman?" Lady Sara asked.

"I hardly noticed her. My attention was riveted on the giant, don't you know." He thought for a moment. "Elderly and stooped, with billowing skirts and a shawl—something out of the National Portrait Gallery. That's the best I can do."

Lady Sara carefully pronounced the critical question. "What shop did they go into?"

"Haven't the faintest," Dempster said. "As they turned in, we started with a jerk, and I forgot about them at once."

"I know the place where they had the street up. Which way were you headed? North? And you saw them on the left-hand side of the street? It should be possible to trace them. Thank you."

Dempster apologized for his memory. "Mind like a sieve," he complained. "Catches this and lets that go. No system to it at all."

"It seems to have caught enough," Lady Sara assured him. "Perhaps this will make you a hero on the side of law and order a second time."

As soon as he left, we were off to Regent Street. Lady Sara not only knew the precise location where the street had been up three weeks before, but she also knew what shops were to be found in the vicinity. "First we'll try Hobbs and Preety, the drapers," she said. "The other choices are a jeweller, a colourman, a perfumer, and a wine merchant."

One of the things most severely lacking in my East End childhood was the romance of London's shops. I rarely glimpsed the inside of even the shabby establishments available there. It was possible to buy almost anything one needed, or wanted, or could afford, from street vendors. That deprivation could never be made up. Long after I reached adulthood, I delighted in joining throngs of children before the windows of Buszard's, the pastry cook in Oxford Street, and gazing with watering mouth at the tiered bride-cakes and other pastries of unbelievable size as well as jam-puffs, cream-buns, and a long miscellany of delicacies unimagined in my youth.

I never saw a draper's shop until after Lady Sara and her mother took charge of me, and by then I was virtually grown up. Even so, the incredible wealth of fabrics in rainbow colours never failed to fascinate me. Equally intriguing was the conduct of the ladies shopping. They seemed to spend infinite amounts of time deciding between this triviality and that, and the shop assistants wisely avoided hurrying them and were always willing to step outside with them to match a bit of ribbon in better light.

But the overwhelming attraction in the draper's shop was the cash railway or overhead change carrier. The assistant packed bill and cash into a wooden ball and sent it spiraling up to an overhead track, where it rolled completely across the shop to drop off the rails onto the cashier's desk. There were dozens of balls rolling unerringly from all parts of the shop, never falling off even at points where the rails intersected. Then came the return journeys with the customers' change. I always regretted never seeing this when I was younger.

While Lady Sara talked with the manager, I renewed my acquaintance with a cash railway and listened with half an ear, as the poets say. The manager was apologetic. He knew nothing about any giants, but of course it was impossible for him to know all of his customers personally. If Lady Sara cared to interview his assistants, he had no objection.

The first assistant we talked with remembered the giant vividly. He was a man about thirty, very sedate and mild looking, but at the mention of a little old woman and her oversized escort, he burst into laughter. Then clapped his hand over his mouth, flushed crimson, and apologized.

"I'm sorry, my lady," he said, "but it was the funniest thing that has happened here in ages."

"It must have been," Lady Sara said sympathetically.

"It was old Miss Chalmer. Miss Penelope Chalmer."

"Of course," Lady Sara said. "Her name would be Penelope."

The assistant swallowed another laugh. "She has been our customer for donkey's years, my lady. Comes in regularly four times a year from some place in the country, I believe. The last time—it couldn't have been more than two or three weeks ago—she brought with her—"

He paused and rearranged his face again. Then, when he noticed the manager watching him, he suddenly became very solemn. "Spring, summer, autumn, and the Christmas season. We could set our calendar by Miss Chalmer. She is a dear old person, really—very temperamental and fussy if she thinks she isn't being looked after with courtesy and dispatch, always threatening to report the assistant but she never does. She'll take an hour to pick out six inches of ribbon and then settle on yards of material with one glance."

"On her last visit, she brought an extremely large man with her," Lady Sara reminded him. "Did she happen to mention who he was or why he was accompanying her?"

"Actually, she did. He was her roomer, and he had never seen London before."

"Did he say anything?"

"Never opened his mouth all the time he was here, my lady. Just stood there watching the cash railway while she made her selections. Then they left with him carrying her packages."

"Would you call him a genuine giant, or was he merely a rather tall man?"

"He was genuine," the assistant said fervently. "Well over seven feet, I am sure."

"And how old a person was he?"

"Difficult to say with him wearing that outlandish suit and keeping his boater pulled down tight on his head. I thought he looked quite young, but perhaps in other clothing—"

Lady Sara nodded. "Where in the country does Miss Chalmer live?"

"I'll find out for you."

He was back three minutes later. "Miss Penelope Chalmer, 9 Green Lane, Whitham. According to our records, she has always lived in Whitham, but she has only been at that address for the past four years."

We went outside, and Old John sprang down to open the carriage door for us. Lady Sara paused with her foot on the step. "After weeks of tedious search, I wonder if this is actually going to be as easy as it looks."

"Probably not," I said. "The giant will have left for Siberia last night."

We drove directly to Liverpool Station and caught the next Great Eastern train to Whitham, pausing only for Lady Sara to telephone Chief Inspector Mewer at Scotland Yard and ask for a favour. Probably this consumed him with curiosity, as did most of her requests, but he promised to comply.

Whitham was a trip of only forty miles, but the distance seemed to be measured in decades as we steamed north. It was a town of no special significance to us except that it harboured a giant. He was not visible from the railway station, however. We took a cab to the police station, where Inspector Vann, the officer in charge, made us welcome. Chief Inspector Mewer's telegram had already provided an introduction for us.

Lady Sara's message was brief. She was looking for a giant. A witness had seen one in London in the company of Miss Penelope Chalmer, of Green Lane. Before interviewing Miss Chalmer, she wanted to know whether there was any official information about this giant.

Inspector Vann pursed his lips thoughtfully. "When did your witness see him in London, my lady?"

"Three weeks ago," Lady Sara said.

The Inspector nodded gravely. "That would have been just before it happened."

"Before what happened?"

"The giant, who was known locally as Rafe Wade, was murdered."

Both of our faces must have registered consternation and astonishment.

"Set upon by thugs, he was," the Inspector continued grimly. "They beat him to death. A very cruel thing it was, my lady. He had lived here for more than a year. He was a gentle soul, never caused any trouble. Because of that, he was often challenged to fight. He steadfastly refused—perhaps he was afraid of what his enormous strength might do to his opponent. As for his murder, no one saw it done, and we are completely without clues. We figure a mob of outsiders was responsible. I don't believe local men would have set upon him so viciously. Those scoundrels must have had a drop too much, and they cornered him on his way home and beat him with clubs. It was a shockingly cruel thing, indeed it was. Only after he was dead did we find out his real identity."

"Who was he?" Lady Sara asked.

"Hob Hagan," the Inspector said.

Lady Sara and I exchanged dumbfounded glances. "Didn't it strike you as a whopping coincidence that you had a giant named Hob Hagan living here in Whitham at the same time that a giant axe murderer of that name was being hanged in London?" she asked.

"Indeed it did," the Inspector admitted. "Our Rafe Wade must have been a relative of the axe murderer. Giantism can run in families or so I've heard. Rafe probably felt so embarrassed by what his relative had done that he changed his name. I would do the same if I were a giant with a name identical to that of a giant axe murderer."

He took us to the churchyard where a white marker of wood had been erected on the site of the new grave. The identification was painted on it in black letters and numerals: "Hob Hagan, 1868-1900," followed by this message: "Sent to his rest by a foul and most unnatural murder."

We went to see Miss Penelope Chalmer, who for the past four years had been living with a nephew and his wife in a fairly new but ugly house near the railway station. Rafe Wade had roomed with them for more than a year before he was murdered.

The tiny Miss Chalmer was indeed something out of a National Portrait Gallery painting—old-fashioned in appearance and dress from her hair to her pointed-toe cloth shoes, billowing skirt, and shawl. I wondered whether her nephew and his wife had a struggle on their hands to keep her from wearing a bustle when she went out.

Mention of the giant brought real tears. Mention of the name Hob Hagan brought an angry response. "His name was Rafe Wade. I know that was his name, my lady. He told me all about himself, and his family, and where he came from."

"Then why was he buried as Hob Hagan?" Lady Sara asked.

"The day after he was killed, a solicitor representng Rafe's family called on us. The family was willing to pay all the expenses of his burial, he said, but it insisted that Rafe be buried under his real name. It sounded fishy to me, but the expenses were a problem because Rafe didn't have any savings and my nephew John and I couldn't afford the nice burial we wanted him to have. So John said to me, 'Aunt, he'll always be Rafe to us. What does it matter what they put on his tombstone?'

"So we consented. The solicitor was nice—he let me choose a line to commemorate Rafe, and he paid for everything. Had the wood marker up in less than a week, and the tombstone is already paid for and ready to set in place as soon as the ground settles."

"Who was the solicitor?" Lady Sara asked.

Miss Chalmer looked at her blankly. "It never occurred to me to ask his name, my lady. We were so upset and all."

"So it was you who picked the line on the grave marker," Lady Sara said. "I noticed you left out the beginning. From Shakespeare's Hamlet, isn't it? It should read, 'Revenge his foul and most unnatural murder.'"

"It didn't seem proper to be mentioning revenge in a churchyard," Miss Chalmer said. "But I thought revenge. I still think revenge. I'll always think revenge. Lady Sara, Rafe was only twenty. He was a sweet boy, gentle and considerate of everyone. Beating him to death like that was a horrible thing, and if there is a just God in heaven, He surely will see that those responsible are punished."

"He surely will," Lady Sara agreed. "And I, for one, am willing to give God a hand in it."

She took down the information Miss Chalmer remembered about Rafe Wade's life before he came to Whitham, after which we walked over to the station and caught the next train to London.

"I wonder what Chief Inspector Mewer will say when we hand him a third Hob Hagan?" she mused as we watched the rich Essex landscape roll past.

I knew the answer to that. What I couldn't account for was the incredible coincidence of this third Hob Hagan being murdered just before we located him.

"Rafe Wade was only twenty years old," Lady Sara said. "Just a boy. Penelope Chalmer wouldn't make a mistake about something like that. The dates on the tombstone were the real Hob Hagan's dates—1868 to 1900. The message is clear enough, isn't it? The person responsible knew we were searching for a giant. There are so few of them around that he also knew we would be certain to learn about Rafe Wade, sooner or later. So he decided to make use of him."

"Who is 'he?'" I asked.

"When we know that, we can wind up all of our cases and clear the board. The solicitor who so generously paid for the funeral—and absent-mindedly neglected to leave his name—is as bogus a character as we have ever encountered. Someone wanted us to believe Hob Hagan is dead and was willing to go to any length at all—even murder—to convince us. Unfortunately for him, the result is the opposite of what he intended. I take this to be incontrovertible proof that Hob Hagan is alive."

There was a momentary diversion when we arrived back in London. One of Lady Sara's maids asked if her mother could come for a consultation. Lady Sara agreed and asked me to be present. Hilda Cruthers was a pleasant-looking, middle-aged woman who had once worked as maid to one of Lady Sara's friends. In her free time she taught herself to typewrite on her master's machine, and now she was a professional typist with her own business office. Lady Sara felt a close affinity for any woman who could achieve such success in an age overwhelmingly dominated by men, and she greeted her warmly.

Mrs. Cruthers's problem was one of the most peculiar we had ever encountered. Her landlord, a Mr. Beveridge, who occupied the downstairs flat just below hers, had taken to burning some kind of incense—"An awful, cinnamon odour," she said—which was making her life miserable. It completely permeated the inside of the building and was even noticeable outside. She complained to the landlord; he said the incense was helpful to his catarrh, and as soon as his condition improved, he would stop burning it. She complained to a constable whose beat that was, and he laughed about it; he thought it a rather pleasant scent. Of course he only smelled it from the street. She didn't want to offend her landlord, but she absolutely could not tolerate the stench any longer. Unless something could be done about it, she would have to move. Could Lady Sara suggest anything?

Lady Sara smiled resignedly. Such requests resulted from her growing reputation for performing all kinds of miracles. They were always a nuisance, but she was sufficiently intrigued by Mrs. Cruthers's problem to visit her flat and experience the stench herself.

It was overwhelming. The house was a dignified building in Bloomsbury. Mrs. Cruthers's flat was fresh-looking and neatly furnished—altogether a pleasant place to live. Her window looked down on her landlord's garden, which was enclosed by walls. He was a meticulous gardener. Gravelled walks led through neatly cropped turf to bird baths, bird feeders, and a careful planting of shrubs and berry bushes that would appeal to birds. Lady Sara gazed at the scene with fascination.

"Sparrows I would have expected, but I see robins, a wood pigeon, a jay, and several finches. Interesting that these birds should be attracted so far from the parks. I take it that Mr. Beveridge is fond of birds."

"Oh, yes, my lady. He also keeps canaries and several other kinds of birds in the house," Mrs. Cruthers said.

"Is he also fond of animals?"

"Oh, yes, he keeps two dogs."

"How long has his catarrh been bothering him?"

"I don't know, my lady. He never mentioned it before."

"Is he married?"

"Yes. His wife is a very nice woman. There would be no problem if she were here, but she is away looking after her mother, who is ill."

Mrs. Cruthers had esteemed her landlord highly until the odour problem started. He had been pleasant and helpful. She loved her flat; she would hate to move, but unless something could be done she would have no choice.

Lady Sara thought for a moment. "Is anyone in the neighbourhood missing a cat?" she asked.

"Why, yes!" Mrs. Cruthers exclaimed. "Mrs. Ibbs, in the building next door, has been looking everywhere for hers."

The denouement came swiftly. Lady Sara, accompanied by the constable, Mrs. Ibbs, and Mrs. Cruthers, called at the landlord's flat. Mr. Beveridge's attitude was one of beligerent denial. Then he broke down and confessed. Day after day the nasty cat somehow got over the wall and stalked birds around his feeders. Seeds would fall to the ground, birds would alight to feed, and the cat would waiting to grab them. The climax came when he found a robin's wing lying under a feeder. The poor little thing had virtually been a pet, and the cat had torn it apart.

The next time he saw the cat, he stalked it and broke its back with a poker. He hadn't thought about disposing of it until after it was dead. Windows of several buildings looked down on his garden, so he had to hurriedly carry the dead cat inside. There was no way he could bury it without spoiling the results of the enormous amount of work he had performed on his garden and also without the danger of being seen. He also was afraid to simply dump it into his dust bin.

At that point he lost his head completely and decided to burn the cat, not realizing what a stench there would be. In desperation, he went out and bought incense, which proved unexpectedly strong, and its odour had lasted longer than he had thought possible. He hadn't burned any for two days, now, but the smell seemed as powerful as ever. He was sure it would go away eventually.

Mrs. Cruthers had to be content with that. The problem of the cat's murder was left for the constable to deal with. Lady Sara received congratulations all around, except from Mr. Beveridge, and added another miracle to her credit.

"Obviously the purpose of the incense was to conceal another odour," she said. "It was difficult to imagine what the respectable Mr. Beveridge had to hide until I saw his garden. He had created a miniature paradise for birds, and his reaction when it attracted a serpent in the form of a cat could be predicted. All I had to do was enquire about a missing cat."

"There were a number of simple solutions available to him," I said. "If he hadn't been so stupid, he could have waited until dark and thrown the cat into the Regent's Canal. Then there would have no odour and no case."

Lady Sara nodded. "It's fortunate that so many criminals are stupid— or unimaginative, which amounts to the same thing. We have the river

thefts to remind us of the difficulties that result when a criminal is brilliant."

CHAPTER 13

The river thefts were continuing. A watch on Prout's Mill still posed difficulties, but we managed as well as we could using street vendors, or passing waggons or cabs, or messengers on bicycles, or by walking past it to a supposed destination further down the river and then returning, or by patronizing the Grapes. Goods arrived openly, by boat; goods were hauled away openly, by boat or waggon. Lady Sara was confident that Eynon Brothers Company could, if challenged, document all of this activity. Nothing improper was observed. There was no night-time loading or unloading of either boats or waggons.

Lady Sara also continued the watch on the headquarters of Eynon Brothers Company and began one on the company's third warehouse and wharf on the Surrey side of the Thames—without results except for the addition of a few more photographs to her collection. Once she had identified the subjects, Rick, Charles, and I investigated further. This added four new names to my list of suspects:

Ralph Bewt was another son who inherited a family concern. The business originally had been John Bewt Ltd. As Bewt's family grew, it became John Bewt & Sons Ltd. The father died, the sons began to die, and as the family diminished, so did the volume of business the firm transacted. Ralph Bewt was the last surviving son. He was elderly and crippled, and he walked with difficulty with a cane, but after seeing how fast he could move in the rain while trying to hail a cab, I became sceptical about the extent of his disabilities. He was grey-haired, with an ornately trimmed beard. He had a reputation for pettiness and for being mean to his employees.

Hollis Ewbank was the gaunt, elderly survivor of two partners who had run Ewbank & Dudding Ltd. for many years with great success. Those days of prosperity were a thing of the past. Bright, ambitious employees looked for jobs elsewhere. Ewbank seemed content to let the business slowly shrink to nothing—except that he had just bought a new estate in the country, and acquaintances were wondering where he had got the money.

Sir Langley Jardin was the head of the Iberian Trading Company Ltd. This was a venerable firm. Jardin had joined it as a boy and rose to the top through merit—and also by pushing his predecessors overboard, according to Lady Sara, who knew him by reputation. He had the look of a leader—sturdy build, neatly trimmed black beard, piercing eyes. On the bridge of any ship, he would have been instantly recognized as the captain.

Fane Malkinson succeeded to the ownership of the Bethume Trading Company by marrying the founder's daughter. He was the type of man who often is said to be too handsome for his own good. Rumour had it that he neglected his business and occupied himself with three mistresses. His perennial financial difficulties surprised no one.

While we investigated suspects and kept an eye on the doings of Eynon Brothers Company from the land side, Ben and Bob Lyle were spending days and nights on the river watching the *Mollie Mae*, the combined sloop and steam-launch. Most of the time it behaved like a perfectly legitimate sloop: It acted as a lighter for shippers needing emergency service; it transported loads about London Harbour from Tilbury to London Bridge, calling at a number of wharves, including those of Eynon Brothers Company; and it brought goods to Prout's Mill from various places. Of course the Lyles couldn't watch the sloop continuously, and when, converted to a steam-launch, it suddenly left Prout's Mill at night, two men rowing a skiff were unable to keep it in sight. They could only wait for it to return.

Lady Sara's search for a better method of following it came to naught. The police needed their launches for routine patroling. They couldn't place a watch on Prout's Mill night after night merely on the chance that something might happen. Lady Sara considered hiring a private launch, but had she done so, everyone on the river would soon have been wondering what she was up to.

Then one night the steam-launch went out and did not return. The sloop *Mollie Mae* disappeared at the same time. The Lyle brothers were unable to locate either of them again, and our investigation of the river thefts ground to a complete halt. This was all the more frustrating because we had seemed on the verge of breaking the case.

Neither had there been any progress with the Shadwell murder or the missing giant. Lady Sara's investigation of the history of Rafe Wade established beyond a doubt that he was a real person and definitely not Hob Hagan, but that left us precisely where we had been before we heard of him.

Our only success concerned Reggie Dempster's ring of burglars. Chief Inspector Mewer quickly caught the principals at work, and from time to time he added the gang's lesser members to his bag. Several of them talked, implicating Clarke-Ivatt, who was Travis McGill in Bristol, and a criminal operation that had gone on successfully for years was about to end in a series of prison sentences.

Then came a day and night of intense fog.

I once heard an artist friend of Lady Sara's berate the National Smoke Abatement Society for its warped sense of values. The Society had calculated that fog cost London five million pounds a year. It was an outrage, the artist thundered, that the English should be willing to sacrifice the dreams and visions of poets and painters to the sordid comforts of six million utterly commonplace citizens. There was no price in pounds and sneezes equal to the value of a Whistler nocturne in fog. An immortal fog madrigal by Monet was surely worth ten times five million pounds. It was nothing less than criminal that anyone should equate ignoble monetary considerations with priceless sonnets in smoke.

After he left, Lady Sara observed philosophically, "He is a portrait painter, and he lives in a remote suburb. It is easy to praise fog from the comfort of a distant studio. He might think differently if he had to move about in it."

I had few poetic thoughts while trying to move about in this fog, the winter's first genuine pea-souper. It descended on us abruptly in late November, a fog of such thickness that England's capital was effectively blindfolded. It looked like a filthy yellow barrier one could push aside with one's hands, and I kept trying to do that as I pursued my list of errands. In the Strand, the churches of St. Clement Danes and St. Mary-le-Strand loomed up like two oversized battleships plunging through a fog-bound sea in single file. Aldwych was a narrow chasm of rolling fog. Waterloo Bridge spewed out or received hazy multitudes of slowly crawling vehicles that came from nowhere or vanished into nowhere. A man roasting chestnuts in an alcove seemed absurdly solid compared with these phantoms of carriages, waggons, and horses.

From the Embankment, the Thames looked caked and encrusted with fog. Ships on the river invisibly honked their signals. Sea-gulls were moving shadows that appeared suddenly and then vanished. Cleopatra's Needle floated elusively like the truncated mast of an invisible ship. I was momentarily startled by a menacing figure that materialized out of the gloom and vanished just as abruptly. It was an old woman with a cane, carrying a large, filthy, much mended cloth bag. She was enshrouded in a shabby cloak that seemed to hold the fog at bay with shuddering, flapping movements. Lady Sara's artist friend doubtless would have told me she was the Witch of Endor and her bag contained spells, charms, love philtres, talismans, and candles made of human fat. Only in thick fog could such be encountered.

There was no reality to be found anywhere. Trafalgar Square was peopled with pedestalled ghosts of kings and generals, and Nelson's column was a shaft of shadow without beginning or end. Even a police constable lacked substance. He loomed up dimly and vanished at once, a belted spectre. Before I completed my errands, I was quite willing for the National Smoke Abatement Society to spend five million or whatever it required to rid London of its foggy days and nights.

When I finally made my way back to Connaught Mews, I found Lady Sara girded for action. "Tonight may be the night we've been waiting for," she said. "The fog will give them cover. I'll be surprised if they don't take advantage of it to move a quantity of stolen goods away from the river. Once these are safe in a nondescript inland warehouse, they can dispose of them pretty much as they like."

She thought Eynon Brothers Company had been concealing small quantities of stolen goods in every waggon load—an amount that could be easily covered by documents concerning the legitimate portion of the load. On a foggy night, with few people about, the firm might be tempted to speed the process.

It seemed to me that any dark night would have done as well, but my logic was no match for hers. "On an ordinary dark night, there is considerable traffic on both the street and the river. Tonight, there will be very little of either—except what we provide ourselves."

We sat down together and made plans for keeping a watch on Prout's Mill in the fog. There would be eight of us—Lady Sara; myself; the two footmen, Charles Tupper and Rick Allward; two of her grooms, Ed Geffen and Tom Ness, who often assisted with investigations; and two street vendors Lady Sara frequently made use of. The latter were known to me only as Artie and Arvin. We would take the four wheeler and the cart so we would have something to follow the stolen goods with if an effort were made to remove them. For the most part, our watch on the mill would be performed on foot and as unobtrusively as possible. Anyone planning to move stolen goods would quickly become alarmed if there were large numbers of vehicles passing.

It seemed like a pathetically small number of watchers, but this was consistent with our objectives: To attract no attention; to follow if merchandise was removed and see where it was taken. Lady Sara easily could have recruited a hundred of her agents to help out. The more watchers, the more likely they were to be detected.

She also could have asked Chief Inspector Mewer for police assistance. There was nothing intrinsically illegal about moving merchandise in the fog, but the Chief Inspector's impulse would have been to make arrests as soon as anyone attempted it. Even if the merchandise proved to be stolen, his bag would contain only a few waggoners and warehouse-men. Neither Lady Sara nor the police would have learned anything we didn't already know. If we could find out where the stolen merchandise was being taken, that would advance our investigation hugely.

So there would be eight of us. "It will be an eerie experience," I said resignedly. "We'll have to walk a short beat if we are to see anything at all in this fog."

"At least you won't have to worry about being noticed yourself," Lady Sara said.

So heavily shrouded was the city of London that by late afternoon it already seemed like night-time along the river. Lady Sara drove the four wheeler with skill, and there was little traffic, but we still had an endless, nerve-racking trip through the city before we drew up at the Grapes as though delivering a passenger. I pretended to be the passenger and went in and had a half-pint just for effect. On that day even the Grapes was subdued. There were few customers. I took my beer to the veranda, where I could hear water lapping at the piles below. Needless to say, I could not see it. I felt the chill, searching wind that blew up from the Channel, but where the river should have been I saw nothing but a darkish, yellowish curtain. I thought about the Wet Bobs, the water constables, faithfully plying their oars down along and up along. On this night they would be wearing their toe bags and squinting into the fog for threatening shadows, but otherwise their duty should be uneventful. Any sensible criminal would keep to the shore.

While Lady Sara remained outside with the four wheeler as though waiting for another fare, Charles drove the cart past Prout's Mill to a waiting place already agreed on, and Rick took charge of the grooms and vendors, who did not know the area, and walked with them as far as the brewery and back again, showing them how the land lay. After that, we settled into our routine.

Lady Sara parked the four wheeler in a cul-de-sac off Narrow Street just west of the stretch we would be watching. The vehicles were to change places every hour, driving past the mill in opposite directions with one of us as a passenger and continuing east all the way to Three Colt Street or west as far as the Regent Canal just in case anyone was curious enough to follow. Then each returned and took over the waiting place the other had vacated. The four of us who were on foot walked back and forth at infrequent intervals, but for long periods of time we rested in convenient doorways across the street from Prout's Mill so there would be no perception of an unusual amount of foot traffic.

It was impossible to see much, but sound travelled well. We could hear the four wheeler or the cart long before either slipped ghost-like from the fog, and we had to walk very carefully to avoid creating the effect of a platoon marching endlessly past Prout's Mill. Other than ourselves, there was little traffic of any kind. The fog had all but immobilized London.

Shortly after midnight, I started another slow-paced trip from the Grapes to the brewery and beyond. It already had been a long night, and what remained seemed to stretch ahead of us endlessly. One of the vendors was riding with Lady Sara, who had just passed us headed west; Charles and the cart, with the other vendor, had already passed Prout's Mill headed east. The two grooms were sheltering invisibly across the street, watching with their ears since it was still impossible to see more than a few feet. Rick was to give me a hundred-foot lead and then follow me.

I had just passed Prout's Mill when I suddenly encountered the devil. He emerged abruptly from the fog, a terrifying, enormous apparition. A cloak enveloped all but his face, but neither cloak nor fog could disguise his enormous form. His face had been artfully rendered hideous. Streaks of phosphorescence accented it and underscored his protruding fangs. He towered over me. Instantly I recoiled sideways into the fog's invisibility, wishing I had brought a revolver.

But he paid me no attention at all. He didn't even break his stride. Perhaps a normal-sized human was beneath his notice; or perhaps, because I was so much smaller than he was, he failed to see me.

My sudden recoil proved fortunate for me. The giant's companions were walking a few paces behind him—a crowd of hulking men who seemed average-sized only because of the immensity of the figure that preceeded them. I continued to edge quietly toward the side of the road, and they passed without noticing me.

"Hold hard!" one of them called guardedly after the giant.

Apparently the giant waited for them, and they moved on together, vanishing into the fog. I stood looking after them confusedly for a moment. Then I suddenly became worried about Rick, who was following me. I hurried cautiously after the men. I should have overtaken them quickly, but I saw nothing at all until, just beyond Prout's Mill, I met Rick.

"Did you see him?" I whispered.

"See who?" he demanded.

I described what I had seen.

"I didn't meet anyone," he said.

We crossed the street and sought out the grooms stationed there. They had heard the vague sounds of someone walking past, and they also had faintly heard the call, "Hold hard," though they hadn't understood it. Neither of them had seen anything. They especially hadn't seen an out-sized, larger-than-human apparition with a made-up face followed by a crowd of ruffians.

"If they didn't come this way, then they vanished through a solid wall, and I refuse to believe that," I told them.

When Lady Sara returned to her cul-de-sac with the four wheeler, I described what I had seen. "There was something supernatural about him," I said. "My hair still feels prickly, but that may be due to the fog."

"You met him and some men following close behind him; Rick, who was some distance behind you, saw nothing. The grooms say no one crossed the street. Is that right?"

It was.

"Then they must have turned off in the other direction," she said.

"The only way they could have done that was to walk through the solid wall of Prout's Mill," I protested.

"Then the solid wall of Prout's Mill isn't solid," Lady Sara said. "We'll have a good look at it by daylight."

"We've already had a good look in every kind of light," I protested.

"True, but we weren't looking for a concealed entrance."

Ed Geffen, one of the grooms, hurried up breathlessly. "Waggons!" he breathed.

It was the moment we had been waiting for. Four wheeler and cart were already positioned so the waggons could be followed in either direction. Ed and I slipped back to Prout's Mill, keeping on the far side of the street where the fog hid us completely. I could see very little of what was happening, but I could hear a great deal. The waggons came crawling out of the fog from the east, one after another, and one at a time they halted by the solid wall of the mill building. Muffled sounds came of goods being loaded, but no light was shown. When the first wagon moved west, another took its place. And then another.

Tom Ness, one of the grooms, approached me where I stood trying vainly to see through the fog. "Ed caught a ride on a wagon," he whispered. "Do you want me to try?"

Together we went to the four wheeler and consulted Lady Sara.

"No," she said firmly. "That is much too dangerous. This is a vicious gang we are dealing with."

She told us what she wanted us to do. She and I would follow after the last waggon. Tom the groom would come with us. Charles and Rick would wait with the cart to see whether another train of waggons arrived. If one did, they were to follow it. The two street vendors, Artie and Arvin, would remain behind to watch Prout's Mill and use their own judgement if anything else happened.

The last waggon was the fourteenth. After it had pulled away, Lady Sara followed. I sat on the box with her; Tom rode inside the cab ready for an errand on foot if we needed one. We plodded along, straining our ears for sounds from the procession of waggons ahead of us, and only Lady Sara's remarkable knowledge of the city kept us oriented. She was able to weave the slightest of clues—a dip in the road, the faint shape of a building, the creak of a swinging pub sign, distant sounds of street repairs—into a detailed map of our route. Occasionally she urged the horse forward until, under a gas lamp, the last waggon loomed dimly ahead of us. Then she dropped back. She whispered the names of invisible streets and landmarks we passed.

At Betcher Street the procession turned north to Brook Street. After a short jog west, it turned north again in Bromley. When we passed Commercial Road, Lady Sara muttered, "They may be headed for somewhere outside of London by way of Mile End Road."

It was an odd pursuit. We weren't trying to catch or overtake the waggons, which we easily could have done. We merely wanted to follow them without their knowing they were followed, and that imposed far more of a strain than a fast chase would have done. At any moment, the driver of the last waggon might sense our presence, and we would suddenly find ourselves pursued instead of pursuing. A gang as well organized as this one certainly would have ready-made plans in case the waggons were followed.

Our journey came to an abrupt end at Oxford Street in Stepney. A four wheeler with a drunken driver charged out of the fog and collided with us. There was a splintering of the two cabs' bodies, a squealing of horses, a threshing of their hooves, and angry shouts from the drunken driver's passengers. Our four wheeler was overturned, and the horses were entangled. Lady Sara and I were thrown free. Tom was battered but not seriously hurt. Everyone concerned worked together to right the four wheeler and get the horses untangled.

Lady Sara had a few words with the drunken driver, who was staggering about forlornly and muttering something about too much gin. Our four wheeler was still useable though wobbly, and we got underway again as quickly as we could. We turned from White Horse Lane into Mile End Road and followed it first east and then west, driving as fast as we could in the fog, but we failed to catch even a ghostly glimpse of the waggon train.

"Now it is up to the others," I said finally. "Perhaps they will have better luck—provided they don't encounter another drunken cab driver."

"What made you think he was drunk?" Lady Sara asked.

I stared at her. "He certainly acted drunk—both the way he drove and the way he staggered about."

"Acting drunk and being drunk are two different things. I thought he drove very skillfully. He cut his horses at just the right moment to hit us a glancing blow that would take us out of the chase while doing a minimal amount of damage. I know he mentioned gin, but there was none on his breath, and he didn't walk the way a drunken man walks. He walked the way a sober man thinks a drunken man would walk. There can be no doubt at all that the collision was deliberate, and the object was to delay us until the waggons escaped. As you said, now it is up to Charles and Rick, and to the vendors."

"And Ed," I reminded her. "Don't forget Ed. Remember—he caught a ride on one of the waggons."

"I am worried about Ed," she said. "He shouldn't have gone off by himself."

We found our way back to Connaught Mews and waited to hear from the others.

Charles and Rick arrived first—without the horse and cart. They looked bruised and battered, and Rick had his arm in a sling. There had been a second train of waggons, sixteen of them, and they had followed it.

"Stupid drunk ran into us," Charles said. "Smashed a wheel on the cart. I left the horse at livery."

"Now it is up to the vendors and Ed," I said.

It was morning when Arvin, one of the two street vendors, telephoned. There had been two more waggon trains after Charles and Rick left—twelve waggons in the first, and fifteen in the second. Artie had followed the second train on foot, thinking he could make at least as good time in the fog as a waggon. Arvin had waited the rest of the night, but there had been no more waggons. He wanted to know if we had heard anything from Artie.

Lady Sara's scowl deepened. She now had two employees to worry about.

Then Artie telephoned. A footpad had waylaid him in the fog and tried to rob him. Artie had taught him a thing or two and left him unconscious. Unfortunately, he lost sight of the waggons while he was fighting. In trying to find them again, he managed to get himself hopelessly lost in Bethnal Green.

This was good news in spite of his failure. All of us brightened, thinking that Ed would be calling soon, but we never heard from him.

The next day the fog lifted, and we drove slowly past Prout's Mill in Lady Sara's carriage. Charles Tupper was on the box. Inside, with Lady

Sara and me, was James Lambert, a builder and an old friend of Lady Sara's. He was a short, tubby man who always had a bowler hat on his head and a cigar in his mouth. I had never seen him without them, even indoors.

He scrutinized the building as we passed it. Then he began to chuckle.

"Got it?" Lady Sara asked.

"Got it," he said. "They weren't even clever about it, my lady."

"Tell me," Lady Sara said.

"They've cut an opening and installed a door. Then they faced the door with bricks. They used old bricks, maybe the same that they removed when they cut the opening. The bricks match perfectly, but they're laid with a different bond. They stand out like a sore thumb."

"Not to me," Lady Sara said.

"Nor to me," I added.

He chuckled again. "Building is Flemish Stretcher Bond, my lady. Two courses of stretchers separated by a course of alternate headers and stretchers. The door facing is a variation of that. Matches well except that the headers don't form a regular pattern. No experienced builder would make such a mistake, but perhaps they were in a hurry and figured no one would notice."

"How would the door work?" Lady Sara asked.

"That took planning, my lady. Door can't swing naturally, you see, because of the thickness—it's a very close fit, has to be to look as though it's bonded to the rest of the building. I figure it slides straight back. In order to do that, they've had to cut the warehouse floor away around the door. Once the door is open, they can roll a platform into place to load wagons and slide it back out of the way when they're ready to close the door again."

"Then a man walking along the street could take advantage of the fog by pushing the door back and vanishing through it," Lady Sara suggested.

"No doubt he could if the door opens easily enough—which it would do if it's well designed and built."

"How long ago was it done?" Lady Sara asked.

Lambert pursed his lips. "That isn't so easy. Not last year. Not a decade ago. Say within the last four or five years."

"Thank you," Lady Sara said. "This is what we needed to know."

Ed Geffen still had not appeared, and late that afternoon I did what had to be done. I began visiting mortuaries and hospitals and examining the debris London's streets had yielded after the fog. In London Hospital, in Whitechapel Road, I found Ed's brutally beaten body among those of starved and diseased derelicts and a scattering of accident victims.

He had been barely alive when found near Whitechapel Station—dumped in the fog a long, long way from where he was assaulted, without a doubt. He hadn't been dead for more than a few minutes when I arrived. "He kept trying to tell us something," the matron said, "but we couldn't understand him. He said, over and over, 'The royal—' but he never told us what royal he meant. Do you know?"

I had no idea, but I promised to speak to his friends and try to find out.

Lady Sara appears most calm when she is furiously angry. She said nothing until she had taken care of notifying Ed's family and arranging for his funeral. Then she sat down to talk with me.

"We have experienced one failure after another in these cases," she said, "but we have learned a great deal despite that. We now we have a good idea of how the gang operates."

"I'm afraid I don't," I said.

"I pointed the clues out to you after our encounter with Alf Rixon, who thought he saw a giant. Both his injured hand and the murder of Bill Havill were connected with the river thefts—that was immediately evident. The murder was an act of terror, intended to frighten men who refused to cooperate. The same type of Cat's Paw that raked Havill's face was used on Rixon, probably by a man of gigantic size, and it put him in such a state of panic that he refused to tell the police anything at all.

"A giant—I think there can be no doubt that it is Hob Hagan—is terrifying workers into cooperating with the thieves. Hagan was returning from some such errand when you saw him in the fog. His face was made up to add to the effect of his gigantic size. Perhaps he had a Cat's Paw up his sleeve. A crowd of thugs was accompanying him. No wonder the poor dock workers fear for their lives.

"This is how the thieves operate: They frighten, bribe, or otherwise coerce night workers into cooperating with them. All of their thefts have occurred at small, independent wharves, but the murdered man worked at the London Docks, and Rixon works at the West India Docks. The thieves are setting their sights higher. Ironic, isn't it, that our search for a giant turned up the most important clue about the river thefts? I told you that all of our Byways would merge."

"It seems to me that we still don't know much about them," I objected.

"We know just enough to deduce the workings of the scheme. Obviously it was devised, and is being carried out, with the touch of a master criminal. The planning is meticulous. The warehouse being victimized is studied carefully, and the timing—to take only those goods that won't be missed at once—is exquisite. The person responsible has amazing intelligence."

"He also is ruthless," I said.

"Totally ruthless. Ruthless enough to murder and mutilate a dock worker just to provide an example for those who won't cooperate. Ruthless enough to have Ed murdered because he may have found out something. He is even ruthless enough to order the brutal murder of Rafe Wade in the hope of putting us off our search for Hob Hagan. That shows you how valuable Hagan is to them."

"Where does 'the royal' come into it?" I asked. "The royal what? I feel certain Ed was trying to leave a message for us."

"So do I. All we can do is keep alert and make certain we recognize the connection when we meet with it." She added determinedly, "We are going to meet with it—but not at Prout's Mill, I think. That has been written off. The *Mollie Mae* went elsewhere and didn't return. The stolen goods the gang had stored there now have been removed. Prout's Mill won't be used again until the gang is convinced we have lost interest in it."

"And—the Vicar, the Reverend Theobald Eynon? Is he the master criminal?"

"That is the puzzler. Is our congenial clergyman a fit character for a great tragedy, risking name and career to do evil so good might ensue? I don't know—yet."

I said slowly, "This means beginning the case over again."

"Not quite," she said. "We have learned more about the gang than it realizes, and a few of those strands remain intact. This certainly is a setback. All the time we were watching Prout's Mill, the gang was watching us. We must take fair warning that they now know at least as much about us as we know about them. Locating the gang's new warehouse will be far more difficult and require more luck than the first did. Chief Inspector Mewer has no awareness of what he is contending with. Breaking up this theft ring is not an assignment. It is a career."

Late that night, Chief Inspector Mewer telephoned. A murdered man had been found near Shadwell Market. His body looked as though he had been attacked by an animal.

Lady Sara said dully, "One mutilated corpse wasn't enough. I wonder how many more will be required."

CHAPTER 14

The murdered man's name was Sid Theaker. His biography read very much like that of the murdered William Havill—he was a decent, reliable night watchman from the East India Docks, highly regarded by his foreman and considered thoroughly honest by all who knew him. It was obvious—to us though not to Chief Inspector Mewer—that the campaign to terrorize dock workers into cooperating with the thieves was continuing.

After examining the site of the murder and viewing the murdered man's body in the company of Sir Thomas Tallmage and myself, Lady Sara commissioned a scrivener to prepare and frame a document for her. She hung it in her study over her desk. It consisted entirely of names, four of them, beautifully executed in florid script: William Havill, Rafe Wade, Ed Geffen, Sid Theaker—the Magnate of Crime's known murder victims.

Still appearing calm—meaning that she was still furiously angry—Lady Sara mused, "I wonder how many more there will be."

We were making plans for renewing our investigation of the river thefts when a diversion came from an unlikely source: Mrs. Mewer, the Chief Inspector's wife. She telephoned Lady Sara and asked for her help.

"She is extremely upset," Lady Sara said. "Her maid has disappeared."

Missing maids were a commonplace in the year 1900. They ran off or eloped with their young men. Or they were unhappy and ran home to their parents. Or they simply ran off. I pointed this out and added, jokingly, "If Mrs. Mewer is genuinely concerned, she should report it to the police."

"This isn't an ordinary disappearance," Lady Sara said. "Eleanor Wellfitt is sixty years old and has been with Mrs. Mewer since the Mewers were married twenty-five years ago. Before she became Mrs. Mewer's maid, she was in service with Mrs. Mewer's mother. She has been loyal, honest, conscientious, and a friend as much as a servant. Suddenly, more than two weeks ago, she vanished. Mrs. Mewer was out that morning, and Eleanor disappeared without so much as leaving a note. As far as

Mrs. Mewer could determine, she dressed as she usually does when she goes out on an errand—coat and bonnet. But she took nothing with her."

"I suppose the Chief Inspector has enquired at the hospitals and morgues," I said.

"Mrs. Mewer was upset enough without having that to worry about, so I didn't ask. Certainly her husband has already thought of it."

"Did Eleanor Wellfitt have any close relatives?"

"None. Her parents died long ago. She had one sister who never married. The sister was in service herself all of her life and died just last year. Eleanor told Mrs. Mewer more than once that she was completely alone in the world and the Mewer family was the only family she had."

"Is it possible that she indulged in politics or had secret riches hidden away?" I asked.

"You would try to make a romance of it," Lady Sara said severely. "We can take it as an absolutely certainty that no one has assasinated her for her politics, or abducted her for her wealth, or murdered her to avenge some sordid scandal. She comes from an obscure but perfectly respectable family. The question is this: What cataclysmic event could have occurred in this woman's life to make her suddenly run off without a word to anyone?"

She allowed me a few moments to reflect on that. Then she asked, "How do you suggest we proceed?"

As far as I was concerned, we didn't. The problem seemed totally perplexing. The only possible course of action was to begin a tortuous job of digging, first searching the Mewers' neighbourhood to find out whether the maid had a friend she might have confided in or if anyone had seen her or talked with her on the day she left.

Lady Sara said, "I asked Mrs. Mewer for two more items of information—the given name of Eleanor's father and the given name and maiden names of her mother. Fortunately, Mrs. Mewer was able to supply both. Her father was James Wellfitt. Her mother, before she married, was Isabel Santer. They lived in Holdford, Sussex."

I snapped my fingers. "Somerset House."

"It took you long enough," Lady Sara said. "Go there the first thing in the morning and see what you can find out."

Somerset House had long been the repository of England's records, and it included the Wills Office and the Registrar-General of Births, Mariages, and Deaths. It took me less than an hour to find the answer. One Winston Wellfitt, of Kesley Green, Sussex, an extremely remote cousin of Eleanor's, had died ten days before Eleanor's disappearance. She was his last surviving relative, and a year before his death he had discovered that fact and added a holograph codicil to his will naming her as his sole heir and giving her address.

The cousin's solicitor, after taking due time to ponder the significance and legality of the codicil, notified Eleanor by letter that she had inherited an estate valued at fifteen thousand pounds, and that was the cataclysmic event that caused her abrupt disappearance without a word to anyone. The moment she read the letter, this loyal servant, who had been at everyone's beck and call and at the mercy of everyone's whims from the moment she went into service at about age twelve, put on her coat and bonnet, took what money she had, and left for Sussex. Neither Lady Sara nor I blamed her. Fifteen thousand pounds was enough to keep Eleanor in luxury with servants of her own for the remainder of her life, which was enough to derange the thinking of anyone in her position, loyalties notwithstanding.

Lady Sara tracked down Eleanor later that day by telephone. It was another triumph for her, but Mrs. Mewer was not grateful. She had lost her servant permanently.

A second diversion occurred immediately afterward. The impressive brougham of Sir Cecil Elliman, with its splendid matched horses and matched, uniformed coachmen, returned to Connaught Mews. Sir Cecil was as expensively turned out as he had been before, but this time he did not bring an earl to introduce him. He seemed far friendlier than he had on his first visit. He asked the favour of a brief interview, and Lady Sara graciously granted it.

She offered tea; Sir Cecil declined to put her to so much trouble. As he had on his first visit, he came to the point immediately. "I don't know, my lady, whether you are aware of the extent of my financial interests. They are extremely diverse, and they include investments in several shipping companies. One of them is the Narramore Importing Company. I know all about the thefts that have plagued London's importing and trading firms. Further, I hold a majority interest in the Thamesside Insurance Company, which has suffered severely from the theft of insured merchandise. Frankly, my personal losses from the thefts have been enormous. Horatio Narramore has discussed with me his firm's recent loss by theft of a large amount of premium quality tea, and he offered the startling information that you had actually witnessed the theft when it was in progress. Is that correct?"

"Along with several of my assistants, I witnessed what we thought was suspicious activity around a wharf. Since this was at night, we had some difficulty in identifying the company concerned. Eventually we did so, and I discussed what we saw with Mr. Narramore as well as the police."

Sir Cecil turned to me. "Were you present? Did you witness the theft?"

I murmured politely, "Yes, sir," and had to restrain myself from adding, "my lord." Even though Sir Cecil was not a peer, one had the feeling that he expected such an indication of respect.

"Narramore described the interview between you and Chief Inspector Mewer. You handed that idiot priceless information, my lady, and he had no notion of what to do with it. As a result, he has made no progress at all in solving the theft—just as the police have made no progress in solving any of the thefts along the river. I have a proposition for you. I represent a consortium of importers, traders, and insurance companies. We would like to hire you to solve the river thefts for us. We would guarantee adequate financial remuneration whether or not you succeed—that part doesn't worry us, we know from diverse sources that you are not in the habit of failing. We also would furnish whatever money you require for expenses. We would expect you to drop all of your other investigations and concentrate your full attention on this with a vastly expanded organization."

"It is a generous offer," Lady Sara said gravely, "and I understand the concern of the importers, traders, and insurance companies in making it. Regretfully, I must decline. I insist on having complete independence in any task I undertake."

Sir Cecil frowned at her. "Perhaps I didn't make myself clear. There would be no attempt whatsoever to interfere with your investigation or to tell you what to do or how to do it. You would simply tell us how much money you need, and we would supply it. You could report progress to us when you had any to report."

"I am not accustomed to reporting to anyone until I am ready to turn a case over to the police," Lady Sara said. "I would not feel comfortable functioning as someone's employee, however lenient my employer. Please assure the members of your consortium that the river thefts will continue to receive my careful attention until they are solved. I will make every effort to bring them to an end and see that the perpetrators are punished, and there will be no financial obligation on their part."

Whereupon Sir Cecil demonstrated one of the qualities that must have contributed substantially to his business success. He recognized an unyielding position when he met with one. He got to his feet, bowed, thanked her for her time, and left. Again she watched his departure from the window.

"He seemed slightly less haughty than the last time," I observed. "The suicide claims were a nuisance, but the thefts are costing him dearly. Why not take his money, hire a thousand agents, and put an end to them?"

"It would require a thousand good agents, not to mention both skill and luck, to break up this theft ring quickly, and where would I find them? Mediocre agents would require more supervision than we could give them and do more harm than good. In the meantime, the thefts would continue. No, until such time as I am convinced that a large number of agents can be used effectively, I will work with the staff I have and report to no one."

Jasper Wightman, the tobacconist, telephoned me the next morning. "I have something that should interest you," he said. "Could you stop by this afternoon?"

I accepted eagerly. He had my complete confidence, and I had discussed the case of the missing giant as well as the river thefts with him. From the bow-fronted shop of Wightman & Company, he had an excellent view of traffic headed to and from the river along narrow, cobbled, steeply-sloping Stibbit Lane. If he had seen anything of interest, I wanted to know about it at once.

When I arrived, the little man greeted me warmly, and then he placed a tiny cloth bag on the counter. He looked at me expectantly.

"What is it?" I asked.

"Tobacco," he said.

I gazed at him blankly. Then I began to laugh. It struck me as hilarious that I had dashed with reckless abandon through London's traffic to be shown a sample of tobacco at a tobacconist's.

Wightman opened the bag and poured some of the contents into his hand. "What does it look like?" he asked me.

"Tobacco," I said. I sniffed it. "It smells like tobacco, too. Rather strong tobacco."

"If you used tobacco, your eyes and nose would tell you far more than that. I have been offered a quantity of this tobacco at a bargain price by a firm calling itself the Unwin Salvage Company. It salvages goods from burned buildings, or from wrecked or sunken ships, or from any kind of mishap, and disposes of portions that are still useable. Have you ever heard of it?"

I had not.

"Nor had I until its representative called here," he said. "This tobacco was represented to me as being of good quality but available at a bargain price because it was salvaged from a warehouse damaged by fire. I was assured that there was no actual damage to the tobacco, either from fire, smoke, or water. The Unwin Salvage Company doesn't profess to know its pedigree—that was the word its representative used—because records and labels were lost or destroyed in the fire. It does know that this is an excellent product because the burned warehouse handled only good quality tobacco. It has been appraised at a price of two shillings per pound, but in order to dispose of it quickly, the Unwin Salvage Company is offering it at a discounted price of ten pounds per hundredweight to tobacconists willing to buy two hundredweight or more."

I must have been looking blank again. Since I knew nothing at all about tobacco, I was wondering why he was telling this to me. Usually I carried a one or two ounce packet to offer to smokers I wanted to talk with, but I only bought the cheapest varieties. That was the extent of my experience.

"Ten pounds per hundredweight," Wightman went on, "is not a discounted salvage price for ordinary good quality tobacco. But this is not ordinary good quality tobacco. This, as any capable tobacconist should know at a glance, is a very special tobacco known as 'Turkish black.' It is a superb tobacco. It is one of the finest tobaccos available, but it is also extremely expensive. The only men who smoke Turkish black are wealthy conoisseurs. It is, however, a uniquely fine tobacco for blending with other tobaccos because of its strong character. An ounce or two per pound enhances the quality of an ordinary blend enormously. I use a great deal of it for blending. Wightman Blend, the best I offer, combines two ounces of Turkish black, two ounces of a special rum-cured tobacco I import from the West Indies, and twelve ounces of good quality American tobacco. I sell tins of this by mail all over the British Isles and to customers living in the colonies. So I use large quantities of Turkish black, and ten pounds per hundredweight is a very good price—a savings of forty or fifty per cent."

I was still wondering what this had to do with me.

"This may be stolen or smuggled tobacco," Mr. Wightman said. "If it were a bona fide salvage offer, and the proprietors really didn't know anything about it, they would be offering it for less—much less. They know exactly what it is, and they are charging accordingly. By pretending not to know, and by giving tobacconists an opportunity to take advantage of their supposed ignorance, they hope to dispose of it quickly at what is, for salvage, a remarkably good price. No doubt there are many who would welcome the prospect of an extra profit whatever the source of the tobacco. Myself, I want nothing to do with this sort of thing."

Light finally dawned on me. Wightman had happened onto something Lady Sara had long been searching for—a glimpse of how the thieves disposed of their stolen goods. "I wish you hadn't turned the offer down," I said.

Mr. Wightman grinned. "I didn't. I told the agent for Unwin and Company that I had to check my inventory and also my bank balance. If both results are satisfactory, I promised to give him a large order. He is to come back at nine tomorrow morning. I thought you might want a look at him."

"Indeed I do," I said. "I'll be here at eight, and I'll bring some colleagues to help me follow him. We want to know all about this Unwin Salvage Company."

"So I thought," Mr. Wightman said. "I'll expect you at eight tomorrow."

"Could I have your sample?" I asked.

"Of course. I certainly don't want it."

I pocketed the little bag of Turkish black, promised to be there promptly at eight in the morning, and left. Thirty minutes later, the bag lay on Lady Sara's desk, and she was sniffing its contents doubtfully.

Then she got to her feet and strolled over to a window where for a time she seemed fascinated by the prosaic activity of Connaught Mews. She often did that when she wanted to think.

"I wonder how many tobacconists—in fact, how many shopkeepers of any variety—are as honest and forthright as your friend Jasper Wightman," she said finally. "How many would turn down an opportunity for a substantial extra profit merely because the goods offered to them might possibly come from a tainted source? Many shopkeepers lead a marginal existence, and the opportunity to buy goods at a bargain price would be severely tempting."

"This isn't the kind of bargain that would tempt the average tobacconist," I said. "He wouldn't be mixing his own blends, he wouldn't have any customers wealthy enough to smoke Turkish black, and he wouldn't have money to tie up in two hundredweight of tobacco even at a bargain price."

"True," she said. "This particular tobacco will be offered only to prosperous shopkeepers with prosperous customers. The question remains: How many of them have sufficient integrity to turn down the opportunity for an extra profit on tainted merchandise? Most will be extremely cautious and take great pains to make certain the quality of the tobacco is as represented, I think, but they won't ask embarrassing questions about where it came from. But wait!"

She went to the telephone and called a good friend who was a newspaper editor. After she talked with him, she announced, "In case a tobacconist is bothered enough by his conscience to check, there was a fire in a tobacco warehouse in Birmingham three months ago."

She returned to her desk. "The planning and execution of the thefts, the handling of the stolen goods and their disposal, are all works of genius. But we are making progress. Take Rick and Charles and see what can be found out about the Unwin Salvage Company and its agent."

We were in Stibbit Lane at eight o'clock the next morning. Charles and I waited in a work-room where Wightman had fashioned an opening that gave him a good view of the shop while he was measuring and blending tobaccos, and it was perfect for our purpose. Rick, who had received a bad sprain the night of the fog and still had his arm in a sling, waited in a doorway across the street. When the young man from the Unwin Salvage Company left Wightman & Company, all three of us would follow him. We had the two cabs waiting for us on Upper Thames Street—Lady Sara's hansom, and a new four wheeler she had bought to replace the one damaged in the fog.

Once again we were prepared for anything except what actually happened, which was nothing. The agent never appeared.

After an hour's wait, Wightman said apologetically, "He said he would be here without fail at nine."

Since it was too early to say whether he had been delayed or somehow been warned off, I sent Charles to tell Rick what had happened. Rick went to warn the two grooms who were driving Lady Sara's private cabs.

We continued to wait. Finally, at noon, we decided we were wasting our time. "If he does come later," I said to Wightman, "I want you to order two hundredweight of the tobacco. Lady Sara will reimburse you. Find out as precisely as you can when it will be delivered, and try to make arrangements for getting in touch with the agent when you are ready for another order. Let me know the result. Perhaps we will be able to follow the deliveryman, and we also can follow the agent on his next visit."

We returned to Connaught Mews. Lady Sara heard my news in silence. "I don't like this," she announced.

"It is one more disappointment," I said. "We've had more than our share of them on this case."

She was shaking her head. "It is something far worse than that. After the agent called, Wightman & Company must have been watched to see whether the proprietor would complain to the authorities. Instead of the police, you arrived, and by this time the gang of thieves knows who its adversaries are and is able to recognize them at sight. They know you report to me, and they knew I would have their agent followed. So he never returned. From this point, we will have to be extremely wary."

She thought for a moment. "I said the thieves were watching us while we were watching them. I was wrong. They are *hunting* us, and they will continued to do so as long as we dog their steps." She glanced up at the elaborately-lettered framed document above her desk. "The gang will be as ruthless toward you and me as it was toward Ed, or Rafe Wade, or

Bill Havill, or Sid Theaker if it chances to catch us frustrating its plans. It is time we took suitable precautions. When Ben Lyle telephones, tell him no more spying from the skiff. I'll find something else for him to do. Right now, Sir William is coming."

Sir William Samper, Professor of Chemistry at London University, was an old friend and mentor of Lady Sara's, and she frequently consulted him on matters where she thought crime and chemistry met—usually with minimal success. He told her, repeatedly, that she was trying to invent a new scientific discipline, the Chemistry of Crime. Perhaps some day it would become a reality. As yet, it was not even in its infancy.

Sir William was a jolly, robust, bouncy man who looked like neither a "sir" nor a professor. Given a choice, he would have been more likely to investigate the chemistries of wine or of gourmet eating than of crime. He arrived in a rush, short of breath and perspiring, and settled himself to learn what impossible problem Lady Sara had for him this time.

"Tobacco," Lady Sara announced.

"That's the most appealing subject you have given me in years, my lady," Sir William said with a grin. He was fond of a good cigar or a pipe himself. "That is far better than a search for clues under the fingernails of decaying corpses."

"I have a sample here," Lady Sara went on. "An expert tobacconist has identified it as a variety known as Turkish black."

"I have smoked Turkish black," Sir William said. "It is very good and also very expensive."

"I suspect this sample came from a quantity of tobacco that was stolen. When this particular gang of thieves steals something, it always leaves some bales or boxes or sacks behind, artfully arranged to conceal the fact that the greater part of an inventory is missing. I want to know whether there is any way you could prove by chemical analysis that this sample came from the same batch of tobacco as one that was left behind."

Sir William fingered his chin thoughtfully. "As far as I know, there is no specialized scientific discipline that studies the chemistry of tobacco. No doubt some day there will be. Some day the chemistry of everything will be studied. What you want is a *portrait parlé* of tobacco comparable to the system Bertillon worked out for humans."

"I would prefer something better than that," Lady Sara said. "The portrait parle is cumbersome and highly unsatisfactory. Sir Francis Galton, in a book called *Finger Prints*, described a much better system of identification eight years ago. A simple and practical method of classifying fingerprints has long been in use in India, and at this moment a Home Office committee is considering adopting it for criminal identification in

England and Wales. I met with the committee yesterday. I would like to know whether every batch of tobacco has its own fingerprints."

"This is a rather small sample, my lady. If I do much experimenting with it, I will quickly use it up. I'll have to acquire a quantity of another tobacco to experiment with. It will be slow going because I have no idea what I will be looking for."

"Various substances are added to tobacco in curing it," Lady Sara said. "Perhaps the amounts vary from batch to batch. You might purchase examples of the same variety of tobacco from different tobaconists and see whether there is any variation in the amounts of the additives."

"Yes," Sir William agreed. "I might try that. Then you feel if I found two different samples with exactly the same amounts of additives they might come from the same batch of tobacco."

"I feel it is an assumption worth testing."

"Then I will test it," Sir William promised. "With pleasure." He took the sample of tobacco and left.

"It will probably come to nothing," Lady Sara said. "As usual. But we are bound to keep trying."

Ben Lyle telephoned late that afternoon. I relayed Lady Sara's instructions about calling off the watch from the skiff.

"You're too late," Ben said grimly. "We were run down by a steam-launch this afternoon. We managed to get clear, but the skiff sank."

"Are both of you all right?" I asked quickly.

"Apart from being wet, we're all right. Peeved, though. It was done deliberately."

"Was it the *Mollie Mae*?"

"No. A launch with a low deckhouse. Didn't get the name. Didn't have much time for reading. It swerved suddenly and steamed right over us."

"Did you report this to the Thames police?"

"What would the police do? Long before they could have got there, we managed to rescue ourselves. If we ever catch sight of that launch again, the crew'll find we're good pay."

"Hold it! If you identify the launch, just tell Lady Sara. She may have her own idea of how best to get even."

I congratulated him on his escape and told him we would be in touch with him as soon as we thought of something for him to do.

Lady Sara received the news with a scowl. "I should have seen this coming. We are almost too late in making arrangements to protect ourselves." She glanced up at the document above her desk. "We narrowly missed having two more names to add. From now on, we will carry revolvers. After tonight, we will have protection of another kind."

Covent Garden, which was filled with market produce, vendors, and customers from the wee hours of the morning until afternoon, was as hushed and still during the evening as Shadwell Market had been when we went to see the two murder victims. There was one significant difference. The area around Covent Garden seethed with night-time activity. Crowds gathered for opera or other events at the Covent Garden Theatre. The Garrick Club, a far livelier establishment than the Army and Navy Club I visited with Reggie Dempster, and the social headquarters for virtually all the prominent actors and literary men of London, was nearby. And on the north-west corner of Covent Garden stood the National Sporting Club.

The clubhouse had a venerable history to rival that of the Garden. This was once considered the centre of London, and magnificent residences were erected here. The building housing the National Sporting Club had a series of titled owners. When the neighbourhood became unfashionable, it became a hotel—the first hotel in London, some said. Later it functioned as a music hall with a theatre celebrated as the Cave of Harmony. It also doubled as a sporting tavern where fights were arranged.

Its present occupant, the National Sporting Club, had only been in existence for a decade or so, but its headquarters were already considered the principal centre in England for the "noble and manly art" of boxing. The former music hall theatre had become the scene of famous pugilistic encounters. Ladies were never to be encountered there except on evenings when the club revived the Cave of Harmony.

As usual, Lady Sara was an exception. She enjoyed studying the science of boxing and often attended matches as a guest of the club's manager, Mr. A. F. Bettinson. On this night, Mr. Bettinson received us in his office.

He was a man of medium build, bald with a well-nourished moustache and a prominent cigar. Since he knew Lady Sara well, he made no apology for continuing to smoke, and she made no complaint. "If women want to associate with men on equal terms, they can't expect special treatment at the same time," she once said.

She described for him the cases we were working on and the result: Our lives were in danger. Mr. Bettinson listened with growing anger. His face turned red.

"Do you mean, my lady, that those scoundrels would actually dare to attack you?"

"Probably with clubs," Lady Sara said cheerfully. "They are cowards, of course, but a crowd of them, armed with clubs, doesn't hesitate to assault someone who is defenceless."

"I see. What is it you want?"

Lady Sara told him. He stared at her for a moment. Then he burst into laughter. "I understand. You want to serve them out good. I think I can find the men you need. The younger boxers would be your best choice. They are thoroughly trained and have considerable experience, but technically they are amateurs. They still lack finesse in the ring, but you won't be needing finesse, and these men are excellent physical specimens—especially those who follow an arduous trade. A man who handles bricks all day develops his arm muscles splendidly, and he has an unequalled knockout punch. In the ring, with a more experienced opponent, he may have difficulty landing it, but in the sort of fight you envisage, with street thugs, he will be deadly."

"How soon can I have them?" Lady Sara asked.

"We are having novice matches this evening, my lady. Come along and make your own selections."

When we returned to Connaught Mews, Lady Sara had added four bodyguards to her payroll, and she had arranged to interview more the next day.

CHAPTER 15

On a chill, rainy day in early December, Ben Lyle rediscovered the missing steam-launch and its incarnation, the sloop Molly Mae. He did this by identifying another small-steam launch called *Vagrant*. He and his brother had long memories, as he had predicted, and when they chanced to see *Vagrant* from the right angle, they immediately recognized the launch that had run them down. With great skill and caution, they succeeded in following it to a wharf below Shadwell Market, one of the Free Trade Wharves.

There was an odd-looking sloop already docked there, and to their astonishment they recognized it as the *Mollie Mae* with her deck house remodelled so as to completely change her lines. She was now called *Clementine*.

"I was," Ben announced, "totally spiflicated. What's to be done?"

I passed the question to Lady Sara, who said, "This time we will profit from our experience and use an entirely different approach."

The first change concerned the Lyle brothers. They gave up their risky water searches and became supervisors, recruiting a crew of a dozen hardbitten retired watermen. Lady Sara explained what she wanted and left the selection entirely to the Lyles. Ben, Bob, and I toured both sides of the Thames, selecting observation points. When we found one we liked, I hired it—a disused storage room; a bedroom in a decrepit lodging house; a former sweatshop in the unheated loft of a warehouse; a grimy, overpriced hotel room. The main requirement was a generously sized window with an excellent view of the river.

In each of these observation points, the Lyles put one of their spies, as Ben called them, equipped with a telescope. They were to log all comings and goings of the two ships that interested us, with date, time, and direction. A comfortable lodging, plenty of food and tobacco, and even a jug of ale when they wanted one, with nothing to do but watch their beloved river, was their idea of paradise. Each of them settled into a routine and worked as many hours as there was light to see by.

The new wharf was in the area still known as Ratcliff although the name of the notorious Ratcliff Highway had been changed to St. George Street long before. It had several warehouses connected with it, all accessible from Broad Street. This occasioned more search for premises on both sides of the river—on the Surrey side, for a vantage point from which every ship calling at the wharf could be logged and described; on the London side, so that a tally could be made of waggon loadings and also so that any interesting visitors could be noted and photographed. The spies had to have cameras and know how to use them. They had to have assistants to bring food and run errands. It quickly became a complicated operation.

Then it became more complicated. The spies succeeded in connecting both *Vagrant* and *Clementine* with two new wharves, one on the Surrey side. Additional spies had to be recruited, trained, and placed in observation posts. The growing complexity of our network was made necessary by the astonishing scope and ingenuity of the river thieves, and Lady Sara never lost sight of that fact.

While we were thus occupied, I suddenly received a wholly unexpected early Christmas present. The morning mail was delivered while I was in conference with Lady Sara. She excused herself so she could quickly look through her own letters. While she was occupied, I glanced at the one letter I had received.

It was typewritten on the same crisply-engraved, expensive stationery I had already seen when Lady Sara received a letter from Sir Cecil Elliman. The Tradesmen Life and Accident Assurance Company informed me that it had decided to establish an investigative branch to consider applications for assurance and also claims. I had been nominated to direct this new branch. The suggested salary was two hundred pounds a year. Would I kindly inform the company at once as to whether I was willing to accept?

Again the signature was that of Sir Cecil Elliman.

Like Ben Lyle, I was totally spiflicated.

Lady Sara glanced across the room at me, glanced again, and asked in alarm, "What is it?"

I took the letter to her. She read it and looked up at me with a smile. "Congratulations. It is a handsome offer. It is far more than that—it is the offer of a splendid career for you."

I shook my head. "I already have a career."

Her face went solemn. "This really is the kind of opportunity that knocks only once in a lifetime. Once ensconced in such a prosperous organization, you would be able to rise as high as your ability would take you—and I have reason to believe that would be extremely high. Thirty years from now, you might be the chairman yourself, signing your letters 'Sir Colin.'"

"And sitting in an office all day telling others what to do?"

She nodded, smiling.

"No, thank you," I said. "A career opened up for me years ago, and I took it—and I intend to keep it. Unless you would like to be rid of me?"

"Certainly not!

There was a stamped, return envelope enclosed for my convenience. I used it immediately, acknowledging the honour and regretting that present commitments would keep me occupied elsewhere.

The collection of photographs of suspects—distinguished-looking men of a type who normally would have sent an employee to transact any business they had in the neighbourhood of the warehouses we were watching but for some reason found it necessary to call there in person—continued to grow slowly. Lady Sara identified them, and, after we had accumulated additional information about them, I added the names to my list of suspects.

Steven Harbisher held the controling interest in the Eastern Asia Trading Company. Despite the name, it was now chiefly concerned with European trade, and Harbisher seemed to be extremely prosperous. As a suspect, he was neither more nor less likely than any of the others, but after only a brief preliminary investigation, I placed him at the top of my list of unpleasant people. He was a small man, and he called himself the Napoleon of Trade. He was a tyrant to his employees, and if one of them chanced to be tall—and he liked to engage tall men—Harbisher was certain to make his life miserable. His appearance was as unpleasant as his manners. Those who knew him well joked that he had been associated with oriental trade for so long that he looked oriental. This wasn't strictly true, but he certainly looked odd.

Sir James Furner owned the Furner Steam-Packet Company. He held extensive interests in trading and importing firms. He was past middle age but more energetic than many younger men. The "sir" came from his political connections. He had twice been a Member of Parliament.

Otis Nicklass was one of five Nicklass brothers who jointly owned and ran the Five Brothers Importing Company Ltd. The others were David, Craig, Lyall, and Roger, but they hardly counted. Otis ran the family and also the company from headquarters located at the Five Brothers Wharf. Originally it had been known as Cakebread Wharf. When the Eynon Brothers renamed the wharf at their headquarters Brothers Wharf, the Nicklass clan also renamed their wharf. Otis seemed like such a total nonentity that a visitor would never have suspected him of being the brother in charge unless he tried to get one of the other brothers to make a decision about something. Otis always had to be consulted. He was slight of stature, with weak eyes and a vague look about him, but employees said his mind was sharp.

Sir Charles Lampson owned Lampson & Company Ltd., which he had established with his wife's money. He was excessively fat, and he puffed and perspired and became red-faced even when relaxing. He looked like a country squire, and he was rumoured to be more concerned with his rural estate and his horses than with his business. Some said his firm was near bankruptcy; some said it was doing well.

An oddity was the occasional appearance of the Reverend Theobald Eynon among photographs taken at the new locations even though Eynon Brothers Company supposedly had no connection with them.

My list, including Eynon, now contained thirteen names, which was ridiculous. We had never experienced such a wealth of suspects.

Lady Sara thought it time to consult with the police—not with Chief Inspector Mewer, whose immediate reaction would have been to object to everything, but with the Home Secretary himself. The fact that he was a remote cousin of hers facilitated matters. They met unofficially and discussed the situation. The problem was the same one we had faced in the beginning. We had no evidence, and the river thieves were too efficient to leave us any. For example, if a police raid on a suspected warehouse should turn up a quantity of the same variety of tea that had been stolen a fortnight earlier, that would prove nothing. There was an enormous amount of tea in Britain, and proof would be needed that this particular tea was the missing tea. We had none, and the thieves would have ample proof they had acquired it legitimately.

Lady Sara and the Home Secretary had their meeting. They agreed to meet again with legal and police advisors. Lady Sara withdrew for a day of meditation and emerged with a new plan for following waggons from the Free Trade Wharves.

Her scheme was complicated, but the fundamental principle was brilliantly simple. Three four wheeler cabs would follow each waggon. Each would contain a driver and a passenger who would change places whenever conveniently possible.

None of them would wait near the warehouses. When a waggon started off, a cart would pull out nearby and follow it. The cart had only one function: To identify the waggon. When the waggon passed one of the waiting cabs, the carter would signal the cab driver and turn off at the first opportunity, leaving the chase to the cabs. The cabs would change places repeatedly, each taking a turn immediately behind the waggon and then turning off to change drivers and disguise the horse, after which it would join the procession again. The waggon would be followed to its destination, but every few streets there would be a different cab doing the following.

I set about making arrangements to put this scheme into practice. At that point, as happened so frequently with Lady Sara's investigations, there was a distraction. Reginald Dempster called to see whether we had made any progress in tracing his Regent Street giant.

"Yes, we traced him," Lady Sara said. "As it turned out, it was the wrong giant, but negative information can be valuable, so it wasn't wasted effort. I'm grateful you told me about him."

"Wrong giant? But there can't be all that many giants around!" Dempster protested.

"There are a few, however, and yours wasn't the one we were looking for."

"Well—sorry about that."

"Not at all," Lady Sara said. "If you see another giant, tell me at once. I'll be grateful, even if it still is not the right one."

"Fair enough," Dempster said. "Though I'm not hopeful about that happening. I mean—up until now, I've seen just one giant in my life. Is there anything else I can do?"

"Not that I can think of at the moment," Lady Sara said.

"I did happen upon something odd recently, but I don't know whether it is your kind of oddity."

Lady Sara smiled. "I welcome all kinds of oddities. Tell me."

"It's about wine," Dempster said. "A man with my income can't afford a cellar. Sometimes I'm hard put to afford a bottle. I usually buy a nice, reliable, Niersteiner at thirteen shillings the dozen. It isn't a wine to be served to royalty, understand, but then—I don't often entertain royalty. I make it do because I have to. One day last week several of us at the club—the Oxford and Cambridge, it is open again—were talking about wine, and I mentioned that my Niersteiner was the best I could afford. Afterward, one of the men took me aside and said, 'I know where you can buy a much better wine than that for about the same price.' I challenged him to show me, and he did. He took me to his wine-merchant—it wasn't far, just off Park Lane—and the wine merchant, name of Beaton, let me sample a glass. It made my Niersteiner taste like factory dregs."

"What kind of wine was it?" Lady Sara asked.

"He told me it was a German wine from a private stock. The bottles have rather plain labels that say, in English, 'Special Import,' and in German, 'Deutscher Tafelwein.'"

"Does the label mention the importer?" Lady Sara asked.

"It does, but I don't remember what the name was."

"'Deutscher Tafelwein' is simple table wine," Lady Sara said. "Usually it is the lowest quality German wine available."

"Maybe so, but not in this instance. It's the best German wine I've ever tasted. He wanted fifteen shillings the dozen, a bit more than I pay for my Niersteiner but a genuine bargain nevertheless. Unfortunately, you've got to have the ready to take advantage of it. Payment with order, a disgusting business practice. Beaton only acts as agent for the importers, and they won't make deliveries unless you put up the cash in advance. I scraped the bottom of my exchequer and bought three dozen bottles. Now you tell me—how can anyone afford to offer such excellent wine at such a low price?"

"There are a number of ways," Lady Sara said. "Most of them are illegal. Did he offer any other varieties at bargain prices?"

"Matter of fact, he did. He had a red French wine and a white Spanish wine, but I prefer German wines, so I took this one. What could be illegal about it?"

"Several things. Before I go into that, I would like to taste the wine."

Dempster nodded wisely. "I'll send you a bottle. The proof of the pudding is in the eating."

"The proof of the wine usually is in the drinking. Thank you, but sending a bottle won't be necessary. Could you arrange for your friend to introduce Colin to this wine merchant? He will purchase some for me."

"Now that I know where the place is, I can introduce him myself. Would you like me to take him now?"

"Yes, please."

"Glad to do it." Dempster grinned. "If I bring in enough business, maybe Beaton will give me a discount."

Lady Sara took me aside and told me, "Order a dozen of each variety, French, Spanish, and German. This may be the opportunity we have been looking for."

We had failed to make contact with the Unwin Salvage Company through Jasper Wightman, and Sir William Samper had made no progress with his chemical analysis of the tobacco sample. Perhaps Reggie Dempster's wine would afford another glimpse of how the river thieves were disposing of their stolen merchandise.

We took Lady Sara's carriage with Old John on the box and two of the new footmen from the group of pugilists Lady Sara hired. She'd had uniforms made for them. The death of Ed Geffen, the groom, was still on everyone's mind, and now none of her staff went anywhere without a bodyguard—which was a nuisance when I was conducting an investigation.

As we drove past Hyde Park, I thought of the earlier outing with Dempster and reflected on the difference a few weeks had made. On this chill December day, there was little reminder of the gay summer atmosphere I had seen then.

I hadn't heard the address Dempster gave to Old John, and I was immensely surprised when we turned from Park Lane into Market Street. A moment later we had arrived—at Shepherd Market, a most unlikely address for a wine-merchant.

It represented the London of a hundred years earlier. It was a neighbourhood of small shopkeepers who carried on flourishing businesses within a stone's throw of one of the world's most expensive thoroughfares, and visiting it was like suddenly finding oneself in a rural town surrounded by the tiny establishments of fishmongers, fruiterers, provision merchants, poulterers, butchers proclaiming bargains in small cuts of beef and mutton, and shops with offerings of leather-work that had spilled onto the pavements or which threatened to exhale cheap crockery through their open doors.

If the address seemed unlikely, so did the wine-merchant. Seth Beaton was a middle-aged man with watery eyes and an unhealthy cough. He wore a shabby suit, and he had an almost comical solemnity. His shop windows displayed wines that were far cheaper than even Reggie Dempster's Niersteiner, but some of the racks inside were stocked with varieties that to my limited knowledge and experience seemed to be of excellent quality.

Beaton greeted Dempster affably, shook my hand with enthusiasm when Dempster introduced me as a friend interested in laying down the foundations of a cellar, and invited us into his tasting parlour. It was a small but comfortable room with surprising furnishings. Four upholstered mahogany dining chairs were arranged about a mahogany tea table with a rectangular top and a tripod base, a piece I judged to be well over a hundred years old. Beaton took six wine glasses from a splendid old, elaborately carved cabinet. Considering the shabby circumstances of the shop, I deduced that either Beaton or his wife had been fortunate enough to inherit furniture from a well-off grandparent.

Beaton brought out three previously opened bottles of wine, one each of the three varieties Dempster had mentioned. He also placed an assortment of biscuits and some very ordinary cheese on the table. Then he poured us small portions of each variety of wine.

I solemnly nibbled a biscuit and tasted the cheese. Then, hoping I wasn't acting too much like a novice, I sampled each of the wines. Dempster did the same. In my non-expert judgement, all three were far better than average.

I left the talking to Dempster. While he was being profuse with his compliments, I slowly finished my samples, taking time between sips to study Beaton and also the wine labels. These latter carried the legend "Special Import" in large type. Below that was the name of the importing firm, Doffrey & Son, and its address in Wellclose Square, London. At the bottom of the label on each bottle was a foreign language description in small type: "Deutscher Tafelwein" on the German bottle, "Vino Corriente" on the Spanish bottle, and "Vin Ordinaire" on the French bottle.

After what I considered proper deliberation, I announced my decision to purchase a dozen bottles of each. Beaton lost his solemnity and brought out an order form. I relieved him of the embarrassment of having to ask for payment in advance by counting out the money. I had expected to take the wine away with me, but he told me regretfully that he stocked only a few bottles for sampling. My order would be delivered to my home on the next delivery date, which was the following Monday.

I took his receipt for two pounds five shillings. I thought it unwise to use my Connaught Mews address, so I gave him the address of a friend who was living in Montagu Place.

Once the purchase had been completed, Beaton relaxed, poured each of us a glass of wine of his choice, poured one for himself, and abruptly changed from a rather shoddy wine merchant into a charming and interesting host. His knowledge of wines was profound, and obviously he loved to talk about them. The names rolled from his tongue—Château varieties of Burgundies, Clarets, and Rhones. The dialects of Champagne. The immense variety of German wines. Dempster protested that he knew little about all that because he simply couldn't afford to educate himself. I confessed that I knew nothing at all about it for the same reason. Beaton gave both of us advice that seemed excellent about developing our palates without ruining our pocketbooks.

I asked him why he had chosen such an unlikely location for his shop, remarking that he must receive very few orders for those superb—and therefore expensive—wines he loved to talk about. "When is the last time you sold a bottle of forty-year-old Burgundy? Or a bottle of vintage Port?"

"More recently than you would expect," he said with a patient smile. "I was a wine-merchant's clerk for more than twenty years. I loved my work; I loved wines, and so did my employer. Then my employer died. His nephew inherited the business. He knew nothing about wines and cared even less. His idea was to turn a larger profit. We imported some of our wines in casks and bottled them ourselves. When I found my new employer deliberately mislabelling those wines, I knew I had to leave.

"Fortunately for me, at that moment my wife came into an inheritance from an aunt she scarcely knew. It was enough to set up a modest shop and to support us until the business was established. I chose my location with care. Shepherd Market may seem unlikely, but it is surrounded by Mayfair. Berkeley and Grosvenor Squares, Park Lane, and similar streets with rows of costly mansions are nearby. The masters and mistresses do not patronize Shepherd Market, but their servants do, and they quickly learned that I keep small quantities of excellent wines on hand. Emergencies can occur even in homes that have well-furnished cellars—extra bottles are suddenly required for a dinner party, or a guest requests something the host's cellar can't provide. When this happens, the servants know they can call on me at any hour since I live at the rear of my shop. In a surprising number of those mansions, there are people who purchase wine only when they are entertaining. They buy a few bottles when needed, and, as I said, their servants know I am here. The wines in the window are only intended for the street trade—for passersby. That's my bread and butter business. I'm doing modestly well, and my business is growing.

"Of course I don't import my own wines—I haven't the capital for that. I act as agent for a few of the larger merchants and occasionally I have the good fortune to make a mutually profitable arrangement with an importer like Doffrey and Son. Eventually—when some of the masters and mistresses begin to call here instead of sending their servants—my business will expand rapidly."

He seemed sincere and absolutely genuine.

We parted friends. I thanked him for the information and promised to see him again and tell him how I liked the wine after drinking a few bottles. I dropped Dempster off at his club, the Oxford and Cambridge, and went to call on my friend in Montagu Place. He wasn't home, but I told his wife, who also was a friend, that on the following Monday she would be receiving three dozen bottles of wine, prepaid, and I would claim it myself or send someone immediately after it was delivered.

Then, with Old John still driving and the two pugilistic footmen still guarding my life, I headed for Wellclose Square.

The neighbourhood, which was close to the dock area, seemed appropriate for an importing firm even if the address did not. Wellclose Square had once been the centre of a Danish settlement. It still had close associations with the sea as evidenced by the numerous seamen's institutes located nearby and the school for seamen's children that stood on the site of the old Danish church. The square's ancient character largely survived, and I expected the firm of Doffrey and Son, an importer pushing bargain wines, to be ridiculously out of place there.

Certainly it would have been had there been any sign of it. I called at the address given on the bottles; the young maid who responded claimed to know nothing of Doffrey and Son or of wines. She was lying. I read it in her face, and she knew that I did, flushed, and turned away. At that instant, another of Reggie Dempster's oddities became a case.

Lady Sara thought so when I described the matter-of-factness of the wine-merchant and the total illusiveness of Doffrey and Son. Her first question was whether at any time I had been followed. I had not been.

"It would be miraculous good fortune to stumble onto another example of the way the river thieves distribute their stolen goods, but sometimes virtue—and hard work—are rewarded," she remarked thoughtfully. "Of course Wellclose Square is only an accommodation address. The thieves have nothing to fear from it as long as the person who collects their mail uses a few simple precautions. We would be wasting our time watching the place. The deliveryman sounds much more promising."

The following Monday, Rick Allward, Charles Tupper, and I—suitably guarded by some of Lady Sara's new footmen—were waiting in carefully chosen locations near my friend's house when the wine was delivered. Charles and I followed the delivery van while Rick Allward collected the three dozen bottles from my friend and took them directly to Lady Sara. Doffrey and Son were doing a flourishing business. The van delivered wine for the remainder of the day. I wondered whether all of those orders had come through Seth Beaton. The empty van finally turned homeward with the horse setting a sharp pace.

"Homeward" was the correct word. I had hoped the driver would lead us to the warehouse the wine had come from, but he was an entrepreneur—he owned his own horse and van. With his deliveries done for the day, he returned horse and van to a mews near Liverpool Street Station and himself to a rickety house in White Lion Street.

It meant hours of tedious watching until he had another commission to deliver wine—probably on the following Monday. I made the arrangements and wearily returned to Connaught Mews.

Lady Sara had already sampled the three different kinds of wine. She opined that the white Spanish wine was really a quite good French Bordeaux, a Sauternes. The other white wine, the one Dempster thought so much better than his Niersteiner, was a very good quality German Rhine wine. The red wine was an excellent claret, also from Bordeaux.

"There are two possible lines of investigation," she said. "One is to find out who is distributing the wines and from where. Hopefully you can accomplish that by following the deliveryman to his source. The other is to identify the kinds of wine as exactly as possible and start enquiries to see whether anyone has reported quantities of them stolen."

"Should we be watching Shepherd Market?" I asked.

"I'll leave that as a last resort. Your wine-merchant may be exactly what he said—an agent for the so-called importers."

"He didn't look like the type to have stolen or smuggled the wine himself," I agreed.

"Not looking like the type can be an enormous advantage," she said impatiently. "But I think you're right. His shop sounds like a marginal business with a very slow rate of growth—exactly as he described it. Any respectable thief or smuggler should be doing far better than that. While we're waiting to find out where the warehouse is, I'll invite Lord Anstee to try the wines. He is far more of a connoisseur than I am."

Lord Anstee made his usual bustling arrival the next morning. He brought a friend with him, a Colonel Maybon, and the Colonel's neatly-trimmed moustache and pointed goatee formed a comical contrast to Lord Anstee's fluttering mutton chop whiskers.

"Still celebrating Mafeking night, Colonel?" Lady Sara asked. Mafeking, which had been under siege by the Boers, had been relieved six months earlier, but it was still an event of the moment for ardent patriots.

Colonel Maybon turned a puzzled gaze on her. "Celebrating..."

"Your cravat," Lady Sara said. "Khaki is an unusual colour for male ornaments. Does that mean you advocate khaki uniforms for the troops?"

"It does, my lady," the Colonel said firmly.

"What about this new book by Arthur Conan Doyle, *The Great Boer War*? It might be subtitled, 'A non-military man's suggestions to the military.' I have heard it called impertinent nonsense."

"It is impertinent common sense," the Colonel growled. "Anyone who has fought on the India frontier could have written it. Those who don't think the army needs reforming still have their minds on the Battle of Waterloo."

Lady Sara changed the subject to wines, and the two elderly men went about the tasting as though they had been doing it all their lives. It was entirely possible that they had.

"What did you pay?" Lord Anstee asked disbelievingly when he had sipped all three varieties.

"Fifteen shillings the dozen," Lady Sara said.

"You stole it," Lord Anstee announced.

"I bought it legally. I have a copy of the order to prove that. The party claiming to be the importer may have stolen it."

"Someone stole it," Lord Anstee insisted. "What is it you want to know?"

"I want to know exactly where it came from." She told him what she had concluded about the wine, and he sipped gravely and nodded. The colonel emulated him.

"The Sauternes is much better than average," Lord Anstee announced. "The Rhine Wine is exceptional. The claret is excellent. I would be willing to lay down a few dozen of the claret myself at fifteen shillings."

"And I would be willing to lay down a few dozen of the Rhine Wine," the colonel said.

"Why don't you?" Lady Sara asked. "Colin will introduce you to the wine merchant. It will be interesting to see how much of this wine he is willing or able to sell and whether there is any hesitation about selling to men in your position. Also, we will know for certain there will be wine to be delivered next Monday in case we want to follow the deliveryman. You can take Colin with you when you leave here and go directly to Shepherd Market. Now tell me—how can I find out exactly where the wine came from?"

"I suppose you would like to know what Bordeaux Châteaux originated the claret and the Sauternes, and what German village or town produced the Rhine Wine," Lord Anstee suggested.

"As near as possible."

"We can't do that for you, but I know someone who can. Do you have a few bottles to spare?"

Lady Sara spoke to her maid, who brought in two bottles of each variety.

"I'll find out as quickly as possible," Lord Anstee said. "Not my line of work at all. I like a more warming drink for winter, but warming drinks have gone sadly out of fashion in London. The old Bull and Bush, on Hamstead Heath, used to offer a brew of barley wine that toasted one from toes to ear lobes. I haven't heard of anything like that for years. How does that poet put it?"

"'Where are the snows of yesteryear?'" Lady Sara suggested.

"Exactly. Where are the hot cordials of yesteryear? They are sorely missed when December winds rack us. Even punch seems to have passed away with Dickens. What was it he said? 'If ever hot punch did fail to act as a preventative, it was merely because the patient fell into the vulgar error of not taking enough of it.' *Pickwick Papers*, isn't it?"

Lady Sara nodded.

"They still compound punch at the Cheshire Cheese but without proper enthusiasm, I think, and it is rarely seen elsewhere. From Samuel Johnson to Charles Dickens, Englishmen of culture and good taste considered a bowl of punch to be one of life's highest felicities and an essential adornment to any social occasion. But these days—when did you last have punch, Colin?"

I couldn't remember ever having any.

"You must visit me this winter. I'll see that you are properly fortified. Here's another forgotten delicacy—pineapple rum, hot with three lumps—nowhere in these degenerate times does one encounter that fragrant concoction unless one makes it oneself. And a port negus—did you ever taste a port negus, Colin?"

"Never, my lord," I said, smiling.

"Lemons, a bottle of port, a pint of boiling water, grated nutmeg, lump sugar to taste. Serve with cinnamon floating on the top like driftwood after a wreck. When I was much younger, the old Ridler's Hotel, in Holborn, had a little inner room where long clay pipes were provided and a stately waiter I would have loved to engage as my butler used to bring a negus that was worth drinking."

Lady Sara regarded him with a mischievous half smile, a certain sign that she was highly amused. "Why didn't you engage him?"

"I was afraid to try. I went there anonymously, and I didn't dare let him know who I was. If my governor had found out about it, he would have sprouted lectures about associations beneath my station. I'd love to go there now, but Ridler's is gone with the snows of yesteryear. The winter announcements of today's publicans don't even carry tidings of mulled ale. It's a damned shame, that's what it is. The best wine is watery stuff in winter. But I'll see what I can do for you."

I took them to Seth Beaton in Shepherd Market, and all three of us solemnly went through the ritual of tasting the three varieties of wine. Then Lord Anstee and Colonel Maybon gave Beaton orders to make his eyes pop—fifteen dozen bottles of the "Vin Ordinaire," the claret, for Lord Anstee, to be delivered to his Park Lane home; and six dozen, immediately amended to ten dozen, bottles of the "Deutscher Tafelwein," the Rhine wine, for Colonel Maybon, to be delivered to his London home in Bayswater.

We knew the deliveryman; we had made certain he would have something to deliver. Now it was up to him to lead us to whatever Doffrey & Son used as a warehouse.

CHAPTER 16

The following Monday, all three of us—Rick, Charles, and I—were waiting before dawn when the waggoner took out his delivery van. We wanted nothing to go wrong on this day. Each of us was equipped differently—with a horse and cart, or the hansom cab, or the four wheeler—and each of us had two of Lady Sara's pugilistic footmen in ordinary clothes as passengers.

During the intervening days, little had happened. Lord Anstee's friend had known precisely where the two French wines originated and approximately where the German wine originated. This was interesting but of little immediate value. We first had to trace the wine back to the source from which it reached London.

Lady Sara had reviewed reports of thefts all over south-eastern England. Small quantities of wine had been stolen from several places, but not those varieties and not in the quantity that had to be involved. There was always the possibility that no one had missed the wine yet, but it did seem strange that so many casks or bottles could vanish without anyone noticing.

Lady Sara continued to enquire; and of course she also was continuing the investigations already in progress. Waggons chosen at random were being followed from the newly discovered warehouses, but thus far their errands had appeared to be routine. The surveillance of ships on the river by the Lyle brothers' spies continued. So did the search for clues to the murders. In addition, all of Lady Sara's agents were still looking for a giant.

Rick, Charles, and I had taken turns watching and following the waggoner who had delivered the wine. We now knew his name was Jem Sutter, and he seemed to lead a tedious and entirely honest life, working with his son, a sturdy boy about twelve, and making deliveries for firms too small to employ their own deliverymen—one day for one firm, the next day for two or three other firms. Thus he ranged all over London, transporting antique furniture that had been refurbished by a French craftsman; or sets of cheap china bought on the payment plan by thrifty housewives; or baskets of fruit or flowers sent to invalids; or an occasional exotic delivery of a rhinoceros's head, a hartebeest's horns, or a tiger skin rug for a taxidermist. As far as we could determine, neither he nor anyone else noticed or even cared that he was being followed. By the end of the week we were waiting eagerly for Monday.

Sutter left earlier than usual that morning and took Commercial Street to Commercial Road, driving briskly through Stepney, Limehouse, and Poplar. When this route drew near the docks, suddenly every public house was a "Jolly Tar" or something similar; slop shops with sailors' clothing and other shops catering for sailors became common—we passed a cheap shoe-mart called "Jack and his Mother"; and the side streets were filled with decrepit doss-houses for sailors, watermen, or dock-workers.

Unsteady sailors returning to their ships after all-night binges and heavy waggon traffic were further indications that the docks were nearby. Foreign sailors became conspicuous: flaxen-haired ones chatting in German; black sailors with cotton handkerchiefs twisted turban-like around their heads talking unidentifiable gibberish. Where Commercial Road divides into East India Dock Road and West India Dock Road, we met a band of five Chinese sailors in dirty blue linen—probably on their way to Limehouse Court, a peculiar little street given up to lodging houses for orientals and grocers' shops kept by discreet, inscrutable Chinese who had married English women and settled in England.

When our waggoner passed the Limehouse Basin of the Regent's Canal, I began to wonder whether his destination was Narrow Street and Prout's Mill, but he kept straight on.

To our right, the line of the Blackwall Railway was visible from time to time, carrying trains on its raised rail level past a stumpy forest of identical chimneys to Blackwall Station, where passengers detraining at the very doorstep of the vast East India Docks found a fresh breeze in their faces and the river at their feet. Our waggoner turned off just before he reached the docks and the station. He took Robinhood Lane and then turned into Wells Street, a short, dilapidated passageway of small buildings. His destination was a shabby warehouse that bore a neatly lettered sign: Poplar Produce Company. There was an exterior loading bay and also a vehicular entrance that permitted inside loading and unloading. The door to the vehicular entrance swung open; Sutter was expected.

He drove into the building with his son walking ahead, guiding the horse. The passageway lead straight through to an exit at the rear, and the warehouse's interior looked remarkably clean. The warehouseman, who wore a white smock, was waiting on a loading platform beside stacks of crates that probably contained bottles of wine.

The moment van and horse were inside, the door was closed on them.

I continued to watch the building. A short time later, a cart arrived drawn by a donkey. It backed up to the outside loading bay. The warehouseman emerged at once, and the driver leaped from cart to the loading level to exchange a few words with him. The two went inside; a moment later they returned, each carrying a large, obviously heavy bag. These were placed in the cart, which promptly drove away. I signalled to Rick Allward, and he and his two footmen followed it. The warehouseman vanished inside to return his attention to Sutter, who was taking on a full van load.

Finally they finished, the door opened, and Sutter drove straight out. This was startling until I learned that there was room behind the warehouse for a waggon to turn around. Sutter had used it and then driven back through the building. He turned into Robinhood Lane, and Charles Tupper followed after him in the four wheeler. Since we now knew all about Sutter's daily routine and also knew at least two of the places he was bound for—Lord Anstee's Park Lane home and Colonel Maybon's Bayswater home—Charles expected to have no difficulties.

Rick Allward returned with the information that the donkey and cart were owned by an apparently respectable greengrocer located a short distance away in Poplar. The two bags had contained potatoes.

"Are you sure?" I asked him.

"As near as could be. Didn't you notice how lumpy the bags looked? Probably there's a hundredweight of potatoes in each bag."

Another cart arrived, this time hitched to a horse. The warehouseman and the driver loaded four large bags that looked identical to those the previous cart had loaded. When the cart left, Rick followed it. I headed for Blackwall Station, where I was certain to find a public telephone, taking one of the pugilistic footmen with me to look after the horse and leaving the other to watch the warehouse. I telephoned Lady Sara.

A serious disadvantage of using telegrams during an investigation was that one never knew how many people would read them and who might be bribing those people for information. The telephone was quicker, and one could convey far more information in a three-minute call than in a telegram, but it also had a disadvantage. One never knew who might be listening.

But Lady Sara never needed detailed explanations. I told her, "The Poplar Produce Company, on Wells Street, seems to be a popular place for greengrocers to buy potatoes." That was enough for her to grasp the entire story—the wine dealing as well as the potato trade.

There was a moment of silence while she reflected. It must have seemed as unlikely to her as it had to me that the same firm selling stolen wine would be dealing in potatoes.

"Are you alone?" she asked.

She wanted to know if anyone had tried to follow us. "Completely," I said.

"There is something peculiar about this," she said. "It simply doesn't seem to fit." She paused. "Who has the horse and cart?"

"I do," I said.

"Since it's a popular place to buy potatoes, try buying some."

When the bodyguard and I returned to Wells Street, Rick was back with the information that the second driver had been a respectable greengrocer in nearby Bromley. Rick had devised a complicated scheme whereby each of the footmen in turn would walk past the warehouse at odd intervals. We felt overly conspicuous; the cramped street probably had not seen that much traffic in years, but no one seemed to notice or care. While I was telling him what Lady Sara wanted me to do, two more carts arrived and loaded bags of potatoes. We didn't bother to follow them. When the carts left, the warehouseman disappeared, and there was neither sign nor sound of activity.

"Good luck," Rick told me with a grin.

I left my two bodyguards with Rick and boldly backed my horse and cart up to the Poplar Produce Company loading bay. A door opened obligingly as I mounted the platform. The warehouseman looked at me enquiringly. He was young, at most twenty-five years old, and I noticed that his white coat had begun to acquire smudges.

I said, "I heard you have a good buy in potatoes."

"We get them from a farmer in East Anglia," he said. He spoke with an accent I couldn't place though his speech was clear enough. "Very good quality. I'll show you."

He led me to a back room containing a heap of potatoes. He had been bagging them; there was a spring scale with a partly filled bag suspended. He took a potato, cut it into quarters, and handed them to me. "Excellent quality," he said. "We'll be able to keep you supplied as long as the crop lasts. We also have vegetable marrows, beets, and turnips from time to time. We sell all of them by the hundredweight. Potatoes are three shillings the bag, sales for cash only. Where are you located?"

"In Limehouse," I said.

He nodded understandingly. "We're more convenient for you than any London market, and, as you already know, we're a lot closer than crossing the river to the Borough Market for potatoes. And we don't mind selling in small quantities. I can let you have one bag or a hundred."

I bought two. I paid him. Then I picked up one, he carried the other, and we loaded them into the cart. I drove off with a wave. The warehouseman called after me, "See you soon."

Once around the corner, I turned into Woolmore Street and waited for Rick to catch up with me. He scrutinized the bags of potatoes. "What are you going to do with them?" he asked.

"They should keep all of our households, including that of the Countess, in potatoes for some time."

"They may last all winter," Rick said.

"At least we now know the business is genuine."

"If anyone had any doubt," Rick said. "How many potato customers does it take to prove a potato business is genuine?" Then he asked, "Why don't you go back and try to buy wine?"

"I'd rather not. Only Jem Sutter is picking up wine. That may be a different operation entirely from the sale of potatoes."

"So where does this leave us?" Rick demanded.

"Mystified," I said.

I took my part in the routine watch on the warehouse. Greengrocers' waggons and carts came and went, buying potatoes. I was parked around the corner with my horse, cart, and bodyguards, resting, when Rick hurried up to me. "The potatoes have arrived," he announced.

I must have looked unusually blank. He chuckled and explained himself. "A waggon just drove up at the Poplar Produce Company with a load of potatoes. Where did you think they got the potatoes they sell? If you still doubt this is a genuine business, go and see for yourself."

I did. I went on foot and arrived just in time to see the load of potatoes disappearing into the vehicle entrance. The waggon had high sides, and its load was covered by a tarpaulin, but the lumpy shape as well as what was visible in gaps along the along the sides left no doubt that it was heaped with potatoes. It was drawn by two horses in tandem. It disappeared inside, and the door closed.

Rick was right, of course—the potatoes the Poplar Produce Company sold had to come from somewhere. We were investigating wine, not potatoes, but for some reason this struck me as an important development. I hurried back to Rick and told him, "I must telephone Lady Sara at once." I drove off at a trot, again taking a bodyguard to watch the horse while I telephoned.

It is difficult to describe the arrival of a load of potatoes in guarded terms, so I simply told Lady Sara what had happened. "The warehouse-man said their potatoes came from East Anglia. Would they be hauling them all the way to London by waggon?"

"I believe London's main source of potatoes is the Borough Market in Southwark, which receives produce by way of the South-East Railway from Kent and maybe by ship from everywhere. I don't know how East Anglian potatoes would reach London. By railway or ship to one of the markets, I suppose. We first must ask ourselves whether there is any connection between the vegetables the Poplar Produce Company sells and product that interests us. Do you see one?"

"No," I admitted.

"There's only one way to find the answers to those questions. You know what to do."

I did. When the waggon left, I would have to follow it.

I dashed back to Wells Street, fearful that I might be too late; but the driver obviously was in no rush. Perhaps the warehouseman was treating him to a sample of wine. I drove around to Woolmore Street, where Rick was waiting, and told him I was going to follow the waggon.

I gave Rick my two bags of potatoes, transferring the problem of their disposal to him. Then I posted three of the footmen where they could relay a signal to me when the waggon was about to depart. While I waited, I arrived at a critical decision. When working with a vehicle, I always carried a bag with several changes of clothing and other items of disguise in case I needed to alter my appearance frequently. I also brought with me items to change the appearance of both horse and cart. Unfortunately, I had nothing with which to transform those hulking, pugilistic footmen, and they couldn't have looked like anything but themselves however they were disguised. A cart with two overly large male passengers would be ridiculously conspicuous. Despite Lady Sara's strict orders, I decided to work alone.

We had a long wait, but eventually the relay worked. I reached the corner of Woolmore Street and Robinhood Lane just as the waggon, now empty except for the neatly folded tarpaulin, passed. I carefully scrutinized the driver as he drove by. Then I gave him a short lead and followed him. He chose his route without hesitation, maintaining a steady, plodding pace, and from the moment he left Robinhood Lane, he mystified me completely. He wasn't headed for any market I was familiar with. He seemed, in fact, to be taking the most direct route out of London. There was no question of his being lost—either he was familiar with the city, or he had delivered potatoes frequently enough to know the way.

I remained sceptical even when he turned east. I hung back far enough to escape his notice if he looked behind him but close enough to keep him in sight. He plodded steadily through Plaistow and turned north at Barking. Only when we reached the principal highway to East Anglia and turned toward Romford and, beyond it, Brentwood, did I reluctantly concede that East Anglia really might be our destination.

But I was still feeling doubtful. If the warehouseman had told me the truth, and the potatoes really did come from East Anglia, why in the name of common sense would someone be hauling them one waggon-load at a time all the way to London? Perhaps potatoes commanded a better price there, but on such a small quantity, would the difference pay the driver's wages and compensate for the wear and tear on horses and waggon?

And surely there were plenty of local markets in East Anglia, not to mention dealers who called there and bought up entire crops from farmers and shipped them to London by rail. There was no rational justification for a farmer hauling his own potatoes to London.

Whatever the logic, if this driver really was headed for East Anglia, then so was I. It was a typical chill December day, but after an hour or so a warming bright sun came out. The potato farmer continued his steady pace. I dropped back almost out of sight, then whipped my horse up to a trot until I had almost overtaken him, and then turned off. After making a few changes in my dress and hanging bright yellow signs on either side of the cart that read, "J. Plover, Ironmonger," I followed him at a distance for a time only to repeat the procedure with different modifications.

The Eastern Counties Railway closely paralleled the road to East Anglia, and as each passing train disappeared into the distance, I watched it with increasing regret. The railway offered a far more comfortable and efficient way to travel if only I had known where I was going. It also offered a far more efficient means of transporting potatoes to London.

It was approaching dusk when we passed through Brentwood—too late to send a telegram. I knew Lady Sara would be worried, but the job came first. For a time the potato waggon continued unwaveringly toward Chelmsford. Finally, as we approached a small village, the driver turned in at an inn calling itself the Boot and Slipper. I drove on past, waited until the driver had had time to have his horse taken care of and get himself settled, and then returned. While I was engaging a room, I announced that I was on my way to London and expected to resume my journey at dawn. In the Inn's register—which I signed using an alias and a false address—the signature above mine read, "John Snell, Great Helmwich." I had no idea where Great Helmwich was. I wondered whether both names were false.

I insisted on putting my own horse and cart away. While doing so, I examined the potato farmer's waggon. There was an odd arrangement of slats nailed to the bottom in parallel rows from front to back. I couldn't think of any useful function for them in transporting potatoes, but they could have had quite a lot to do with hauling wine. The slats would keep rows of wine casks in position. Other rows would be loaded on top, and the whole buried under a mound of potatoes and covered with a tarpaulin. As easily as that, I discovered the connection between the potatoes and the wine. My trip no longer seemed like a wild-goose chase.

I asked the innkeeper about telephones. When he told me there were none in the village, I wrote out an ambiguous telegram for Lady Sara, telling her I was travelling in the direction of East Anglia and might actually go there. This I sealed into an envelope with enough pence for the tariff. I gave it to the inn's boots with sixpence for himself in exchange for his solemn promise to hand it in the moment the post office opened in the morning. I promised I would come back and skin him alive if he failed to do so.

Later, while eating my dinner, I watched John Snell playing at darts. He was close to forty years old, robustly built, and a fine specimen of a man. Either he was well known there, or he had the gift of friendliness. Those playing with him treated him like an old acquaintance.

It was a comfortable little inn. The food was fairly good, and the bed gave me a restful night's sleep. The maid awakened me at dawn, as I had requested; and, when I came down, she had breakfast ready for me: Hot tea, scones, cold sliced ham, and freshly baked bread. It was far from the worst meal I had ever had.

I paid my bill, tipped the maid who had given me breakfast and the groom who had permitted me to look after my own horse—both seemed astonished—and I conspicuously drove off in the direction of London. I took the first turning, and at a convenient place I converted myself into a bearded man wearing a different coat and hat. I reversed the signs on the cart; now they proclaimed, in black and white letters, "Endmore Company, Sewing Machines."

Then I drove past the Boot and Slipper and found a place where I could loiter inconspicuously. There was grass on the verge for my horse to munch. Both of us composed ourselves for a long wait. At no time had John Snell behaved like a man in a hurry.

It was almost nine o'clock when he appeared. I gave him a good lead and then followed, repeating my performance of the previous day. On we plodded—through Chelmsford, through Whitham—where I saluted the ghost of the gentle giant, Rafe Wade—and through Colchester. There were things well worth seeing in all three towns—the celebrated Roman ruins in Colchester, for example, and the Norman castle—but I caught nary a glimpse of them. I had to be constantly alert, always keeping that distant waggon in sight so I could react at once should Snell make a turning.

On this day the land looked desolate under a sweep of cold December air from the North Sea. It would have been lovely in summer, however, with charming water meadows freshened by pools and streams and much favoured by ducks. Splashes of colour were furnished by picturesque pink country cottages with yellow thatched roofs. Such scenes were well worth painting, and probably Constable had already done so. I had to keep a tight rein on such unseasonable fancies, however. Snell and his waggon required my constant attention. Just when I concluded we were going all the way to Ipswich, he made his turn.

Between Colchester and Ipswich, the sea made broad indentations at the mouths of the Rivers Stour, Orwell and the smaller Rosan. There were lesser indentations all along the coast marking the mouths of other inlets and creeks. Toward the sea, the land became marshy; but it was excellent for hay and livestock, and there were highly productive farms in the area. As we traveled eastward, the road became narrower, and there were villages rather than towns to thread our way through. Snell seemed to drive with his eyes set straight ahead. Perhaps his horses knew the route well enough to find their own way, and he was able to doze. In any event, he showed no awareness of being followed.

Finally the road veered to the right, and a town appeared on the high ground ahead of us. It was Great Helmwich, which Snell had used as his address in the inn register. A short distance to the north was Little Helmwich, a small fishing village located around the harbour where the River Rosan flowed into a narrow North Sea inlet. Snell drove straight through Great Helmwich, which had the usual clutter of shops on a drowsy High Street and a scattering of imposing old Georgian houses. Everything else—streets, houses, buildings—looked nondescript except for a charming group of thatched cottages on the outskirts.

Snell was well known there. Pedestrians waved or called greetings to him. Drivers he met saluted him with their whips, and he responded.

Beyond the town, the land seemed to be sliding down a gradual slope into the sea. There were creeks that probably were tidal inlets, and on the low marshy land, the rich crop of hay had already been cut. Low-lying pastures were laced with dykes for drainage.

Snell took another turning into a road that wound off toward the sea, and the taste of salt in the breeze warned me it must be nearby. When I reached the turning, I halted and looked after him doubtfully. For the past hour he had acted very much like a man headed for home and in a hurry to get there, and I had no desire to fetch up on his doorstep.

Before I could reach a decision, another waggon approached. The driver nodded at me and then, recognizing a stranger, pulled up his horses. "Looking for something?" he asked.

"Yes," I said with a smile. "I'm an estate agent. I'm looking for land to buy." Neither the horse and cart nor my dress were in character, but I took a chance on the uncritical hospitality and politeness with which rural people everywhere treat well-spoken strangers. I nodded in the direction Snell had taken. "Is there anything down that way worth seeing?"

"There's nothing in that direction but Abner Snell's farm," the driver said. "It's a good farm, but I'm sure it isn't for sale. Abner is getting on, but he has five boys to leave it to."

"Is it a prosperous farm?"

"All farms have good years and bad. This has been a good year, and Abner has a rare good crop of potatoes. His boys are hauling them to London—Abner says he gets a much better price that way. That's all right if you have five boys and can let one take the time to do that."

I asked him about other farms, and he answered politely. As far as he knew, none were for sale. He drove on, and I turned my cart and started back to Great Helmwich. First I had to find a telephone, and then I had to find a place to stay. My instinct told me I was likely to be there for some time.

The Snell family appeared to be completely above-board. Certainly it had made no attempt to conceal anything, and perhaps hauling potatoes all the way to London one waggon-load at a time really was a shrewd way to market them. Even so, the slats nailed to the bottom of the waggon had to be accounted for. If my deduction about their use was wrong, they still were an oddity, and Lady Sara's philosophy was to leave no oddity unturned.

The one public telephone in Great Helmwich was in the post office. It was almost too public for my purpose, but I had no choice. I called Lady Sara. I told her where I was and talked like a land agent, mentioning the farms I'd heard referred to—including that of Abner Snell, whose sons were hauling his potatoes to London.

"That's interesting," she said. "I recently encountered the name 'Snell' here in London. There's a warehouseman in Poplar who calls himself James Snell. He has the reputation of being a steady worker with no bad habits." She paused. "Great Helmwich. I believe my friend Lady Roulson has a country place somewhere nearby. She might be spending Christmas there."

I asked the post office assistant. She had overheard my land agent conversation, and she said, "Oh, but Lady Roulson would never sell. The estate has been in her family for centuries."

"How close to the coast is the Abner Snell farm?" Lady Sara asked.

"It may be right on it," I said. "I'll investigate that as soon as I get myself settled." The post office assistant was still listening, so I had to be more circumspect than usual. "This sounds like an excellent location for owlers," I said. Owlers were the famous smugglers of the Romney Marsh, so-called because they used the cry of an owl as a signal.

"Almost every place on the coast has at least a minor history of smuggling," Lady Sara said. "If you find an elderly citizen of Great Helmwich who is willing to talk, he will tell you all about smuggling and smugglers in olden times. No one will mention today's smugglers, of course, but none of that has anything to do with us. I'll explain when I see you. I'll send Rick and Charles to help you, and I'll arrive myself as soon as I can arrange a visit to Lady Roulson."

I asked her to have Rick or Charles pack some clothing for me. She would know what sort of clothing I meant. If I were to impersonate a prosperous estate agent, I would have to look the part. I promised to call back as soon as I had arranged for a place to stay.

The postmaster, a genial old fellow named Prout, let me study an Ordnance Survey map of the region, and I finally got the geography firmly in mind. Many of the names of the scattered towns and villages in the area were paired as "great" and "little." The River Rosan threaded its way across the land to a long, narrow inlet at the head of which Little Helmwich was located—a mere half mile from Great Helmwich.

"But it isn't much of a harbour," Mr. Prout said regretfully. "Once it was, I am told, but not these days—not with Harwich and Felixstowe nearby with an excellent harbour where the rivers Stour and Orwell meet the sea and the railway as well. The railway misses us, and the Little Helmwich harbour is suitable only for small boats. Also, the sands along this coast are tricky, and the Rosan keeps rearranging them. Local fishermen can keep track of that, but visiting captains would consider this a risky port of call even if the harbour were large enough and deep enough for them."

I asked about the locations of various farms, and Mr. Prout pointed them out to me. The Abner Snell farm fronted on the inlet close to the sea. There were various creeks crossing his land; probably they were filled to the brim at high tide. I considered the sand banks and decided I wouldn't want the job of trying to reach the Snell farm by ship. Apparently no one else would have wanted it, either. Mr. Prowse assured me there was only one channel, and it approximately followed the centre line of the inlet to the North Sea.

The coast had a gnawed look about it. I said as much, and Mr. Prout nodded wisely. "'Gnawed' is the word. The sea has been gnawing at this land for centuries. Further north, there was the coastal city of Dunwich, which dated back to Roman times and was a considerable place in the Middle Ages, with a good harbour, churches, a monastery, a town hall, a hospital, palaces, elaborate houses, even a mint. Now all of that has been taken by the sea—including the harbour, there's hardly anything left but a few ruins. Much more recently, Walton-on-the-Naze lost its old church to the sea. But—" He shrugged and added cheerfully, "If you're thinking of investing in land hereabouts, Great Helmwich should be safe for another thousand years or so."

I thanked him and went to see about my lodging.

Great Helmwich had an inn appropriately called the Ship and Plough, a tribute to the formerly prosperous harbour and the presently prosperous surrounding farms. I engaged rooms for myself and two associates who would be joining me on the morrow, identifying myself as an estate agent in the inn's register. I saw that my cart and horse were looked after, and then I set out to learn what I could about Great Helmwich.

CHAPTER 17

The shops were displaying lavish Christmas plumage, with stars formed of gas jets over their doors and evergreen branches trimming their windows. I introduced myself as a visiting estate agent, and the shopkeepers greeted me enthusiastically and told me as much as they knew about land around Great Helmwich. Like those I had talked with in Pangstead when I was investigating the Reverend Theobald Eynon, the possibility of money coming into the community from outside delighted them, and they had immediate visions of a "great house" that would provide lavish entertainments for titled guests, purchasing all of its supplies locally. I carefully said nothing to contradict this.

There was Harlock the apothecary, a brisk, clean-shaven man who was welcoming the Christmas season with a window display in which jars of various colours were arranged to spell the message "Merry Christmas." He wore a frock coat at work to emphasize his professional standing, and his shop was an enchanting curiosity trove of remarkable odds and ends. Every kind of medicine, or herb, or medical appliance was intermingled with toothbrushes, dog pills, flea powders, and curry-combs. Blake, the local constable, told me in seeming seriousness that the same had been true of Harlock's predecessor, and his predecessor's predecessor, and so on back into time. None of them had ever discarded anything. If I searched the shop diligently enough, he said, I would be certain to find a chastity belt. There was no dentist in Great Helmwich, and Harlock was considered a highly skilled drawer of teeth.

When, in our discussion of available land, I chanced to mention Abner Snell's farm, Harlock shook his head emphatically. "No. Abner has his boys to think of, and the farm is doing well. He's the rare old dog who's always learning new tricks. Hauls his potatoes to London to sell—no one else in these parts would think of doing something like that. Abner isn't selling land, he's buying it. Bought a piece of the neighbouring farm from Ev Atter last year and built a house on it for his eldest son, John."

Next-door was Musard, the tailor. Tall and lank, he spent his day perched cross-legged on a counter. He could have been more prosperous if he had done poorer work; his clothes lasted forever, I was told. His salute to the Christmas season was a window decorated with Japanese lanterns. He gave me the names of several farmers who might be willing to sell—Abner Snell wasn't mentioned—and I learned later that all of them were customers who were slow in settling their accounts.

Further along the street was Rucker's confectionery shop, whose window featured delicious-looking jam puffs arranged around a display of Christmas cakes. Just beyond it was Pateman the draper, who had spelled out his Christmas message with spools of thread. His shop was furnished with shining wood counters, and there were gloves and reels of ribbon dangling from overhead rods as well as fat rolls of goods on rollers, but a change carrier such as I had admired in London shops was lacking.

Pateman looked a bit of a dandy despite his fifty odd years—neatly dressed with a natty moustache and a curl in his hair that almost certainly was not natural. He gave the impression of being something of a ladies' man, and his conversation reflected the fact that he dealt almost exclusively with the women of Great Helmwich. He didn't say Abner Snell wouldn't sell his farm. He said Lila Snell would never let him sell it.

Across the street was Ablett the grocer, whose window was welcoming the Christmas season and promoting his business at the same time with the motto "Eat, Drink, and be Merry!" This was surrounded by a display of delicacies with little cardboard images of Father Christmas peeping out between sugar mice. Ablett was a gaunt, bald man seventy-six years old, and he was proud enough of that fact to tell it to a stranger in the second sentence he spoke. He thought highly of the Snells. "Pay their bills promptly," he said. "Abner has been through some hard times, though. Several of his boys went away to sea because there didn't seem to be any future for them here, and even three, four years ago there were rumours he might lose the farm. But he got things straightened out, paid all his back bills, and now he's doing real well. I don't think he would sell for any price."

At the other end of the High Street was the ornate shop of Layfield the butcher, whose window featured a glazed pig's head with an apple in its mouth, the whole decorated with coloured icing. The shop's interior was festooned with hanging geese and porkers, and a waggon backed up to the yard entrance was unloading Christmas bullocks destined for the community's yule feasts—to the considerable interest of passers-by.

Because most farmers butchered their own meat, Layfield knew little about the Snell family, but Frearson, the elderly blacksmith who had his shop across the street, knew everything about every farmer in the area. Other tradesmen could tell you which farmers weren't paying their bills; Frearson knew why—which had been unlucky, which were lazy, and which were merely poor farmers. When I asked him about available land, he recited a round dozen farms that were not paying and whose owners might be amenable to an offer.

He didn't mention Abner Snell. When I did, he shook his head firmly. "Abner is doing well, now. I don't think he would sell. A few years back he went through some tough times, but that's all behind him. Abner's problem was never laziness—he and all of his boys are hard workers. Abner tends to be reckless. Always wants to try something new—new crops, new breeds of animals, newfangled methods for this or that. Sometimes they work. More often than not, the time-tested ways prove best. Once he lost his whole crop and was in deep trouble. He got around it, but it was catch and do for a time. I don't suppose he learned a thing."

I continued to make the rounds, talking with anyone willing to spare me a few minutes: the baker, who delivered his own bread from a cart pulled by a goat; two old ladies who kept the Penny Bazaar, which had a window full of dolls and toy soldiers; the proprietor of the Forge and Hammer, a pub near the blacksmith shop; the cobbler; the harness maker. There also were cottage industries—a woman who caned chairs; several seamstresses; a locksmith; a milkman who made his round with a hand churn mounted on two large wheels.

Such was Great Helmwich. I liked it at once, and I quickly determined that no one in town was aware of any untoward doings out at the Abner Snell farm. Snell was a hardworking farmer who had survived good years and bad, raised a family, and made trouble for no one. He was a withdrawn sort of person, but perhaps his age and frail physical condition contributed to that. His sons were friendly enough. Three of them were married; the eldest, John, had built a home for his own family on the new land his father had bought, and the other married sons were talking about doing the same. Four of the five sons had gone to sea for a spell—something common enough among boys growing up near the coast—but they quickly learned that a sailor's life was no easier than a farmer's life, and now all four were back home. When I mentioned meeting one of them in London recently, the response was, "Ah—that'll be them potatoes. Abner has a rare good crop this year, and his boys are always driving off to London to market a load."

The only exceptional thing about the Snells seemed to be their astuteness in marketing potatoes in London. The previous year they'd done the same with an excellent crop of turnips. Sometimes, if they were able to make room on the waggon, they obliged neighbouring farmers who had a surplus to dispose of.

Before the post office closed, I telephoned Lady Sara again, gave her my address, and cautiously summarized what I had learned. She informed me that Rick and Charles would take the train to Colchester early next morning, and each of them would hire a horse and trap there and drive to Great Helmwich.

"I'm not sure I'll have anything for them to do," I said.

"They already know what to do," Lady Sara said. "I've discussed it with them." She added, "I'm sorry we have to be occupied with a case in East Anglia when there is unfinished work in London, but it now looks as though we have a capital matter to deal with there." This was the first suggestion I'd had that the Snells were involved in crimes far more serious than wine stealing. She silenced me when I tried to ask for more information; obviously it was not a proper subject to discuss on the telephone.

Walking back to the inn, I was astonished to recognize a familiar figure on the pavement just ahead of me. It was Malcolm Gavin, the London trader who had always looked like a pirate to me. In Great Helmwich, with his swashbuckling figure and drooping moustaches, he looked even more like a pirate. He was wearing an old-fashioned cloak with a shoulder cape, and he had a country cap perched on his head.

I had carefully kept out of sight when I investigated him in London, so I had no hesitation in following him about boldly. It came as no surprise that he was staying at the inn—there was only one. I ate my dinner at the table next to his and was completely ignored by him. The following morning, I was up early and waiting for him when he finally appeared. He took a leisurely breakfast, after which I followed him to Little Helmwich—he in a hired trap and me in my cart.

As Postmaster Prout had remarked, the harbour at Little Helmwich was a small one, and the port had been slowly decaying for many years. It was home to a small group of fishing smacks that worked the North Sea for herring and sole or dredged for succulent east coast oysters. There also were a few barges laden with timber and general goods for local trade. The growing interest in pleasure boats had brought prosperity to many a moribund seaside community, but the harbour at Little Helmwich was far too small and the channel from the sea too dangerous. Its principal enterprises were pubs (four) and fishmongers (two). One of the pub owners sold a few groceries to residents who couldn't spare the time to shop in Great Helmwich.

I watched Malcolm Gavin board two of the barges, apparently to inspect them. He conferred at length with their captains. Then he drove off in a northerly direction, perhaps to call at other ports. I couldn't follow him because Rick and Charles were to arrive shortly, and we had the unfinished business of the Snell family to take care of.

I made a few enquiries before I left the port—not about Abner Snell, but about his sons who had gone to sea. They were highly thought of.

Rick Allward and Charler Tupper arrived before noon, driving their hired horses and traps. They brought the clothing I had requested, three cameras, and a quantity of roll film.

They also brought the most recent results of the enquiries concerning the Poplar Produce Company. The firm had occupied the Wells Street building for more than three years, selling assorted vegetables when available. Lady Sara suspected it of buying from local markets when the East Anglia farm's supply was exhausted and selling at cost as a continuing cover for the wine business. She also thought the Snells may have distributed wine from some other address before they thought of using the produce business as cover.

No one had noticed wine being delivered there—but then, no one had noticed it being hauled away, either, in Jem Sutter's van. Anything illicit had been loaded or unloaded inside. A careful inspection of the premises after hours had discovered intriguing modifications to the old building— bars on windows, stout new doors, and good quality locks.

The cameras were supposed to give us an aura of professionalism in our masquerade as estate agents. We used both traps to travel widely about the countryside, asking questions of all we met, informing anyone who would listen of our interest in buying property, pretending to take numerous photographs, and making ourselves as conspicuous as possible. Our hope was that word of this activity would get back to Abner Snell before we called on him at the end of the day.

All of our film was reserved for the Snell farm, but I insisted on stopping for a real photograph of the picturesque, thatched roof cottages when we passed them. Dr. Edmund Eubank, the parish's elderly, cantankerous, and much-loved physician, happened by and wanted to know what the devil I thought I was doing. When I waxed poetic about the beauties of the scene, the good doctor snorted.

"Why don't you photograph the dampness, the lack of drains, the leaky roofs, the rat-infested walls, and the poverty—especially the poverty. Those families are always short of food and poorly clothed. Sometimes the children eat nothing but bread and jam for weeks on end and feel fortunate to have the jam. Believe you me, there is nothing picturesque or beautiful about that."

By late afternoon, we felt ready to confront Abner Snell. As soon as we had his farm buildings in sight, Charles turned his trap aside, tied his horse, and began taking pictures. He was to circle widely and photograph the farm as extensively as possible.

Rick and I drove on and arrived, in a businesslike way, at Abner Snell's front door. We got out; Rick immediately began taking pictures while I approached the house.

It was a sturdy old timber-framed building, and the weather-boarded barn, built entirely from wood, was immense, dating from a time when every farm had to have an enclosed threshing floor. Some barns had several, and this one looked large enough to have three or more. Around the perimeter of a rectangle, whose ends were formed by the house and the barn, there were other buildings, also of wood—storage and animal sheds. The wood surprised me. I learned only later that farms near that coast were often constructed of wood salvaged from the frequent maritime disasters in the neighbourhood. Old planks, beams, and timbers became the farmer's studs, joists, and wall-boards.

Abner Snell bounded out and confronted me before I reached the door. He demanded, "Whatcha want?"

I introduced myself and began my talk about putting together a country estate for a rich and titled client. Snell interrupted me. He had just noticed Rick at work with his camera.

"What's he doin'?"

I started over again, explaining that photographs were necessary so the rich and titled client could use them to form his decision.

Snell interruped a second time. He pointed a trembling finger. "Get!"

I attempted to remonstrate; suddenly he whistled shrilly, and in an instant we were surrounded by dogs.

"I heard about you," he growled. "Nothin' here is for sale. Get, or I'll set the dogs on you."

He meant it. It is a true saying there is no mistaking a tyrant on his own dung heap. I retreated to the trap; he and the dogs followed. Rick had already taken in the situation and was waiting for me. As we drove off, I noticed that the house's door and windows were filled with faces—women and children and at least two other adult males who were watching our departure.

Charles had photographed the farm as well as he could from a distance and was waiting for us. The three of us left together.

Our elaborate scheme had gone for naught. I could have got myself run off the farm just as effectively the day before with no preparation at all.

We still had work to do. The neighbouring farmers realized they had nothing to lose by letting us use our cameras, and they made us welcome. If the wealthy nobleman we represented decided to make them an offer, they still had the option of accepting or refusing.

So we took numerous photographs, but all of them were views of the Snell farm seen from a distance. Unfortunately, we had no notion at all of what we were trying to accomplish. We knew nothing about farming, and one farm in winter, with fallow fields, hayricks, land ploughed and harrowed for winter planting, and cattle feeding on stubble, looked just like another. When we finished, Charles left with the exposed film. A Colchester chemist Lady Sara knew would develop it and make enlarged prints immediately.

That evening Rick and I had visitors at the Ship and Plough—Lady Sara and Lady Roulson. The awed landlord gave us the use of his private parlour for a conference. I had hoped to have something more positive to report than my total failure at the Abner Snell farm, but Lady Sara had a reassuring way of converting failures into successes.

Lady Roulson was a florid, bosomy woman of about fifty who was dressed in men's clothing. She was the widow of a mere knight, the lowest of the titled ranks, but that meant little in her case because she was wealthy enough to do whatever she chose. At a time when it was still a scandal for women to wear trousers when they went riding, Lady Roulson wore them whenever she felt like it, riding or no. She also smoked cigars, eschewed the traditional lady's side-saddle or any saddle at all when she rode, and, with suitable provocation, swore like a docker. She admired Lady Sara immensely and at the same time was jealous of her. Lady Sara achieved all of the freedom Lady Roulson aspired for, but Lady Sara did it while remaining every bit as lady-like as a situation called for and commanding everyone's respect. She regarded Lady Roulson with affectionate amusement.

Lady Roulson knew the surrounding country and its people intimately. She took part in every local celebration, organized activities for charity, helped the poor, nursed the sick, and offered a helping hand to anyone who deserved one. She knew all about everyone, including the Abner Snell family.

I first described my encounter with the pirate, Malcolm Gavin, in Great Helmwich's High Street and his subsequent errand to Little Helmwich.

"Several of the London traders have East Anglian connections," she said. "The Reverend Theobald Eynon sometimes trades pulpits for a week or two with the Vicar of Far Vanley, who is an old school chum. That is only ten miles from Great Helmwich. Sir Langley Jardin's wife came from Harwich, and her family is prominent there. Sir James Furner goes to Norfolk each winter to shoot geese. Malcolm Gavin operates a fleet of barges, and his business here is certainly legitimate. All of that is coincidental. I feel certain that the wine has nothing to do with the river thefts. I also feel certain that the wine wasn't smuggled. Rather, it was smuggled, but it was stolen first."

"How can you know?" I asked.

"Think! There would be no tariff on smuggled wine, but the smugglers would still have to buy it on the continent for its normal price. Not only would they be fully aware of its value, but they certainly couldn't sell it for fifteen shillings the dozen without losing money. The wine was stolen, but not in London, and it was stolen by someone who doesn't know much about wine. Remember what Jasper Wightman said about the stolen tobacco—whoever was selling it knew its value and priced it accordingly. If the river thieves were selling the stolen wine, the price would reflect its true value. Also, if they wanted to move wine from East Anglia to London, they certainly wouldn't do it one waggon-load at a time disguised as potatoes. This is an entirely different group of thieves—but they are thieves, and they are guilty of far worse crimes than theft, and we must put a stop to crime wherever we encounter it. Tell us about the Snell farm."

The two of them listened attentively to my description of our futile attempts to make ourselves acquainted with it. Lady Sara frowned when I mentioned the pack of dogs and the larger pack of humans.

"That is what I was afraid of. I had hoped to contrive some means of approaching the farm buildings by stealth, but obviously this would be impossible. I have no doubt the wine is stored there, but it will be difficult to prove if we don't have access to the premises."

"I find all of this hard to comprehend," Lady Roulson announced. "Abner has always been headstrong. He resents having anyone try to tell him anything, but he is law-abiding as anyone else in these parts. The law gets winked at in a lot of ways by country people, but you are imputing serious crimes to him and to his entire family. If anyone else had told me, I wouldn't have believed it."

"You can't know a man well until you have seen how he reacts to failure," Lady Sara said. "Snell was about to lose everything. This is how he reacted, but it may have been his sons' idea, rather than his, and apart from the fact that one of the sons is disposing of the booty in London, we still haven't a scrap of evidence."

Charles arrived in the nick of time with the finished photographs. Lady Sara and Lady Roulson studied them.

"These old buildings look sturdy enough to serve as a fort if the Snells decide to fight," Lady Sara observed. "Let's hope it doesn't come to that. We first must discover the route by which the wine reaches the farm. Of course it is arriving by ship, but the buildings are at the extreme opposite end of the farm from the water. The Snells certainly wouldn't dump an entire shipload of wine casks on the shore to be disposed of at their leisure. People would notice them and talk. On the other hand, moving those casks all that distance across fields is more than a night's work even for six men. I'm curious about this hayrick. Doesn't it look unusually large?"

Lady Roulson scowled at the photograph. "Hard to say—there's nothing in the picture to compare it with."

"They've caught it in three other photographs," Lady Sara said.

Lady Roulson put the photographs side by side. "You think there is something odd about that hayrick?"

"I do. Not only is it unusually large, but it is in an awkward place. Why would a farmer put a hayrick on low ground in a remote corner of a farm?"

"I wouldn't," Lady Roulson said. "But what a farmer has in mind sometimes isn't immediately evident."

"I'm searching for the key to a puzzle," Lady Sara said impatiently. "The hayrick is the only thing that fits."

"Then we will have a look at it," Lady Roulson said matter-of-factly. "Since we have to take soundings anyway, we might as well do both at once."

She turned to Charles, Rick, and me. "The three of you are to lunch with me tomorrow. Afterward, we will take soundings in the inlet to see whether there has been secret dredging to give a deep water ship passage to the farm. Also, we will look at the hayrick."

"We will need directions for finding your house, my lady," I told her.

"I will send a boat for you. Of course."

I started to protest, but she silenced me with a gesture. "The road is terrible—through marshes and over rickety bridges. The boat is much quicker and far more comfortable. Shall we say—eleven-thirty at the harbour pier?"

"Yes, my lady," I agreed. "Eleven-thirty at the harbour pier." She was only the widow of a knight, but it was obvious that in this small corner of England she wielded the full authority of a duchess.

CHAPTER 18

Lady Roulson sent a large dinghy for us, rowed by servants who obviously were experienced watermen, and they took us at high speed along the north shore of the inlet to Lady Roulson's pier. It was a pleasantly sunny day despite the cold wind off the North Sea. The tide was going out, and a broad expanse of mud lined the shore, but there was enough water at the end of the pier to float the dinghy. Lady Roulson's country home was a splendid old moated farmhouse, a pseudo castle with a turret at each corner. It was roofed with pantiles—tiles imported from Holland at some forgotten period of history and used extensively in eastern England. There was a broad lawn stretching down to the water, and, off to one side, an unpopulated duck pond and a tennis court. In the rear was a large stable. Lady Roulson was a famous horsewoman.

She couldn't have greeted us more warmly if we had been minor peers ourselves. For the moment we were her guests, and, whatever our pedigrees, she belonged to that noble rural tradition that knew only one way to treat a guest—nobly.

There was one other guest present. Lady Roulson introduced him to us as Lieutenant Juster, a naval officer. He was a man about thirty, tall and muscular, and he looked as though he climbed trees for practice when there were no masts available.

That was before Lady Roulson offered him one of her cigars. Afterward, he took on an unhealthy greenish tint and acted seasick. Charles, Rick, and I declined cigars on the grounds that we didn't smoke, which Lady Roulson clearly considered an inadequate excuse. She suggested cigarettes and then snuff before she decided to drop the matter.

We had what Lady Roulson called a small luncheon. It consisted of roast beef, leg of lamb, pork pie, mutton chops, veal cutlets, three kinds of fish, oyster pie, and assorted vegetable dishes, all fortified with a quantity of breads, buns, and crumpets and followed by a sideboard that groaned under the weight of cakes, puddings, tarts, muffins, and fruits. Each phase of the meal was marked off with ale or wine. While we ate, Lady Roulson and Lady Sara talked about horses. From their own expertise, Rick and Charles were able to contribute occasional remarks about methods of breeding, breaking, and training horses in the Midlands. The naval lieutenant and I, having nothing to say, occupied ourselves with eating. When, immediately after the luncheon, Lady Sara called a strategy session, I felt almost too comatose to participate, and Lieutenant Juster had difficulty removing himself from the table.

Lady Sara gave me a sympathetic look. "Any meal with Lady Roulson is likely to be a feast," she said. Then she added, "I hope Lieutenant Juster is able to function. He has been sent to help us by the Admiralty."

"Then it is a case of smuggling," I exclaimed.

She shook her head. "The Snells are guilty of far worse crimes than that, and they committed them on the high seas, which explains the Admiralty's interest."

The lieutenant studied the photographs of the Snell farm like a ship's captain scowling at foul weather. I suspected he was having difficulty focusing his thoughts after all that food and wine. "Were you thinking of a raid?" he asked finally.

"That can be decided later," Lady Sara said. "First we must find out what the problem is."

Lady Roulson made certain all of us were dressed warmly enough for an excursion on the chill North Sea waters. Then Lady Sara led the way down to the pier and got everyone arranged in the dingy to her satisfaction. Rick and Charles sat amidships, each with a pair of oars; Lady Roulson and I took the bow, she with a chart and me with a lead line, a contrivance I had never used before; Lady Sara and the lieutenant sat in the stern with Lady Sara handling the tiller. There was a small mast with a single sail, but we kept the sail furled. Oars were best for the kind of mission Lady Sara had planned.

Lady Roulson's dignified butler handed a large hamper aboard just before we started. It contained a picnic meal, but that was only for show in case we were challenged. Certainly none of us felt like eating. More to the point, Lady Roulson passed out revolvers to all of us and concealed two rifles under the decking at the bow.

She addressed the lieutenant. "What do we do if we are fired upon?"

"Over the side," the lieutenant said, "with the boat between us and wherever the bullets are coming from."

"Can everyone swim?" Lady Roulson asked. "Right enough. Let's go."

The sea inlet was a hundred yards wide at Lady Roulson's estate. Inland, it gradually narrowed until it reached the mouth of the River Rosan at Little Helmwich. In the other direction, after a sharp bend, its width increased until it became difficult to say at what point one left the inlet and moved into the North Sea.

With only a single, narrow channel deep enough for navigation, the inlet was too hazardous for coasting ships, though the captains of the small fishing boats harbouring at Little Helmwich knew it well and had no difficulties.

We headed east with Rick and Charles maintaining a steady but leisurely pace. Lady Roulson sat poised with the chart in her lap and a pencil in her hand. Lady Sara had that look of intense concentration she always wore when she was in close pursuit of law violators. Lieutenant Juster kept looking about him as though considering the best way to maneuver two battleships of the Royal Sovereign class in that narrow inlet. When we reached the point where the inlet opened widely to the sea, we turned south. For some reason comprehensible only to sailors, the land about us was considered the north side of the mouth of the river Thames, even though that stream was as remote and invisible as the coast of Holland.

We crossed the inlet slowly with me working the lead line—awkwardly, at first, and then, with practice, a bit less awkwardly—and Lady Roulson recording my findings on her chart. The profile of the inlet's bottom was precisely as expected. It had a channel of moderate depth in the centre, and it rapidly became shallow toward either shore.

Then we turned inland and moved quietly along the southern shore. Again the profile was as expected. No one had been secretly dredging a channel to make one of the tidal creeks navigable. Beyond mud-flats that were already diminishing as the tide turned, the shore was overgrown with a tangle of shrubs. Several creeks wound their way through the flats. At high tide, seawater would fill them far inland. We passed by the first; the second looked broad enough to be a small river.

"Possible," Lady Sara murmured. "Definitely possible."

But we passed it by, also, to see what the other possibilities were. We scrutinized two other creeks that meandered across the Snell farm, but neither of them interested Lady Sara, so we turned back for another look at the one she had called possible. I continued to work the lead line as she pointed the dinghy into it. There was no sign of dredging, but the creek had washed a modest channel of its own through the mudbanks. With me taking repeated soundings, we moved cautiously between overgrown banks that were a tangle of brushwood and young trees until we rounded a bend and suddenly came upon shallow water. Lady Sara turned the dinghy toward the bank, where a stretch of the brushwood had been cut away.

"Obviously they didn't bring a sea-going ship in here," she remarked. "Is there enough water for a heavily laden gig or long-boat?"

"They might want a bit more than this just to be sure," the lieutenant said. "In another hour they would have no problem at all."

Lady Sara stood up. "You can see where planks were laid to make it easier to move the casks—probably in barrows. They would want to move the wine to a place of concealment quickly, and there's the hayrick, twenty feet away. Once the casks were safely out of sight, they could take their time moving them to the farm."

It looked to me like a logical enough place for a hayrick. The field was a hayfield with the year's crop recently cut. Lady Roulson scrutinized it with a scowl.

"You are right, dear. It is an odd place for a hayrick, and that isn't hay from this year or even last year. It has been there at least three years. Why pile up hay in this damp place and not use it? They should have taken it to a pasture on higher ground or to the farm for storage."

"Odd that it has held its shape so well," Lady Sara said. "We'll have a look. Do you have a yarn ready in case someone sees us?"

"Leave that to me. I know all of these people."

Lady Sara asked me to accompany her. We circled the hayrick widely and then approached it from the rear where we couldn't be observed from the distant farm buildings. Back at the dinghy, Lady Roulson was acting as sentry, peering about alertly with a hand shading her eyes.

As we came closer to the hayrick, I could see that the hay was old and beaten down by the weather. We moved around it slowly, pausing frequently while Lady Sara worked her hand into the hay.

"There'll be an entrance somewhere," she explained. "Probably on the side nearest the creek."

We had moved halfway around it and were easily visible from the farm when she suddenly announced, "Here's the door."

It had a large padlock on it. The mechanism was simple, and I had it picked in an instant. As the door swung open, a section of the hayrick swung open with it. Lady Sara darted inside; I remained in the opening, looking about warily. I heard her strike a vesta, and I turned just in time to catch a glimpse of the interior before she blew it out. The hayrick had been built around and over a building made of poles and slats. The building was empty.

Lady Sara emerged at once; I closed the door and snapped the padlock, and we quickly walked away. We had almost reached the boat when a man's voice bellowed.

Abner Snell came striding toward us with three dogs at his heels. He carried some kind of gun with a long barrel—perhaps a fowling piece. Since he already had warned me off his place, I felt apprehensive.

I need not have worried. Lady Roulson was out of the boat in a flash and striding toward him. "Hello Abner," she called.

He came to a halt. "Oh. Hello, Lady Roulson."

"I had no idea we'd got this far west. We were headed for a picnic on the shore, but one thing led to another. How do we get to Trigg's meadow?"

"That's the creek east of here," Snell said. "There's only one."

"Right. We cut directly across the inlet and hit the wrong creek. Sorry to have bothered you. Give my regards to Lila."

She returned to the dinghy, and we backed slowly down the creek to the inlet. Snell followed along. It was a tense moment. If the Snells really were murderers, and if they thought we had found them out, they wouldn't hesitate to do it again. Lieutenant Juster had talked nonchalantly about putting the boat between us and wherever the bullets were coming from, which sounded well enough in theory, but with us trapped in the creek, Abner Snell and his five sons could easily shoot from either side.

Nothing happened, but Abner continued to follow until we reached the inlet, and he stood watching us when we turned east.

We quickly picked up speed, but no one said anything. Sound carries well over water, and for all we knew, Snell was continuing to follow us along the shore. When we found the right creek, we thought it wise to go through the motions of having a picnic, hungry or no. We carried the picnic hamper to a short stretch of sandy beach and pretended to eat. It was just as well that we did so. We caught a glimpse of a skiff nosing along the shore of the inlet. Whoever was in it saw us about the same time we sighted it. It turned back before it reached open water and vanished from our sight. A few minutes later, Lady Roulson thought she saw someone—probably Abner Snell—playing Red Indian and skulking behind bushes and trees. He, too, turned back as soon as he saw what we were doing.

We didn't discuss the hayrick until we were safely back at Lady Roulson's house.

"What do you make of it?" Lieutenant Juster asked Lady Sara.

"Obviously the wine was brought to the hayrick in small boats," she said. "Would the Snells have had any problem anchoring a schooner off-shore at night while they unloaded it?"

"Not in good weather. Since they know the sandbanks perfectly, they could bring it in closer than most ships would dare to come. They wouldn't even have to set riding lights—nothing would be running into them there."

"Then they unloaded the cargo into small boats, brought it up the creek, and got it out of sight quickly by hiding it in the fake hayrick. Could five boys and the father unload a ship in a single night?"

"If they couldn't, they could drop down to the Channel, coast until it was time to turn back, and finish the job the next night," Lieutenant Juster said.

"Then that's what they did," Lady Sara said. "Once they had the wine hidden in the hayrick, they could take their time moving it to the farm—concealed under loads of hay during the day or openly at night. It's their farm, and they have plenty of dogs to keep intruders away. They probably have a huge cellar under the farmhouse where they store the wine. This takes care of every problem except one. They still had to dispose of the ship. Would they sink it?"

"Why sink a valuable ship?" the lieutenant asked. "They could paint a new name on it and sail it over to Walcheren or the Frisian Islands, where there are markets for ships with uncertain pedigrees—or so I've heard."

"Then they picked up a chunk of cash for each ship they stole, and they are gradually building a market in London for the cargoes of wine. The wine costs them nothing to begin with, so they probably clear a pound on every two dozen bottles. They may be selling a hundred dozen a week, which gives them a clear profit of fifty pounds—added to what they gain from selling the ships. No wonder Adam Snell has paid off all of the notes on his farm and begun to add land and new buildings."

"But where are they getting the ships?" I asked.

"That is the tragedy. There is an elderly wine merchant in Edinburgh—head of a venerable firm—who believes firmly that the quality of wine is improved when it is transported in small sailing ships. The wave action keeps the wine sloshing in the casks. He imports his own wines in sufficient quantity to make up the entire cargo of such a ship. During recent years, four of these ships have disappeared."

"Without a trace?" I asked.

"Apparently without a trace. All four were written off as having sunk. There weren't any storms to account for it, but the east coast of England can be treacherous enough even in good weather, especially for sailing ships. It isn't unusual to have two or three hundred ships lost each year between the Thames and the Wash, which includes this stretch of coast, so no one thought anything unusual about a small wine schooner vanishing every year or two.

"But after the last loss, a nude body washed up on the coast of Belgium. It was a middle-aged man who'd had his throat cut. By coincidence, he was recognized. He was born and grew up in the vicinity. It was the captain of a missing wine ship. Four of the Snell brothers are former seamen. My theory is that they signed on those missing ships under assumed names. They would make up the entire crew of a small cargo ship. Picking their time, they would murder the captain and mate, throw their nude bodies overboard, bring the ship here at night on a favourable tide, unload her, bring her back the next night if necessary to finish the unloading, and then sail her to wherever they could get a good price for her. Then they would return to the farm."

I tried to envisage a quiet, clannish East Anglian farm family deliberately setting out on a program of mutiny and murder to recoup its fortunes. I found the notion staggering.

"It would take at least a rudimentary knowledge of the wine business to operate as they do," I said. "Certainly they didn't acquire that in Great Helmwich."

"Of course not. One of the Snell sons worked for a wine merchant in London before he went to sea. Obviously he didn't learn much about the quality of wines, but he learned the rudiments of handling them, and gluing labels on bottles, and filling bottles from casks. Probably he picked up a smattering of information about marketing them. Then all he had to do was build a list of small, independent wine merchants like Seth Beaton, collect their orders and money once a week, and arrange for the deliveries. Chief Inspector Mewer has found the firm that printed the wine labels for them and also the firm that sells bottles to them. Of course those four shiploads contained more than three varieties of wine, but the Snell brothers probably pay little attention to which wine goes with which label. At that price, their customers aren't likely to complain as long as all of the wines are of good quality. Their list of agents is growing rapidly—and so is the amount of wine they sell. I wonder how long it will be before they need another shipload."

I shuddered. Probably all of us did. The combination of cold-blooded murder and thievery, repeatedly carried out, is fortunately rare in England.

"The question is how to put a stop to it with so little evidence," Lady Sara said. "Chief Inspector Mewer is coming this evening. We should be able to contrive something."

CHAPTER 19

The Chief Inspector had outfitted himself for the country. He was wearing a deerstalker and brightly checked plus-fours. If he intended these as a disguise, they were a great success. No one could possibly have suspected him of being a police officer. Unfortunately, no one could have failed to notice him, either, wherever he went.

"I had a conference with Rear Admiral Gossard, my lady," he said to Lady Sara after Lady Roulson had made him welcome. "Even though the ships involved were foreign, the Admiralty is most anxious to have this matter successfully resolved—especially since the culprits seem to have been English."

"The Admiralty takes an understandably dim view of mutiny and murder on the high seas," Lady Sara murmured.

"To be sure, but it isn't clear to me just where I come into this. I assumed I was to act as your liaison with the local police, but I talked with an inspector in Colchester, and he knew even less than I do. What do we have to work with?"

"Very little except an impeccable chain of logic."

"No evidence?"

"Nothing as specific as we would like. We will have to contrive something."

The Chief Inspector scowled.

"The only things required are a little acting and a few lies," Lady Sara said lightly. "One of the Snell brothers is due to take another load of potatoes—or turnips, or vegetable marrows, or whatever—to London any day now. He makes this trip weekly but not always on the same day. He travels as far as the Boot and Slipper, on the other side of Ingatestone, and stays there overnight. He goes on to London the next day, unloads, and returns as far as the Boot and Slipper for another overnight stay on his way home. Obviously this is how the wine gets to London. The heaping load of vegetables conceals a considerable waggon-load of wine casks. Can you arrange an announcement tonight that a vicious murderer has escaped from Her Majesty's Prison in Chelmsford and may be headed for the coast in an attempt to make his way out of the country?"

The Chief Inspector gazed at her open-mouthed. "What good would that do?"

"Tomorrow, it will be reported that the escaped murderer has been seen in the vicinity of Colchester and may soon be passing through this neighbourhood. Everyone will be asked to be on the lookout for him. Describe him any way you like. The state of alert will be maintained until John Snell heads for London with his waggon-load of vegetables. The local constabulary will stop the waggon at a properly secluded place and insist that it be unloaded. A heaped waggon-load of vegetables is an ideal place for an escaped prisoner to hide, especially if he has changed his mind and decided to make for London—or so the constables will explain when Snell protests heatedly. If they find casks of wine under the potatoes, as we expect, they will take no official notice of them. It is a man they are searching for. Actually, they will count the casks carefully and look for distinguishing marks on them. Then, having satisfied themselves that the casks are too small to contain the escaped prisoner, they will apologize, carefully reload the vegetables, and allow Snell to proceed to London."

"So what does all that accomplish?" Chief Inspector Mewer demanded.

"That waggon is of critical importance. It connects the farm, which is the source of the stolen wine, with the Poplar Produce Company, in London, from which the wine is distributed. A number of witnesses will have seen wine casks hidden in the waggon and be able to describe them. Their testimony will be evidence enough to obtain warrants to search both the Snell farm and the produce company."

"I see," Chief Inspector Mewer said, but his tone indicated that he did not see at all. Not only did he consider Lady Sara's approach to detective work to be unladylike, but she made of it a job not quite suitable for a gentleman, and he resented that. "Do you mean, my lady, that you are willing to terrorize the countryside with a false report about an escaped murderer just to get evidence about a few casks of wine?"

"Didn't the Admiralty tell you how many murders have been committed by the wine thieves? If we don't secure evidence for a warrant and put a stop to this business, there certainly will be more murders. The countryside won't be terrorized for long. As soon as the Snell waggon has been inspected, you can circulate a notice that the escaped murderer has been recaptured. And as soon as we can obtain warrants, we will set about capturing the Snells, who are as cold-blooded a gang of murderers as any you have encountered in London."

"Why all the pother about reloading the waggon and letting Snell proceed?" the Chief Inspector demanded. "Why not just arrest the bloke and then go get the others?"

"That might work in London but not here. As we have found out, anyone setting foot on that farm is carefully scrutinized. A squad of police would be met by bullets, and I don't want casualties. The Snells know there are ropes waiting for them, and if cornered, they will fight rather than surrender. It would be foolhardy to approach the Snell property without a proper warrant and sufficient force to handle any eventuality. Even in London, where customers are coming and going all the time, it would be better to choose a moment when James Snell is fully occupied. The best time for a raid will be shortly after his brother has arrived with another waggon-load of wine. Then both men will be working to unload it quickly, and they won't notice what is happening until it is too late."

The Chief Inspector's face was a study. It was slowing dawning on him that he now was in the position of having to take orders from Lady Sara. With the Admiralty backing her so emphatically, he had no choice but to do what she asked. He left for a conference with local police about the notice concerning a fictitious escaped murderer. Rick, Charles, and I went back to Great Helmwich to circulate the notice on our own. I called at all of the shops in the High Street. Rick and Charles made the rounds of the farmers they had met and arranged for one of them to inform the Snells.

On the morrow, we made the rounds again to warn everyone that the escaped murderer had been seen only a few miles away. The constables placed a guard around the harbour, supposedly to prevent him from stealing a boat. It was all very realistic, and the good citizens of both Great and Little Helmwich talked of nothing else.

The following morning we watched—from a carefully chosen hiding place in some shrubbery along the road—while a group of constables halted John Snell's waggon and insisted on unloading his potatoes. He protested vehemently. He had loaded the waggon himself, he said, and he knew there was no one hiding under the potatoes. The constables and their sergeant, all of whom knew John Snell well, were extremely sorry. Orders were orders; escaped murderers were not to be trifled with. They had to unload the potatoes, but they would do it carefully and not delay him a moment longer than necessary.

They drove another waggon alongside and quickly transferred John Snell's potatoes to it. As Snell's waggon was emptied, it quickly became evident that it contained a far greater volume of wine casks than potatoes.

Snell began what was probably a carefully prepared explanation, but the sergeant waved it aside. "That's your business," he said. "We're looking for a man. As long as your casks are too small to contain the escaped prisoner, which they are, they don't interest us."

The constables checked them carefully anyway and then reloaded the potatoes. The sergeant thanked Snell and allowed him to proceed.

"What's to be done now?" he asked me.

"Write your report," I said. "Be sure to describe the wine casks carefully. Have all of your men sign it. We will spread word that the escaped murderer has been recaptured."

At Lady Roulson's, Chief Inspector Mewer was further daunted to learn that Lady Sara now had the backing of the War Office, which was furnishing a battalion of infantry. To her considerable credit, Lady Sara had persuaded the authorities to send in sufficient force before it was needed. During the long series of riots and insurrections that had blighted English history during the nineteenth century, troops had rarely been called out before serious damage and bloodshed occurred.

The battalion's commander, Colonel Millward, a tall, ramrod erect officer, had just reported to Lady Sara. The Admiralty remained deeply concerned, and Lieutenant Juster's presence indicated that a combined land and naval manoeuvre was contemplated. Lady Sara spread an Ordnance Survey map on a splendid old mahogany drum-topped library table and took command.

Lady Roulson produced a neighbouring farmer who knew the Snells' farm intimately and was able to describe in great detail every creek, drainage ditch, and fence line. He also knew which were sufficiently overgrown to offer cover for advancing soldiers.

"We want these people taken alive," Lady Sara told the Colonel. "We certainly don't want any of the women and children injured or killed. At the same time, we have to consider the men scoundrels who will stop at nothing. Four of the brothers murdered their shipmates—in four different ships—by catching them asleep and cutting their throats, and they won't hesitate to shoot a few soldiers if we give them the opportunity. If the Snells insist on being killed, we have no choice but to accommodate them, but I don't want any casualties among your men, and I don't want to escalate this into a war."

"I understand, my lady. The idea is to display enough force to convince the Snells it is futile to resist."

"Precisely. If they insist on resisting anyway, we will put them under siege, and if that doesn't work—which it probably won't, they have the farm animals and a full winter's provisions on hand—we may have to burn them out."

The operation envisaged by Lady Sara involved two detachments of troops. One would be transported by the navy in small boats that would reach the Snell farm by way of creeks that flowed into the inlet. The other would approach on foot from the land side. Once in position, each detachment would form two sides of a rectangle as its troops moved quickly to surround the buildings. What happened after that was up to the Snells. They would be served with a warrant—by a police officer, the Chief Inspector thought; by Lady Sara herself, she thought, since the Snells would be less likely to shoot a woman without a parley. The soldiers were to be highly visible but take no active part unless the Snells forced that on them.

In London, police would close in on the Poplar Produce Company as soon as John Snell arrived there. Since there would be only the two Snell brothers in the building, Chief Inspector Mewer doubted that the army would be needed, but he promised to have plenty of police on hand.

Colonel Millward had a distinct advantage over Chief Inspector Mewer. He had a sense of humour. He said to me, with a twinkle in his eyes, "Your employer would make a fine general."

Unfortunately for him, the War Office had placed him under Lady Sara's orders when it sent him to report to her, and he had not yet fully grasped the implications of that fact. The possibility that she might ask him to do something he disagreed with simply had not occurred to him. Actually, Lady Sara was a fine general, and, given that authority, she had every intention of exercising it.

She asked me to sketch a map of the Snell farm and make as many copies as possible. I consulted with the farmer and also with Colonel Millward, and then I quickly produced a pencil sketch that included every important feature. When both the farmer and the Colonel were satisfied, I copied it in ink and began making tracings.

While I worked, I listened to the hubbub of discussion and debate. I was waiting to find out what Lady Sara was going to do. Then I intended to do the same thing.

Colonel Millward was trying to make certain she did nothing at all. In his view, she had already located the culprits, reconnoitred their farm, and planned the attack, which should have been sufficient to satisfy any woman, even one with enormous political influence. Now it was time for the men to take over. She listened patiently, and then she coolly gave him his orders, informing him that if he refused to follow them, she would ask the War Office for another battalion.

I had been tempted to join the detachment of soldiers that would be landed from boats simply because there would be far less walking that way, but Lady Sara had a better idea. She intended to drive a trap right up to the farmhouse door, which meant virtually no walking at all. I told her I was coming with her, and so were Rick and Charles, and all three of us would be well-armed.

"Very well," she said. "That might be a better idea. I'll borrow Lady Roulson's carriage. Rick and Charles can sit on the box as coachmen. You can be a footman. All three of you should be in uniform. I'll see if Lady Roulson can find something for you. Arm yourselves however you like, but make certain you don't show any weapons."

In the end, everything was done precisely the way Lady Sara wanted it. The morning was cold but clear, with a stiff wind off the sea. The operation, launched just before dawn, went smoothly, and the soldiers were in position when Rick and Charles drove Lady Roulson's carriage at a slow pace down the long, bumpy, narrow road to the door of the Snell farmhouse. The carriage had been new about the time of Queen Victoria's coronation and was ornate enough for a Lord Mayor's procession. It made me feel ridiculous. The uniforms Lady Roulson had found for us had been in storage for years, in that damp climate, and they smelled of mildew and decay and looked about as venerable as the carriage, and of course they didn't fit, so I also felt uncomfortable.

When the carriage stopped, I climbed down stiffly and ceremoniously handed Lady Sara down. She was dressed in a gown Lady Roulson had inherited from a frivolous ancestor—all frills, ribbons, billowing skirts, and violent colours. Her hat, also borrowed from Lady Roulson, was a colossal construction of artificial fruit, flowers, and feathers. She must have felt as foolish as I did, but she considered the total effect of uniforms, dress, and carriage to be critically important.

I went to the door with Lady Sara and worked the old, corroded knocker energetically. Then I stepped back and folded my hands behind me.

The door opened a crack, and Abner Snell's sharp nose appeared. "What'cha want?" he demanded.

"Take a look," Lady Sara said. "There are four hundred soldiers surrounding the farm."

Probably Snell had already seen them—we already knew that very little happened on the farm without his knowledge—but he opened the door wider and looked out. The soldiers were standing motionless in a line a hundred yards distant that now curved completely around the farm buildings. They were placed where they could take cover instantly if trouble developed.

"Trespassin'," Snell growled. "All of ye are trespassin'. I'm orderin' ye to get."

Lady Sara presented him with a copy of the warrant. "We know what happened to the missing wine ships," she said, speaking slowly and very distinctly. "We also know what happen to their crews—the members who weren't Snell brothers. We know how you got the wine ashore and how you have been disposing of it in London. Your sons James and John are about to be arrested there. I'm calling on you and your other sons to surrender peacefully."

Abner Snell pointed a finger. "Get."

"If you want to make damn fools of yourselves, that's all right with me," Lady Sara said. She sounded superbly indifferent. "We have enough guns, including artillary, to pound your farm buildings to rubble. But we don't want to harm the women and children. You have no right to make them suffer just because you are feeling reckless. Send them out, and I'll see that they get to a safe place. If you and your sons surrender now, the women and children will still have a home when this is over with. If you decide to fight, there won't be any farm buildings left."

The door closed. For a few minutes nothing happened. I hoped Snell and his sons were conferring inside. Then the door opened again. Abner said again, "Get!"

"Don't be a bloody idiot," Lady Sara said impatiently. "The women and children are innocent. Why needlessly destroy their home and their means of earning a living? At least send them out and let me take them to a safe place."

The door closed again. Then it opened on a parade of frightened, crying children and frightened, white-faced women. Lady Sara got busy at once, packing the smallest children and one woman who was heavily pregnant into the carriage.

The last woman remained in the doorway for a sharp altercation with Abner. It was his wife, Lila. She didn't want to leave him. She was stooped and grey and looked more like his mother than his wife, which demonstrated how hard farm life could be on a woman. Finally he slapped her face with a sharp crack. "Get!" he said.

She staggered out, sobbing, and Lady Sara found a place for her in the carriage. When Lady Sara turned to remonstrate again with Snell, he threatened her with a rifle. She shrugged and signalled to Charles to drive off. She and I followed on foot, and two women and the older children walked with us. Rick walked behind, acting as rear guard.

We passed the line of soldiers. Out of sight of the farm buildings, Lady Roulson was waiting for us with another carriage. We got the walking refugees packed into it, and the two carriages headed for the harbour, where boats would take them to Lady Roulson's home. Lady Sara turned her attention to the farm.

"Your men are not to shoot unless they are shot at," she said to Colonel Millward. "Do they understand that?"

"Perfectly, my lady," Colonel Millward said.

"Very well. They can start moving up."

One or two at a time the men began dashing forward to the next cover or working along overgrown fence lines or drainage ditches, Gradually they drew closer to the house.

Shots rang out; one of the soldiers fell wounded. Two of his mates carried him to safety; the others sought concealment. For a time nothing at all happened, and it looked as though we had a stalemate. The soldiers could rush the farm buildings at any time and overwhelm the Snells, but there certainly would be more casualties.

The carriages returned. Lady Sara mounted into one, drew its curtains, and exchanged her frilly dress for a practical woman's riding habit. She emerged wearing a close-fitting, plain jacket, a foot-length, tight skirt, Wellington boots, and her own adaptation of a deerstalker. Lady Roulson joined us wearing men's clothing.

Two of Lady Roulson's grooms led horses forward. Lady Roulson vaulted onto one that was equipped with a man's saddle. Lady Sara gracefully mounted the one with a woman's saddle. A box-like container was secured behind the saddle of each horse.

At that moment Colonel Millward rode up and began to remonstrate with Lady Sara. He wanted her and Lady Roulson to remain in a safe place and let two of his men undertake whatever it was she was planning to do. I joined in with a different kind of argument. I wanted to come along.

She didn't bother to answer me. We both knew I was able to keep my seat on a horse only with the horse's full consent and cooperation.

She told the Colonel, "Nonsense! We've spent hours practising this manoeuvre. I wouldn't trust it to your men. Maybe it will work; maybe it won't. Better to do something than to sit and do nothing."

He changed his tone. It would humiliate his men, he said, if they had to stand and watch two women do a job they had been trained for.

Lady Sara shook her head. "In a military operaton, which this now is, delay is always costly."

"At least give us a little time to plan a diversion," the Colonel pleaded. "Then the men can feel that they have helped."

Lady Sara studied him gravely. "What sort of diversion?"

"Something to keep the Snells occupied."

"Very well," Lady Sara said. "Plan your diversion."

The two women dismounted again. The Colonel gave his orders. The diversion required preparation, and both women were becoming impatient before the Colonel finally was ready. An old abandoned sledge that stood beside the drive leading to the farm had given him an idea.

Messengers had been sent galloping. Finally two waggon-loads of hay bales arrived along with another sledge drawn by a team of horses. The hay was loaded onto the sledges to a height that would give the soldiers cover. Several sturdy individuals were told off to push each sledge. One sledge was to approach the farm along the road. The other was to move across a field and approach from a different angle.

"Move slowly and steadily," the Colonel told his men. "Make certain you stay under cover. Your job is to attract the Snells' attention and keep it."

They certainly attracted the Snells' attention. As soon as the moving hay bales came into sight, fusillades were directed at them. The soldiers lowered their heads, braced their legs, and kept the sledges inching forward. One caught a bullet in an exposed arm; the others remained safe behind the rows of hay bales. The Snells kept shooting.

While that was going on, the two women rode off at a trot, widely circling the farm buildings. Rick, Charles, and I ran after them trying to keep them in sight. They were a study in contrasts. Lady Roulson sat astride her horse as erect and at ease as any man. She rode superbly. Lady Sara, though riding side-saddle, sat on her horse with the same ease and somehow managed to look wonderfully ladylike and far more graceful.

They vanished from sight behind a small grove of trees. When they appeared again, the containers were billowing smoke. They rode at a gallop toward the farm buildings, approaching the windward side of storage and animal sheds at an angle. The stiff wind whipped the smoke ahead of them almost like a curtain.

But the Colonel's diversion was such an overwhelming success that the women's approach was unnoticed. It was one of the few times in my memory that Lady Sara had been outmanoeuvered by a man. The Snells' attention remained focused on the sledges; they were firing as rapidly as they could. Further, the Colonel ordered his men to discharge their rifles into the air when the women approached the farm buildings. The battalion's artillary began firing guns loaded only with powder, but they certainly sounded warlike. The racket became thunderous, and the approaching horsewomen were both unseen and unheard. They did not attract a single shot. When they came close to the buildings, they wheeled sharply, dropping the containers, and left at a gallop. The wind quickly enshrouded the farm in thick, oily smoke.

The women rode back to their starting point and coolly dismounted.

Under the cover of smoke, the soldiers began to move forward. Those who had been pushing the sledges abandoned them and ran to a rickety outbuilding that offered a good measure of concealment. They began peering around its corners toward the farm building.

Suddenly several shots rang out. Lady Sara took a rifle and carefully sighted it at the house. After a few minutes, she put it down again without firing. There were no more shots.

The soldiers were becoming bolder. Finally one of them walked up to the door and tried the latch. It was locked. He backed up and crashed into it with his shoulder. The door splintered and flew open; the soldier leaped aside and peered in cautiously, rifle at the ready. Then he gingerly vanished into the house.

He emerged a moment later and called something to his sergeant. The sergeant passed the message along, and eventually it reached us. Abner Snell and the three sons who were with him had shot themselves. All were dead.

Lady Sara shook her head regretfully. "The wine would have brought them long prison terms in any case," she said. "If the Admiralty succeeded in connecting the sons with just one of the vanished ships, they would have been hanged for mutiny and murder. Abner, because of his age and the fact that he had no direct part in those crimes, might have been let off easy."

"No doubt they all expected to be hanged, my lady," the Colonel said. "Otherwise, why shoot themselves?"

"It was a silly thing to do," Lady Sara said. "We still don't know how much of a case could be made against them."

When the burning containers had been dragged away and doused with water, she insisted on searching the farm buildings. In a cellar we found enough wine to keep the Poplar Produce Company in business for a year or more.

"When supplies got low, there would have been more murders and another ship stolen," Lady Sara said soberly. "What a horrible ending to a horrible business."

"It isn't ended yet, my lady," I reminded her. "The two brothers in London should have been captured alive."

"It is ended for us," Lady Sara said. "The eldest son, John, wasn't a sailor. He may escape with a prison term. His brother will be hanged if the Admiralty can produce the evidence. Certainly it will try, but none of that is any concern of ours. Let's get back to London. We have work to do."

The Admiralty gave Lady Sara a special commendation and medal, which amused her greatly. Reginald Dempster also received a commendation as well as a substantial reward for his role in the recovery of a large quantity of stolen wine. He was overwhelmed. "My word!" he exclaimed to Lady Sara afterward. "I had no idea law and order could be so profitable. You've been holding out on me. I'd have taken this up years ago if I had known."

"It is never too late to start," she said. "Neither of us will live long enough to exhaust the supply of criminals."

"I'll have to give it serious thought and maybe even work at it," Dempster said. "Until now, I've only taken what came my way." He looked at his cheque again. "My word! Cicely and I will be able to afford Bath next year and the year after that. She'll be pleased. Do you have anything else in hand I could help with?"

"Thus far you have exposed a ring of housebreakers and brought a family of murderers to justice," Lady Sara said. "Your information about the Whitham giant came to nothing, but two out of three is a score the most expert detective would be proud of. Just keep your eyes open for oddities."

"I will," Dempster promised fervently.

CHAPTER 20

The case of the wine thefts was finished. On the giant cribbage board, its pegs had been moved all the way to the game holes and off the board in a surprisingly short time considering the seriousness of the offenses and the convolutions of the investigation: A number of murders solved that the authorities had not even known about; an enormous quantity of valuable merchandise recovered; the culprits either in custody or dead by their own hands. It was a tremendous achievement, but there was no time to celebrate. As Lady Sara had said, we had plenty of unfinished business in London.

The moment we arrived there, she resumed her routine: the morning coffee hours and problems of her friends to solve, most of them trivial; the evenings as Madam Zarno, with a gleaning of information on commonplace events in the London underworld; and countless tips and bits of information from her own informers.

But the framed document remained over her desk with the names of the river thieves' victims. Lady Sara looked up at it from time to time as she spent her free moments contemplating photographs of the river theft suspects, arranging them in rows on the table and shuffling them around as though she were playing a game of Patience. At one side was an additional pile of photographs, evidence of repeated visits by these same suspects to the warehouses we were having watched. At the other was a blank piece of paper trimmed to the same size as a photograph.

The paper, Lady Sara said, was to remind her that a master criminal might have his business so well organized that he never had to appear at any of the addresses connected with stolen goods.

"If that is true, one of the other men could be his assistant," I suggested. "Or several could be his assistants."

Lady Sara agreed. "The problem is that all of them are men with good reputations and well-established businesses of their own. All of them could have plausible business reasons for calling at the warehouses. So which of them is the master criminal? We are looking for a man who is brilliant, extremely rich, extremely greedy for more riches, and totally ruthless, with no moral sense at all. He is impersonating an upright, responsible citizen so effectively that no one suspects his true character.

We may know him well, or we may never have set eyes on him. Even if we trap his confederates and smash his illegal businesses, we may not find a single thread that leads to him. The river thefts may be only one of the illicit activities he directs. There is no way of knowing how many others there are."

I looked over the list of names again: Ralph Bewt, of John Bewt Ltd.; Innes Cameron, of Cameron & Company Ltd.; Hollis Ewbank, of Ewbank and Dudding Ltd.; Sir James Furner, of the Furner Steam-Packet Company; Malcolm Gavin, of Malcolm Gavin Ltd.; Steven Harbisher, of the Eastern Asia Trading Company; Sir Langley Jardin, of the Iberian Trading Company Ltd.; Sir Charles Lampson, of Lampson & Company; Fane Malkinson, of Bethume Trading Company Ltd.; Otis Nicklass, of the Five Brothers Importing Company Ltd.; Alban Ryman, of Manley Ryman Ltd.; Grant Stoffer, of George Stoffer & Company; and the Reverend Theobald Eynon, of Eynon Brothers Company.

My investigations had turned up the interesting fact that several of them were in financial difficulties about the time the river thefts began and now were prospering. "Shouldn't they head our list of suspects?" I asked. "I'm referring to Sir Charles Lampson, Alban Ryman, and Grant Stoffer. I would add Malcolm Gavin, who seems to have got rich with a very small business and certainly looks villainous."

Lady Sara shook her head. "There also are several men on your list who were prosperous at the time the river thefts started and now are even more prosperous. They, also, should head our list of suspects."

"I have a difficult time matching the Reverend Theobald Eynon with those qualities you mentioned," I said. "But then—I also have a difficult time understanding how he could suddenly take over a prosperous shipping company and run it successfully."

"Many business firms have capable employees who are able to run them without supervision, at least for a time. The Reverend Theobald's brothers may have left him an extremely competent staff. You already have raised a more pertinent question—whether he could suddenly develop a hugely successful theft operation about the time he took over the shipping company. As far as we know, he had no background at all for that."

She paused, and I waited. Actually, I was waiting for instructions, but she seemed to have none for me.

"It may be," she said finally, "that you and I are too innocent to unravel the dealings of such a depraved mentality. Still—every man has his weaknesses and blind spots. For the present, we will follow the lines we have already laid out. Perhaps one of the ring's operations will miscarry. Or perhaps we will have another stroke of luck."

I was still examining the photographs. "I have the feeling I should be able to read more into these. The camera doesn't lie. Or does it?"

"It doesn't lie, but it is easily fooled," Lady Sara said. "The problem is that it catches the exact truth without approaching reality—because reality is a lie made up of dozens of flickers of truth. The camera catches only one of those flickers, and the result may be far more deceptive than an outright lie. Whistler said one who paints only what he sees is no artist, but that is what the camera does—it paints only what it sees."

"Of what use are the photographs, then?"

"For identification, not for insights into character."

"Even if we don't have enough evidence to determine which suspect is guilty, there may be some among them who obviously aren't guilty," I said. "We ought to be able to eliminate them. We have a ridiculous number of suspects."

She looked at me with interest. "That is a good thought. Why don't you try it?"

I spent three days going over all of our information and looking for new evidence, and then I took my list of names to Lady Sara. "Sir Charles Lampson," I said. "His firm is doing well after several very shaky years, but that is due to his manager, who runs it for him. Sir Charles spends more time in the country than the Reverend Theobald Eynon. Lampson and Company is only a hobby, and its success doesn't matter to him because his wife brought him a fortune. Horses are his business. He has neither the time nor the intelligence to be a Magnate of Crime."

"Are you crossing him off?"

"I am."

"I have him marked 'doubtful,' but it is too early to cross him off completely. The manager who is making a success of Lampson and Company has a prison record—for burglary of warehouses. Who else?"

"Hollis Ewbank. He is virtually senile. His is an old, successful firm, and its reputation still carries it, but its employees are responsible for almost all of its operations, and even they wonder how much longer Ewbank can pretend to be in charge."

"I also have him marked 'doubtful,' but not all of the firm's recent success can be accounted for by its reputation. For some unexplained reason, it suddenly began to make money. Who else?"

"Fane Malkinson. He may have more than three mistresses. He hasn't time to be a Magnate of Crime."

She nodded. "Another doubtful one—except that those mistresses mean his need for money is greater than that of anyone else on the list. Who else?"

"Ralph Bewt. He isn't as senile as Hollis Ewbank, but he certainly lacks the energy to run a huge criminal enterprise in addition to this business. He isn't even running John Bewt and Sons successfully. According to his employees, the firm is 'dying on its feet.'"

"His lack of energy could be made up for by one energetic assistant, and he has a criminal mentality—he has always been as dishonest as he dared to be. Put him on the 'doubtful' list. Who else?"

"Sir James Furner—for a surprising reason. He has an astonishing reputation for forthrightness and honesty. He failed as a politician because of it. His steam packet company represents a wise investment he made a number of years ago, and it virtually runs itself. He has never shown the slightest interest in expanding it. He is so different from the others that he simply doesn't belong on the list."

"Mark him 'doubtful' and hope he hasn't been trying to correct his failings where his honesty is concerned. Who else?"

"Grant Stoffer. We thought he had almost ruined his firm with mergers but was now recovering. I just learned that the recovery was exaggerated. He is on the verge of bankruptcy. If he were a Magnate of Crime, he would have enough money to keep his business afloat."

"True enough," Lady Sara said. "It is also true that being on the verge of bankruptcy would be an excellent cover for a Magnate of Crime. Who would suspect him of making millions illegally? Mark him doubtful. What about the Reverend Theobald Eynon running his successful importing business and also an ingenious criminal scheme on two days a week in London? Do you consider him doubtful?"

"I would like to," I said, "but Eynon Brothers Company is too deeply involved with the thefts."

"While we were frivolling in East Anglia, Tom Ness went to Pangstead to find out how the Reverend Theobald occupies himself on the five days he is not in London. The answer was interesting. No one knows. With three competent curates to perform all of the parish's routine work, he can take as much time off as he likes. He usually manages to be on hand on Sunday morning to deliver a stirring sermon paternally admonishing his parishioners to be good, but he may leave again as early as Sunday afternoon and return as late as Saturday night. He is supposed to be travelling about, visiting distant parishes in search of ideas for improving Pangstead. His parishioners consider this noble of him—to spend all of his time working for them when he could stay at home and do nothing. I am giving some thought to the best way to follow him on his excursions. It will have to be done with extreme care. In the meantime, there is nothing doubtful about him as a suspect. Where does that leave us?"

"With seven suspects and six that are doubtful."

"Do you have a favorite candidate among the seven?"

"Apart from the Reverend Theobald, I have three. I still like Malcolm Gavin, whose business is a small one and who is far wealthier than he should be, and now I have other reasons. Not only does his business give him an excuse for dropping out of sight for days at a time, like the Reverend Theobald, but he is rarely home at night. We have been watching suspected warehouses during the day, and noting the occasional appearance of suspects there, but the river theft business occurs mainly at night. We should be following our suspects on their nighttime excursions."

"Who are the other two?" Lady Sara asked.

"Another is Langley Jardin, who is both ruthless and resourceful and who also has an unusual amount of nocturnal activity—his servants say he socializes a great deal."

"Who else?"

"Steven Harbisher. He, also, is strangely unavailable several nights of the week. Supposedly he visits one of his clubs, but he comes home too late for that, and on the one night I was able to check, he hadn't been near his clubs. He is a petty tyrant in his legitimate business, which could have functioned as an apprenticeship for being a real tyrant in an illegitimate business. I think a Magnate of Crime would have to be a real tyrant. Perhaps the title of Napoleon of Trade wasn't distinction enough for Harbisher, and he also decided to become the Napoleon of Crime."

"Definitely a possibility," she agreed. "Anyone else?"

"Three—plus the Reverend Theobald—are enough for now. There is one more thing. I think our Magnate of Crime would also have to be a natural leader, and I think all three of these men qualify. Most of the other suspects don't."

She nodded gravely. "Very well reasoned. I have been having the homes and businesses of all of our suspects watched by street people for several weeks and records made of their comings and goings. This was easily arranged. Having the suspects followed on their nighttime excursions would be another matter entirely. Like following the Reverend Theobald, it would have to be done with extreme care. At the point where our Magnate of Crime crosses the line from legitimate to illegitimate activity, we are likely to encounter bullies of the same sort that were protecting the giant on the night of the fog and that Ed Geffer and Rafe Wade encountered. We don't want to lose any more people. You might give some thought to how we could manage this while you are catching up on what has been happening while we were in East Anglia."

I was still supposed to be accompanied by two pugilistic footmen whenever I went out, but I found them such a nuisance I preferred to take my chances without them. I had seen no evidence that anyone had the slightest interest in my movements.

I went to see what Ben and Bob Lyle had been doing, and they took me for a tour of the spy stations they had established along the river. I also called on the watchers stationed around the warehouses. I quickly learned that both spies and watchers had got so accustomed to having nothing happen that they were virtually sleeping while they worked. On my own initiative, I started switching them around, telling them to look for people or ships they had already seen at their former locations. Even if it accomplished nothing, I thought it would wake them up temporarily.

There was one immediate result: It woke Ben and Bob Lyle up. Supervising people who had nothing to do but sit at windows was not their style. They resumed going out on the river at night, and after their first excursion, Ben telephoned me.

"I think maybe we've got something," he said.

I went to see them at their lodgings, which they had changed since we first met. Their mishap with the steam launch had given them the idea that someone actively disliked them, so they "disappeared" into new lodgings. They now lived on the north side of the Thames in a Limehouse sailors' home. Their room was cramped but scrupulously clean, and they seemed thoroughly at home.

"Being as we'd rowed our arms off without seeing anything, we decided to stay in one place and see what would come to us," Ben said. "So we got a new skiff. We were going to drop down the river at night one reach at a time and sit still and watch."

"We figured nothing was going to happen during the first hours after dark, so we started about midnight," Bob added. "We anchored off Fountain Stairs, which is a little way below Tower Bridge on the Surrey side. Do you know the place?"

"I remember seeing a sign," I said. "Isn't there a 'Fountain Stairs Wharf?'"

Ben nodded. "It's all granary buildings there. Nothing unusual about them, but the stairs are interesting. There's an old right of way to the river at that place. When they built the granaries they had to preserve the right of way, so they left a passage through one of the buildings. At the foot of the stairs, there's a stone causeway where a small boat can land at low tide without getting its passengers' feet wet. Not many people travel in small boats these days, of course. Anyway, that's where we were—off Fountain Stairs. There's a good view of Tower Bridge from there, which as you know is well-lit. We were hidden in shadows alongside an anchored timber barge. We sat there most of the night enjoying the view."

They had to be allowed their own good time to tell their story. "Was it boring?" I asked.

"Not bad. We each had a jug of ale. Also, some apples and sausage rolls."

"So what happened?" I asked.

"It was a good lay," Ben said. "Bridge lit, us in the shadows, we could see anything moving on the river between us and the bridge, whether it was lighted or not."

"About two in the morning, we saw something that was not," Bob said. "It came up the river lighted and then doused its lights and veered toward the south shore. And vanished. Into St. Saviour's Dock, we reckoned. An hour and a half later, or a bit more, it came out again."

When I said I didn't know St. Saviour's Dock, they offered to take me down the river and show it to me. At first I was reluctant. "If you really have found something, it won't do to hang around and gawk," I said.

"There's no cause to worrit," Ben said. "You'll be a passenger, you're supposed to gawk."

I learned afterward that St. Saviour's Dock is the former mouth of one of London's lost rivers, the Neckinger. As we moved slowly past it, I immediately understood why the men wanted me to see it for myself. It was a mere gap, a narrow chasm lined with tall granaries, warehouses, and flour and seed mills, some of them seven storeys high or higher. The dock was a tidal inlet stretching back three hundred yards or so to the Dockhead, and it looked like a cramped city street where one had to look straight up to see the sky. The buildings were packed closely against one another, and there was hardly room for lighters to pass each other even when the water level permitted it. At low water, the barges lay untidily on the mud.

"You saw a boat go in there at night?" I asked doubtfully.

"It was high tide," Ben said. "But that's the point—St. Saviour's is only navigable for an hour or so each side of high water."

"Depending on the boat, of course, and how much cargo it carries," Bob added.

"So it looks to us like they've got things carefully timed," Ben said. "They've got to load the stolen goods and get to St. Saviour's precisely an hour before high water if they want to get in, and unload, and leave while they can still get out."

"Which means," Bob interposed, "since they probably don't want to pull this caper early at night or close to daylight when there may be people about, they can only work when there's high water during the first few hours after midnight."

"I see," I said. "It sounds like an unlikely place to be taking stolen goods."

"Which probably is why they're doing it," Ben said. "What do we do now? Snoop around on the land side for places to put spies?"

"No," I said. "We did that before and got nowhere. I'll report this to Lady Sara and let her decide."

I described the situation to her, and, as I expected, she knew St. Saviour's and the area around it well. "It wouldn't be difficult for them to get a small steam launch in and out of there at night. A single lamp or an occasional flash of light at end of passage would give the launch something to steer by, and no doubt there are lights along the north side of the river that would guide it out again. As for watching the place, I agree. The surrounding streets are complicated, and there is no single point that all the dock traffic has to pass. Even if there were, and if we were able to discover what warehouse they are using, there would be no way to know which waggons came from there."

"So what do we do?" I asked.

She first telephoned Chief Inspector Mewer. He had no report of a warehouse theft on the previous night.

"Which means they are still cleverly concealing their thefts," Lady Sara said. "When this one is finally discovered, no one will know when it occurred. Tell Ben and Bob to watch again tonight from the same place."

They did, and again they saw an unlighted launch enter St. Saviour's Dock about the same time. Lady Sara and I risked a quick drive through the area in a carriage, looping around the dock by following Shad Thames Street to Dockhead and then taking Mill Street to Bermondsey Wall. We saw nothing but the clutter of heavy traffic usually found near the river.

We tried again, driving a waggon. Christmas was almost upon us; there was a cold, cutting wind, and both of us were bundled in heavy seamen's coats. She drove, and I rode on the box beside her. We travelled through the entire dock area as though we had business there, one of many waggons coming and going. All we accomplished was to get a first hand idea of the layout.

"We have never encountered this situation before," Lady Sara remarked irritably. "If we identify the warehouse and post a watch, they will quickly detect that and move their operation somewhere else. We won't have learned a thing. The most we could accomplish would be to inconvenience them. We have done nothing more than that from the start of our investigation."

"So what do we do?" I asked.

"I'll try to think of something. Have Ben and Bob keep watching."

They did, and they added the interesting information that this set of thieves worked on Christmas and also on Boxing Day.

During this futile surveillance of the River Thames, it was some consolation to me that Lady Sara had continued to have the homes and businesses of all of the suspects watched. When, eventually, we devised a safe procedure for following them, we should be on our way to winding up the case. Until then, she would not hear of my trying to follow them at night.

The day after Boxing Day, a diversion arrived in the form of an official-looking letter from the Cutter and Ramsey Assurance Company. If I would call on the following morning at ten o'clock and ask for Mr. Walshman, I could learn something to my advantage.

Lady Sara encouraged me to go. The Cutter and Ramsey Assurance Company had an excellent business reputation.

It occupied staid quarters in the centre of London's business community on Throgmorton Street. Mr. Walshman proved to be a lank, elderly, white-haired gentleman who peered at me narrowly through a gold pince-nez.

He thanked me for coming to see him, asked about my health, asked about Lady Sara's health, and eventually came to the point. "I understand you refused an extremely generous offer from the Tradesmen Life and Accident Assurance Company. You said your present commitments prevented your accepting it. Is that correct?"

"It is," I said.

He nodded thoughtfully. "Our problem is similar to theirs. We are convinced we are inviting serious losses by failing to scrutinize our clients carefully. We have looked into your credentials—rather, into Lady Sara's credentials. They are impressive, and our informants tell us that you are principally responsible for her successes. This doesn't surprise us, of course. After all, she is only a woman, albeit a wealthy one from a distinguished family, and it is to be expected that an assistant would be performing most of the work her success is based upon. I don't know what she pays you, but I am certain we could better it. If you don't care to break your connection with Lady Sara, we would like to explore the possibility of your undertaking selected investigations for us in your free time."

I smiled. "Investigating is not a free-time occupation and could not be. It is a total-time occupation. There are no 'hours.' One is completely occupied until an investigation is completed. Then one begins another."

"I see. Then you wouldn't consider undertaking an investigation for us from time to time?"

"Not at present," I said.

"Very well. If your situation changes, come and see me."

We shook hands.

I returned to Connaught Mews and described the interview to Lady Sara, carefully omitting the remark about her being only a woman. She seemed perplexed.

"Knowing your capabilities as well as I do, I am not surprised that such glowing opportunities are being extended to you. What does surprise me is that businessmen like Sir Cecil and this Mr. Walshman have found out enough about you to confidently make such offers. As you well know, most of our work is done anonymously. If you would like to accept this latest offer on a trial basis, I will see that you have time available."

"No, thank you," I said. "I'm happy working on your investigations."

"It might be interesting to see what they would ask you to do. Let's give some thought to it."

We were interrupted by Reginald Dempster. Lady Sara greeted him with a smile. "Do you have another oddity for us?"

But Reggie was the picture of gloom. "I say—look at this," he said. He held out a five-pound banknote.

Lady Sara took it and examined it.

"Is it queer?" Reggie asked anxiously.

Lady Sara nodded. "It is. Where did you get it?"

"At the bank. Stopped to get some money to buy a birthday gift for Cicely. Then I went to Garrard and Company, the Haymarket jewellers, and decided on a brooch and was about to pay for it when I noticed this note had an odd look about it. Seemed a bit blurry and pinkish under the light there. So I told them to hold the brooch and hared over here to ask you about it."

"What bank was it?" Lady Sara asked.

"Drummond's in Charing Cross."

"You could take it back there. Or complain to the police."

"The police would confiscate it, wouldn't they?"

"I'm afraid they would."

"And the bank—awkward thing, my word against theirs. What if they were to claim they hadn't given it to me and accuse me of trying to pass it? Same with the jeweller. If the jeweller had accepted it, wouldn't I be guilty of shoving the queer the moment they realized they'd got a bad bill? And if they detected it at once and refused to take it, wouldn't they call the police? Either way I'm in trouble and out a fiver, and I don't have all that many fivers. What a piece of bad luck!"

"I'll give you five pounds for it. Then you won't be out anything and I can try to trace its history without embarrassing you."

"Would you? I say—that's sporting of you!"

The exchange was made in a moment. Dempster left for Garrand and Company to complete his purchase, trailing clouds of thanks. Lady Sara handed the note to me to examine.

"It looks like an extremely competent forgery," I said.

"Unusually competent," she agreed. "What do you think of Reggie's story?"

"It's a little hard to believe the bank would hand out a forged note. I thought bank clerks were trained to detect forgeries."

"Do you remember that story we heard last month about a new ring of coiners?"

"Yes," I said. "It was going to operate on the unusual principle of not being greedy. Those shoving the queer, or dealing smash, always try to get rid of as much as possible, which inevitably leads to their being caught. This gang was going to use restraint and work for small, safe, and steady profits. They thought their scheme was foolproof."

"I am wondering if perhaps my informer got it wrong and the ring is shoving counterfeit banknotes instead of coins. We didn't take the report seriously because the reward would be so small. The profit on a sovereign or two a week, split several ways, wouldn't encourage restraint. If banknotes are involved, we have a different situation entirely. I need to think about this."

She did her thinking in the same intense way she surveyed the scene of a crime—quietly but with total concentration. While she thought, I busied myself with bringing records up to date on payments to her agents. More than an hour passed, and during all of that time she was completely oblivious to my presence. I could not imagine what sort of problem a queer banknote could pose that required such a measure of deliberation.

Finally she turned to me. "This is something for Chief Inspector Mewer," she announced.

She telephoned him at once, leaving me totally perplexed. It was not often that she surrendered a promising investigation to the police without first having a careful look at it. The Chief Inspector arrived promptly, bringing with him a C.I.D. Inspector Jones, a short, sturdily built man with black hair and eyes and a smile that he turned on whenever he thought someone was looking at him. When Lady Sara presented them with the forged note, they were very interested indeed. She explained the tip we'd received and our reason for believing the informer had it wrong.

"A bank clerk easily could find situations in which a forged fiver could be exchanged for a real one," she said. "Say a packet of notes was being made up for storage or transfer. He could remove one and slip a forged note into the middle of the packet. His profit on the transaction might be as much as three pounds. If he has restraint to limit himself to one or two completely safe transactions a week and also to restrain himself from a suspicious display of affluence, he will gain a very useful supplement to his salary."

"That would be highly unusual behavior, my lady," Chief Inspector Mewer said. "If the clerk doesn't spend that illegal income, what does he do with it? Save it for his old age?"

"Or for a nest egg, or for marriage, or for whatever. That's the rub, of course. How many would have the restraint to exchange only one forged note if the opportunity were there to insert six or eight into a packet? If someone has recruited a ring of exceptional agents, then you have a considerable problem. The ringleader, gaining two to four pounds a week from each member, wouldn't need many agents to improve his level of comfort considerably. The difficulty will be in finding out which clerk is the agent."

The Chief Inspector said sourly, "I think it amuses you to underestimate a situation."

"Cheer up, Chief Inspector. It is a foolproof scheme, but already it has come unravelled. The note I just gave you was handed to a private customer, either inadvertently or on purpose."

The two officers thanked her and left—presumably to rush to Drummond's and start their investigation. "Why are you looking so puzzled?" she asked.

"I can't remember the last time you handed an interesting case to the police without even taking a look at it," I said.

"We have something else to work on. Reggie Dempster actually gave us two oddities today. We wouldn't have time for both, so we will let the police investigate the banknote case. We will concentrate on the other."

"What other?" I asked blankly.

"Think! What else did Reggie tell us?"

I thought hard, but blankness was the only result.

"Never mind," she said. "Just for a beginning, I want you to start following Reggie. Rick and Charles will help you. You will have to plan it carefully, because he knows all three of you."

"Follow Reggie?" I exclaimed. "What are we supposed to accomplish by that?"

"The first thing you will accomplish is to be bored to death. Day after day. I'm afraid Reggie leads an almost totally uneventful life. What you will be looking for is the rare occasion when his life becomes interesting. Sooner or later that is certain to happen. You see—the second oddity Reggie gave us today was himself."

CHAPTER 21

I began by reviewing everything I knew about Reginald Dempster, and when I finished, my imagination still refused to connect him with any kind of criminal operation in any capacity whatsoever.

I always regarded him with amused contempt, and he seemed to view himself in much the same light. He belonged to that special category Lady Sara labelled "well-born parasites." The possibility that he was a brilliant, ruthless, master criminal seemed preposterous.

He lived in a London suburb. Suburbs had sprouted like mushrooms all around London during the nineteenth century, and they were often dismissed, in a derogatory way, as "Suburbia." Reginald Dempster went this term one better, derisively referring to his own address in Notting Hill as "Stucco Gardens" because of the prevalent building material on display there. He was, he would say sadly, one of the least significant and hopelessly mired units of the Great Middle Class, and he would bring in references to nearby piggeries and otherwise make his situation sound like an awful come down from his youthful days in the country before his marriage when, as first cousin and heir presumptive of a baronet, he was a welcome guest at every wealthy home in the entire region that had an unmarried daughter.

His marriage had brought him face to face with reality. His wife's family, on the strength of his Third in law at Oxford and the fact that he had been called to the bar, assumed that he would practise law and insisted on his residing near his work, so a portion of his and his wife's patrimony was invested in a Notting Hill home. That was twenty years before. Ever since then, while attempting to live on a fixed income in the face of rising rates and taxes—rising everything, he would moan dramatically—he had been steadily sinking in the direction of the piggeries. Those piggeries had once actually existed in Notting Hill but had long-since been abolished.

Despite his constant laments about his precarious financial position, Dempster managed to retain a few shreds of dignity. His home was, in fact, a quite comfortable semi-detached villa. His door was opened by a venerable retainer in a dingy, well-worn dress suit who acted as butler and also as Dempster's valet when he needed one. The retainer's wife functioned as housekeeper and Cicely Dempster's personal maid. There were, in addition, a cook and an "up and down" maid, or tweeny.

Dempster's wife, Cicely, was considered the most stylishly dressed of her suburban circle. Dempster himself belonged to two clubs. Such undeniable marks of affluence were a puzzling contradiction of his complaints about his strained circumstances. For example, every summer the head of his family sent him a haunch of venison, which should have enabled him to add a feudal air to his modest mode of entertaining and at the same time pay off some of his accumulated debtedness in unreturned dinner invitations. Instead, with loud moans about his pinched finances, he would turn the haunch over to his fishmonger or his butcher in payment of his account.

Dempster and his wife were not "carriage people," and it was a matter of deep regret for him that Cicely was compelled to make her social outings by underground train rather than by chartering a victoria for the afternoon. Even so, he found the underground invaluable. Notting Hill had access to both the "inner circle" and the newly opened Central London Railway, and the Dempsters' exile was softened somewhat by the fact that they were only half-an-hour away from the centre of London. Dempster's attitude toward many things was so childish I had to keep reminding myself that he was encroaching on middle age and that what his tailor kindly referred to as the lower part of his chest had undergone considerable development.

This was the Reginald Dempster I had been casually aware of for many years. In my attempt to understand why Lady Sara wanted him investigated, I carefully reviewed our most recent contacts with him. He had given us a valuable tip that resulted in the smashing of a ring of burglars, but that happened only because the putter-up had the bad luck to impersonate a friend of Dempster's in his presence. No one but an imbecile could have overlooked that. Dempster also had given us a tip on a giant when Lady Sara mentioned that we were looking for one. The tip had been bona fide even though Rafe Wade wasn't the giant we wanted. As for the vital clue that led to the exposure of the Snell family's unsavoury history of mutiny and murder on the high seas, Dempster picked it up unknowingly when he took advantage of a remarkable bargain in wine. Finally, he had been a victim himself of a counterfeit note handed out by a bank clerk, and certainly his conduct was above suspicion in that.

In each of these instances, Dempster's involvement was not merely passive but accidental. It wouldn't have been in character for him to take any kind of decisive action about anything. He had unlimited time on his hands and nothing much to do but keep his eyes open, and in those circumstances anyone could have compiled a similar record with only a small amount of luck.

When I asked myself what Dempster had done to arouse Lady Sara's curiosity, I could only answer, "Nothing."

Whatever the cause, she went to work on him thoroughly. Dempster's neighbourhood was not the sort of place where one could loiter on a street corner waiting for a subject to make his appearance. Constant surveillance would have been not merely difficult but impossible. Through Lady Sara's numerous contacts, she learned that a neighbour of Dempster's sometimes let his residence during the Season, furnished and complete with servants, to families with marriageable daughters who wanted a convenient base for thrusting their offspring into the London social whirl that functioned as a marriage market. In order to take advantage of this, Lady Sara produced a respectable country family from Berkshire, the Brownsons, old friends of hers who had three attractive daughters.

She arranged for the Brownsons to occupy the neighbour's house for three months on his terms except that the Brownsons insisted on bringing their own servants—which meant, of course, Lady Sara's servants. Any others would have cramped her investigation. The Brownsons moved in and quickly were caught up in the London Season and also in Notting Hill's rather limited social scene, and Rick, Charles, and I, suitably disguised, assumed places in their household as footmen who doubled as coachmen when needed. We thus had a convenient base of our own for keeping an eye on Dempster.

This required very little effort. Dempster kept to his rails as reliably as any railway train and followed a timetable just as faithfully. At ten A.M. he strolled to the underground station, took a train to the West End, lunched at one of his clubs, and returned home at six, ready to assume whatever social obligations his wife had arranged for him.

Those of us who were having our first close look at the strange world of suburbia were awed by Notting Hill's pretentious social and cultural climate. Many of its activities centred on the church, St. Eustella's, whose vicar, the Reverend Justin Stick, was a personality in his own right. While other churchmen were espousing or denouncing the "High," "Low," or "Broad" approaches to the Church of England ritual, the Reverend Stick ignored all that and avowed himself to be of the "Deep Church." This sounded so profound that he never felt it necessary to explain himself. He garnished his preaching with quotations from Browning, Matthew Arnold, Shakespeare—whom he always referred to as the National Bard—and Jowett's Plato, and he had recently held his congregation spellbound with Wednesday night lectures on such stirring topics as "The Theological Aspects of Restoration Drama," and "The

Religious Basis of Punch and Judy." Nor did the vicar keep his gaze on the past. He had welcomed the new year with a novel devotion that was announced as "Voices of Eminent Preachers heard through the Phonograph, with Illustrative Comments."

His wife had what is politely called "a little money," which enabled her to assume social leadership in the parish with summer garden parties—ornamented with a brass band and ices from Whiteleys—or, in inclement weather, with drawing room teas at which tea and cress-sandwiches were served.

Dempster and his wife were regarded as pillars of the congregation. They invariably attended the Sunday morning and Wednesday evening services and were prominent at all church events as well as at the Town Hall lecture series. We found it difficult to believe, but so important a figure did Reggie Dempster cut locally that rival politicians competed for his support. All of this was duly reported to us by the Brownson family, whose members were able to observe the Dempsters in situations where it would have been awkward for Rick, Charles, or I to be present.

The notion that a ruthless gang of thieves who took murder as a matter of course could somehow be connected with this harmlessly pretentious suburb seemed totally unreal. I reminded myself, however, that Lady Sara had not claimed any deep involvement in crime for Reggie. She merely implied that on occasion he might rub elbows with it.

Our one diversion from this humdrum routine came when the police arrested a clerk at Drummond's for passing counterfeit fivers. The clerk insisted he had merely exchanged an occasional bad note for a good one within the bank and had never given one to a customer, so Reggie Dempster's mishap had been purely accidental. Even so, the clerk's confession had led to the apprehension of principal members of a major counterfeiting ring, which added up to yet another inadvertent coup for Dempster with the possibility of another reward. Lady Sara shrugged and told us to keep digging.

The only dissonant note we discerned in Dempster's behaviour came on a Saturday or a Sunday afternoon when the weather was fine and he wasn't otherwise occupied. Then, wearing an old tweed suit and smoking a pipe, he would stroll as far as Hyde Park and walk about there, pausing to chat with habitues, each of whom seemed to have his own bench where he held "at-homes." Dempster could have been passing or receiving communications of some sort, but after carefully investigating the people he talked with, we came to the conclusion that he was simply fond of conversation with anyone. His wife, who was a tartar and the dominant figure in their household, kept him firmly under her thumb at home.

Lady Sara took another tack. As a rag and bone lady, offering premium prices because of her supposed contacts with a new industry that processed these homely items into chemicals, she became familiar with the servants in every house in the vicinity, including Dempster's. She made her regular rounds and even managed to purchase the contents of the Dempsters' waste baskets on some pretext or other.

We diligently sorted through the resultant clutter, but the only intelligence we gained came from various notices of winter sales in which Cicely Dempster had indicated items that interested her with slashes of violet ink: "Pink Chiffon Princess Gown, bodice embroidered corals and pearls, handsomely trimmed lace, flowing overtrain. 20 gns. White soft satin, with lace-embroidered violets in baskets and pearls, embroidered sequins, straps of velvet, applique lace and velvet flowers, baby bodice embroidered jet and steel, with primula garniture. 30 gns. Red Faced Cloth Zouave, fancy strappings of own material, white embroidered cloth collar, facings and cuffs studded with quaint buttons, skirt strapped and studded to match coat. 25 gns." And on and on.

Not even Rick and Charles, both of whom had wives, had been aware of the existence of such notices. All three of us found the prices, twenty to thirty guineas for a gown, staggering. It was enough to make a man decide to remain a bachelor. After a few pages of such reading, we felt much more sympathetic toward Dempster's constant financial complaints, but this could not be said to have advanced our investigation.

A gleaning of servant's chatter provided further insights into the Dempsters' home life. Cicely's sister was staying with them—and carrying on a warm friendship with the curate. This had been discouraged by Cicely until she found the curate's father prominently mentioned in Burke's Landed Gentry. After that, she made the young man welcome at every opportunity. Thus did the marriage market flourish on every level of English society, but none of this connected Reginald Dempster with a crime wave along the river.

As we diligently compiled all sorts of information about Dempster and Cicely, we succeeded only in becoming increasingly bored with our subjects, which was what Lady Sara had anticipated in the beginning.

In mid-January, the first oddity occurred. Each weekday morning, Dempster took the underground train to St. James's Park station. He then strolled leisurely across the park to one of his clubs. Only in the worst weather did he take a cab.

On the day in question, Rick was following him. We had adopted various disguises, and our procedure was to arrive at the Notting Hill underground station well ahead of Dempster so he would find us waiting on the platform when he arrived and thus not suspect that he was being followed. Dempster always took a third-class ticket. As he remarked—in the hearing of his servants—the carriages were not crowded at that time of day, the ride was anyway a short one, and why not save a few pence? We sometimes rode in a different car, even a first-class car, and since we knew for certain where he would detrain, we made our way to the street ahead of him and then followed him.

On that day, he surprised Rick. Rick reached the street and waited for him; he did not appear. Rick hurried back into the station, but there was no sign of Dempster, and the train had long since departed.

Obviously Dempster had failed to get off at his usual stop. By the time Rick discovered this, Dempster could have reached the next inner circle station in either direction. The only thing Rick could do was alert street watchers at both of Dempster's clubs in the hope that eventually he would make an appearance at one of them.

This he did. He arrived in midafternoon, carrying several packages and sporting a much more impressive buttonhole than was his wont. Not until that evening, when Dempster and Cicely dined at Rule's in Maiden Lane, a startling expenditure for them, and then attended a special performance of *Samson et Dalila*, by Saint-Saëns, at the Covent Garden Theatre, did his morning expedition became clear to us. He had gone to Covent Garden to purchase the tickets, and he also did some shopping in the vicinity—and acquired his buttonhole from one of the flower girls there. It further emerged that the vicar, the Reverend Justin Stick, had earnestly recommended Samson et Dalila to his congregation because of its theological theme. Since Dempster and his wife were the only ones who attended, they were socially one up on everyone else in Stucco Gardens for the remainder of the month.

It seemed clear enough, but Lady Sara received the explanation with a scowl. "Even if he did exactly what you think he did, you still have no idea what else he might have done," she said. "Buying tickets and making a few purchases didn't occupy him until mid-afternoon. And why should he travel all the way to Covent Garden to purchase tickets when they are readily available at any of the numerous Keith, Prowse, and Company offices or from other agents?"

She also was intrigued by his sudden affluence—the shopping as well as dining out and attending the opera. She revised our procedures to make certain that there were always two of us following Dempster, and one of us was not to leave the train until he did.

Immediately after this, a pall was suddenly cast over this blithe suburb by word of Queen Victoria's illness. The Queen was at Osborne House on the Isle of Wight; news seemed to be sketchy and tardy, but there could be no doubt she was gravely ill. Even the Emperor of Germany, her grandson, was sufficiently alarmed to rush to her bedside.

The Queen died on January 22nd, setting off an extended period of national mourning. Stucco Gardens participated in its own way, apparently attempting to emulate whatever the court made fashionable. Lady Sara was both amused and touched. Maids' caps were crowned with black bows; menservants wore crape bands around their arms. Formal entertaining was abandoned, and even the informal gatherings in the vicarage drawing room were curtailed.

First the royal funeral and then the new King and his court became the subjects of gossip that was faithfully related to us by the Brownsons. Their own plans for putting their marriageable daughters on display had been blighted by this sudden turn of events, but Lady Sara, who was providing the house for them, had no difficulty in persuading them to stay on in London. The social prizes of the moment were places from which the King's procession at the opening of Parliament could be observed, and—thanks to Lady Sara—the Brownsons were among those who succeeded in snatching these and were much envied. The Dempsters were not among the favoured.

After the one aberration in which Reggie escaped our surveillance, he returned to his regular rails, visiting his clubs, taking Saturday or Sunday walks to the park, and participating in such social events as were available during the period of national mourning. The attention Lady Sara was giving to him seemed more and more inexplicable.

The river thefts were continuing. Word reached us of drastic measures taken by shippers and importers to curtail them—entirely without success. The police were as baffled as ever. There seemed to be no predicting where the thieves would strike next nor any way to prevent it. The Lyle brothers impatiently continued to note nocturnal visits of a steam launch to St. Saviour's Dock and several private wharves. They braved January and February nights on the Thames in order to continue their observations, and they kept demanding that something be done. Then the visits suddenly ceased and they had to start anew to trace the thieves to another wharf. In the face of all this, Lady Sara persisted in investing our energy and time in watching a man whose existence was as boring and uneventful as any in London.

As the middle of February approached, Lady Sara suddenly insisted that all three of us follow Dempster each morning. On Friday, February 15, he again failed to detrain at St. James's Park. We lost Charles there—he had hurried on ahead so as to be waiting when Dempster emerged from the station. Rick and I remained on the train and rode with Dempster as far as Cannon Street.

Leaving the Cannon Street station, he hurried on foot toward London's financial district, but he proceeded only a short distance before he turned into a side street and entered the premises of a Scottish firm with the unlikely name of Gow & Son. I'd had one previous encounter with that firm. In its mottled history it had dabbled in many things—as estate agent, insurance agent, commission agent, and also moneylender. In the latter guise, it narrowly escaped a usury charge. This seemed a most improper place for the respectable Reginald Dempster to be doing business of any kind, but business he must have done. When he emerged, he was sufficiently affluent to hail the first passing hansom.

Rick and I emulated him, each of us taking a cab, and to my total astonishment, we followed Dempster all across London, finally skirting Regent's Park on Park Road and entering yet another London suburb, this one far wealthier than Dempster's own Stucco Gardens, St. John's Wood.

It came as no surprise to us to learn that Dempster was cultivating someone in London's most affluent suburb. He was a man perpetually on the make as could be seen from his hovering about Lady Sara's mother, the Countess. The oddity was that he took the long trip to St. John's Wood by cab.

We followed his cab along attractive wooded streets populated by Italianate and Gothic villas. Eventually it fetched up at a detached villa surrounded by a high brick wall. Dempster evidently was expected; the gate opened as his cab approached.

Rick and I stopped around the next corner for a conference. The identity of the person Dempster was calling on might be of critical importance to us, or it might be of no importance, but we had to find out who it was. I volunteered to learn what I could about the occupant of the walled villa. Rick would follow Dempster when he left.

My task required some preparation, and fortunately St. John's Wood was no great distance from Connaught Mews by a rather direct route, down Park Road and Gloucester Place to Oxford Street. I began by going home and equipping myself appropriately.

At Connaught Mews, I recruited Tom Ness, Lady Sara's groom, to help me. He was glad to have something to do. Things had been dull there with Lady Sara concentrating on Notting Hill. The problem we faced was the Notting Hill problem all over again. One couldn't loiter on a street corner in St. John's Wood hoping to pick up information. Unlike Notting Hill, where we had known who our subject was and where he lived and simply wanted to learn whether there were dark secrets in his life, in St. John's Wood we had no idea whom we were investigating.

Tom and I loaded the equipment we thought we needed into the cart, hitched up a horse, and started for St. John's Wood. I had an experiment I wanted to try, so I stopped along the way and bought a selection of the latest magazines—the gossip variety that servants love. We parked the cart in the next street, and I strolled around to the address where Reginald Dempster's hansom had called.

The gate was locked, and there was no way to inform the occupants of the villa that someone was calling there. Neither was there any way to find out whether Dempster was still there except that Rick Alward and his hansom were nowhere in sight. The locked gate seemed suspiciously inhospitable.

I went to the villa next door. A maid answered my knock, a pert young lady of about eighteen. I told her I was conducting a survey of householder services for the London County Council and offered her a choice of the magazines, free, for a few simple answers. She was suspicious but willing and permitted me to ask several "yes or no" type questions: Was the gas service reliable? Was their refuse collected regularly? Were they ever bothered by street noises? Were there any delays in mail deliveries?

When I finished, and she had delightedly selected one of the magazines, I asked one more question as an afterthought. "By the way, I tried to call next door, but the gate is locked and of course no one responded to a knock at that distance. Who lives there?"

She now was fully convinced of my bona fides, and she talked freely. "The Hathaways live there," she said. "Mr. Hathaway is a police official and works nights, so they don't encourage daytime callers."

I said, "Really? How interesting. Do you know them?"

"I don't know Mr. Hathaway. He is always working or sleeping. But Mrs. Hathaway is very friendly and nice, and they have two pretty little girls."

"You have saved me some trouble," I said. "I won't try to call there again." I gave her another magazine for her help and left.

I rejoined Tom and told him what I had learned.

"So what are we trying to accomplish?" he asked.

"I must have a look inside that wall," I said. "If I have to look the house over closely, it will be useful to know where the obstacles are and what the best route is in and out."

Tom shrugged. "Better you than me."

We got our props out of the cart, including a surveyor's transit. Lady Sara had suggested that I try it on a difficult case two years before. I had found it a highly effective means of obtaining access to restricted places, but it had to be used with care.

With our instrument and a few other items, we called at the villa whose backyard abutted on that of the mysterious Hathaways. My question was not one for a maid to decide. I asked for the housekeeper. "Running a quick survey line," I said. "We would like permission to pass through your property."

"Goodness!" she exclaimed. "Is anything wrong?"

"Nothing at all," I assured her. "It has nothing to do with you. The problem is at the end of the street, but we have to work through here, you see, in order to get there."

She decided to consult her mistress. When she returned, she asked, "Will it take long?"

"Only a few minutes," I assured her.

She told us to go ahead.

We did so in a thoroughly professional manner despite the fact that our equipment included something few surveyors have any use for, a folding ladder. We crossed the back of the property with Tom operating the transit and me making mysterious measurements and occasionally mounting the ladder so Tom could take a high sighting.

Ten minutes and it was done. I had a detailed map of the Hathaways' backyard in my head, and I transferred it to paper when we returned to the cart.

I also had committed to memory the profile of Mr. Hathaway, the mysterious police official. He had been pottering in his garden and fortunately had not noticed the several incursions I made on his privacy when I mounted the ladder.

His profile was impressive. There was no doubt about it whatsoever—the gardener, a thoroughly robust individual, was working nearby and could be used for comparison. Besides, I had seen the drawings of both Stephen Lynes and Evan Vaughan, and I knew there could be no mistake.

We had found Hob Hagan, our missing giant.

CHAPTER 22

Reginald Dempster had served his purpose, and Lady Sara dropped him at once. We transferred our attention to St. John's Wood, leaving Notting Hill to the Brownson family and its attractive daughters. Several times I attempted to learn the basis for Lady Sara's conclusion that Dempster, of all people, might lead us to the elusive giant Hob Hagan. I wanted to know whether she had arrived at it by divination, incantation, wild guess, or masterful deduction. She parried every effort with a smile.

As I already noted, the St. John's Wood problem was the Notting Hill problem over again only worse. With its pretty, wooded streets and villas surrounded by high walls, it was the most fashionable of the London suburbs. There were no loiterers there. One could not keep an address under surveillance in St. John's Wood by idling away a morning or an afternoon unless one could impersonate a tree or a lamppost. Otherwise, someone would call the police.

Fortunately we did not have to do that. Mr. Hathaway, the mysterious police official, held no interest for us as long as he was in St. John's Wood, but we very much wanted to know where he went, and what he did, when he left. Since he worked nights and remained quietly at home during the day, we could do our idling after dark, lurking behind the neighbourhood's numerous trees and shrubs while waiting for his departure.

We quickly learned that he, also, had a set of rails, and up to a point he followed them as faithfully as did Reggie Dempster. At nine o'clock each night, Monday till Saturday, the gate opened and a closed carriage drove out. It always turned in the same direction. Rick, Charles, or I would be on watch at Hagan's villa and would signal with a lantern Lady Sara had designed. It was modeled on a spout lantern, and its momentary pinpoint of light was visible only to those positioned directly in front of it. Three flashes warned the person on watch at distant Park Road that the vehicle now headed that way was Hagan's. When Hagan's carriage made its turning, a hansom or a four wheeler parked unobtrusively some distance from the corner would be prepared to follow it.

Hagan's route was always the same: Across London to the Minories and then south to the docks. From that point, following him became tricky because his destination changed each night. It was always somewhere near the river, but it varied from a shabby slop shop near St. Katherine's Docks to a decrepit factory near Blackwall Station. Twice he crossed the Thames at Tower Bridge, and on one of those occasions he travelled all the way to Woolwich. Once, shades of our distant past, he drove directly to Prout's Mill.

Sometimes he entered a building and never left until his carriage drove him back to St. John's Wood. On other nights he went prowling, and following him became not merely tricky but dangerous.

For one thing, he moved through narrow alleys that contained the foul roosts and drinking dens of the worst ruffians of the city. The stench of the river was nearby; the stench and slime of the neighbourhood's refuse was underfoot. A solitary pedestrian dressed a cut above the ordinary or one who had incautiously allowed a few pence to tinkle in his purse might have his throat cut for his indiscretion. With the river so near, the disposal of his stripped body would be a casual afterthought. Even the police went about in pairs and wished it could have been squadrons.

For another thing, Hob Hagan never went unescorted. He was always the centre of a group of thugs, and he kept himself heavily muffled and moved at a crouch to disguise his enormous size. In the concealing darkness, this tactic was so successful that at first we had difficulty recognizing him. I questioned Lady Sara as to why he was so carefully guarded once he reached the docks.

"He is their trump," she said. "Anyone caught trying to follow him will be in serious trouble."

My own encounter with him—at Prout's Mill the night of the fog— had been an exception. Apparently he was walking a few strides ahead of his escort only because the fog was so thick no one was likely to be about.

Rick, Charles, and I were forbidden to even try to follow Hagan. Lady Sara made her own special arrangements for that: Ben and Bob Lyle found her some elderly dockers who were at home in such surroundings and could wander drunkenly in the wake of Hagan and his ruffians without attracting attention. In this manner, after two weeks of fumbling effort during which Hagan led them to all manner of low drinking dens, untenanted shops, and abandoned buildings, they turned up one bright gem of information. Hagan occasionally made short trips by water, stepping into a skiff and being rowed to his next destination.

When Lady Sara heard this, she nodded wisely. "That explains why he wasn't seen again after he disappeared into Prout's Mill the night of the fog."

Another week of watching, and she decided she was as ready as she ever would be. There was a long conference with Chief Inspector Mewer and the Home Secretary, and she took me with her for a lesson in bureaucratic pettifogging. There was indeed the most tut-tutting I had ever heard in a short space of time, and certainly Lady Sara had very little evidence to offer. She was proposing a raid on a private residence, and the Home Secretary gave her to understand that the law protected giants in the same degree that it protected citizens of ordinary stature. What, really, had the man done? Driving down to the docks six nights a week, or even letting it be falsely rumoured about the neighbourhood that he was a police official—if in fact he had done so—were not statutory offences. Lady Sara's claim that ample evidence would be forthcoming the moment Hob Hagan was in custody wasn't relevant.

Lady Sara pointed out acidly that it didn't need to be. The mere fact that Hob Hagan was at large and going about his affairs—or someone's affairs—seven months after he was supposed to have been hanged for a triple murder surely justified detaining him for questioning.

That was the cause of more tut-tutting. Eventually the truth emerged. The Home Secretary was deeply concerned that the rearrest of a man who had already been hanged was certain to embarrass the government whatever the outcome. Did Lady Sara have any inkling of the legal complications involved if for some reason they would have to hang him twice?

Lady Sara's complete confidence finally carried the day—that and her assertion that leaving Hob Hagan at large was likely to embarrass the government far more than rearresting him would. The Home Secretary told the Chief Inspector to do what she wanted. There remained only the matter of choosing a time, and Lady Sara was emphatic about that. She wanted Hob Hagan arrested early on a Sunday morning on his return home from his usual Saturday night foray. One time was as good as another for the Chief Inspector, and he agreed.

As a result, the following Sunday morning found the trees and shrubs of St. John's Wood very nearly overpopulated with police constables. Hob Hagan's closed carriage plodded its monotonous way along a seemingly peaceful, slumbering street; his gate was opened from the inside; the carriage turned in.

As the gate began to swing shut, a picked squad of constables rushed through and quickly overpowered the gardener who was closing it. A second squad of picked constables swarmed after the carriage, which, oblivious to the turmoil behind it, had moved ahead and come to a halt at the side of the house under a stylishly columned portico that protected a carriage entrance.

Hob Hagan stepped down tiredly—and was swarmed over by the police. He reacted with a roar of rage, and the fight that followed flattened no less than four constables and a sergeant and left Chief Inspector Mewer with a battered eye that promised to achieve spectacular shades of blackness.

Standing on the outskirts of the fracas, I suddenly became aware of a second figure looming in the door of the carriage. It was enveloped in a heavy coat and shrouded in darkness as well, but when a lantern flashed in that direction, I saw that it was a woman. Only quick intervention by two constables kept her from leaping to Hob Hagan's assistance. As she struggled, she screamed, "Why can't you leave him alone? No one will leave him alone!" Then Lady Sara spoke to her, and she quieted at once.

Lady Sara watched the battle calmly and restrained me with a hand on my arm when she thought I was tempted to take part. She spoke into my ear. "This is only the preliminary. The main bout comes later today." I desisted and watched the police finally subdue Hob Hagan.

Bloody and manacled, he was dragged into his house and into the drawing room and thrust into a chair. Obviously it was his chair; it was enormous. The woman followed along. While the Chief Inspector, Lady Sara, and I were finding chairs for ourselves, the woman brought a towel and tenderly mopped the blood from Hob Hagan's face. Then she seated herself. Police officers crowded around us, ready to subdue Hagan a second time if it proved necessary.

It was my first close look at Hagan, and I noticed the birthmark on his left cheek at once, a small port wine blotch that looked like a bug.

No one said anything. Everyone was waiting for Lady Sara, and she was merely waiting. Finally a constable pushed his way through the throng and handed her something.

Two somethings.

"Found 'em under the carriage," he explained.

They were Cat's Paws or Spanish Ticklers—differing from Lord Anstee's model in that each had a looping handle a hand could grasp. Lady Sara held them up for Chief Inspector Mewer to see.

"Are you still looking for evidence in the William Havill and Sid Theaker murder cases?" she asked.

"I'm always looking for evidence in unsolved murder cases, my lady," he growled. He took the Spanish ticklers from Lady Sara and examined them carefully. "So that's the way it happened!" he exclaimed.

Hob Hagan burst into tears. He looked nothing like the enraged wild beast of the wax museum. This giant was a bewildered child. Lady Sara silenced the Chief Inspector with a glance and said to Hagan, "Why don't you tell us about it? You can't hold your tongue now. That only will make things worse for you."

Hagan said nothing.

Lady Sara turned to the woman. "Is he your husband?"

She nodded.

"You have children? Two little girls?"

She nodded again.

"Try to make him tell the truth. Things may work out all right if he does. Otherwise, he will be in deep trouble."

The woman looked at Hagan imploringly. He said nothing.

"Bring in the witness," Lady Sara said.

The Chief Inspector snapped an order. There was pushing and shoving from the rear, and a man was thrust into the circle: Alf Rixon, the West India Docks worker who had screamed, "The giant!" when an ordinary-sized robber accosted him.

"Have you met this character before?" Lady Sara asked him.

Rixon looked about him for reassurance. Seeing more than a dozen constables ready to spring the moment Hagan moved, he growled, "Sure—I met him. His face was fixed different, and his teeth stuck out, but it was him, all right."

"Tell us about it," Lady Sara said.

"'Twas the night that robber jumped me. Thugs grabbed me on my way to work and took me—took me somewhere. Vacant room. There was a crowd of them and him." He pointed at Hagan. "Showed me his claws, he did, and they said if I wouldn't play he would do to me and my face like he did to the man he'd killed."

"Play what" Lady Sara wanted to know.

"Look the other way while they looted the docks."

"And you refused?"

"I did, my lady. Then they held me while he raked his claw across my hand, and they told me I'd better keep my mouth shut."

"As a result of the wound, you couldn't work, so you went to your friend's house and got drunk, and then you were robbed on your way home."

Rixon nodded.

"You didn't play, but you did keep your mouth shut."

Rixon nodded again.

"Would you be willing to testify in court that they told you Hob Hagan did the murder?"

Hagan leaped to his feet and had to be subdued.

Rixon said, "They didn't call him Hob Hagan, my lady, but it was him they were talking about. Sure, I'll testify."

"That's all for now," Lady Sara told a police sergeant. "Take him home." As Rixon was led out, she said to Chief Inspector Mewer, "He should have a police guard until this is settled.

Chief Inspector Mewer nodded and spoke to the sergeant. Then he asked, "How much more do you have, my lady?"

"The evening is still young," Lady Sara said with a smile. "Now it is Hagan's turn to talk."

All of us looked at the giant. "I didn't kill nobody," he blubbered.

"Who did?" Lady Sara asked.

"Don't know. It's Mort's fault."

"Mort was your brother?"

Hagan nodded. Perhaps from agitation, he began lapsing into his native Yorkshire dialect. At times I lost his meaning, but Lady Sara seemed to follow him with ease. "We allus fratched when we was bairns, my lady. He hated me 'cause I tried to do right. He was allus faal. After he came to London, he told people he was me."

"Was he calling himself Hob Hagan when he committed all those crimes?"

Hagan nodded.

"But finally he was caught and hanged. What happened then?"

Hagan had lost his tongue again, so the woman spoke up. "It started before Mort was hanged, my lady. Right after he was caught, a man came to see us. He told us Mort would be hanged, but it was really Hob Hagan as did those bad things, 'cause that was what Mort was calling himself. If the police caught Hob, they would hang him, too."

"He offered to look after you?" Lady Sara asked.

She nodded.

"He moved you and your family into this fine home?"

She nodded again.

"Who hired the servants?"

"He did, my lady. He took care of everything."

"And—what did you have to do in return?"

Both were silent.

"Come—no one can help you unless you tell us everything," Lady Sara said impatiently. "What did you have to do in return?"

"Scare people," Hagan blurted.

"Every night the carriage takes you somewhere near the river, and sometimes you walk or go by boat to other places. Is that what happens?"

Hagan nodded.

"Is that all? You simply stand there and scare people?"

"They paint my face," Hagan said, "'n give me teeth that stick out. 'N sometimes I make noises. 'N I wear the claws."

"Do you know why they want you to scare people?"

Hagan nodded. "To make them do bad things."

"Do you enjoy that? Scaring people into violating the law?"

"I hate it," Hagan said fervently.

"Don't you like having good wages and living in this fine villa with servants?"

"I never wanted to do it," Hagan burst out. "He said I could frame, 'n addle piles of brass, 'n I told him I'd rather clam. He threeped me down an' made me do it. He said the police would find me 'n hang me if I didn't. I hate it! It's worse than jail. They're his servants, 'n I have to do what they say. He won't let me quit. Now the police will hang me anyway. I was gaumless."

"Never mind that," Lady Sara said. "No one is going to hang you. Who is 'he?' Does he have a name?"

"He's the Royal."

"Is that all? The Royal?"

Hagan nodded.

"Can you describe him?"

Hagan shook his head bewilderedly.

"What colour is his hair?" Lady Sara persisted.

"He allus wears a hat. A funny, furry thing."

"Is he fat or skinny?"

Hagan considered that. "Don't know. He allus wears one of them flappy things."

"A cloak?" Lady Sara suggested.

Hagan nodded.

"Is he tall?"

Hagan raised both hands. Probably no normally tall person seemed tall to him. "Middlin'," he said finally.

"So what we have is a man calling himself the Royal. He is of average height, and he always wears a fur hat of some kind and a cloak. That doesn't help us much. Isn't there anything distinctive about him?"

Hagan shook his head.

"Is he clean-shaven?"

Hagan brightened. "He has a moustache and beard."

"What color are they?"

Hagan considered that. "Darkish."

"You must have seen him occasionally with other people around. He was the chief, the man in charge. What did the others call him? How did they address him?"

"They called him 'the Royal,' my lady," Hagan said.

"It's an appropriate name," Lady Sara mused. "He certainly is the king of criminals. Here is the critical question. If you see him again, do you think you will recognize him?"

Hagan considered that. "I think so."

"He might be wearing something other than a fur hat and a cloak. The beard and moustache may be false. He will look entirely different. Do you still think you will recognize him?"

"I'll know his eyes," Hagan said. "They're faal. They scare me."

Lady Sara turned to the woman. "Do you always accompany him on these outings?"

"Not all the way, my lady," she said. "As far as they let me. Some-times I wait in the carriage, and he goes off with his guard. He needs someone to look after him, and I do the best I can."

"Have you met the Royal?"

"Oh, yes! I've met him."

"Would you know him if you saw him again."

"I would know him anywhere," she said bitterly.

Lady Sara turned to Hagan. "You and your family will stay here for the present. The police will look after you, and they will take your servants away and keep them locked up where they can't bother you. Sometime later today I may bring the Royal to see both of you just to find out whether you can recognize him."

"What's going to happen?" Hagan's wife demanded.

"It's too early to try to sort things out," Lady Sara said, "but I promise you Hob won't have to scare people any longer."

We went outside with the Chief Inspector.

"Hagan was the giant in Spitalfields," I told Lady Sara. "The one who rescued Mrs. Ungles from the intruder."

"Of course," Lady Sara said. "The gentle giant who became aroused when he saw someone mistreating an animal—or a woman." She turned to Chief Inspector Mewer. "Obviously our next problem is find the Royal. As I told you, only a gigantic hoax will bring this off. If even a whisper gets out that Hob Hagan has been captured, the hoax will fail."

"These are picked men, my lady," the Chief Inspector said. "They know something very important is at stake here. They won't breathe a word of it."

"Good. I'm counting on you to make certain they don't."

The Home Secretary called on Lady Sara later for a report on the night's work. By getting up early on a Sunday morning, he demonstrated how concerned he had been. The report was far more satisfactory than he had expected. She emphasized to him, also, the necessity for secrecy.

"What are you going to do now?" he asked.

"We must find the Royal, and speed is essential. I am going to organize a search that will be intensive beyond anything England's police are capable of. It also will be extremely expensive. Some months back, a man named Sir Cecil Elliman made me a proposal. Do you know Sir Cecil?"

"I know Sir Cecil well."

"Sir Cecil offered to form a consortium of businessmen to finance my investigation. At the time, nothing I was doing required that measure of financial outlay, but this is entirely different. I need a large number of investigators—good investigators—and I need them immediately. I'm going to accept Sir Cecil's offer—with the proviso that it be my consortium, rather than his, and that I select the members. I wonder how he will react to that."

"I can tell you. It would be better not to count on him—not if you are expecting to get money from him. Sir Cecil has a reputation for taking a long look at a pound before he parts with it."

"In this instance, he shouldn't hesitate," Lady Sara said. "The river thefts have caused him severe financial losses."

The Home Secretary reflected for a moment. "If that is true, you may be right. A good businessman is always willing to spend money to make money—or to save money. It comes to the same thing. And Sir Cecil is a very good businessman. If the thefts really have caused him heavy losses, he just may give you anything you ask for."

"I'm counting on that," Lady Sara said. "He may consult you first. If he does, make certain you don't divulge anything at all about the capture of Hob Hagan."

The Home Secretary said indignantly, "Don't you think I can keep a secret?"

"Most men can't," Lady Sara said.

CHAPTER 23

Lady Sara telephoned Sir Cecil at nine o'clock—at home, of course, since it was Sunday morning. I was present and so heard her half the conversation, and I overheard much of his. Lady Sara reminded Sir Cecil of his kind offer to form a consortium to finance an investigation into the thefts along the river and asked him if the matter still interested him. Obviously it did.

"I now am ready to take advantage of your offer," she told him. "There have been important developments, and it looks as though we may be able to put an end to this problem if we act at once with the kind of support you envisaged. I insist on selecting the members of the consortium myself, but since it was your idea, I am offering you the chairmanship. May I tell the members I choose that you have accepted? Your presence is certain to have a positive effect on their decision to join."

Sir Cecil demonstrated once more that a good executive knows how to execute. He accepted at once and added, "If you need a place to meet, my lady, I should be honoured to provide one—the offices of the Tradesmen Life and Accident Assurance Company in Cornhill."

"Thank you," Lady Sara said. "That should serve our purpose nicely. We will meet there this evening at eight-thirty o'clock. I will ask everyone to be prompt."

That ended the conversation.

"He surely is aware that this is going to cost him a considerable amount of money, but he didn't even hesitate," I observed. "By the way—exactly how much money are you planning on asking for?"

"Fifty thousand pounds," she said. "Of course Sir Cecil would be responsible for only one share of that. If all of those I invite accept, it should amount to slightly less than four thousand pounds each."

"For a common labourer, that would be the equivalent of twice the earnings of a lifetime!" I exclaimed. "How will you justify asking for so much?"

"Fifty thousand pounds will provide a hundred and fifty pounds each for three hundred skilled investigators plus a reserve for expenses. Skilled investigators do not come cheap—as Reggie Dempster would say, the labourer is worthy of his hire—and it would be dangerous to try to use unskilled ones. I will make it clear to the consortium that this opportunity certainly will knock only once, and frugality would be idiotic." She added thoughtfully, "To an importer or trader who has had repeated theft losses, it should seem like a bargain. If one of them doesn't think so, that in itself would be an important clue."

We got out the names and photographs we had been studying for so long, including those that had been marked "doubtful" and also including my four most likely choices: The Reverend Theobald Eynon; Malcolm Gavin, the pirate; Sir Langley Jardin, with his "captain" profile; and Steven Harbisher, the odd looking Napoleon. Lady Sara ran down the complete list: the elderly, bent Ralph Bewt who had been so agile in catching a cab; Innes Cameron, the dour Scotchman; Hollis Ewbank, whose prosperity had grown mysteriously while his business faded; Sir James Furner, the honest politician; Sir Charles Lampson, the horsy squire; the handsome Fane Malkinson; Otis Nicklass, the dominant one of five brothers; Alban Ryman, who had almost ruined his inherited businesses and then, in the past few years, made a miraculous recovery; and Grant Stoffer, who, as far as we knew, had remained ruined. Sir Cecil Elliman would bring the total to fourteen if all of them came. I wondered what Lady Sara's object was in bringing them together and whether the Royal, the King of Criminals, was actually on our list. In a case as convoluted as this one, we were dealing in possibilities, not certainties.

Our first problem concerned the Reverend Theobald Eynon, who would be conducting services down in Pangstead, Kent, on this Sunday morning and could well have commitments for the entire day. I knew Pangstead was remote, but I was surprised to find it was not even on the telephone. Lady Sara told me to dispatch a telegram from the Marylebone Station, where the office was open Sunday mornings until 11.30.

"Send it with reply prepaid," she said. "I have a feeling the Reverend Theobald will appreciate that."

Then, as I started off, she called me back. "Some of the others may not have telephones in their homes. Better wait until I've tried the whole list."

She reached nine of the men by telephone; all agreed to attend. The only reluctant one was Alban Ryman, the Baltic trader, who flatly refused at first and then, when Lady Sara politely expressed her regrets, changed his mind. I arrived at Marylebone Station before 11 A.M. and dispatched four telegrams, all of them with replies prepaid. Oddly enough, the first response came from the Reverend Theobald Eynon. He promised to be there though he cautioned that he might be a mite late because of an awkward train schedule.

"Perhaps he welcomes an opportunity to get down to London," Lady Sara said.

By early afternoon all of the invitations had been accepted, but our work for the day was only begun. Lady Sara's notion of a main bout required extensive preparations, and she called Rick, Charles, and me into conference to plan them.

"Our assumption is that the Royal keeps his life in carefully separated compartments," she told us. "The description Hob Hagan and his wife have given us is of a man carefully disguised. None of his colleagues in the river theft ring will have the faintest notion of his identity in that other compartment where he is a successful man of business. None of his business associates, friends, family, or servants will have the slightest notion that in another compartment he is the Royal, the Magnate of Crime. He cannot—he dare not—permit any leakage at all from one compartment to another. If those in the crime compartment knew his real identity, they would blackmail him ruthlessly. Anyone in his 'good citizen' compartment who gained even an inkling that he practised crime on the side would gossip just as ruthlessly and destroy him just as thoroughly. He absolutely must keep those compartments sealed off from each other. Is that understood?"

"Perfectly," I said, and Rick and Charles nodded their assent.

"If the Royal really is among those invited to the meeting this evening, I am going to present him with a dilemma. He will be attending in a relaxed mood as a supposed good citizen, prepared to laugh inwardly at yet another attempt to solve the river thefts while pretending to support it fully. Suddenly he will learn that he is in great peril. He must act at once, and for the moment he will be trapped in the wrong compartment. He must change his identity—and his compartment—at the earliest possible moment. If his coachman drove him to the meeting, the coachman must be sent home and other transportation found. He must disguise himself—not necessarily with the elaboration the Royal used for Hob Hagan, but sufficiently to conceal his real identity. He may carry the Royal's fake moustache and beard in his pocket, ready for any contingency. It will be interesting to see how he manages."

She seemed to know exactly what choices the Royal would have, and she made her arrangements accordingly, sending the three of us scrambling all over London. She developed her plans with the same devotion to detail she had employed in the military operation at Great Helmwich, but this time the army and navy were not involved.

Chief Inspector Mewer promised her ample police reinforcements if she would tell him when and where she wanted them. It quickly became obvious that she was not going to tell him anything at all until the last moment. She had never lost sight of the possibility that the Royal had spies in various police headquarters. She and the Chief Inspector finally settled on several locations where constables would be kept on the alert from eight o'clock on waiting for her orders. Total secrecy was to be maintained. For her own personal staff, she already had assembled all of her pugilistic bodyguards and recruited more.

As I left on a late afternoon errand, I received a special assignment. I was to return to Connaught Mews by a specific route and ask myself: If you wanted to ambush someone along this route, what place would you choose?

When I returned, Lady Sara asked me what I had decided.

"Holborn Circus," I said. "Five streets come together there, and several others intersect either Holborn or Holborn Viaduct within a very short distance. It would be possible to hide a small army just off the route, either on foot or in carriages, and pour it into Holborn Circus on a moment's notice."

She smiled. "Excellent! That is what I decided. The only question now is whether the Royal knows London well enough to make the same choice without studying the route. I think he does."

Rick and Charles had received the same assignment. Each of them, when he was asked, "What did you decide," responded, "Holborn Circus."

Our unanimity made me feel doubtful. "Are we in the position of the gambler who risks everything on one card?" I asked.

Lady Sara shook her head. "Not at all. We are in the position of a sharper who keeps extra cards in reserve. The question is whether they are the right cards. We can only wait and see. Now I want all of you to rest yourselves. You know what you have to do. Arm yourselves well before you start. Two revolvers each—you may need them both. At eight-thirty this evening, I want all of you fully alert and ready for whatever might happen."

The City, a mere square mile in extent but the historic heart of London and the business and financial centre of an empire, was all but deserted on a Sunday night. The stately old building that housed the offices of the Tradesmen Life and Accident Assurance Company was the only one in sight that was well-lighted when we drove up at eight-thirty. A row of waiting carriages were evidence that many of the traders Lady Sara invited were there ahead of us.

Lady Sara and I arrived in her own carriage with Old John on the box. An elderly porter darted out to open the door and greet us with a smile and a sweeping bow. "Lady Sara? Sir Cecil is waiting for you. A number of the gentlemen have arrived."

Lady Sara thanked him with a smile that made him forever beholden to her. "Where are we meeting?" she asked.

"In the directors' room, my lady."

"First storey front?" Lady Sara asked.

The porter nodded.

"I can see the lights," Lady Sara said.

We moved on, and Sir Cecil himself stepped forward to greet us before we reached the stairway. He escorted us the rest of the way. The directors' room at front of the first storey was furnished with a thick carpet, a long, highly polished table with comfortable chairs, and numerous book cabinets. The entire company of suspects was already assembled except for the Reverend Theobald Eynon.

"Do you want to wait for him?" Sir Cecil asked.

"Since he promised to come, it would be the polite thing to do," Lady Sara said.

Sir Cecil had provided a sideboard containing refreshments of all kinds, including an impressive assortment of bottles, so no one seemed to be in a hurry. He already knew everyone in the room from business as well as social occasions, and he escorted us from one trader to another performing introductions. It seemed odd indeed to be meeting formally with these men I had already investigated privately and speculated so much about.

None of them had the air of being a Magnate of Crime, not even the three men who topped my list of suspects; and, except for the fact that all were well dressed, there was nothing in the manner or appearance of any of them that suggested exceptional business ability. As for those private qualities I had meditated on for so long, I could readily believe that Steven Harbisher, the Napoleon of Trade, was the petty tyrant he was alleged to be; that the handsome Fane Malkinson was indeed a lady's man, whether or not he had the number of mistresses that rumour gave him; that Sir Langley Jardin had risen to the top of his company by merit and also through whatever fair or foul means he found necessary; that Hollis Ewbank, a weak-looking, watery-eyed old man, had all of his successes behind him; that Innes Cameron was indeed a dangerous enemy, though I had my doubts as to his generosity as a friend.

Malcolm Gavin, with his powerful body and sinister, drooping moustaches, still looked like a pirate to me. Otis Nicklass, with his slight stature and weak, oddly coloured eyes, seemed as vague in person as he had in his photos. Sir James Furner, who had twice been a Member of Parliament, obviously had at least one speech left over and was eager to deliver it. The grey-haired, ornately bearded Ralph Bewt was as bent with the burden of years as his photos showed, and he did indeed walk hesitantly with a stick, but I noticed at once that it was a sword-stick, and he had the air of knowing how to use it.

My inventory of those present was interrupted by the arrival of the Reverend Theobald Eynon. Plump and perspiring, he rushed in murmuring apologies, shook Sir Cecil's hand, shook Lady Sara's hand, almost shook my hand but decided in time that I was someone's lackey and instead shook the hand of the nearest trader, the dour Innes Cameron, thus proving he was present in his role as a shipping magnate and not as the Vicar of Pangstead.

Sir Cecil raised his voice and invited everyone to be seated. He had thoughtfully provided two chairs at the head of the long table so Lady Sara could share the position of honour with him. When everyone was comfortably settled, he rose and spoke a few words. Though he had accepted the position of chairman, he really knew very little about the subject or purpose of the meeting, he said. He did know a great deal about the abilities and accomplishments of Lady Sara Varnley, and he had been assured by no less a person than the Home Secretary himself that her work on the problem of the river thefts, a matter of great concern to everyone present, was of vital importance. Sir Cecil understood that Lady Sara was familiar with all of them by reputation, and on the basis of their reputations she had invited them there to ask for their help. He would leave it to her to explain what she was attempting and how they could best assist her.

He seated himself, and Lady Sara spoke without getting to her feet. She described the river thefts, the helplessness of the police in solving them, and the total cost to London's business community that could reach millions of pounds. Her investigation—made at her own expense and at the cost of the life of one of her employees—had turned up a quantity of information not known to the police. "I know how the gang operates. I even know the name by which the members of the gang refer to their leader. He is the 'Royal.' They are afraid of him, of course, because he is completely ruthless, but once we have him in custody, they will talk."

She described her discovery that there were two giants and her search for the missing Hob Hagan. Then she talked about the three dock workers, the murdered Bill Havill and Sid Theaker and the injured Alf Rixon, and the probable links of these crimes to the giant as well as the river thefts.

"After weeks of investigation, we have traced the giant to the most unlikely address in the world, St. John's Wood, or somewhere nearby," she said. "Unfortunately, St. John's Wood and its surroundings cover a considerable area. It is critically important to locate him at once and apprehend him before he slips away and finds a new haven. This will literally require a house-to-house search in which all residents and their servants are adroitly questioned about their own activities and those of their neighbours. We are looking for a mysterious person who hides by day, goes out regularly at night, and never permits anyone to see him. Given people's natural curiosity about those living nearby, I think it unlikely that our giant could reside in one place for many weeks without his odd behaviour being noticed and talked about.

"Described in that way, such an investigation may sound simple, but it will be extremely difficult—the more so because it must be done so quickly. It will require at least three hundred trained and experienced investigators. Both the training and the experience are critically important. Once we identify the correct house, it is not to be expected that the giant will answer the door. Our investigators will need to know how to obtain entry and apprehend him. I am convinced that Hob Hagan has personal knowledge of the Royal. He should be able to describe him and furnish valuable details about his person and his methods. On the basis of that information, we will soon have the Royal in custody, and Hagan will be able to identify him. I have information indicating that Hagan is living with a woman who also will be able to supply important evidence. When we arrest Hagan, both of them will talk. With their joint testimony, we surely can put an end to this gang of thieves. Gentlemen, this is a opportunity that may come only once, and it must be seized now—tonight.

"Thus far, I have financed the entire investigation myself. I ask no return for that. I ask no reward for myself in the event of success. But now I must launch the most extensive search in the nation's history to locate and apprehend the missing giant quickly. This will require money. Experienced and capable investigators are difficult to find. I can find them, but they are expensive, and I do not have the resources to hire the number I need. I must have, immediately, fifty thousand pounds. All of it will be used to pay investigators and their expenses."

Sir Cecil interrupted. "Will fifty thousand pounds be sufficient, my lady?"

"I believe that it will," Lady Sara said. "Naturally I will render a full accounting when the case is finally resolved. Fifty thousand pounds is a small amount compared with the enormous loses all of you are suffering from the river thieves, but of course it would be a considerable sum of money for one person to provide on the spur of the moment. That is why I asked Sir Cecil to form a consortium. Now I am going to leave so you can discuss this matter without the embarrassment of my presence. I'll ask Sir Cecil to telephone me first thing in the morning to tell me your decision so I can know whether I should proceed."

She got to her feet.

"Please wait one moment, my lady," Sir Cecil said. He hurried from the room. A short time later he returned. "Here is my cheque for fifty thousand pounds," he said. "I want you to leave here knowing you have the necessary support. These gentlemen can decide how much of the fifty thousand each will contribute, and I will assume responsibility for the balance, whatever it is."

Lady Sara took the cheque. "Thank you," she said. "I will start at once, this evening, to recruit the expert investigators I need. By early tomorrow morning, they should be at work on the most intensive search possible of St. John's Wood."

She touched my arm as she turned away, and I hurried after her. We swept down the stairs, and the elderly porter bowed us out of the building.

"That went well," Lady Sara said, "but it is too early to say whether it worked. Keeping track of all fourteen when they come out will be a chore, and we don't dare make a mistake. Unless, that is—"

"Unless what?" I asked.

"We can only wait and see what happens."

"I thought Sir Cecil messed it up for you," I said. "Now you won't know whether any of them refuse to participate."

"If that turns out to be important, I can easily find out later."

I handed her into the carriage, Old John cracked his whip, and we were off—ostensibly for Connaught Mews but actually to circle back as soon as we were out of sight of the Tradesmen Life and Accident Assurance Company's building.

The four wheeler—this time drawn by two horses—was waiting just off Cornhill by the Royal Exchange in Threadneedle Street. Four hulking pugilists were in charge—two on the box and two lurking in a nearby doorway. Old John and the carriage were sent back to Connaught Mews. Along the way, he was to carry a message to Chief Inspector Mewer, telling him to begin moving his men into the positions Lady Sara had chosen. Lady Sara quickly changed to men's clothing inside the cab. Then the two of us walked to the corner. Lights still blazed in the directors' room of the Tradesmen Life and Accident Assurance Company.

Lady Sara struck a vesta. From across the street came an answering flash of light; from a watch-post opposite the assurance company came another. Everyone was in place; everything was ready.

We returned to the cab. Lady Sara mounted the box, I took my place beside her, and the pugilists, who were almost too large for it, crowded inside.

Now, as Lady Sara had observed, we could only wait and see what happened.

Some fifteen minutes passed, twenty, half-an-hour. Suddenly there were several flashes of light—a signal from the watch-post opposite the assurance company, relayed to us on one of Lady Sara's special lanterns by a watcher waiting on the corner by the Bank of England.

"He has sent his carriage away empty!" Lady Sara exclaimed. "Now we will see if he contrives an excuse to leave before the others."

Another fifteen minutes, and there were more flashes.

"He did leave before the others!" Lady Sara exulted. "He called a cab—a hansom. Now we have him!"

The hansom flashed past us headed along Cheapside. Lady Sara cracked her whip, and we rushed in pursuit. Behind us, the entire apparatus she had spent the day organizing spun into motion: cabs and carriages hurried after us; messages were telephoned; messengers raced away by bicycle; reinforcements began moving in from the north and the south. As it turned out, an entirely different apparatus, craftily constructed by the Royal, had also been set in motion by telephone, and these two elaborate mechanisms were now rushing toward each other.

An enormously long stretch of straight thoroughfare, one of few to be found in London, extends from Cornhill through Cheapside and then along Newgate Street, Holborn Viaduct, Holborn, High Holborn, New Oxford Street, and Oxford Street. From the westward extent of Oxford Street, there is a choice of routes to St. John's Wood depending on whether one wants to approach it from the east or the west.

We dashed at top speed through a deserted City—along Cheapside, along Newgate Street, along Holborn Viaduct. Such traffic as we encountered was all headed in the other direction, toward the docks. Even in one of the world's most brightly lit cities, there were unfortunate patches of dimness between lamps, and the hansom sometimes stood out sharply and sometimes faded into gloom. We continued to rush after it. A hansom is much faster than a four wheeler, which placed us at a disadvantage, but we had the enormous advantage of two carefully selected horses. The hansom evidently had been hired off the street. Its driver was eager—probably he had been promised a large bonus; its horse was willing but outmatched.

Lady Sara was playing a game of her own. She could have overtaken the hanson easily, but she contented herself with slowly narrowing the gap between us. We rushed at high speed along Holborn Viaduct, and that was the velocity at which those two intricate mechanisms collided.

Holborn Circus loomed ahead of us. The hansom rushed through. As we reached it, a gang of ruffians suddenly closed off the street, recklessly dashing out to seize our horses' bridles. They hauled our rearing horses to a stop—but before we quite lost momentum, our friendly pugilists poured from the cab. At the same time, I drew a revolver and fired several shots into the air. Carriages began to overtake us from behind, and each of them erupted squads of pugilists. From the sides, companies of police began to close in.

A gap suddenly opened ahead of us. Lady Sara cracked her whip, and we put the rumpus far behind. We heard only later how the pugilists had lined the street with bodies as they administered one knock-out punch after another. Police officers closed in to handcuff the fallen, and the ruffians' resistance quickly collapsed.

Once clear of Holborn Circus, Lady Sara made no effort to hold back the horses. We passed along Holborn and High Holborn at a speed that probably had never been equaled on those usually crowded thoroughfares. Only when we got that fleeing hansom in sight again did she slow our pace. The hansom driver, figuring he was in the clear, had settled down to a steady trot to save his horse, and we emulated him.

"The Royal suspected a trap," Lady Sara explained. "We will let him think he escaped it—and hope he doesn't suspect two traps."

We followed him at the same speed almost the full length of a deserted Oxford Street, still making no further effort to overtake him. Finally the hansom made a sweeping turn into Portman Street, which led directly to Gloucester Place and then Upper Gloucester Place—one of the most direct routes to St. John's Wood.

"He's in a hurry," Lady Sara observed. "And well he might be."

She had considered the possibility that he might take Edgware Road and approach St. John's Wood from the west—a more devious but much longer route. It really made no difference which way he went except to reveal his state of mind. She had all of the routes covered, but none of the waiting police would reveal themselves unless the Royal tried to turn aside and flee.

He took Upper Gloucester Place to Park Road and made the turning into St. John's Wood. At that point, Lady Sara slowed our horses to a walk. She wanted the Royal to feel certain he had given us the slip. I signalled with one of Lady Sara's special lanterns as we approached the intersection. A hansom cab hurried toward us with Tom Ness, one of Lady Sara's grooms, driving. Another groom, Joe Hovel, was the passenger. Joe took over the four wheeler; Lady Sara and I boarded the hansom.

The two horses would have made our four wheeler instantly recognizable even in a dim street. If we had driven it past Hob Hagan's villa, the Royal would have known we were still on his trail. Hence the change to the hansom. We clipped sedately past Hob Hagan's address, where all looked quiet. There was no signal for us, so we continued at a moderate clip to the first turning. There Lady Sara and I got out and waited at the corner. Still there was no signal.

Finally it came—a pinpoint of light flashed and repeated. We hurried toward it on foot.

Chief Inspector Mewer met us. "It's all right, my lady," he said. "We've got him."

"What took so long?" Lady Sara asked.

"He's a crafty one. He got out and dismissed his cab, first telling the driver the route he wanted him to follow back to the City. Then he stood behind a bush and waited, looking the entire neighbourhood over as well as he could in the dark. Twice he walked to the gate and studied Hagan's villa and grounds. He seemed almost convinced that everything was all right, but when your hansom approached, he ducked behind the bush again. Finally, after you turned the corner, he went to the gate again, opened it with a key, and went on in. As he approached the villa, we grabbed him and took him inside. He is being watched very carefully."

"Your men did a superb job of keeping out of sight," Lady Sara said. "He suspected a trap, and he would have bolted at the slightest sign of it and ruined everything. You must congratulate them for me. Has the Royal said anything?"

"Not a syllable. Wrapped up in a greatcoat, he was, with a scarf around his face. Underneath, he's dressed like something out of a play."

"Good. Now we will conduct what I hope will be the final experiment."

We entered the house along with the Chief Inspector. Seated in the drawing room, hands manacled behind him, was the Royal—a moustached and bearded man wearing a cloak and an odd fur hat that definitely was not English. It looked like an animal curled around his head, and flaps extended down the sides of his face and partially concealed his cheeks. He did not turn in our direction when we entered.

"He was carrying both a revolver and a knife," Chief Inspector Mewer said. "We relieved him of them. Are you ready?"

"'Now or never,' as Reggie Dempster would say. Some of Reggie's cliches have excellent pedigrees. That one is Chaucer, but Reggie never has the faintest idea whom he is quoting. Go ahead."

The Chief Inspector nodded at a sergeant, who left the room and returned a moment later, urging Hob Hagan and his wife along in front of him. Hagan saw the cloaked figure, came to an abrupt stop, and recoiled.

"The Royal!" he gasped.

He brushed the sergeant aside and fled.

His wife stood her ground. She spoke to the Royal directly. "I know you. I heard and saw you trying to goad Hob into killing those men, and

I heard the men you sent to do it tell you it was done. You are evil, and you tried to turn my gentle husband into a monster. Everything you touch turns to evil, but you couldn't corrupt Hob."

The police took her away.

"That should be enough to start with," Lady Sara told the Chief Inspector. "There will be more evidence than you can handle once it becomes known you have arrested him."

The Royal turned a gaze of sheer hatred on us.

The Chief Inspector walked over to him, removed the odd hat, and unceremoniously ripped off the beard. "So that's who you are," he said. "I'll keep these as evidence. Your cloak, too."

Lady Sara may have known—or guessed—who it was when she began the investigation of Reginald Dempster, but I hadn't an inkling until the moment I entered the room and saw him. It was Sir Cecil Elliman.

CHAPTER 24

There was no time for celebration or even for questions. All across the East End, workers who had been employed at the looted warehouses were routed out of bed and questioned. Sir Cecil's associates—including Reginald Dempster—were treated in the same manner.

The message, everywhere, was a simple one: The Royal and the giant have been arrested. The warehouse thefts are only part of the charge—there were murders done, and more than one will swing. Peach now while you still do yourself some good. Once the talking's done, it'll be the last drop for anyone left.

Enough of them saw it that way to give the police their busiest week in history, taking statements, obtaining warrants, raiding suspicious premises, recovering stolen property.

Once the investigation was effectively launched, Lady Sara returned to her own affairs. Her first act was to ceremoniously move all of the pegs on the giant cribbage board to the game holes. As she had predicted long before, our Byways had merged.

Her second act was to write letters to the thirteen businessmen who had been suspects for so long, explaining her object with that odd Sunday night meeting and thanking them for their help. She also informed them that they would not be called upon to honour the pledges they had made, which must have been a relief to some of them.

Sir Cecil's cheque for fifty thousand pounds was never cashed. I asked Lady Sara whether she intended to frame it as a memento. She said no, it would be evidence in the case against him.

There was a quantity of unfinished business to deal with from her coffee hours and also from her evenings as Madam Zarno. It was Wednesday of the next week before I had a moment of leisure when I could sit down with Lady Sara and ask a few questions. Before I had fairly begun, we were interrupted by Stephen Lynes, the artist, who called seeking technical assistance.

Lynes's waxworks was now open and flourishing, and he wanted to add an effigy of the Royal to his dungeon to take advantage of the public sensation of the moment.

"Is Sir Cecil willing to pose for you?" Lady Sara asked. "Not he!" Lynes said bitterly. "He's not seeing anyone. But I have found several portraits of him—newspaper photos and drawings—and all I need is a little help in getting his disguise right."

Our memories of that cloaked figure were still vivid, and, following our descriptions, Lynes's pencil soon produced a commendable likeness. Lady Sara promised to arrange with Chief Inspector Mewer for him to examine the Royal's strange hat and cloak long enough to enable him to make exact duplicates. Lynes headed back to his waxworks in an elated mood to begin sculpting the Royal in wax, and I was able to resume my questions about the ins and outs of the Byways that had finally merged.

"By now, you should have been able to work things out for yourself," Lady Sara said severely. "What is it you want to know?"

"Reggie Dempster," I said. "What made you suspect him?"

"For a long time, I didn't. Those were excellent tips he gave us, and they were exactly the sort of thing he might have happened onto. It finally occurred to me that the only cases for the board we were able to solve were the ones Reggie brought to us. That seemed like a strange coincidence. When I reflected on it, I decided there were too many of them, and they were too timely. This gave me pause. Did you notice how timely they were?"

"No," I confessed. "I never gave that a thought. What do you mean by 'timely?'"

"In the first instance, we hadn't seen Reggie in Connaught Mews for years. He knew he wasn't going to get anything out of his visits here, so he stopped coming. Can you remember the day he returned?"

I thought for a moment. "He was with your mother, wasn't he? Lord Anstee was here, and the Chief Inspector, and Sir Thomas. Also, the artists."

"Right. And the occasion?"

I thought again. "It was to discuss the giants. That's why the artists were there. Also, Lord Anstee had brought his Cat's Paw, so it was the day after the first Shadwell murder."

"Right again. The Royal had informants at Scotland Yard, and word reached him early on the morning after the Shadwell murder that Lady Sara had taken an interest and promised Chief Inspector Mewer vital information if he would call on her that day. Sir Cecil wanted to know what I was up to, so he consulted his list of lackeys, noted that Reggie Dempster claimed a remote connection with our family and also casual friendship with my mother—Reggie probably called himself her confidant—and he sent Reggie to see what was going on.

Of course Reggie knew Sir Cecil only as the Royal, and he never knew who the Royal was. Sir Cecil's instinct for self preservation prevented him from confiding anything Reggie didn't need to know. They probably met at the offices of Gow & Son whenever he needed to see Reggie personally. Of course that was where Reggie picked up Hob Hagan's monthly stipend and his own as well and got instructions for both of them. Gow & Son is located only a short walk from the offices of the Tradesmen Life and Accident Assurance Company in Cornhill. The Royal had his office there—and a place in between where he could transform himself from one to the other.

"Reggie's report must have alarmed him. For one thing, Lord Anstee was there. His collection of medieval torture instruments is well known, and the inevitable conclusion was that I somehow had penetrated the secret of the animal claw marks. Immediately after that, Sir Cecil learned from one of his spies at the Yard of my interest in giants and my request for information about them. I had put my finger on two of the river thieves' best-kept secrets. Sir Cecil decided to visit me as quickly as possible in order to form his own opinion of me, and he persuaded the Earl of Spalton to come along and introduce him. The interview must have reassured him. He decided I was no more than a minor nuisance, and he tried to buy me off by offering me trivial investigating chores. Do you see what I meant by 'timely?' Everything Reggie—or Sir Cecil—did, then and later, was in reaction to something we had done. Of course it was a long time before that pattern became evident. Even so, I should have seen it far sooner than I did.

"We happened onto Alf Rixon, the injured docker. The next morning I told the Chief Inspector that his hand had been wounded by the same instrument that had torn the murdered Bill Havill's face. The Scotland Yard informer passed this along, and it convinced Sir Cecil I might be dangerous. Since he had failed in his attempt to buy me off, he decided to provide me with another case to distract me from meddling with the river thefts. That afternoon, Reggie called on us with 'something queer'—the fact that his friend Clarke was being impersonated by another man at the Army and Navy Club.

"The Royal of course had a vast knowledge of crime in London. The more of it there was, and the more efficiently it was carried out, the less attention the police could give his doings. He knew all about the ring of burglars and where they got their leads. In actual fact, Reggie and Clarke were not friends, but because they belonged to the same club, Reggie, who wouldn't have noticed the impersonation if the Royal hadn't put him onto it, could pretend he had discovered it accidentally. The distraction worked, but like all of the others, only until I solved the case.

"The pattern continued. Shortly after we discovered Prout's Mill and the Eynon Brothers Company steam-launch, Sir Cecil invited me to become a director of the Tradesmen Life and Accident Assurance Company. Probably he hoped to keep me occupied with trival business problems. Can you work out the rest of the pattern yourself?"

"The moment Clarke-Ivatt and his associates were arrested, Reggie was there with information about a third giant," I suggested.

She nodded. "Actually, it was Sir Cecil or one of his lackeys who noticed Rafe Wade on Regent Street. Sir Cecil immediately saw a use for Wade and had him murdered as further protection for Hob Hagan. At the first opportunity, Reggie called on me and pretended to have seen Wade himself. He made it convincing—Sir Cecil had coached him well. Remember? Reggie didn't volunteer the information. He kept asking if there was anything else he could help us with until I mentioned the giant search. Then he told us about seeing Wade. It gave us another distraction, but only a momentary one, and the result was the opposite of what was intended. It convinced me Hob Hagan was alive."

"And then—right after the fog, when we tried to follow waggons away from Prout's Mill, Sir Cecil offered you the help of a consortium," I suggested.

"He would have helped me in such a way as to adroitly cripple my investigation—or tried to. Our discoveries must have seemed uncanny to him. We actually witnessed a theft in progress. We discovered Prout's Mill and the dual role of the *Mollie Mae*, and we placed a watch on Prout's Mill, all of which caused him serious inconvenience. He kept trying to find some means of distracting me.

"As yet I had no idea he was the Royal or even that there was such a person. Ed's dying message was too vague. I may have been wrong about one thing. Probably we had no need for bodyguards. I now think Ed's murder was done accidentally by ruffians not accustomed to controlling their violence. I can imagine one of them remonstrating, 'Don't do him in. The Royal won't like that.' Ed heard the reference to 'the Royal' and knew it was important, so he kept repeating the word. But his death certainly wasn't intended. He hadn't learned anything—he was caught on the waggon before it reached its destination. Sir Cecil wouldn't hesitate to order a murder, but only after he had calculated profit and loss. An attack on me would have aroused the city, and he certainly didn't want that."

"Next Sir Cecil tried to hire me," I said.

"It was in character for him to conclude that a mere woman such as myself must be relying heavily on her male assistants. He thought he could cripple my investigation by offering you a position you couldn't refuse. You refused it anyway, which certainly perplexed him, and my investigation continued. Ben and Bob Lyle kept making discoveries and giving us more warehouses to watch, which must have seemed like further uncanniness to Sir Cecil. He responded by sending Reggie to us with a tale of unusually cheap wines."

"And again it worked," I pointed out.

"Indeed it did. It sent us chasing off to Great Helmwich, and it further delayed the investigation of the river thefts. The respite was only a brief one, however. When we returned, Ben and Bob discovered Sir Cecil's use of St. Saviour's Dock, which must have been a blow to him. His own watchers probably recognized us when we drove through the area. He reacted at once, prodding a friend of his to offer you employment with the Cutter and Ramsey Assurance Company. When that failed, Reggie Dempster called right on schedule with a counterfeit five-pound banknote."

"Was it really passed to him by a clerk at Drummond's?" I asked.

"I think that unlikely. The clerk would have been taking an enormous risk, and he knew it. Sir Cecil had access to the counterfeit notes, perhaps he dabbled in them himself—even yet the police have no idea of the full extent of his criminal interests—and he knew a clerk at Drummond's was involved. So he sent Reggie to us with another diversion. Like all of the others, it was an excellent tip. Unfortunately for Sir Cecil, at that point the pattern became all too obvious. I passed the tip to Chief Inspector Mewer and investigated Reggie Dempster instead."

"Did you know he would lead you to Hob Hagan?"

"No. That surprised me. Sir Cecil is an excellent judge of character. A man who could be successful in both legitimate and illegitimate businesses would have to be. I was and am surprised that he would trust Reggie with a really important task. Probably he had two reasons for it. One was because he needed someone presentable enough to make daytime calls in St. John's Wood. One of his river thugs might have caused talk.

"The other reason was the difficulty he was having with Hob Hagan's wife. Hagan is simple-minded and easily intimidated. Not so his wife. She looked after him as well as she could, and she insisted on accompanying him to the river each night and reviewing what they wanted him to do. She was the weak point in Sir Cecil's arrangements, and he knew it. She was the one likely to rebel. Whatever else can be said about Reggie, his manners are impeccable, and he is completely at ease in soothing ruffled feeling of those he considers underlings. Mrs. Hagan insisted that Hob's salary be placed in her hands, regularly, at the same time each month. Reggie was given the task of drawing the money, taking it to her, listening to her complaints, and reassuring her. Perhaps he delivered instructions to the Hagans' servants at the same time. We will soon know all about it. Reggie certainly will talk."

"How did Sir Cecil arrange the riot so quickly on Sunday night?"

"That only took a telephone call. He was afraid something was up when I called the meeting, and he had his men standing by. Once he heard what I had to say, he knew he had to deal with the situation quickly. At the same time, he suspected a trap, and he ordered the riot in order to delay anyone following him until he'd had a chance to get free. Of course he didn't know we had already found Hob Hagan, and the last thing he wanted to do was lead us to him. When he reached Hagan's residence, he was still deeply suspicious. He hesitated a long time before he decided to enter the villa and confront the Hagans. In the end, he had to do it. He realized that Hagan and his wife posed a deadly threat to him."

"Would he have murdered them?"

"He would have had to. Hagan and his wife as well. As valuable as Hagan was to him, his usefulness was finished the moment the police began an all-out search for him, and from that point his very existence was dangerous to Sir Cecil."

"But why did he go himself?" I asked. "Why didn't he just send one of his thugs to do the murders and lead us a merry chase in the wrong direction?"

"He was caught in a trap of his own making. Those numerous, highly efficient servants of the Hagan family were actually bodyguards. They were to protect Hagan from any outside contact, and they worked at it. There was no telephone in the Hagan house. No callers were permitted. Mrs. Hagan was permitted a few contacts with neighbours to keep them from being suspicious, but that was all. You were fortunate that your peeking over the wall caught the guards in a moment of laxity.

"If Sir Cecil had sent assassins to deal with Hagan and his wife, they would have been dealt with summarily. Even if they produced a written order from Sir Cecil, the guards simply wouldn't have believed it. Anyway, Sir Cecil knew better than to put an order like that in writing. Hagan was a monster Sir Cecil created himself, and only Sir Cecil could destroy him.

"So he had to make the trip to St. John's Wood himself, and he had to do it that night. My presentation to the consortium convinced him that by morning I would have three hundred trained agents searching for Hob Hagan, and from my description—a mysterious person who hides by day, goes out regularly at night, and never permits anyone to see him—Sir Cecil knew they would quickly find the right residence. He had to eliminate Hagan himself, and quickly, so he arranged the ambush for anyone trying to follow him. He couldn't take his own carriage—he didn't want to give his coachman something to gossip about. He left the meeting shortly after I did on the same pretext, letting the others determine their contributions without the embarrassment of his presence, sent his carriage home, told the porter to wait on the gentlemen who remained in case they needed something, disguised himself in his office, ordered a hansom cab by telephone, and slipped out without the porter seeing him. You know the rest."

"In retrospect, it all seems simple," I said.

"Most cases do. In retrospect, all of the mystery is eliminated."

"All except one thing. Why Sir Cecil? He had success and respect and the distinction of being knighted for his public services. He had power and wealth. Why throw all that away by becoming involved in a criminal scheme that at best brought him additional wealth, which he shouldn't have needed, and power and influence with the underworld, which he shouldn't have wanted?"

Lady Sara shrugged. "Who can say? Probably Sir Cecil would have difficulty explaining it himself. He didn't decide suddenly to become the Royal, the king of crime. What we've been able to find out suggests that he slipped into it gradually. First, his own affairs hadn't been going well, and he was dangerously short of money. He met that problem by establishing a new insurance company, Thameside Insurance, to supply theft insurance to shippers and importers in and about the Port of London. The company did not prosper—the competition, from Lloyd's and others, is formidable. In looking into the reason for the company's failure to grow, Sir Cecil made a discovery. Before quoting a premium, an insurance company has the right of inspection to evaluate the risk it would be assuming. In looking for ways to keep thieves out, it was also possible to search out easy ways for thieves to get in. Sir Cecil balanced that fact with another: The more thefts there are, the greater the demand for insurance. He decided to promote a few river thefts to give warehouse and dock owners more incentive to buy insurance and thus give a boost to his insurance company.

"Both of these enterprises flourished mightily, and he managed them with ease. If a warehouse could be easily and profitably looted, he would refuse to insure it—and do the looting himself. If, on the other hand, he did decide to insure it, it automatically became immune to his thievery—to such an extent that the low rate of theft among his insurance customers was talked about. It was attributed to the very sound suggestions Sir Cecil's company made for reducing the risk of theft. In no time at all, his river thefts had become a serious crime wave, the profits astonished him, and he had become the Royal, the king of crime. Perhaps that title reflected his pique over the fact that his chances of elevation to the peerage were virtually nil despite his wealth and accomplishments. On the illegitimate side, it must have seemed to him that there was no limit to how high he could rise."

"What about the giants?" I asked.

"Very early in his enterprise, Sir Cecil encountered Mort Hagan, Hob's brother, who already was a terror, and he found a natural use for him—terrorizing night workers into cooperating with his thieves. We know how effective that was. Even those who refused were too terrified to say anything. When Mort Hagan was arrested and hanged, Sir Cecil coerced his innocent brother into continuing the role.

"We can see how valuable Hagan was to him by the expense Sir Cecil incurred in establishing a secret existence for him in St. John's Wood. We also can understand why they didn't bother to fake animal tracks around the murdered Bill Havill and Sid Theaker. They weren't concerned about what the police would think. They were trying to impress the dock workers. Those who had already met the giant, and seen his claws, knew at once that the monster had claimed a victim."

"What was Sir Cecil's connection with the Eynon Brothers Company and the Reverend Theobald?" I asked. "The river thieves certainly made free use of their warehouses."

"As soon as Sir Cecil's thieves began to flourish, he needed places to store stolen goods until they could be disposed of or moved inland. About that time, the two elder Eynon brothers, the principal operators of Eynon Brothers Company, were lost at sea. The Reverend Theobald took charge of the company himself and thought he could run it efficiently by working two days a week. The notion was patently ridiculous, but for some strange reason the firm continued to prosper. My guess is that Sir Cecil saw this as an opportunity. He virtually took control of the company without the Reverend Theobald's knowledge. He ran its ships, operated its warehouses, and handled its trade to his own advantage so as to store and dispose of stolen goods.

"So firm was Sir Cecil's control of Eynon Brothers Company that he even remodelled Prout's Mill to provide facilities for quickly loading stolen goods, and the giant and his escort made frequent use of it. Sir Cecil allowed the firm to continue to show good profits simply because that was profitable to him, and the innocent Reverend Theobald thought it was all his doing. Of course Sir Cecil used other locations as well, making frequent changes to foil investigators. Chief Inspector Mewer may never get hold of the whole story, but he will dig up a good part of it if he persists."

"I wonder what the Reverend Theobald Eynon will think about this?"

"I have had a talk with him. He was astonished. He also was crushed to learn he had been a principal tool in a crime wave. He has decided to sell Eynon Brothers Company and devote his attention to his most important business, being Vicar of Pangstead. And now—the board is clear, and it is time we found new problems to consider."

That night, as she did every Wednesday night, Lady Sara dressed in her flowing, brilliantly patterned gown and shawl, did strange things to her face with make-up, and became Madam Zarno. We called first on Madam Furneaux, who welcomed us with a list of waiting clients.

One of them was Sally Smeed, one of Lady Sara's regulars. She was devastated. Despite her efforts, and those of Lady Sara, her husband had persisted in helping his cousin Mannie deal smash and had been caught. Now he was in prison. Lady Sara listened sympathetically, but the case had reached a point where there was nothing she could do but help out with a few shillings.

Sally added some items of gossip to her tale of woe. Then, as she was about to leave, she remarked, "I see'd somethin' funny on my way here. There was a 'orse pushin' a waggon."

"Pushing a waggon?" Lady Sara echoed.

Sally nodded. "'E was hitched up all right, but 'is nose was right in the driver's lap, so to speak, 'n 'e was pushin' 'stead of pullin'."

"Where was this happening?"

"Nicholas Street."

"After dark?"

"Yes."

"Thank you."

The moment she left, Lady Sara told Rick Allward and Charles Tupper, "Go over to Nicholas Street quickly and see if you can find this horse pushing a waggon. Follow it."

By the end of the week, Lady Sara had solved a sensational jewellery theft with much of the loot recovered and all of the members of the gang under arrest. They had smashed a jeweller's window in Regent Street. The window looked as though a heavy waggon had been backed into it. The members of the gang had leaped inside, grabbed everything they could, had a quick go at the safe, and made their escape. There was, of course, no sign of the waggon, which seemed to have driven away the moment the window was broken. The case had caused speculation and doubt as to whether a horse could back up with sufficient force to severely damage a shop front.

The Nicholas Street incident revealed the answer. The horse had been trained to push the waggon; probably he could go at a gallop for a short distance. The thieves had invented a easy-change harnass that enabled them to turn the horse around quickly. Less than a minute after the waggon hit the store front, they had reversed the horse and were quietly driving away while their mates quickly finished looting the store.

It had seemed like a foolproof plan, but a flaw or two had been revealed in the first theft, and they had the horse out after dark on a quiet street to practise for their next job.

It was, as Lady Sara remarked when Chief Inspector Mewer came to congratulate her, a simple and obvious case. On the other hand, another case, which developed out of a visit from Lord Anstee, proved to be extremely complicated and almost worthy of a place on the board.

Lord Anstee made a flustered, out-of-breath appearance and informed Lady Sara that he had just discovered a wombat in his wine cellar.

Lady Sara regarded him gravely. "Congratulations. They make excellent pets. Dante Gabriel Rossetti, the artist and poet, owned one. I saw it when I was a child. It was a great favourite with his artist friends, and Lewis Carroll is supposed to have modeled the dormouse in Alice in Wonderland on it. It did one thing that I admired fervently. It ate my nurse's hat."

"I had no thought of keeping it," Lord Anstee said testily. "I complained to the Zoological Society, and they sent someone for it."

"Are you certain it was a wombat?"

"Positive. Fellow from the Zoological Society agreed. Looked like a small bear. But why my wine cellar, and why a wombat?"

"Are any of your neighbours from Australia?" Lady Sara asked.

"Not to my knowledge?"

"Or any of their servants?" Lady Sara persisted.

Lord Anstee reflected. "I believe my next-door neighbour has a coachman who comes from there."

Lady Sara nodded gravely. "Is any of your wine missing?"

"Not that I know of. Of course I don't take daily inventories."

"It might be wise to do so today."

"Because of the wombat?"

"No. Because of the coachman. Let's do it now."

There was wine missing and evidence of tunnelling from the adjacent cellar. The wombat must have slipped through the tunnel unobserved by its master, the coachman. Some of Lord Anstee's most priceless bottles had been taken—indication that the coachman wasn't stealing for himself. Probably he wouldn't have known the difference. Lord Anstee's wombat thus introduced us to another case involving stolen wine, this one far more complicated and sinister than the one that took us to Great Helmwich.

But that is another story.

ENVOI

In postscripts to my two earlier novels set in this period, *The Quallsford Inheritance* and *The Glendower Conspiracy*, I described the difficulties one encounters in attempting to evoke Great Britain at the beginning of the twentieth century: It exists "...in pieces—sometimes very small pieces—in a million books and public records and photographs and postcards and letters, and the search takes one to libraries and museums and private collections and the reminiscences of the elderly. It sometimes seems that the one essential small piece that the author needs is the one that is impossible to find."

Byways to Evil repeats these problems except that with this later book I have expanded my resources and found materials that were new to me, and one begins to suspect that the sources in which all of those very small pieces are contained number in the billions rather than the millions.

As with my earlier books, I am deeply indebted to two classes of authors who wrote in vivid detail concerning life in Britain during the first decade of this century. One group consists of those who described their own contemporary world. The other group consists of those who experienced the first decade of this century as children and described it later in reminiscences. There is a third group, often anonymous, consisting of contemporary travelers and travel writers who provided descriptions of Britain in books as well as guides such as those of Baedeker. As I wrote earlier, "...the material may exist only in very small pieces, for descriptions of places seen in passing are likely to be limited to a sentence here, a paragraph there, and nothing in several other books. Where it is found, however, it is sometimes pure gold." Without the vivid eyewitness reports of all of these writers, this book could not have been written.

The child's vision is sometimes sharper than the adult's. Thomas Burke's London in My Time,, published in 1934, contains an enthusiastic description of draper's shops at the turn of the century, where the cash railways "...used to reconcile me to otherwise dreary half-hours in those dim, pokey shops when Aunt Jane and the assistant were out on the pavement matching a ribbon by daylight..." None of the adult authors I have found who wrote about their own time bothered to describe such a triviality—but I met and corresponded with elderly people who had encountered the cash railway as children and remembered it with enormous pleasure.

Burke also describes Buzzard's, the Oxford Street pastrycook, which, at the time of his writing, in the 1930s, still stood just as he remembered it as a child. Even the windows looked unchanged—and this in a London in which much was sadly altered by that date. An English friend of today, who kindly read this manuscript, also has fond memories of Buzzard's "before the war." Neither she nor any of the contemporaries she consulted could remember the exact spelling of the name, but all of them remembered the cakes.

I should note in addition my indebtedness to the specialized dictionaries of Eric Partridge, invaluable in determining the meanings of slang words and expressions and the period in which they were used. The Oxford Dictionaries fulfilled the same function with regular English English.

An American writing about England—at any date—has the enormous handicap of a different heritage—historical, cultural, and linguistic—to overcome. I am deeply indebted to two friends in Britain, Douglas Morgan, of Cardiff, and Joan Temple, of Folkestone, who, as they did with my earlier books set in Britain, generously invested the considerable time and effort necessary to read the manuscript and correct and delete my vulgar Americanisms. Robert Morrison, of Reading, kindly assisted in tracking down some of those elusive pieces of information. My literary agent, George Schithers, generously performed a similar analysis based on his own extensive knowledge of Britain. In American, among those who kindly read the manuscript were Allan M. Hayes and Theodore Reynolds, both who contributed their own specialized knowledge.

There have been other attempts to present female detectives in this time period. Having read in enormous detail of the trials women faced in the late nineteenth and early twentieth centuries in forcing any kind of a beachhead in the professions or even in society if they defied the rigid customs of the day, I found these stories singularly unconvincing. It seemed to me that the only way it could have been done was for a woman to be sufficiently wealthy, and sufficiently well-born, and sufficiently gifted to make a unique niche for herself. Even then she would have had to pay lip service to the conventions if she were not to add ostracism to the heavy burden she already bore in being a woman.

Hence Lady Sara Varnley.

—Lloyd Biggle, Jr.
Ypsilanti, Michigan
October 25, 1995

268 | LLOYD BIGGLE, JR.

www.ingramcontent.com/pod-product-compliance
Lightning Source LLC
Chambersburg PA
CBHW020613260626
47157CB00003B/988